Gwendoline

Cover illustration by Simon Barlow

Ralph Thomas was born in Monmouthshire and educated at Pontllanfraith Grammar School. In 1936 he went to work in London, then into the Army, serving for six years mostly in North Africa and Italy. He and Kathleen were married in 1947. They returned to Wales where their two children were born and where he worked until 1985.

On his retirement he took up writing and his first book, a history of a mining village was published in 1986. He has lectured on local history and this book is the fulfilment of a long harboured wish to write a historical novel.

The Black Domain

by Ralph Thomas

OLD BAKEHOUSE
PUBLICATIONS

First published in July 1992

ISBN 0 9512181 7 4

Published in the U.K. by
Old Bakehouse Publications
Church Street,
Abertillery, Gwent NP3 1EA
Telephone: 0495 212600   Fax: 0495 216222

Made and printed in the U.K.
by J.R. Davies (Printers) Ltd.

FOR
KATHLEEN

PROLOGUE

The feeble light that came from the stub of candle, wavered in a draught. Like an invisible metronome, beating time, the steady drip, drip, of water, was the only sound in the cold wet darkness that surrounded him.

Hunched into the ragged overcoat that had once belonged to his Dad, the doorboy sniffed, trying to halt the mucous that trickled from his nostrils. Failing, he wiped his sleeve across his upper lip, then spat into the space between the faintly gleaming rails. His stomach rumbled. He rose from the seat that had been fashioned from a large block of wood. It had been there almost as long as the NantyGwrhay colliery had been working, and had been passed on from one door-boy to the next. Again the candle flame flickered. Somebody or something was coming. His feet, bare in the oversized boots, were cold and wet, and he stamped in an effort to bring some feeling back into them. He beat his thin arms about his scrawny body like some little bird beating its wings. 'Jesu mawr' it was cold.

He stopped his efforts to get warm as his ears detected the rumble of a tub being dragged along. He waited, then came the call, 'Ieuan! Open the bloody door'.

He grasped the rope handle and pulled the wooden door towards him. The rush of cold air whistled into the tunnel making the shadows cast by the candle, dance. The owner of the voice, gasping as it struggled to maintain the momentum of the tub's forward movement, moved through the door and passed him in the gloom. Only then was it possible to recognise the figure as that of a female.

When he had first seen one of these creatures, it had been like watching something from a nightmare come to life. He had been so frightened that he had released his hold on the rope handle of the door and it had swung shut as he cowered, shielding his head and eyes with his arms. The cackle of laughter had frightened him even more as he huddled in the darkness, eyes closed, awaiting he knew not what.

That had been a year ago. Now he had become accustomed to the appearance of these human horses looming out of the darkness, like goblins, struggling and straining to keep their burdens moving. Pausing only to adjust the chain that passed between her legs to the shackle on the tub, the filthy bedraggled creature then bent forward, almost parallel to the floor and with a grunt threw herself forward in a effort to get the tub moving forward once more. As she strained she gasped, 'Gissa a shove Ieuan bach'.

He made no move to help her, but waited for her next remark. 'Lazy little sod. You wait 'til I catch you sleepin'. I'll 'ave you down and cut it off.'

This threat, which at one time had put the fear of God into him, had long since lost its power to frighten and had now become a mechanical response to his refusal to help.

He laughed and let go the rope, allowing the door to slam back into place, shutting off the current of cold air. Muttering to herself as she strained and heaved in her harness, the woman vanished into the darkness that lay beyond the candle's feeble light.

His nose was running once more and with practised ease, he pinched the end then blew through it, expelling the watery mucous of his cold. Hawking noisily in his throat he spat out the dust laden phlegm and wiping his fingers on his coat he returned to his seat. Pulling the ragged coat tight about him, he sat down to await the next tub.

Someday soon, he hoped his Dad would tell him that he was to work with him on the coal. He would be released from this cold dark world and join other boys like Robert Morgan, who had been doing this job before him. Until that happy day he would sit in the candle's fitful light and dream. Always it was the same dream. At eight years of age, Ieuan Evans, had already learned that the best way to exist in this halfworld below ground, was to dream of the blue skies and green grass of the world above.

While Ieuan squatted on his block of wood, huddled in his overcoat, sniffing as the mucous trickled down his upper lip, John Moggridge, owner of the NantGwrhay mine and Ieuan's employer, dabbed at his mouth with a napkin, pushed back his chair from the dining table and announced to his wife Sarah that it was about time he started work.

There were reports to be read, sent by Paget the mine manager, not to mention the output figures that needed to be checked. 'I need a bookkeeper' he had declared more than once.

Matthew his son did not show any great interest in the mine, being more interested in studying the plants and flowers that abounded in this Welsh valley and already attaining a reputation as a botanist of some note. Quite a few of the exotic shrubs and plants that he had introduced into the grounds surrounding the house, bore strange and beautiful flowers. As befitted a young man of good breeding and education, his interests extended beyond the boundary of the coal mining industry. His father had hoped that the interest he himself had in geology might surface in his son but Matthew seemed to show greater delight in the things on the surface rather than those buried deep in the rock and soil from which the family's wealth was dug.

Sitting at his desk, unwilling to start reading the report that Paget sent him every day, he gazed out of the window at the blue sky. Against it, the topmost branches of the trees in the park waved gently in the breeze. Near the house, the shaven lawns spread outward until almost imperceptibly they merged with the grassland that supplied grazing to the sheep and horses. He sighed contentedly. When he had announced his intention to leave Dymock and move to the border county of Monmouthshire, there were several of his friends who had tried to dissuade him. However his belief that beneath the hills and mountains of that county there existed rich seams of coal, had convinced him that he could do no better than to buy some land there and engage in the coal mining industry. He had had a good life in Gloucestershire and when he had become Lord of the Manor at Dymock, followed shortly after by the honour of being named High Sheriff of Gloucestershire, it seemed he had reached the pinnacle of attainment. But in 1810 he knew he had done the right thing when he sold the Dymock estate and after a little while managed to purchase the Plas Bedwellty estate from the powerful Morgan family. While this lovely house they lived in, was being built, he and Sarah had lived at Llanrumney Hall but as soon as possible they had come to this secluded valley. He had no regrets. He had been able to engage in politics, though that row with Frost had shown him that one couldn't be too careful in choosing friends. He had tried to do his best as a magistrate and he admitted to a quiet pride in his achieving some success with the Village System. He had improved life for some of the poor devils who lived in Blackwood. A man could only do so much and at fifty five there were times when he felt he would like to let someone else take up the burden.

As he broke the wax seal on the rolled report that Paget had sent, he turned for a last look at the blue skies and green grass. What fun it would be to be eight or nine years old again and able to spend the day playing out there.

CHAPTER 1

1826. The sixth year of the reign of King George IV. The traumas of the war against Napoleon and the threat of invasion were now things of the past. The wooden walls of the navy and the triumph of the Iron Duke at Waterloo had made sure that his Majesty's subjects could sleep undisturbed at night. Now was the time for the British giant to stir itself and change the face of the world. The Industrial Revolution was about to replace the horrors of the Revolution across the Channel. The revolution that had promised the common man so much, that had been praised in England's Parliament at its outset. A revolution that had degenerated into a mad nightmare, wherein thousands had ended their lives climbing the steps to be embraced in the insatiable arms of Madame La Guillotine.

In the coffee houses of the City of London, gentlemen sat discussing the possibilities for enrichment that beckoned them. Plans were laid in the studies and smoking rooms of the big houses that overlooked the royal parks. With the discovery of power that was contained in a jet of steam, farseeing men of business talked of the need to fuel the fires of industry with the rich black diamonds that lay buried beneath the green countryside of Britain. Coal. A gift that would make rich men such as Sir Henry Siston even richer, bringing wealth to a favoured few, and misery, death, and unrest to many. The scene was being set for the enactment of what was to be Britain's last armed rebellion, and the awakening of love in the hearts of two people, one hardly more than a child, the other only a few years older, but already doing a man's work in one of the holes in the ground that proudly called itself a colliery.

Six men sat at the large table, which until a few minutes earlier had been the scene of a sumptuous meal. Their womenfolk had retired to the drawing room, there to discuss and gossip about friends and enemies. Not for them the endless talk about money and how to make it. That was the business of men. Ladies' talk was of the latest fashions; of new dresses and who was doing what and where and with whom.

Of the men, now passing the port around the table, Sir Henry was not only the wealthiest, but the one who had greatest influence in places where it mattered most. He was speaking about the need for business men to get together and open up the areas where coal was to be had for little financial outlay.

'Gentlemen. I have a few interests in the west country and earlier I instructed my agent in Bristol to do some investigating in Newport. I have now received his report. He informs me that it is possible to pick coal from amongst the grass in some parts of Monmouthshire. The few people, farmers mostly, who live in the area, are not interested in recovering this new source of fuel. I believe that anyone, for a not very large outlay, stands to make a fortune by forming a group to dig this stuff out and transport it to the towns, foundries and factories. That is why I asked you to dinner tonight. We are all friends and business men. With the iron industry calling for a more efficient method of smelting, this is a golden opportunity. We can establish ourselves as suppliers of what will,'I am sure, become the main fuel in this land of ours for the next century. We have a chance to put our hands on a source of riches undreamed of.'

His friends nodded in agreement. It was well known that Sir Henry had an uncanny nose for smelling out new sources of wealth. If he was going into this, then it behove them to hang on to his coattails.

His wife Susannah meanwhile, listened as the wives of her husband's friends, regaled each other with the latest reports on what was going on, in that part of fashionable London in which they lived and played. She was quite heavily pregnant, but her couturier, who employed a whole host of grossly underpaid but highly proficient needle women, had so far cleverly disguised the fact.

Her female guests, sat in the comfortable chairs and chattered. Some of the more elderly who had eaten too well, strove to disguise the genteel belches they gave, while wishing that it were possible to loosen the strings of the corsets that fashion dictated they should wear. Susannah with a polite smile on her face strove to answer the questions directed at her. At the same time her attention kept wandering as her mind dwelt on the forthcoming event, now only a few months away. This would be her fifth child and she hoped that it would be another girl. Her husband was anxious to establish a firm line of heirs and she was equally anxious, but for different reasons. It would be nice to have another daughter. Gwendoline was now almost within a few years of her own age when Henry had sought her hand in marriage. Susannah missed the pleasure of having a little girl about, to spoil and dress in pretty things. Henry had shown his displeasure when Gwendoline had been the first born, and had the young Henry been another girl, she often wondered what his reaction would have been. True, he had been happy when Henry had arrived thus ensuring the continuation of the line, but she had noticed that once more, he had taken to talking about the unborn child as 'he', completely disregarding the fact that there was an equal chance of it being a girl. The arrivals of Jeremy and Simon had seemed to quell his fears that the Siston line would suddenly die out and had induced in him a joviality that was unusual. The successive births of three sons had undoubtedly gone a long way in helping to change his attitude toward Gwendoline. Not only did he now treat her with affection but at times seemed inordinately proud of her good looks and spirit. Almost fourteen years of age, she was already showing signs that, in a few years, her beauty would attract many a young beau. Her mother's one fear was that her spirit might prove a drawback. Susannah however, well knew, that should the new baby be another girl, Sir Henry might be displeased and that this time next year, he would be expecting her to be well on the way to producing another son. She sighed as she half listened to the words of wisdom pouring from Mrs. Denton, mother of nine. How to avoid too many of those occasions that men demanded as their rights. Mrs. Denton's advice it seemed hadn't proved very efficacious in view of the brood of Denton children. Others went into detail about the difficult times they had undergone producing their offspring. How different it was from her girlish dreams. The daughter of an Anglican Canon, Susannah Timperley one of five children, had been swept into marriage, unprepared, hardly more than a schoolgirl. They had been married only six months when she knew she was pregnant. Sir Henry had been delighted, and to her relief, did not press her to continue the love making that had been slightly distasteful to her. Instead, he enjoyed the favours of several ladies of his acquaintance, a fact unknown to Susannah, but common talk among those who comprised the set in which he moved. When her mother had indicated that she hoped that Susannah would soon make her a grandmother, she had been happy and relieved to tell her that she was now expecting.

The conversation of the assembled ladies was interrupted by the entrance of their menfolk, all looking flushed and in what seemed to be good spirits. With their arrival, the evening took on a somewhat predictable course. One of the wives played the pianoforte. Another sang. A third recited some poems. At ten o'clock they began to take their leave and soon Sir Henry and his wife were alone. Feeling tired, Susannah slowly climbed the stairs, leaving her husband to finish the bottle of port that he had brought with him from the dining room. He had periodically refilled his glass from it during the evening, and it was quite likely that Jevons the butler would be needed to help him into bed.

The plans which Sir Henry and his friends had made at the dinner table were quickly put into effect. Before the end of the year, papers had been prepared by his lawyers, enabling him and his friends to become the owners of over one hundred acres of land in a valley that ran north from Newport. This valley, one of several that were a feature of the county, was a lush green stretch of unspoiled countryside, home to nothing more than a few isolated farms and some sheep. A pleasant river, rich with trout, flowed quietly along its floor, linking the towns of Newport and Tredegar. The first, a small town with pretensions to be a large port, lay at the mouth of the river Usk. The other, already beginning to flex its industrial muscle, had been the home of iron works for some years. The great Morgan family who owned all the land thereabouts, had leased parts that lay in the vicinity of Tredegar, to Richard Homfray a Welsh industrialist. He, with his partners had taken the opportunity to set up forges and furnaces in the area, manufacturing iron.

The problem that had faced them was how to get their products from the furnaces to the canal which ran in the adjoining valley. Eventually, in 1805 a tramroad had been constructed to run down the western side of the river from Tredegar to a point just nine miles from Newport. The way was now open to exploit the coal and iron that lay beneath the hillsides and fields that bordered the valley. By 1806 another tramroad had been laid on the other side of the valley to deal with the output of coal from the area in which Sir Henry and his associates were interested. A man with whom Sir Henry was to have many dealings, recognising the potential wealth of the sparsely populated area, had also bought himself a large piece of land from the Morgan family, and had leased parts of it for the purpose of extracting the coal known to be lying there. Such had been the amount dug out that there now existed collieries employing considerable numbers of men.

Sir Henry, being the largest holder of shares in the newly formed London Fuel Company, decided to see for himself the piece of land situated in the hills, which he hoped would bring him additional wealth. Bidding goodbye to his wife, now nearly at her time, he set off for Wales.

Although travelling inside as befitted his rank, the journey to Newport had taken its toll and when he stepped stiffly down from the coach at the entrance to the Westgate Hotel, all he wanted was a meal and a comfortable bed; the former to be accompanied by a bottle of port. He was greeted by his agent, Daniel Morgan, who assured him that he would be most comfortable at this prestigious hotel. Sir Henry was in no mood for idle chatter and after being escorted to the room he was to occupy that night, dismissed Morgan, with instructions to come to see him the next morning at ten o'clock. He wished, he said, to travel up the valley to inspect his purchase and return to the hotel that same day. He did not wish to spend too much time in what he considered to be a backwater of civilisation.

Having eaten a surprisingly good dinner and drank the

best part of a bottle of port, he had slept well, and had not long arisen from his bed when his agent tapped at his bedroom door. Never one to let anyone he considered a menial interfere with his pleasures, Morgan was told to await his employer's pleasure. The next hour was spent in dressing carefully and then partaking of a good breakfast before he summoned his agent once more. Morgan had not wasted his time. He had spoken to a considerable number of people and had gained considerable knowledge about the area they proposed visiting and also about some of its better known inhabitants. He enquired if Sir Henry had slept well and then plunged immediately into briefing him on what he had been able to find out.

'I have spoken to several of my acquaintances Sir Henry, regarding the gentry who live in and around the area you are interested in. One of the most influential men in that particular area, is a gentleman by the name of John Hodder Moggridge. I understand, he owns quite a large expanse of land in the immediate vicinity of that purchased by you, much of which he leases for mining. They say he has built a fine mansion in a large park and besides being a successful industrialist, is a political figure and is a Magistrate. There is just one thing Sir Henry. Mr. Moggridge is I'm afraid, something of a Whig in his political beliefs. He was at one time a friend of some dubious characters in this town. Two well known local Radicals, John Frost who was at one time the mayor, and Samuel Ethridge. In fact, they supported him when he stood for Parliament. However, it appears that a year or so later, they became his bitter enemies. Frost went so far as to call Mr. Moggridge's sincerity into question in print. I thought it wise you should be aware of this sir.'

'Hm. It might be a good idea Morgan if I made the acquaintance of this Moggridge. It would be as well to have an influential friend in the area, even someone of this man's political persuasion. Not that I have ever known politics to hinder business unduly. I have heard some tales of unrest amongst the workers hereabouts and someone with local knowledge and a seat on the Bench would be invaluable.'

'If you would be prepared to stay for a night or two at The

Rock Inn nearby, perhaps I could arrange a meeting sir? It is well recommended. This would allow me to take a letter to Mr. Moggridge, explaining your reason for being in the area and the mutual benefits to be derived from a meeting before you return to London. One other point Sir Henry. The countryside in that area is thinly settled and such roads as there are, are little better than tracks. I fear it may be necessary for you to travel on horseback to reach some parts. Shall I arrange for the necessary horses when we get to the inn?'

'Very well Morgan. Tell the landlord that I shall not be returning tonight, and tell him to send up someone for my trunk. We might as well make a start.'

Half an hour later the carriage carrying Sir Henry and his agent was bowling along the road past Tredegar Park, the home of Sir Charles Morgan. He fervently hoped that his piece of land would net him a fortune that compared favourably. Sir Charles had been very fortunate. In the Act which allowed the original tramway to be built from Tredegar to Newport, the tramway entered his estate and he was allowed to levy a charge of one penny per ton per mile for maintenance on all the traffic passing over his section of the tramway. With the ever increasing amounts of coal pouring down the valley, this very lucrative toll caused the name the 'Golden Mile' to be bestowed on that section of the tramway, adding yet further to the fortunes of the Morgan family. He settled back against the cushions of the carriage. Perhaps if he could have foreseen the events which were to take place, he might have had second thoughts about the venture and returned to London.

CHAPTER 2

The journey northward up the long winding valley was pleasant in the sunshine. They stopped only once en route, at a little village where a sign post indicated that, the traveller needed to take the road that bore away to the left. Here they stopped to give the horses a breather. Sir Henry took the opportunity to instruct the driver to hand down the luncheon basket. Morgan under Sir Henry's guidance, opened both the wine and the port and laid out the contents of the basket on the carriage seat. The driver was despatched to find himself some food and drink at a local beerhouse while his passengers settled down to their lunch. Knowing Sir Henry's liking for port, Morgan having drunk two glasses of wine, thanked him for his offer but declined to share the bottle. Sir Henry was not put out by his agent's refusal and proceeded to lower the level of the bottle before declaring himself satisfied. With the driver refreshed and the horses now rested and fed, they set off once more. Perhaps due to the gentle jogging of the carriage and the amount of drink he had consumed, Sir Henry dozed off, leaving Morgan to look about him as they continued up the valley. Had Sir Henry been awake, he would have been aware of the tramway track that marched alongside the road. After about an hour's travel the outskirts of what looked like a much larger village appeared. Sir Henry awoke and enquired of his agent its name?

'That is Blackwood Sir Henry. I know very little about it, except that my informant in Newport gave most credit to Mr. Moggridge as being the person responsible for its establishment. It appears to be a very thriving little town sir, and is said to have grown because of the tramway and the scheme that Mr. Moggridge brought into being. I shall make it my business to find out all I can about it during our stay at the Rock Inn.'

Sir Henry listened to Morgan's explanation, nodded, then sat silent looking about him at the wooded countryside on either side of the river. He was surprised at the natural beauty of the valley having imagined that since industry had been established at its head, its effects would have been felt. As if to reinforce Morgan's statement about the importance of the tramway, they became aware of a rumbling noise approaching rapidly. Alongside, the steel rails stretched in both directions. Their purpose was soon made abundantly clear. Ahead of them along the track there appeared a long line of what Sir Henry assumed were trams, being pulled by horses. The trams were nothing more than large square boxes on wheels. Each tram was piled high with iron and coal. Their driver had climbed down from his perch and stood holding the horses' heads while the convoy passed. Sir Henry and Morgan sat in silence until it had passed from view. They sat for a while each thinking about what they had just encountered, then Sir Henry nodded to the driver to carry on.

Before they had reached the outskirts of the town, they were forced to stop once more by the passage of another convoy. Their driver apologised for the need for him to dismount and hold the horses' heads, but the noise and appearance of these long lines of loaded trams was having an effect upon them and he had no wish to have them frighten and bolt. At last they entered the town and Sir Henry was immediately struck by the contrast between it and its surroundings. Smoke clouded everything despite the sunshine and both he and Morgan began to cough. Worse was yet to come. As they approached what seemed to be the centre of the town, the rumble of yet another journey of trams became audible. Peering through the gloom Sir Henry was able to see the first of the trams. There were no horses at the front yet the line of trams was hurtling along. He realised then that it was the gradient that was responsible for their speed. Somehow they clung to the rails despite the curves where the rails followed the natural contours. Men ran alongside, all carrying large pieces of wood, presumably to push into the wheels to slow down the speed of the tubs when they were travelling downhill. Each tram, like those that had gone before, carried a full load. The driver had once more climbed down and stood holding the horses' heads. Sir Henry looked about him. Marooned in the carriage, he had ample time to study his surroundings. He was no stranger to the sights of towns which had suddenly had industrial development thrust upon them.

Having travelled extensively in the pursuit of his business interests, he was used to seeing the poverty which seemed to go hand in hand with the wealth of the nation, but his first impression of this comparatively new town, was one which he admitted to himself, surpassed all others in its picture of degradation. Despite the dry weather, underfoot was a sea of almost black mud and pools of scummy water. That it was the continuous passage of the tubs of coal that was responsible for the colour of the mud was clear, but the presence of so much water, in which floated filth of every sort, was not immediately obvious.

The town, which seemed to consist of an extended row of buildings either side of the track, was built on the sloping side of the valley, and the tramway, its central feature, laid along what had probably been an original footpath. He could see two streams that ran between the cottages, down to the river in the valley bottom. It was the overflow from these that had caused the puddles.

The dwellings were not much better than hovels and comprised the majority of the buildings. From their squat chimneys smoke belched forth, adding to the gloom that hung over the scene, and to the general grime that had long since changed the original whitewashed walls to a uniform dirty grey. Each cottage had but one window facing the track, but like everything else, this was covered in a coating of dirt that would make it impossible to see either in or out. Despite this, the inhabitants had tried to add to their privacy by hanging nondescript pieces of material to act as curtains. Dirty and torn, they only added to the general air of squalor and miserable poverty. Doorways, opening direct on to the muddy track, were mostly open, but again the smoke within, allowed little or no light to penetrate and nothing could be seen of the interiors.

There was a large number of people passing to and fro and he had never set eyes on a scruffier collection. For the most part, they did not spare him more than a brief glance and such conversation as he heard was unintelligible. There was none of the life and vitality that was normally displayed on even the meanest London street. Instead, a conspiratorial grimness seemed to pervade the very air. The men wore an expression he could not put a name to. They were unshaven and dark featured, many clenching clay pipes in their teeth, slouching as they walked. He searched for the word. Dour? No. Sullen. That was it! Like curs with their tails between their legs, but likely to turn and snap back. The women, for the most part clad in unbecoming black, except for their mop caps and shawls, were at least brighter in their aspect, but even they had a despairing look about them. They clutched a basket or held their skirts, trying to avoid contact with the mud and filth that floated in the water, but the majority of the crowd, unheeding, ploughed back and forth, their clothes bespattered and wet. Overall hung the stench. It was appalling and he held his handkerchief to his nose.

At last the train of tubs came to an end with the last of the tubs being nothing more than a flat bottomed platform. On this were tethered two horses, obviously not required on the part of the journey just completed. Their driver resumed his perch, shook the reins and a sudden jerk signalled the continuation of their journey. Sir Henry settled back in his seat, glad to be leaving the sights and smells of the new town.

This was their first view of what would become a common sight in the industrialised areas that business men were turning these pleasant valleys into. About a half hour later they pulled into the courtyard of the Rock Inn.

As soon as he had seen Sir Henry settled in his room, Morgan broached the subject of the letter to Mr. Moggridge. With Sir Henry installed before the fire, a glass of port to hand, Morgan sharpened a quill, and wrote as his employer dictated. Having checked what had been written, Sir Henry scribbled the name 'Siston' above the neatly written signature inscribed by Morgan. Sanding the letter, Morgan sealed it with wax. Assuring his master that he would return as quickly as possible, he left Sir Henry to his thoughts, and went to seek the landlord to hire a horse and obtain directions to the mansion that Mr. Moggridge was said to inhabit somewhere nearby. It was now just two o'clock in the afternoon and, after studying a rough map that the landlord had drawn for him, he set off.

The first part of his journey involved crossing the river in the valley bottom. Apparently, his destination was a large house situated in a piece of woodland known as Woodfield Park. To reach this, necessitated climbing to the summit of the hill on the opposite side of the valley, then following the track that wound along the flank of the hillside. He was glad to note that the map showed an inn called the Ivy Bush stood on the side of the track about halfway to his destination. Another hostelry called the Angel Inn stood very near to a church and marked the end of his journey. A lodge which marked the side entrance to Mr. Moggridge's residence, was shown as being within a very short distance of the last named inn. Sat on the horse's back, he was glad that he did not have to walk the track that led down to the river. It was a narrow pathway that was composed mainly of sharp edged stones and protruding.rock, flanked by hedges that overgrew the path to meet overhead in parts. At the bottom, a stone built bridge crossed the swiftly flowing river. His map named this as Pont Syr Dafydd. Once over the bridge, the track led sharply upward, climbing continuously. This would be Rhiw Syr Dafydd he thought. When he had asked the landlord why that name had been bestowed on the hill, he had been told of the band of Welsh archers who had fought at Agincourt and whose leader Dafydd Gam had died while saving King Henry V. He had been knighted as he lay dying and the hill and the bridge had been named after him. Some said it was because some of his band of archers had come from the area and wanted his gallant act to be remembered. So steep was the hill that Morgan was forced to get down from the saddle and walk alongside his horse as its metal shoes rang against the stone underfoot. By the time he had climbed until he met another track coming from the right, he was panting with exertion and took the opportunity to rest. The only signs of habitation were some farm buildings set back from the track away to his left. Remounting he rode slowly along until he came to a gate with a sign on it declaring this to be Penrhiw Farm. Knowing that he was proceeding in the right direction, he nudged his mount and soon found himself passing the little inn called the Ivy Bush. Despite the warm day, wishing to complete his journey as quickly as possible, he did not stop. Soon another farm appeared, then a church, badly in need of repair. Several weatherbeaten stones, marking the resting places of some of its worshippers, testified to its having occupied the spot for some years. The track sloped away quite sharply and further down he could see smoke rising from the chimneys of a long low building which he assumed to be the Angel Inn. To its right, was a tract of wooded countryside, and assured now that he had arrived, he urged his horse forward. After passing the inn, he saw, fifty or sixty yards away to his right, the white walled thatched cottage, which he knew must be the lodge he was seeking. Dismounting, he approached the little building and knocked at the door. A woman opened it and stood looking at him. He greeted her in Welsh, aware that this was the language most in use hereabout. She replied in the same language. In reply to his inquiry she said, that 'Yes this was Mr. Moggridge's estate and if he would follow the driveway it would take him to the house. The master was at home.' He thanked her and remounting rode along the grassy drive with its two wheel tracks toward the building that he could make out amongst the trees. A dog came running towards him barking loudly, but stopped when someone shouted and it slunk quietly back. He was met by the owner of the voice before he had reached the house.

'Please excuse my dog. We do not get many visitors and he gets excited. Can I help you? My name is Moggridge. John Moggridge. This is my home.'

Morgan dismounted and introduced himself. Mr Moggridge interrupted him saying,

'I'm forgetting my manners Mr. Morgan. Please come in. I'm sure you must be thirsty and a little saddle sore from our so called roads.'

As they made their way around the house, Morgan studied it carefully. The driveway he had come in by was really a side entrance. Away to his left he could see a drive which ended at the same entrance but disappeared into the wooded park stretching away down the hill in a southerly direction. As they were about to enter the house, Morgan was able to appreciate its size. Six gabled rooftops gave him some indication of its dimensions and when they got inside he noted the beauty of the interior with its magnificent staircase and carving. Mr. Moggridge led the way to a room that he obviously used as a study. Racks of books lined the walls, and a writing bureau whose pigeon holes were stuffed with papers, indicated that it was the centre of his activities. From a cabinet he withdrew a decanter and glasses.

'Some brandy Mr. Morgan?'

'Thank you sir. I must admit climbing up that hill from the river below the Rock Inn has given me a thirst.'

Settled in their chairs, Morgan withdrew the letter and passed it to his host.

'Sir Henry Siston, my employer, has instructed me to hand this to you. It is self explanatory and if it is possible I am to return with an answer.'

Moggridge broke the seal and began reading. Morgan sipped his brandy and sat silent, studying his surroundings. This was the room of a well read man. The books looked as if they had been used and unlike some houses he had been in, the books were not in orderly rows, but higgledy piggledy as if put back after use wherever there was room. His thoughts were interrupted by Mr. Moggridge.

'I take it you are aware of the contents of this letter Mr. Morgan?'

'Yes Mr. Moggridge. As you can see from the signature, Sir Henry has signed it but the handwriting is mine.'

'You have worked for him for some time?'

'I've had the privilege of acting as his agent in the west country for quite a few years, so when he became interested in purchasing or leasing land in this area, I was detailed to find out what I could before Sir Henry came down himself to look around.'

'Where is Sir Henry staying?'

'We have rooms at the Rock Inn.'

'Quite a good hostelry so I understand. But I feel Sir Henry would be much happier here. I shall put pen to paper immediately Mr. Morgan and extend an invitation to him to spend the remainder of his stay here. You too of course. If you will

24

excuse me, I will write the letter now. Perhaps you could manage a bite to eat while I do so?'

He lifted a hand bell and in answer to its tinkle, a maid appeared.

'Gwynneth. Prepare something to eat for Mr. Morgan.'

The maid bobbed a curtsy and disappeared.

Mr. Moggridge busied himself at his desk. After a short while, a tap at the door heralded the entrance of the maid bearing a tray. Mr. Morgan was glad to see that among the plates, a pewter tankard indicated that whoever had prepared the tray, reckoned that anyone who had arrived on horseback and had endured the dust and heat, was more in need of a long drink of ale than the master's brandy.

'Carry on Mr. Morgan. I shall be busy for a while but we can talk while you eat. Have you personally visited the area that Sir Henry has purchased?'

'No sir. I only know that it is situated in an area known as the Gwrhay. We had intended asking the landlord of the Rock Inn to supply us with a guide.'

'Well if Sir Henry accepts my invitation, it will give me the greatest pleasure to take you myself. I trust he is in no great hurry to get back to London?'

'I know he is prepared to stop in the area for a couple of days but as to his plans beyond that I cannot help you.'

'No matter. I can talk the matter over with him when we meet.'

He had continued writing while he was talking, and picking up a small pewter pot, shook some sand on to the paper then blew it off.

He sealed the missive and addressed it, then handed it to Morgan, who had now finished the piece of pie and pickles that had been under the cover. Raising the tankard, he drained it and wiping his fingers on a surprisingly delicate handkerchief that he withdrew from his coat pocket, he placed the letter inside his coat.

'Should Sir Henry give me the honour to accept my invitation, I would suggest that you take a different route to reach here. I cannot imagine that Sir Henry would relish climbing the Rhiw even with the help of his horse.'

Daniel Morgan could not suppress the smile that sprung to his lips at the mental picture of his employer struggling to make his way up the incline which would have made a goat struggle.

'When you know his intention, get the landlord to give you directions to reach Woodfield Park through Blackwood. You will find the track much easier to follow and much less fatiguing. I hope I shall have the pleasure of seeing you again tomorrow and having you as my guest for a few days.'

After a few more words, Morgan took his departure, and now knowing the route, was soon at the head of the hill leading down to the river. It was indeed quite an incline and he dismounted, fearful of the horse slipping on the stony surface. It would not do to take a tumble here, he could lie for ages waiting for some wayfarer to espy him on this lonely road.

At last he was able to remount the horse and was soon handing it back to the care of the ostler. He hurried to Sir Henry's room and found him sitting where he had left him, an empty bottle on the small table. The only sound was a gentle snore from the occupant of the chair. He gently shook Sir Henry's shoulder and when he was awake, handed him the letter. Sir Henry took it from him and opening it, quickly read it.

'Damned civil of the man. He's invited me to stay with him Morgan. Expects me for lunch tomorrow.'

'Very good Sir Henry.'

'What sort of person is he Morgan?'

'Oh a gentleman sir. No doubt of that. Well to do and from my brief acquaintance, a clever and well read man sir. If the house is anything to judge him by sir, he's somebody of great consequence in the area.'

'Well I see no reason not to accept his invitation. This is a comfortable place but I would appreciate the company of a gentleman at the table, and to hear civilized talk. Most of what I've heard sounds like gibberish. We'll leave tomorrow then Morgan.'

'One thing Sir Henry. Mr. Moggridge suggests we travel a different route to the one I took...'

Sir Henry interrupted him, 'Very well Morgan. I leave all that to you. Now I think it's time I had something to eat. Go and see what the landlord has for me, there's a good man.'

After ensuring that Sir Henry was well provided for, both in the eating and drinking manner, Morgan made arrangements with the landlord to supply two good horses to enable them to reach Woodfield Park. The question of Sir Henry's trunk was solved by the landlord offering, to hire a cart for a small sum, to precede them carrying the heavy article. Satisfied that he had made all the necessary arrangements and his immediate duties done, Morgan invited the landlord to join him, and together they stood either side of the bar talking and drinking until Morgan bade him good night and retired to bed.

They had no difficulty in following the new route, thanks to the cart whose horse plodded quietly along ahead of them. This time they retraced their path back to Blackwood and as they came to the end of the row of cottages, shops and beer houses that lined the track through the town, they turned downhill toward the river. It was no more than a grassy track and they dismounted, allowing the horses to lead them down the slope. Morgan shouted to the driver of the cart, 'What's the name of this river?'
'This be the Sirhowy.'

Immediately after crossing the river, they were confronted by a hill track that to Morgan's eyes, looked as steep as the Rhiw he had climbed from the Rock Inn. Sir Henry too looked at it with horror. When Morgan suggested they dismount and walk, he refused point blank.
'I'll ride on the cart' he said.

It was the driver's turn to refuse.
'I be sorry m'lord but the old nag 'ont pull the cart and your trunk up this slope.'
Morgan solved the problem by suggesting that he accompany the cart to the top where he and the driver would unload the luggage then the cart could come back down and pick up Sir Henry. The horses could be fastenend to the back of the cart. There being no better solution this was undertaken and eventually they were all once more together on the

road that ran past the lodge gates.

An elderly woman opened the large iron gates, and they rode through wooded land separating the main house from the public highway. Seen from this side, the house presented a magnificent picture. It was surrounded by trees and shrubs, many of which were in flower. One tree, whose trunk and branches were sheathed in broad pointed bladelike leaves, was unlike anything either of them had seen before. Their arrival was greeted with the barking of the dog, but it did not appear. When they neared the house, they could see the brute was chained. No doubt, Mr. Moggridge expecting them, had taken the precaution of ensuring that Sir Henry Siston was not disturbed by a dog threatening to tear him limb from limb. They were greeted by Mr. Moggridge, and his wife. Servants scurried about picking up Sir Henry's trunk and Morgan's smaller bags. Soon the guests had been installed in adjoining rooms. Sir Henry was impressed by the luxury of the appointments and hoped that his host was a man who kept a cellar equally well furnished. The visitors were summoned to a lunch that confirmed Sir Henry's hopes, that, in accepting the invitation to stay here, he had every prospect of enjoying the sort of food and drink that he was used to. Mr. Moggridge invited them to look over the part of his estate immediately adjacent to the house, and in the afternoon sun the three of them strolled amongst the trees. While Morgan enjoyed the tour, his employer who very rarely walked any further than necessary, excused himself and retired to his room to rest. Mr. Moggridge and Morgan walked leisurely on, talking, about the surrounding countryside and of Mr. Moggridge's Village System, the scheme which he had initiated in the years after the Napoleonic war. Mr. Moggridge was someone to whom it was easy to listen while he talked. The agent was a good listener and the afternoon passed quickly while his host spoke of the things that had happened in this supposedly backward part of the country. Morgan chanced to remark on the disrepair into which the church nearby had fallen, and his companion seized upon this to enlighten him about the history of that building. His first impression of John Moggridge had been correct. Not only was he a good business man, but a man of considerable culture whose farsightedness had caused a miniature revolution in a quiet valley. He determined that when he was alone he would write down what he had heard today and perhaps one day he might learn from it and, like his host, profit therefrom. The evening too was well spent. A meal that would have done credit to any of the best eating places in London was enjoyed by Sir Henry and Morgan. The latter felt slightly uncomfortable at first, but as the meal progressed and the wine flowed, he relaxed and began to enjoy himself. Sir Henry did justice to the meal and the wine, and when Mr. Moggridge suggested that they retire to his study to talk over their plans for the morrow, Sir Henry was very happy to note that Mr. Moggridge instructed the serving girl to bring the port. It was at this point that Sir Henry subtly brought to his host's attention, that, while he had no objection to Morgan being seated at the Moggridge table, he, Sir Henry, had no intention of allowing his agent, however trustworthy, to be party to whatever was discussed in the study. As Morgan followed them from the dining room, Sir Henry, turned and said,

'Ah. Morgan. I don't think we need involve you in our talk. I am sure you must have things to see to. I'll see you in the morning.'

Aware that he had been dismissed, Morgan thanked his host for an excellent meal and made his way to his room.

Downstairs, the two men settled down to their talk about coal and the best means of getting it out of the ground cheaply, and selling it at a good profit.

CHAPTER 3

While Sir Henry and Mr. Moggridge discussed ways and means to enable them to cut costs, increase output and thus increase profit, Daniel Morgan determined to put down on paper as much as he' could remember about the things his host had disclosed during their conversation that afternoon. It was obvious that modesty had forced Mr. Moggridge to speak in general terms about his scheme to develop the workers' natural independence, but Morgan was astute enough to be able to discern much that had been left unsaid. He sat thinking for a while then began writing:-

'When the following was disclosed to me today, I was intrigued. John Hodder Moggridge of whom I write, is a man who has much to recommend him. Here is a man who has, by virtue of his concern for his fellow men, brought into being a village. Where once stood one or two mean dwellings within the confines of a large wood, known as Coed Duon, there now stands the village of Blackwood. A village so rapidly growing that within a very short time it will attain the status of a town. Mr. Moggridge, business man, Magistrate, politician, and philanthropist, though he will deny the last, can truly be said to be the father of the new village within the Black Wood. Born in 1771 in Bradford upon Avon, he is no stranger to high office. In 1809 he served as High Sheriff of Gloucestershire, then moved to Wales. He purchased the Plas Newydd estate in the parishes of Bedwellty and Mynyddislwyn and has built for himself, a magnificent home in the Sirhowy valley. Although a stranger in the area, such is the man's capabilities, he took his place on the Bench just over two years after relinquishing his high office to move here. He is well known for his interest in politics, and in 1820 stood for Parliament in the Monmouth Boroughs with the active support of that well known Radical Mr. John Frost. Mr. Moggridge has confessed that he has changed direction since then and now is of the Whig party persuasion. In the depression following the wars against Napoleon, he was an enthusiastic Reformer and strove to lighten the burdens that rested so heavily upon the shoulders of the less fortunate labouring classes. Not only did he speak out in print about the causes of their misfortune but he took action in a practical way. This was his 'Village System.' He offered suitable workmen, the chance to lease a small area of ground on condition that they paid a small ground rent, built a cottage thereon and cultivated the garden and repaid the money advanced with interest at stipulated intervals. The benefit to the men concerned can be seen by the fact that the ground rent, plus the repayment of the loan and interest, amounted to much less than was normally paid in rent annually for a cottage. From a small start the scheme has grown by leaps and bounds. None of his chosen workmen have failed to repay him and since the inception of this novel scheme, this public benefactor has caused to be built, a market hall in 1822 and every year new houses have been added. A similar system has been started at Ynysddu and ground has been laid out for another village in the Rhymney valley to be called Trelyn. It is estimated that the three villages in his scheme have a total of more than two thousand inhabitants. Blackwood is by far the largest, harbouring well over one thousand souls. Mr. Moggridge has confessed that contrary to popular belief, his schemes have not caused him any financial loss. On the contrary. He states that they have produced an increase in the rental of his estate. He is also more than happy to be able to boast that, there is now a 'Colony of valuable workmen' available to work in the collieries in the valleys, something greatly to be desired, as what had been a vagrant and migratory population has become stationary and steady. This social experiment of John Hodder Moggridge is one that deserves recognition and one that could well be copied in other areas.'

Morgan put down his pen and read what lay before him. He did not think that what he had written differed in any great extent to that which he had been told that afternoon. What had not been revealed of course, was his host's motives for having introduced the scheme. In the course of his dealings as agent for Sir Henry, Daniel Morgan had learned that not everything was as at first appeared in business. Why therefore, had Mr. Moggridge apparently been prepared to risk losing large amounts of money, on what appeared to be a scheme that went against the normal run of business practice? As a member of the Bench he would have seen plenty of the problems that a poor society would have to face, and concerned as he may have been about the conditions under which the poor lived, he was only too well aware of the burden they were on the rates and how discontented workers could cause instability in society, thus giving rise to strikes that directly effected the output of his coal bearing properties. Despite the benefits that such a scheme as he had introduced would bring to those of his workers who lived in Blackwood, in the strike of 1822 his coalmining profits must have suffered. It was said that the strike had been engineered by the gangs known as Scotch Cattle who operated in the area. Despite his workers' willingness to work, they had been scared off by the desperate men who wreaked vengeance on all those who stood against them. Morgan came to the conclusion that his host's motives were a mixture of philanthropic benevolence and self interest. The first having a direct and beneficial effect on the second. Happy with his reasoning and aware that what he had written gave him an insight into the way Moggridge's mind worked, he carefully rolled the paper, bound it and placed it in his bag. He had promised Sir Henry that he would find out as much as possible about their host and what better source than the gentleman himself? Of course, nobody was likely to reveal anything that might damage their reputation but perhaps his employer might see fit to reward him for bringing this information to his attention? Maybe Morgan had dealt with business men for too long. He gave no thought to the fact that Moggridge's system perhaps bestowed greater benefits on those participating in it than on Moggridge himself. Thinking only that business men always had ulterior motives for anything they did.

In the study below, Sir Henry and his host were discussing plans for a tour of inspection of Sir Henry's acquisition. As Morgan had forseen, it would have to be carried out on horseback. Mr. Moggridge assured his guest that he would be able to provide horses for all of them. His description of the output of coal from the other collieries nearby had raised Sir

Henry's hopes that in the near future, he too would be participating in the sharing of wealth that this latest business venture promised. They talked for a long time, discussing wages,
hours, deduction for various benefits such as surgeons attention, and what action Sir Henry, as a new participant in the
coal mining industry, should take to ensure that the owners
maintained a united front, in the event of industrial unrest.
At last, satisfied that they had discussed as many as possible
of the problems that confronted businessmen, they parted to
dress for dinner. That evening, Morgan gave his employer
his written report on their host. In the privacy of his bedroom
Sir Henry studied it and was inclined to agree with Morgan's
conclusions. Mr. Moggridge had not acquired a reputation
for being an excellent businessman without having an eye for
the main chance. It was always as well to know as much as
possible about your business friends and rivals, and what
Morgan had written had made him aware that his host was
not to be taken lightly.

CHAPTER 4

At the same time that Mr. Moggridge, his family and guests sat down and asked the blessing of God on the table groaning beneath the weight of the food they intended eating, three miles away, Robert Morgan aged fifteen gathered up his tools, put on a jacket and wound a kerchief around his neck; then along with the hundred or so others who worked in the sodden but still dust laden hole in the ground, that went under the imposing name of the NantGwrhay Colliery, made his way out into the evening air and started his two miles walk home.

Along with his workmates, he talked about the problems he had faced during his twelve hours hacking away at the seam of coal. Of the foul mouthed Dai Williams who was in charge of the several yards of coal that comprised the face where he worked. When Robert had pointed out the likelihood of flooding from the water that leaked from the coal face, water which gathered around them until they stood up to their knees in it, Williams had given him a choice. Either he carried on, or he could finish that same day. There were plenty who would be glad to take his place. Both knew, that in fact there was no choice. If he chose to finish, his six brothers and sisters and widowed mother would starve. Since the day, now nearly three years ago, when Evan Morgan had been buried beneath the rock fall, Robert had been the breadwinner. But for the fact that his father had sent him fifty yards down the tunnel to fetch a post to prop up the roof and his jack of water, he too would have been buried under the massive fall that had killed his father. Even now, he still awoke with screams ringing in his ears. There had been two others who had died that day, Emrys Evans and his nine year old son Ieuan, dreamer of blue skies and green grass, had worked alongside Robert and his father. The creaks and groans from the roof above them were a part of life underground and to the experienced collier represented nothing more than constant warnings that above their heads, thousands of tons of earth waited to crash down on them. They were warnings that were noted but ignored. No man could afford to pay too much attention to them. It was hard enough trying to keep up with the demands made by Williams, without constantly stopping to listen to the threatening sounds from above. The day the roof had caved in had been the same as any other. At five o'clock on that fateful day his mother had shaken him awake and he had crawled from the warm bed he shared with his three brothers. Shivering as he pulled on the workclothes that his mother had laid on the ragmat in front of the fire. Never as long as he could remember had he ever seen the fireplace cold and empty. It was the only source of warmth in the cottage and before he had gone to join his father in the pit, as the eldest, it had been his job to make sure that there was always enough coal and wood in the 'cwtch' in the corner of the room to ensure that the fire never died. Now that duty had fallen upon Dafydd, whilst he spent most of his waking hours in the mine trying desperately to make sure that there was enough money handed over to Mam to keep them in food. With eight mouths to feed, there was very little to spare and he was well aware that there were times when his mother had untruthfully protested that she was not hungry and had divided up her share of the evening meal between the youngest of her brood.

It was this aspect of his family's life that was foremost in his mind that evening as he trudged wearily alongside the tramway that led from the colliery. Laid down by the renowned engineer Benjamin Hall, it hugged the valley side, winding its way along to Abercarn where it would link up with that marvel of engineering, the Monmouthshire Canal. When they came to the Rhiw, Robert and one or two others, left the main flood of workers, and made their way down the rocky track to the main highway, running from Tredegar further up the valley. The same track up which his namesake, Sir Henry's agent, had stumbled clinging to his horse, the previous day. While Morgan had been careful where he placed his feet for fear of falling, Robert after years of walking this path to the colliery, hardly noticed where he put his feet. With his empty jack swinging from one hip and tommy box hanging on the other, he moved along with his eyes half closed. He was bone weary and the clammy feel of the water sodden trousers against his flesh only served to add to his misery. Six days a week for the last six years he had trudged this way. At first, as a pale underfed boy of nine, he had held his father's hand as they walked from Coed Duon to the colliery. He had been handed over to tender mercies of Joshua Walters at the colliery shaft to be initiated into the mysteries of working as a 'door boy.' Barely able to keep his eyes open after a night with not much sleep, a night spent wondering what the morrow would bring, he had been given some hot ale and a hunk of bread for his breakfast, and a jack of water and more bread and a piece of cheese to eat at work by his mother. Then, they had trudged off into the winter's darkness, to join similar couples.

His duties were to open and shut the ventilation doors to allow the passage of coal out and timber and other supplies into the coal face. In itself the duty was not hard, but to crouch there in the darkness, sometimes numb with cold, alone, waiting for the sound of someone coming, to bring the blessed relief of the sound and sight of another human being. Not that any time could be spent in idle chatter. Usually the creature dragging the tub of coal was too breathless and eager to get on, to do anything other than to curse him for being so slow to open the door. Cursing and sobbing for breath, these creatures were hardly recognisable as women and young girls. Harnessed like horses to the tubs of coal, they dragged them from the coal face to the bottom of the shaft, there to be lifted up to the daylight by other women straining to wind the handle of the windlass that supplied the power to raise the burden. When first the young Robert had seen these human horses, he hardly recognised them for what they really were. Never in his short life had he seen any woman or girl who looked as these did. With a harness made of rope or leather tied around their waist, fastened to a chain that hung between their legs, then hooked on to the tub of coal, they crawled forward dragging their loads. Some edged forwards on hands and knees. Others, bent forward just touching the floor with their knuckles, gasping in the dusty air, sweat and coal dust streaking every part of the body that was exposed. Their faces contorted with the effort, they threw their weight forward in an effort to keep the tub moving. Any natural modesty these women might have had had long since been abandoned in their efforts to lessen the sweating brought about by their labours. It was not uncommon for them to appear before the young boy in a half naked state as they struggled in the semi darkness to maintain movement. He was witness too, to the indecencies to which they were subjected. Both by the miners, who might have been expected to show sympathy toward a fellow worker, and the likes of Dai Williams. Working in conditions that were little short of cruel slavery, they were treated like animals, cursed and reviled for not moving fast enough; threatened with the loss of their job if they protested when liberties were taken with their bodies. Little wonder then that, when the doorboy was slow in unbarring the way for them, they in turn cursed him and said other things that brought a blush to his dusty cheeks. He had heard tales of other doorboys, younger even than he, who had begun their first day's work being carried on their father's shoulders, too young even to walk as far as the colliery. Like those working at the coal face Robert and his companions faced the same dangers. Roof falls. Being crushed by the tubs of coal as the women struggled to gain momentum. Scummy water, running from the face swirling along the tunnel soaking and freezing their skinny illclad bodies; and always the ever present danger of rats attracted by any food that could be foraged. All these dangers were as nothing compared to the one of falling asleep and being caught by one of the bosses. That meant the loss of the job and the few shillings wages. Sometimes, it had been almost impossible to stop his eyelids from closing and succumbing to the temptation to sneak just a few minutes blessed sleep. No matter that, as soon as he had washed and eaten at night, curled up in his bed he shared and sunk into sleep, next morning he had to be dragged out still asleep and would stumble alongside his father, still trying to unglue his eyes.

That had been six years ago and now he was the man of the house. Even now, still only fifteen, his mother and family looked to him to provide the wherewithal to keep body and soul together. Dafydd was now ten and if he could persuade Williams, he might be able to get him a start alongside him. Deri, his helper since he had been given a place at the face, was nearly as old as himself and ready to take over a place of his own. He would ask Williams tomorrow, but he was well aware that he might be asked to pay a bribe that he could not afford. There were, as Williams had pointed out, plenty waiting to take his place if he wasn't satisfied, and it was not uncommon for a price to be extracted for any favours granted. Since the rise in demand for coal to meet the iron industry's insatiable hunger, villages had sprung up around each new colliery; villages populated by thousands of immigrant workers from all parts of the British Isles, all seeking work in the new collieries. Those who could not find homes of their own, shared the cottages that sprang up, helping to pay the rents demanded by rapacious landlords. He would have to wait and see whether Williams would be prepared to make up for the death of his father by employing another son. All these things went through his mind as he trudged along. It was with relief that he spotted the first of the mean cottages that were the outskirts of the village that had been Coed Duon, but which had now become the rapidly growing town of Blackwood.

CHAPTER 5

The cottage that Robert called home was little more than a
hovel. Indeed, some five years previously, a famous man had
proclaimed in a report on the conditions under which the
mining workers and their families lived, that 'Their dwellings
are little better than pig-beds' and in the intervening time,
there had been no improvement. It defied the efforts of his
mother and the eldest of his sisters, to make it into anything
other than the meanest of dwellings. No amount of sweeping
with the homemade besom could cope with the dirt and
muck that came in from the outside and the smoke which
rose from the fire. In the one cluttered room which comprised the living space for the whole family, Myfanwy Morgan had laboured day after day to feed her family, nurse the
baby that suckled at her breast, or in the brief respite granted
her by nature, acted as wife to his father, and mother and
nurse to the rest of the brood that, every two years since her
marriage, had been born into a world that seemed to try its
hardest to kill them. Married nearly eighteen years, at thirty
five she looked an old woman. Small to start with, the years
of child bearing and unremitting toil had bent her and drawn
lines on her face. The pain in her back had now become as familiar as an old friend. To stand up straight caused the beast
that dwelt within her to make her gasp with pain, so she
passed most of the time, back curved like a bow, head sunk
to her chest. Her day, as befitted a dutiful wife, started at
four thirty each morning, winter or summer, and ended
when her husband fell asleep in the bed separated from the
rest of the family, by a few feet of dirt floor. Now it was her
eldest son who had to be roused at five o'clock to trudge off
to work. Soon perhaps, Dafydd would accompany his big
brother. Whatever pitiful wage he brought home, it would
make a great difference. Thank God Evan had somehow
managed to keep them out of the grasp of the Truck Shop. If
once they had become entangled in the web of that unholy
place, they would have starved when Evan was killed. She
had heard tales of families who had had their meagre belongings taken to pay what was said to be owing. Whatever might

be said about 'Squire' Moggridge, he, thank God, paid his workmen in coin, and not the tokens that some mineowners hereabouts gave their men. Tokens only changeable in the Truck Shop, where the goods were much dearer than anywhere else and not always of the same quality. There had been riots and strikes at some collieries where the Truck Shop held the workmen to ransom by this system of payment. Whenever Myfanwy Morgan thanked God for the few benefits that befell her family, she always thanked Him that the Morgan men, however poorly paid, were working for the man who lived in Woodfield Park.

The three years since her husband's death had dulled the mental pain and now and again she smiled in a sad sort of way. A smile that said, 'I have lost my husband. I have lost two children with the cholera. Perhaps God will grant me a few years peace now.' She was not happy. When Evan had brought her from North Wales in 1810, a bride of six months, her belly already swollen with Robert, she had been happy. She had been young and strong then. The change, from life on a farm, to being the wife of a miner had been enough to cause her to weep when she was alone, but still she had been happy; at least, most of the time. Even when the twins, only months old, had been taken in the cholera that had swept through the valley like a plague, she had, after the initial grief, somehow seemed content. Now she wasn't happy or content, not since the day her husband's body had been carried home from the NantGwrhay on a rough litter. Still in sodden workclothes, one arm hanging limply from under the filthy blanket that covered his broken body, they had brought him to his wife; they had laid the litter on the dirt floor of the cottage, and mumbling their sympathy, had retreated, leaving her to weep. Robert, his face streaked with dirt and tears had walked behind the six men who had borne his father home still clutching the jack of water his father had sent him to fetch only a minute or so before the roof had collapsed, burying him and his two workmates.

A neighbour had come and shooed the children outside, then had led away his mother to her equally depressing home. Robert had stood silent, watching as a dirt ridden hag, who had arrived proclaiming herself to be the woman who laid out the dead, undressed the broken body of Evan Morgan, washed him, crossed his arms on his chest and wrapped him in a bed sheet. After asking him if he wanted her to tell the coffin maker he was needed straight away and receiving a nod, she had left, taking with her the dirty bloodstained blanket and the two pence he took from the purse he carried in a pocket of his best Sunday suit, which she claimed was her usual charge. When the coffin maker had come and made his measurements, promising to return in a short while, Robert had fetched his mother knowing she would want to see her husband for the last time before the coffin was nailed down.

After kissing Evan goodbye, she had wiped away her tears. When the undertaker and his helper arrived in company with the coffin and its maker, she had stood silent and dry eyed while they performed their tasks. When they had gone the habits of years took over and while the coffin stood on two trestles along one wall, she had begun preparing the day's meal for her children, and Robert had taken off his clothes and washed away the filth.

Being of Welsh chapel stock, and a regular worshipper with her husband and family at the Independent chapel perched on the side of the hill. Myfanwy had sent her eldest son to Ty Gronow, the minister's house at Penmaen, to ask the minister to conduct the burial. Three days later, Evan Morgan was laid to rest in the churchyard there, in the same grave that held the tiny coffins of his twin sons. When Robert went back to work the day after the burial, and asked that he be given his father's place and wage, Dai Williams had laughed. 'You be only a boy. That be man's work. See me in a couple of years when you be grown,' then informed him that he was to work as helper to Jeremiah Davies at the face. Two new men were already working at that part of the face where Emrys Evans and his son had died alongside Evan Morgan. Apart from the sympathy offered by Jeremiah nothing more was said. Robert stored up the hatred he felt for Dai Williams and went to work. Myfanwy Morgan, no longer happy or contented, was now resigned to whatever life held in store for her, and did her best to keep house for her son in the same way that she had done for her husband, albeit with even less money. Somehow they had survived.

CHAPTER 6

Being on the outskirts, the cottage escaped the worst of the conditions that prevailed in some parts of the village. What passed for the main throughfare was little more than a muddy track running alongside the tramway. A track rutted by the passage of carts, ruts filled to overflowing with water, in which floated all sorts of unspeakable matter. Stinking water lay in pools or swirled slowly along the ruts, carrying with it the refuse and rubbish that was hurled from the doors of the overcrowded dwellings that lined the roadway. Huddled cheek by jowl, the oldest buildings stood mixed with those erected since the advent of the tramway. Most were one-storey cottages, having the bare essentials, usually surrounded by accumulated household rubbish. A place to eat and sleep, little else. Water was drawn from the stream that ran down the slope to the river. An industrious few had sunk the odd well, but most depended for their water on the stream. Sanitation was practically non-existent. A communal cesspit was shared by some lucky ones, but for the majority even this basic need was missing, and the calls of nature were answered wherever and whenever the need arose. Having lived on a farm, Mrs. Morgan had known the stench of the farmyard ever since she could remember, and had been determined that when they were fortunate enough to be able to move into their cottage, she would not suffer the all prevading smells of her youth. She had insisted that Evan dug a pit at the end of the little garden as far away from the house as possible. He was to shovel in dirt at least once a week. She had seen and smelled the cesspits used in the village and had no intention of suffering from the vile smells and clouds of flies that the summer weather would bring. She often wished that Evan had been offered the chance to lease some of 'Squire' Moggridge's land and build a home on it. She was sure that he had the qualities demanded. Somehow the chance had never come and they had been forced to bring up their family in the hovel they still occupied; totally inadequate, dirty and in bad repair. Nevertheless, this was the place that Robert Morgan trudged to from work and the place that he called home.

The youngest children were playing around the doorway waiting for the familiar routine to be carried out before they could group themselves at the rough table set in the centre of the room. As he bent to enter the cottage doorway, he could smell the stew that his mother was cooking in the big pot hanging from the irons across the mouth of the chimney. It had probably been simmering since early morning, taking on extra smells and flavours as his mother had added to it. This would be the main meal of the day for the whole family. As his eyes became accustomed to the smoke and gloom that filled the room, he could see his mother standing by the pot, stirring it now and again. Her face turned toward him as he entered and a brief smile showed. Her son was home. He was safe again for another night. God willing, he would come through the door again tomorrow. Taking off his jacket and shirt, both grimy and wet, and the heavy sodden boots, he looked about him. His mother gestured to Eirwen his eldest sister and obedient to the role of woman in the household, she carried a kettle of hot water outside and poured it into a bowl that lay there. Re-filling it from the bucket of water, collected that morning from one of the streams that ran nearby, she took it indoors and placed it on the fire. Robert strode outside and began the task of removing some of the dirt and coal dust from his face and hands. Wiping himself in the piece of sacking that hung from a nail, he threw the dirty water over the garden and returned indoors to take his place at the head of the table, followed now by his brothers and sisters. Helped by Eirwen, his mother brought the smoke blackened pot to the table and ladled out a portion to each, starting with Robert. No-one moved until Mrs. Morgan, with a quick glance around the table to ensure that everyone's head was bowed over his or her plate, said a quick Grace. With the help of the chunks of bread carved from the loaf with a huge knife, the family quickly emptied their plates, mopping up the gravy. Once finished, Eirwen gathered the plates and spoons and took them outside to be washed, at the same time urging the smaller ones outside once more and remaining there herself. Robert, trousers steaming in the warmth of the fire, rose

44

from the table and collected the bowl and bucket of water from outside. While his mother busied herself at various tasks, he stripped and began the daily task of washing away the coal dust and muck accumulated in the candlelit darkness of the NantGwrhay Colliery. The unremitting labour of the last four years, ever since he had gone to work alongside his father had added slabs of muscle to his bony frame. He was tall, nearing six feet, with a deep chest bearing the beginnings of a matting of dark hair, and broad shoulders that tapered to a waist rippling with ridges of stomach muscles. His legs, in places bearing the blue scars that were the legacy of the miner, were in proportion, carrying his weight easily. While he dried himself, his mother carried the bowl to the doorway, emptied it on the already muddy track, and brought it back indoors. He knelt on the floor, while his mother poured cold water from the bucket over his head into the bowl as he strove to wash away as much as possible of the coal dust that blackened his scalp. Finished at last, he donned a flannel shirt and rough corduroy trousers and seating himself alongside the fireplace, stretched out his legs. He glanced at the clock. it was nearly a quarter to eight. Soon the smaller children would be tucked up in bed. At nine o'clock the others would follow. His mother would then begin the task of cutting the bread and cheese with which she filled his tommy box, and prepare for the morning. The fire would be raked out, leaving only the larger glowing cokes. A couple of shovelfulls of small and rubble coal would be added to 'bank it up.' In the morning, a few pieces of wood and a poke or two would be enough to start the flames leaping, ready for another day. By ten o'clock the cottage would be quiet.

As he sat there, he thought back to the day that his father had been killed. Once they had nailed down the lid of his coffin, his mother had wiped away her tears and taken control. She had fed them. He had washed and she had sent him to Penmaen. Having lost her twins, Mrs. Morgan was already familiar with the tragic business of arranging for someone to place a loved one in the earth. All these things she did without shedding another tear. Perhaps she had no more to shed. Dry eyed, she had walked to the chapel behind the bier that

45

held the coffin, with her eldest son holding her arm, and Eirwen sobbing quietly on the other side. The younger children had been left in the care of Dafydd and his other sister. Apart from themselves, the minister and the two men who had pushed and pulled the bier, no-one else attended. As he had stood watching while the gravedigger and his helper lowered the coffin into the grave, his mind had already began to grapple with the fact that he was now the head of the household. Upon him would fall the burden of ensuring that his mother and brothers and sisters, had enough to eat and that each week his mother could pay the rent demanded. He would have to speak to Dai Williams, nay almost beg, to be given his father's place at the coalface. It was the sound of his mother's half stifled sobs that had brought him back to the tearful scene in which they were engaged, and putting his arm about her he made a silent vow to try to take over his father's duties. He had never forgotten Williams's answer to his request. Some day there would be a reckoning. Despite his mistaken wish to appear manly, he had not been able to hold back the tears that sprang to his eyes as the first shovel of dirt rattled on the lid of the coffin. Wiping his eyes with his sleeve, he turned from the grave, leading his mother and sister up the slope toward the chapel. The minister had walked on ahead leaving them to say their farewells, and now stood waiting at the gate. After speaking a few words of comfort and expressing his sympathy for the loss of a God fearing, hardworking husband, he had bidden them goodbye and strode away down the hill.

As they walked slowly back, Robert's young mind had tried hard to reconcile the differences which existed between his family and that of the man for whom he worked. There through the trees, he could see the mansion where 'Squire' Moggridge lived. The huge house, surrounded by out buildings, probably had more rooms than the whole row of cottages that he and the others like him lived in. What made it right for one man and his family to live in such luxury, while those who sweated and slaved in the mines from which his wealth came, lived in squalor? Wasn't his family as entitled to a decent life as the 'Squire'? Hadn't his Dad and he worked hard for the wages they received? Now his Dad was lying in Penmaen churchyard. Killed by rocks that fell from a roof weakened by the water that constantly seeped through. And 'Squire' Moggridge, what did he care? Probably didn't even know. Dai Williams wasn't likely to go running to him and say, 'Please Mr. Moggridge. Evan Morgan was killed in the mine by a roof fall. He's left a widow and seven children, living in a cottage that you wouldn't keep your pigs in.' No. More likely he'd just cross Dad's name off the list and forget him. Thus ran the grieving boy's mind.

How strange that at almost the same moment that these rebellious thoughts coursed through his brain, not far away, the minister too was asking some very similar questions. Walking away from the churchyard, he could not help but reflect on the sorrows which God had laid upon his flock. He had just helped lay Evan Morgan to rest. He had been a good man. Hardworking. A man who raised his family as Christians. He sighed. He supposed it was God's will. This afternoon he had another burial, a father and son, killed alongside Evan Morgan in the NantGwrhay.

Quite a lot of people had much to thank Mr. Moggridge for. Those who now lived in their own cottages thanks to the scheme the 'Squire' had brought into being, and he himself. When he had come here first, Ty Gronow where he lived as minister to his flock, had not long been erected, on land sold cheaply to the chapel. Despite this, as a man of God, he sometimes wondered at the price demanded for the coal which enabled people like Mr. Moggridge to carry out their acts of philanthropy.

CHAPTER 7

Sitting in the chair which had been his father's seat, legs out-stretched, Robert Morgan gazed unseeing at the fire, deeply confused. He could still remember what had passed through his mind when walking back from the burial. What did the minister think when he buried men and boys who had been killed in the mines that littered the country roundabout? Was it just a job to him? A job which he was paid to do. Like I'm paid for cutting coal? Did he think about what was going to happen to the families left behind? What happened to them if there was nobody to earn any money? He had heard men talking about the ties that existed between the clergy and the gentry who supplied them with their living. How, in return for a comfortable living, the clergy saw to it that through their sermons and prayers, their congregations were kept down-trodden and ignorant, thankful to be employed and as will-ing to put up with their condition as the gentry wished. As one who had been brought up to look up to the minister and attend chapel every Sunday, he was unwilling to ally himself with these stories. Yet, when he sat in the chapel seat and lis-tened to this same minister call for prayers for the wellbeing of those who gave employment, and also call down the wrath of God on those who tried to stir up the working man against his employers, he was confused. Surely the employment of a man in a dangerous job should place a bounden duty on both the employer and the employed? The worker should work hard and give value for his wage. Equally the employer should pay properly for a job well done. Why then were wages so small while profits seemed to be such that the iron-masters and coalowners lived in luxury? Did not the mi-neowner have a duty to ensure that his mine was as safe as regular maintenance could make it? There would always be accidents but when danger was pointed out, then for bosses like Dai Williams to scoff, or worse, threaten them with the loss of their jobs, that must be wrong surely? Was it any wonder that amongst the workers there were hotheads who could wreak revenge on the mineowners and their equally guilty servants? During the troubled times that had existed in the coalfield since the strike in 1816 there had arisen a sort of secret society calling itself, the 'Scotch Cattle.' The men who belonged to this movement were violent men. Some people said that it was because of their actions that the strike of 1822 had happened. From what his father had told him, the miners who belonged to this society were formed into bands called 'herds', with a leader who was known as the 'bull'. These bands had sworn secret oaths to defend the rights of the working miners. It was not uncommon for the mineowners to make a cut in the wages without warning and in defiance of any agreement. It was against such practices and the attempted strikebreaking by 'scab' workers that they took violent action. Nobody seemed to know where they had got their name from. Some said it was because the members disguised themselves by wearing skins said to be taken from cattle. Others said it was because the leaders of the bands wore cows horns. Many people in the area lived in fear of being victims of these bands. Any man suspected of being a scab or working for less than the accepted wages was likely to find himself warned, then, if he persisted in working, his home could well be ransacked, possibly fired, and he himself beaten. Nobody could recognise them. They had a system whereby a 'scotching' as it was called, due to be carried out in Blackwood, would be undertaken by a band from Risca or some other local area. His father would have nothing to do with them, but like others who felt as he did, when a strike was called at NantGwrhay Colliery, he came out. One or two who worked, were badly beaten.

Despite the terror which they inspired in many of the valley's inhabitants, there were many who had pledged allegiance to a local 'herd'. Many who had questioned the Cattle's right to act as the miners' champions, were convinced when they listened to the long list of wrongs inflicted on the mineworkers by the agents and contractors who managed the collieries on behalf of the absentee English mineowners. One major source of despair was the so called 'long pay' system whereby a contractor settled with men at lengthy intervals of anything from four to seven weeks. Men were forced to resort to asking for advances in the form of tokens which were only exchangeable at the Truck Shop, either owned or encouraged by the contractors. Another ploy was for wages settlements to be made in the Company Shop where the men were expected to change their money immediately for goods of dubious quality and weight. In areas where the nonconformist chapels held sway, the attitude of those who worshipped there was another reason for the militancy of the Cattle. Being a working class combination, the Union clubs which had been formed during periods of unemployment as an aid to resisting reductions in wages, felt the full weight of the chapels' displeasure. They regarded the oaths taken by the union members as blasphemous and showed further disapproval because the clubs met in public houses. The Calvinistic Methodist chapels prohibited church membership to any union club member. The unions had no funds and any member who was sacked for being a member received neither pay from the union nor could claim parish relief. These and other complaints of low wages, job insecurity, bad housing, swelled the ranks of the Scotch Cattle.

Robert had first hand knowledge of the methods used by the Cattle to enforce their rules. A strike had been called at NantGwrhay over a pay dispute and all had walked out except for two or three. The Cattle had immediately warned these miners threatening them and their families. This had been sufficient for two of them to remain at home. One however, braver or more foolish, living not more than fifty yards from Robert, had tried once more to enter the mine.

The first warning that there was trouble brewing came not long after he had made his attempt. Robert and his father were returning home after a day spent picking coal off the tip that now stretched from the colliery down to the river. Where once there had been a large grove of oak trees, there now stood the ever growing mounds of spoil, that came from the area where the tubs of coal from underground were screened, to remove the stones and slag. Little nuggets of coal spilled out when the tubs were tipped and became mixed with the rubbish that the women working on the screens threw out. Daily, the rubbish was put into tubs and tipped thus forming the mounds. It was forbidden for anyone to search these tips for coal, as the mineowners claimed that any coal taken belonged to them. This however did not deter those who had need of coal to fuel their fires, both for cooking and warmth, and every day dozens would collect at the foot of the tip, then spread out like gleaners in the stubble of a cornfield. Although the mineowners employed bailiffs to ensure the striking miners did not steal this coal, the bailiffs whether through sympathy or fear always ensured that the pickers always had plenty of warning of their approach and never pursued them as they scurried away carrying their sacks of precious rubble.

On this particular occasion, as Robert and his father neared their home, they could hear and see a large crowd gathered to watch what was happening at the home of the accused scab miner. Shouting and waving clubs, the mob had gathered in front of the cottage occupied by one Will Daniels, and were screaming for him to come out and take his punishment. The door of the cottage remained closed and as they drew nearer, the identity of those in the front became clear. All were covered in what looked like large animal skins, pulled up to cover their heads and disguise their features. One however was distinguished by his headdress of a pair of horns. Undoubtedly it was a 'herd' of the Scotch Cattle under the leadership of a 'Bull' and they were intent on meting out punishment to the miner who had broken the rules. Evan Morgan stopped on the outskirts of the crowd and dropped his sack of coal at his feet. As Robert tried to press forward to get a better view, he felt the restraining hand of his father on his shoulder.

'No further Rob. They be Cattle.'

'But Dad...'

'Stay here lad, out of the way. The poor devil is going to be scotched. We mustn't get mixed up in it.'

'That's Mr. Daniels's cottage Dad.'

'Aye lad. Come in here boy, out of sight.'

They stood in the shelter of a cottage whose door was shut and curtains drawn.

Already those in front were hammering at the door of the Daniels's cottage and the mob was screaming even louder for him to show himself. There was no response and the 'Bull' pointed at the door and shouted something. From where they stood, the shouting of the crowd made it impossible to hear what he had said, but the crowd's reaction soon made it clear. There was a concerted rush at the door but despite their attack it remained standing. Suddenly those in front parted and made way for a broad shouldered man who strode forward hefting a huge hammer. He cleared a space around him then swung it at the door. With a crash, one of the panels gave way. Again he swung and another panel split. Urged on by the crowd he spat on his hands and with all his strength swung the hammer in a round arm swing. The iron head crashed against the door then broke through the woodwork. Tugging at it, he released it then like a man possessed, crashed blow after blow against the wood until at last the beam which held it shut, finally broke and the door swung open. With a shout four men jumped into the opening and vanished into the gloom of the interior.

From the inside there came a confused shouting and crashing then the screams of a woman. Someone in the crowd determined to make their presence felt, hurled a stone at the window. Others followed suit and a volley smashed the glass adding to the general confusion. There was more screaming from the woman, and shouts and curses as the attackers struggled to bring out their victim. At last to the roar of approval from the onlookers, the four men emerged dragging the struggling, cursing Daniels. His wife was beating at the head of one of the men holding him, and with a cry of rage, he swung round and dealt her a blow to the face that knocked her to the ground. Daniels was hauled before the 'Bull' and was crouched as if awaiting his punishment. Now that the hapless victim had been brought out, the shouting died down and everyone could hear what the leader of the mob was saying. In a loud voice he cried;

'Will Daniels! You were warned. You 'ave broke the rules of our union. You been scabbing and you be going to be punished.' He turned to face the mob.

'This scab 'ave been trying to work at the Nant. We warned 'im but 'e took no notice. Now 'e be going to be beaten as a punishment and a warning to any other scab what tries to break the rules. Strip 'im lads'

Two of his followers grabbed the unfortunate man and tore his clothes from him, leaving him naked. As he tried to cover his nakedness with his arms and hands, there were hoots of laughter and shouted ribald remarks hurled at him. The 'Bull' however was determined that physical punishment should replace the mirth that was being levelled at their captive. He signalled to one of the men who stepped forward, holding a strap that had been slit to resemble the dreaded cat-o-nine-tails, so beloved for dealing out punishment in the King's ships. Two men grasped Daniels's arms and holding him with arms fully outstretched, cleared a space around them. The man holding the leather strap flicked it with his wrist, causing it to snap with a vicious 'crack'. Satisfied he measured his distance from the whimpering man, then began a savage beating. At the first contact of the leather against his flesh, he screamed and writhed in the grasp of his tormentors, but there was no mercy shown. As if used to dealing out such punishment, the wielder of the whiplike strap beat him until his back was crisscrossed with weals, some of which began to bleed. From his shoulders to his buttocks, the leather weapon flayed him until the pain was too much for him to bear, and he collapsed to lie unconscious at the feet of the 'Bull'. The crowd which had been baying for his punishment, had become silent as the thrashing went on. Perhaps sensing that if he allowed it to continue the crowd might turn upon them and try and rescue the man, the 'Bull' signalled that the punishment was to stop, then stepped forward and stirred the unconscious man's body with his boot. There was no response. He turned to the crowd, then once more, roused them with a cry of 'Right lads. Chuck out the bits and pieces. Let's 'ave a bonfire.'

Ignoring the pitiful figure huddled in the mud, several of the mob entered the cottage and began throwing out the few pieces of furniture they found within. These were piled up, then followed by articles of clothing and bedclothes. The curtains which still hung from the shattered windows were torn down and thrown upon the heap. Satisfied they had stripped the cottage, someone set the pile ablaze.

Mrs. Daniels, having recovered from the blow that had floored her, crawled through the filth and mud to her husband's side, and placing her arms about his naked bloodied body, began rocking him like a mother with a child, all the while watching with tears running down her face, as her home was consumed by the flames. Satisfied that the scotching had served to demonstrate how far the 'Cattle' would go if anyone tried to defy them, the 'herd' began to move away singing and shouting, leaving the local inhabitants to gaze at the fire that burned their neighbours' few possessions, and the pitiful picture of them lying in the mud. Ashamed or frightened the crowd quickly broke up and hurried away. Without looking at his son, Evan Morgan shouldered his sack and together they made their way home in silence, each busy with his own thoughts.

There were some, who when the Cattle attacked and ransacked the Truck Shops felt a certain sympathy with them and their methods.

He awoke with a start. He must have dozed off. The fire had died down and the room was silent except for the breathing of his sleeping brothers and sisters, and the ticking of the clock. The clock had been there as long as he could remember. His mother had brought it to her first married home from North Wales and not a day passed that she did not carefully dust it. It was the only thing of value that the family ever possessed and when she had spoken to him about it, she hoped that the girl he married, would look after it. In the semi-darkness he could see his mother sitting at the table, her head resting on her forearms. As he rose, she stirred, then sat up. In the glow of the fire he could just see it was past ten o'clock. His mother moved to the fire and raked at it to clear the ash, leaving only a few glowing coals. On top of these she placed some rubble. No words had passed between them. Words were not necessary. At this time of night they would naturally seek their beds, to be ready for the next day. Despite his tiredness he did not fall asleep immediately. Why he wondered had he spent the whole evening going over the events of the past? Was it the refusal of Dai Williams to do anything about the water that leaked ceaselessly from the roof, that had sent his mind back over the years? Things were every bit as bad now as then. The only good thing that had happened was when he was told there was to be a new face opened and he was to be given a place of his own to work. Williams had made it plain that he was not in favour of a fourteen year old being given such a position, although there were already at least two such cases in the colliery. He had obviously been over-ruled by the manager, so he had taken great delight in warning Robert, that if he came up with any evidence that Robert wasn't capable of doing the job, he would see to it that he would find himself looking for work somewhere else. Robert wondered what it was that made Williams hate him so much. Was it because like his father before him, he did his job, and did not curry favour with the bullying face boss? Some there were, who could be found buying Williams a tankard of ale, laughing at his coarse jokes. Since he did not frequent the alehouses and had no wish to spend any time in his company, there was no point of contact between them. Williams was a big man with shoulders that betokened considerable strength, but a large belly that hung over the thick leather belt holding up his trousers, was further evidence that much of the bulk was fat. He was loud mouthed and his bullying manner ensured that at least some of those working under him, would kowtow to him. Perhaps it was his failure to do this last that was responsible for the dislike he had for Robert.

Although only fourteen when given the new job, the boy for such he was, was tall and well muscled. Now at sixteen, there was no surplus fat on him, and having worked on the coal face for nearly five years, his muscles were thickest around the upper arms and shoulders. Robert knew that should he ever get involved in a fight with Williams, his best policy would be to evade the bearlike grip he knew the man possessed, and use his youthful speed to keep away from him while he hit him as hard and as often as possible. That the prospect of such a fight was possible, did not alarm him unduly. One day, he had promised himself long ago, there would be a day of reckoning. The time was not yet though.

He had other things to do first. Williams could wait.

When he had begun working at the new face, he had hoped that the new face boss might agree to allow his brother Dafydd to work with him. This was not to be however and when he arrived he found a young lad waiting for him. He had seen him before and knew him to be one of the door-boys. He was about ten or eleven years old, and said he was called Deri Jones. Together they trudged into the tunnel, the candles fixed to their caps giving a feeble light. The new face had already been pierced in several places by his new work-mates, cutting and hammering away at the thin seam of coal that showed between the rock. It was estimated that the seam would widen considerably once the initial rock had been cut away. In the meantime, all the men were too well aware that, while only a thin seam was workable, there would be very little output, hence small wages. In the gutter-ing light from their candles, they wielded their picks and shovels, stopping only to prop up the roof with the timber posts that their young helpers dragged in to the face from where they had been dumped. There was universal thanks for the fact that the new face was as least dry. No longer were they working in evil smelling water. There was however the problem of height. In no place was the roof higher than four feet, which meant that almost everything they did had to be carried out while bent nearly double, or by squatting on their haunches. Again it had been said that this difficulty would be lessened once the seam thickened; in the meantime, they crouched, or knelt, their shoulders moving in rhythm to the swing of their picks as they prised the coal from between the rock layers.

Things had continued like this for some time until it was decided that quicker progress would be made if the rock layer was loosened by the use of blasting powder. This was a dan-gerous procedure and when the face boss had prepared his charges and laid a trail of the black powder back along the tunnel, they had all retreated well beyond the junction with the main tunnel. As they crouched there, awaiting the explo-sion that they hoped would result in bringing down the rock and revealing the thick seam of coal said to lay beyond, Deri spoke in a low voice to Robert.

'Won't all the roof come in when it blows up?'

He had assured him that Jonas Pritchard was a good man with blasting powder, and would only put in enough to break up the rock which was causing the problem.

'What if there's water waiting to flood in?'

The young boy was evidently frightened, never having been anywhere near a coal face before.

'There's no water behind this face' he had told him confident-ly, 'it would have seeped through before now.'

Deri had seemed satisfied with this explanation but moved to stand behind him. There was a shout from Jonas and ever-ybody crouched down as he applied the flame of his candle to the trail of powder. The spluttering flame moved off into the darkness vanishing from sight as it rounded a bend. Ro-bert became aware that he was holding his breath as they wa-ited for the explosion. Suddenly the darkness was rent by a red flame and a crash that deafened them. Smoke poured to-ward them and showers of rock splinters whistled and whirred in the tunnel. As the echoes died away and the smoke began to clear, it was with delight mixed with some apprehension they were able to survey the results of Jonas's blasting. Where previously they had been faced with a sand-wich of rock and coal, now the face lay revealed as promised. From floor to floor, a solid seam of coal, at least five foot thick, faced them. However, emerging slowly from the top of the seam a trickle of water splashed the ground at their feet. Jonas took a pick and began gently tapping at the coal. The ooze of water did not increase. Stepping back he swung the pick so that it sunk into the coal. Leavering gently he en-larged the hole, then withdrew it. For a moment nothing happened, then a stream of water shot out, arcing to a dis-tance of some feet. They watched in dismay as the jet con-tinued spurting forcefully out of the coal. Jonas repeated his action at another point slightly lower, then retreated to watch the result. Another stream of water shot out to land some feet away. However much was there behind the coal, was debate-able, but there was no doubt about the pressure under which it was being held. It might only be a pocket, but it could also be the forerunner of a flood that would swamp the workings and make the face unworkable. Anxiously they waited, willing the two jets to decrease but they continued to pour forth with undiminished force. There was nothing to do but wait. Meanwhile the resulting flow had begun to make its way along the tunnel, like a snake crawling and twisting. If the present rate kept up, there was a danger that the main tunnel would be flooded when the new water joined up with that already lying inches deep in places. Too big an increase would mean that it would be impossible for the women and girls to drag the tubs back to the shaft, and the whole colliery could be in grave danger of flooding! Jonas decided that it was time the situation was brought to the attention of someone higher up.

'Morgan. Get back to the shaft and send someone to get Mr. Paget, the manager. Wait for him and when he comes bring him back here. Tell him what's happened. We'll stay here and see if there's anything we can do. You'd better take your boy with you, he isn't going to be much help here. Look sharp now, this could be serious.'

He remembered how he and Deri had started back along the tunnel, trotting, their shadows dancing along the sides. Underfoot, the water splashed as they ran. Twice when they reached the main tunnel, they had to squeeze past the twisted figures of the women as they lunged against the straps of the harness, gasping for breath and cursing both the tub and the two hurrying boys. Behind one woman, the tub of coal had become wedged against the side and the half naked creature was almost screaming in anger as it defied every effort she made to dislodge it. Shouting to her to get back in front of her burden, they grasped at the heavy tub and dragged it back on to the floor of the tunnel, then ran on, leaving her to continue pulling and cursing. At last they reached the bottom of the shaft. There were several tubs of coal waiting to be tipped into the huge iron bucket that hung from the iron links that stretched up a couple of hundred feet into the daylight. As they had tried to get to the foot of the shaft and speak to the man who signalled those above that there was a full bucket waiting to be hoisted, several women tried to stop them, shouting and screaming at them to wait their turn. He smiled as he recollected how he had pushed his way roughly through them. That had been no time to be polite! At last he had confronted the man he wanted.

'I've got to get a message to the manager. There's flooding in the new face. It's serious and Jonas Pritchard wants him down here straight away.'

The man had argued. 'You'll have to wait. The bucket's full.' Knowing that at any moment, back there in the darkness, what had been a trickle when they left, could well now be growing to a flood, he had turned and given Deri his instructions, ignoring the man's protests,

'Deri. Climb up on top of the coal and hang on. When you get to the top, tell the winder you've got to speak to the manager. Tell him Jonas Pritchard says there's water coming in the new face, and it's serious. Bring Mr. Paget back down here. Tell him I'll be waiting for him to take him in. Can you remember that?'

The boy nodded. Robert helped him climb onto the loaded bucket and the man gave a couple of tugs on the wire that disappeared up the shaft. With a rasping of metal as the links took the weight, the bucket began slowly to climb up the shaft, Deri hanging on to the metal shackle. Some of the women had gone quiet now sensing that something serious was happening. One or two at the front of the queue began asking him questions.

'What's going on? What's all the hurry?'

Others further back started shouting, demanding to know what the hold up was.

'We've got tubs waiting to unload. How would you like dragging a bleeding tub of coal and then have to wait while some bloody kid scoots up the shaft?'

He had waited an anxious twenty minutes before the bucket had descended and the manager had climbed from it. He was a short burly man, who had learned his mining in the pits of the Forest of Dean. He had been in charge for several years but Robert could not remember ever having seen him except at a distance. Now he was in a hurry.

'Morgan? What's the problem? That lad of yours said Jonas

Pritchard had trouble in the new face. Come on let's see what it's all about.'

They had pushed a way through the now increased crowd of women and tubs. As they had gone he had told Mr. Paget what had happened.

'How bad was the water spouting out when you left?'

He had told him that in his opinion that if it didn't slow down, there was a chance that the whole face and the main tunnel could be flooded.

'How many men working in the face?'

'About a dozen.'

The manager had said no more until they arrived at the junction of the two tunnels. Several men were waiting there.

'What are you lot doing here?'

One had replied that Jonas had told them to clear the face until it was decided what to do. Paget grunted but said no more. Beckoning Robert he had gone into the tunnel splashing through the water that was now a steady stream. Telling Deri to stay with the others, he had followed the manager into the darkness. A few minutes later they met the face boss.

'What's happening Pritchard?'

'It's as bad as ever Mr. Paget.' Jonas had replied.

'Come on. Let's go and have a look',

Paget had said and strode away, Jonas and Robert following. They had gone but a few yards when they became aware of the sound of water splashing. A few yards more and they were able to see the two jets of water still describing arcs as they poured out from the coal. The manager studied the face for a moment then gestured for Jonas to hand him a pick. Taking it he sloshed through the water, then raising it he drove it into the coal near the bottom of the seam. No sooner had he withdrawn it than another stream of water shot out. He stepped back and studied the three streams of water.

'If it's a pocket, the top flow should begin to slow in a bit, once it gets below the level of the hole.'

They waited in silence, their eyes never leaving the stream of water. Ten minutes or so went by. Still the water poured forth. Paget made no move staring intently. Suddenly he pointed. The top stream was not reaching out as far as before. As if a tap was being slowly closed, the force of the jet gradually decreased until it had become not much more than a trickle down the coal face.

'It looks like a pocket, Jonas. Probably seepage from the stream and built up between the rock. Keep your eye on it though. Get the men back in here, there's posts want putting up or you'll have the roof in.' He had gone almost as soon as he had finished speaking and Jonas had sent him to fetch the others back to the coalface. They had spent the rest of their shift clearing up the debris from the explosion and putting up new roof supports. The water had continued running but by the end of the shift only the stream from the bottom of the seam continued, and when they had returned the next morning, that too had finished running.

That had been nearly a year ago and things had been better for a while. The thick seam of coal that had been revealed when Jonas had set off his explosion, had remained. He and Deri and the rest of his workmates had been able to hack away at the seemingly inexhaustable supply of coal. Tub after tub, loaded with the shiny black lumps, was dragged in an almost endless chain by the sweating, filthy half clad women and girls away into the darkness, their places being taken by others waiting to repeat the process. Working under Jonas, who was a hard task master but not given to bullying those under him, had restored some of the faith in his fellow men and when he heard that the faceboss was leaving them to work as Mr. Paget's assistant, he prayed they would get somebody else who would carry on in the same manner. Alas, for reasons best known to those in charge, it was decided that Williams was to be put in charge. Almost from the day he had assumed his new position, Williams began hectoring the men. No matter that the output from the new face exceeded anything dreamed of, he demanded more and more coal be cut. When the men broke off cutting coal in order to put up posts or make things a little bit safer, he hounded them until they abandoned these essential tasks and went back to cutting more coal. As a result more and more falls occured and in one of them, Moses Watkins who was working just a few yards from Deri, was partially buried.

After frantic digging, they uncovered him but it was obvious from the way his leg was twisted that it was badly broken. Even then, Williams insisted that only two of them should carry him out.

The thing they all feared more than anything else, another flood of water, was always uppermost in their minds, and when droplets began once more to fall from the roof, they watched it each day with fearful eyes. It did not develop any more. Just enough to make them aware of its presence. It lay in small puddles around them. Williams's attention was drawn to it and one of the men told him of the time when Mr. Paget had come to inspect it. Williams scoffed at them, calling them a lot of women worrying about a few drops of water.

So it went on for some months, then one day when they entered the face, it was to find their fears realised. A continuous trickle now crawled down one part of the coal face and the leaking from the roof was no longer to be measured in droplets. It was to this increase he had drawn Williams's attention and it was the faceboss's reply that had made him determined that one day there would be a settling of their long standing feud.

All around him he could make out the breathing of his brothers and sisters as they lay wrapped in slumber. He shrugged the blanket further up around his shoulders and turned on his side. Time enough to worry about tomorrow when it came.

Two feet away, sharing a bed with Eirwen, Mrs. Morgan wondered what it was that had been occupying her eldest son's mind since he had settled in front of the fire. Uttering a silent prayer that He watch over Robert while he toiled, she closed her eyes. At half past four she knew she would awake. The habit of years would arouse her. She would get up, stir the fire and get her eldest son out of his bed to face another day of toil and danger. She slept.

At half past four next morning she had awakened as she had known she would. She moved quietly about the dark room mechanically doing the tasks she had done for years. At five o'clock she had aroused him, ignoring his efforts to remain asleep. Eventually he had climbed from the bed and dressed in his work clothes while she cut a large slice of bread from the loaf and warmed some ale. Hardly aware of what he was eating he had filled his jack with water from the bucket and kissing her goodbye he had gone out into the dawn. At a quarter past six he drove the blade of his pick into the coal. Another day of toil had started at the NantGwrhay Colliery, one of the many which he reckoned would stretch into the future.

He was greatly suprised therefore, one Sunday, when accompanying his mother, and sisters and brothers, to chapel as usual, to be hailed by the minister as they were leaving and asked if he had time to discuss something important. Assuring Mrs. Morgan that he would not detain her son, the minister had spoken to Robert as they walked down the hill. 'Robert. How would you like to have a job working outside the colliery? Before you answer I must tell you that the pay would be no better than you earn now, but there will be other advantages.'

'Doing what sir?'

'Well to start with, it would be a sort of assistant steward's job working on Mr. Moggridge's estate. The present steward is getting on and as minister, I was asked if I knew of anyone who might be trained to take over the job. It might be another year or two before you'd be in charge. In the meantime, if you take the position there are one or two things I might be able to help you with. I know you can read and write English thanks to your father bringing you to my lessons and this would be a great advantage, but you would need to know other things, and these I can teach you.'

'What about my family?'

'The lodgekeeper at the south end of the park died recently and his wife is going to live with her daughter, so it will be vacant shortly and you can all live there. One thing however. Whoever lives there has to act as lodge keeper and attend to all the traffic passing through the gate to the house.'

'Eirwen could manage that sir, and Dafydd could help.'

'Well then I see no problems. Mind you. You will have to pass Mr. Moggridge's scrutiny. Before you make your mind up, you'd better speak to your mother. Let me know your answer next Sunday.'

'Thank you sir.'

Robert hurried after his family, eager to talk to his mother about the unexpected good fortune that seemed to be beckoning them. To get out of that hellhole and away from the likes of Williams. To breathe fresh air and live in a proper cottage with running water. He caught up with them and as much as he wanted to impart the good news, he said nothing until they arrived home. Once there he revealed the content of his conversation with the minister and as expected, his mother's face lit up. True there would not be any increase in the income of the family as might have been expected if Dafydd had been taken on at the colliery. Against that however was the knowledge that unlike him, his brother would not have to sit in the dark and wet, in constant danger of being injured, and witness to the unspeakable degradation of the women and girls who toiled there. The minister had said that there would probably be other advantages which would compensate for the loss of Dafydd's wage. Before they went to bed that night, Robert and his mother decided that next Sunday, he would tell the minister that he would give up his job in NantGwrhay whenever it suited Mr. Moggridge to advise the minister that he now needed an assistant steward.

CHAPTER 8

Lady Gwendoline was annoyed. She had wanted to go for a drive in the park that morning. Yesterday, driving along, her carriage had been overtaken by two uniformed young men on spirited horses. They had studied her carefully as they had ridden past and both had raised their hands to their shako style headgear. Pretending not to have noticed them, as befitted a young unchaperoned lady, she had looked straight ahead after one swift glance, a glance that had been sufficient to imprint upon her memory, the dark curly hair, and fresh moustachioed features of the young Lancer officer nearest. That had been yesterday. Today she had announced her intention of once again taking a drive in the park, only to be told by her mother, that it was unseemly for a young girl to spend too much time driving about unaccompanied.

'Mama. I am grown up, and perfectly well aware how a young lady should act. Also I shall not be alone. Reynolds will be driving the carriage. I cannot remain cooped up in this house every day.'

'Gwendoline. I wasn't aware that you spent much time cooped up here. Most afternoons you go out to your friends' houses.'

'But it's so dull Mama just meeting the same people all the time, and doing the same things every day.'

'You know very well Gwendoline that until you are sixteen, your father will not allow you to go to any public functions unless he accompanies you. He doesn't want you riding unless he's with you. I only permitted you to take the carriage because your father is not here and I know how you enjoy being with horses. You are too young to be gadding about. When I was your age, I had a full day learning the right things.'

'Mama. You know that I am hopeless at embroidery and I detest poetry. When is Papa coming back?'

'I don't know. He was only going for a day or so but as you'll find out when you are married my girl, men say one thing and do another. I hope he's back before I'm confined. Not that he's any help but it's nice to know he's in the house.

Ring for Jevons, I'll have to give him the menu to give to the cook for tomorrow.'

Gwendoline crossed the room and tugged at the bellrope, then went and sat next to her mother.

'Mama. If Papa is going to have business to do in Wales, and you are going to be busy with my new brother or sister, I shall have nobody to talk to.'

'You have three brothers.'

'Mama. They are boys. What do they know? Do you think Papa would take me with him the next time he goes.'

'To Wales?'

'Yes.'

'My dear child. Do you realise what you are saying? Young ladies of your age do not go traipsing off to places like that. From what your father has told me, it's hardly civilized there. Half of them don't even speak English. Besides, your father would be much too busy to be able to look after you. It's out of the question.'

'Papa must have acquaintances down there. I've heard him talking about somebody called Sir Charles Morgan who's very rich and he said he was hoping to meet some other business people.'

'You are talking nonsense Gwendoline. You can't just go off into the wilds and stay with complete strangers. You'll just have to wait until your father returns home and see what his plans are. Now be a good girl and don't bother me with such nonsense. Look dear. Don't think I don't sympathise. In a few months you'll be sixteen and things will be different then, you'll be able to go out a lot more to balls, and the theatre. Perhaps by then, your father will have finished his business in Wales and he'll take us all away somewhere. Once the baby's born things will be better you'll see. I'll get a wet nurse and I'll be able to take you out to buy new clothes. You'll need a whole new wardrobe. Ballgowns, dresses, hats and if we do go away somewhere in the country, perhaps we'll be able to get your father to buy you a riding habit, and you'll be able to ride out.'

'Oh Mama do you really mean that?'

'Yes dear. Young ladies must have the right clothes for every occasion. Who knows who you may meet? You'll soon be mixing with the very best people, not to mention the young men who'll be coming here once we start our very own entertaining.'

'Do you mean we are going to have dinners and dancing with an orchestra?'

'Why yes child. You are nearly sixteen and it's time for you to enter society. In a couple of years you'll be married. Now is the time to start looking round for a suitable husband for you.'

'But I don't want to get married for years and years. I want to enjoy life first. There's so much to do and see.'

'Gwendoline. It is a woman's lot to marry well and be a faithful and dutiful wife. You will have at least two years to 'enjoy life' as you put it. You don't want to be an old maid do you?'

'No Mama, but...'

'Your father and I have talked about this. We only want you to be happy dear. I had the same foolish dreams as you before your father married me. You'll see we are right once you're wed and have a family. Don't expect too much from life my dear.'

The door opened and Jevons appeared.

'You rang M'Lady?'

'Yes Jevons. Take this list down to the cook and tell Reynolds that Lady Gwendoline will not be needing the carriage this morning after all.'

She handed him the piece of paper then resumed talking to her daughter,

'Isn't it your morning for a music lesson?'

Realising that there was no more to be gained by arguing, Gwendoline dutifully kissed her mother's cheek and left the room.

CHAPTER 9

Sir Henry, Mr. Moggridge and Morgan were gathered out-side the house preparing to mount their respective horses. It was the following morning and aware that his guest would want to see as much as possible, Mr. Moggridge had suggest-ed that they start immediately after breakfast, inspect the land acquired, and return to Woodfield Park for a late lunch. It would be too late for his guests to depart for Newport on the first leg of the return journey to London and it would give him more time to discuss a certain matter that he felt might interest Sir Henry. They had found much to talk about re-garding their respective business activities and had agreed on most aspects when it came to dealing with the people who worked for them. Mr. Moggridge however did feel that as this line of business was a new one for Sir Henry, it behove him to warn him that he would be dealing with a completely different type of worker from that with which he was normal-ly familiar. He hoped that his erstwhile guest might even be tempted to come and live in the area. The natives were a clan-nish lot, with their weird language, but there was an ever in-creasing amount of English being spoken. Unfortunately, there were very few of the gentry hereabouts, and the arrival of Sir Henry had emphasised this. He didn't want to frighten them off with stories of those damned Scotch Cattle, but the man should be told of some of the things that had happened. Lord knows he had done all he could to lighten the burden of his workers but there would always be hotheads who no matter what you did for them, would demand more. He would try and inform Sir Henry without causing him too much worry after lunch. Perhaps with a good lunch and some of his best port to wash it down, his guest would be in a receptive frame of mind. Joined by his steward whose saddle bags bulged with sandwiches and a couple of bottles, they set off. It was decided that in order that his guests should see as much of the countryside as possible, they would stick to the regular tracks and not make it a cross country journey. It was a sunny morning as they jogged along, the steward leading followed by Mr. Moggridge and Sir Henry with Morgan trailing in the rear. Mr. Moggridge pointed out the various land-marks and explained who the land belonged to. There were one or two large farms belonging to small estates but the majority of the country they passed through seemed to belonged to the Morgan family.

After about half an hour's ride they sighted a long low building and nearby another, outside which hung a sign identifying it as the Maypole Inn. Together with a couple of barns and cottages, the buildings formed a small hamlet at the junction of several tracks. Mr. Moggridge explained that this was called Croespenmaen and was one of the main junctions for the roads leading to all parts of the county. He said nothing about it being one of the main meeting places also for huge crowds of miners belonging to the Scotch Cattle, and a place to be avoided by people like himself and his fellow travellers. They turned north at this point, then, at a junction in the road where stood another small beerhouse called the Cherry Tree, changed direction once more, almost completing a large circle. They immediately started to descend toward the valley bottom, but as leader of the expedition, Mr. Moggridge stopped them to point out the headgears of several small workings, almost hidden amongst the wooded countryside. The massive oak trees which made up practically all the wooded areas, swept away in a dale toward the river which could be seen flashing in the sunshine away to their left. He named the little collieries marked by the mounds of spoil, including his own, the NantGwrhay Colliery. Nearby stood a larger one called the Gwrhay. Both names, despite the spelling were pronounced 'Gray' he said. Another, the Waterloo was quite large, and probably named after the famous battle. Sir Henry's land was not yet visible. Nearer and on the track along which they would pass, stood a small farm. That said Mr. Moggridge was the Darren and if they looked carefully to the left of the farm they would just be able to make out some of the buildings that went to make up the little village which bore the same name as the colliery.

Having given them some idea of the lie of the land, they rode on, soon reaching the farm, then passing close to the cottages which lay alongside a tramway running both north and south. Mr. Moggridge explained that there were coal-mines further up the valley and it was to these that the tram-way ran. Sir Henry's land lay about a half mile up the tram-way so he would not have to lay much track to join with this. Despite having dealings with a great number of businesses, this was Sir Henry's first venture into mining and he looked about him with great interest. His first impression was of the squalor that surrounded the cottages. No matter where he looked, rubbish and smelling refuse lay. Pools of water, in which innumerable, small, dirty, partially clad, children played, lay everywhere. From several of the cottages' door-ways, unkempt slatternly women watched the party as they sat on their horses. Two or three held clay pipes between their teeth and puffed smoke as they watched in silence. Never had he seen such filth. He had once or twice had occa-sion to visit the London Docks in his carriage and the scenes there had been bad enough, but this was worse. Even in the sunshine, the whole place reeked with filth, and by the look of them, water was something they weren't very fond of.

'By Gad Mr. Moggridge. Let's get on. The stink of this place is upsetting my stomach.'

They wheeled their horses away from the the scene and followed the path of the tramway around the breast of the small hill. Mr. Moggridge pointed as they came abreast the junction of the tramway with that that led to his mine,

'That's my place up there.'

They went on and after about ten minutes riding came to another junction. Nearby was a mound of what looked like small coal and just beyond it the entrance to a level driven in-to the side of the hill.

'This must be your piece of land Sir Henry. At least part of it. Have you got the map?'

Morgan urged his horse forward and climbed down from the saddle. He reached into his saddle bag and took out a sheet folded several times. Opening it out, he held it out for his employer to look at. Studying the map then looking about him, Sir Henry said,

'It seems I've got the land from here up to some stream or other in the wood. Along the tramway for a hundred yards northward, and back to the stream again. The stream must be the boundary and it curves round in a semicircle.'

'That'll be the Nant as they call it. It bounds my piece in the wood, so we share a common boundary. Do you want to have a look at the mine Sir Henry? We shan't go in. Too dangerous. It hasn't been worked for years to my knowledge, but if you've got the seam that runs along beneath the stream then you've bought yourself a good coal mine. It's five feet thick on my side and easy to work. There's some water but nothing these fellows aren't used to working in. Mind you, I think you would do better to sink a shaft down to the seam rather than go down an incline. Much quicker and cheaper in the long run. Shall we go and look at the rest of your land?'

They spent the next couple of hours inspecting Sir Henry's purchase. It was mostly covered in stunted trees and undergrowth and they found it difficult to break through in parts. There was evidence of old workings, but as Moggridge said, 'There's been digging for coal in these parts going back for many many years.'

At last, satisfied that they had seen all that was to be seen on the surface, they returned to the mine entrance. Mr. Moggridge instructed his steward to unpack the refreshments from his saddle bags and while they stood discussing what they had seen, Morgan and the steward lay the food and drink out on an old upturned tub. It was obvious that quite a lot of work would need to be done before there was any prospect of commencing working below the surface, and it was this point that Sir Henry was anxious to talk about.

'By George Mr. Moggridge, it seems to me that it will be months before we'll be getting any return on our money.'

'Well Sir Henry a lot will depend on the men you get to do the preliminary work. If you can get a good manager, somebody who will drive the men hard, you can probably cut down on the amount of time needed to make it ready. I'll have a word with Paget my manager. He may know somebody who'll fit the bill. In the meantime, I suggest you think seriously about whether you're going to sink a shaft. If you can let me know I can arrange for a team of sinkers to start as soon as you give the word.'

'That's civil of you Mr. Moggridge. Frankly I've no idea where to start first on this business, more at home raising money.'

'Sir Henry. Coal mining is a tricky business. You can make a fortune or lose the lot just because a seam of coal goes one way instead of the other. I was surprised when I got your letter from Morgan to learn that you intended to go into the coal industry. Not many from London get mixed up in it. I can make a suggestion that might benefit us both. I'd like to discuss it with you when we get back. There's not much more we can do here. You've seen the area so you'll have some idea of what you're up against. I think what I have in mind will appeal to you.'

They finished the snack and very soon after, mounted the horses and started on the journey back.

That afternoon, in Mr. Moggridge's study, Sir Henry and his host engaged in a conversation that was to solve many problems for both men. Sir Henry and Morgan stayed the night and early next morning took their leave of Mr. Moggridge travelling down the valley in their host's carriage, back to Newport. Sir Henry did not disclose to his agent that he and his family had received an invitation from Mr. Moggridge to spend a month or more if necessary at Woodfield while preliminary work went on. However he did tell him that, after he had returned to London and spoken to his fellow directors, Morgan was to await a letter advising him of what had been arranged and to make whatever arrangements were considered necessary.

The following morning Sir Henry boarded the mail coach back to London. Within the week he had met his fellow investors and laid before them the plans discussed with Mr. Moggridge. Interested only in the profits to be made from the venture they were investing in, they agreed to the suggestions put forward and Sir Henry instructed his lawyer to draw up the necessary papers. These were dispatched to Mr. Moggridge and signed by him. Under the agreement contained in these papers, the NantGwrhay Colliery, would be leased to the London Fuel Company and the Company would then have the right to extract coal both from the

NantGwrhay and the land recently purchased by Sir Henry Siston and his associates. The agreement would come into force on the first day of January 1828. In the meantime, it was agreed that the London Fuel Company would have the right to purchase coal from Mr. Moggridge at a price well below the market price, for resale as they thought fit. This would recompense Sir Henry and his friends for the time they would have to wait until they could operate the colliery as they saw fit. Mr. Moggridge was happy with the agreement, as he had for some time been considering retiring from the troubled coal mining industry and he could foresee even more trouble in the future. If things continued as they were, he had even thought about moving away from his beloved Woodfield Park and setting up home somewhere else. Somewhere he could enjoy a well deserved rest, free from the responsibilities of public life and the stress of engaging in the coal mining industry.

CHAPTER 10

While all this had been going on, Robert Morgan's life had gone on little changed. Rise at five, at the coal face at six and twelve hours of unremitting toil until he stumbled from the bucket that carried him up the shaft into the evening sunlight. Now that there was a chance that he would be able to escape from the hell of life spent underground in the darkness, he had become more wary of the dangers that hung over him as he swung his pick and shovel. More aware that the creak of the timber, the steady trickle of water that gathered around their feet, all were warnings, that the chance to work as steward to the man who owned the colliery, could be dashed in a split second. Every day, Dai Williams shouted at them whenever he thought they weren't working fast enough. Time and again he threatened to deduct payment if they persisted in stopping to put up new posts, or cleared away what they considered dangerous hazards. Williams was determined that his position as boss of the new face would not be endangered if he could help it.

There had been some changes. Robert had spoken to the minister immediately after the service at the chapel on the Sunday. Rather than wait until he was to face Mr. Moggridge, he had asked the minister if there was anything he could do that would enhance his chances of obtaining the post. The minister had asked him to come to the manse each Sunday after the evening service to be taught the mysteries of addition, subtraction and multiplication. If he could face his prospective employer, secure in the knowledge that he could convince him that he was capable of doing simple bookkeeping, then his chances would be greatly increased. Robert surprised the cleric by his natural ability with figures, and had soon progressed so well that his teacher decided it would be of greater benefit to his pupil if he taught him how to speak properly in English. Like many of the mining families, Welsh was Robert's first language and was the one spoken at home. The use of English however had increased tremendously with the invasion of miners from outside Wales, and since practically all the coal owners were English, it was the language used in issuing orders and in the big houses belonging to them. Week after week he walked to and from the manse, spending an hour or so each visit trying to understand why he should say this rather than say that.

Unknown to him events were taking shape that were to have an influence on the lives of many people. All through the period from the beginning of the decade, trouble had been brewing in the coalfield. The miners were becoming more and more frustrated by the conditions under which they lived and worked. Apart from the progress that had been made by the introduction of Mr. Moggridge's system of leasing land to help families build their own dwellings, the majority still lived in the hovels that comprised most mining communities. Added to this, the iniquitous system of the Truck Shop, the slavelike employment of women and girls, and the poor pay and dangerous conditions of the miners themselves, it was little wonder that the Scotch Cattle found plenty of recruits. While Mr. Moggridge and Sir Henry Siston were busy arriving at an agreement that would benefit them both financially, and Robert Morgan tried in his way to better himself, meetings of discontented miners were taking place in isolated places and plans were being laid that would hasten Mr. Moggridge's decision to rid himself of the burden of being employer and coal owner.

In the early part of 1827 a huge crowd of miners and iron-workers, congregated on the mountain top at Croespen-maen. Fortified by the beer they had drunk, the gathering was in an ugly mood and ready for trouble. There were 'herds' from several mining communities in the area and it would have been obvious to any onlooker that the feelings of all those present ran high. Successive speakers further in-flamed their already fiery tempers. Speaker after speaker leapt up on to the 'gambo' that served as a platform and poured forth tales of double dealing and cheating by the managements of the collieries they worked in. Others shout-ed to the crowd of the treatment received at the Truck Shops. Others spoke passionately of the low wages and squalor they lived in while the coal owners lived in luxury. Bottles of ale and cider circulated amongst the crowd, every swallow serving to help whip up their feelings against those they considered their enemies. Cries went up for action. One who spoke, a huge muscular man seemed to dominate the other speakers. A large hat pulled well down over his forehead, partially obscured his features and with his collar pulled well up, it was impossible to identify him. That he was known to many there became obvious when the cry went up to listen to 'The Bull'. He moved to the front of the platform and raised his hands for silence.

'Fellow workers. A lot of you know me, and just in case there's spies amongst you, I'm not taking off my hat. If I do they might see my horns.'

The crowd laughed at this reference to his leadership of a 'herd'. He went on,

'We be gathered here tonight to make a plan how to strike a telling blow against the mine owners about here. Now I'm not going to stand here and shout out what we're going to do. I'm asking that all those who've been up here on this cart tonight, to meet with me at the Maypole in half an hour. Ask the landlord to bring you up to Mister Bull's room. We'll be able to sit quiet there and work out the best way to show the likes of John Moggridge and his pals what the Cattle can do. We've put up with enough from them. It's our turn now. When we've decided, your bulls will let you know when and where. Go home quiet now and wait. It won't be long.'

He jumped down from the cart and with two or three others strode off toward the nearby inn. The crowd began to disperse, going off in groups talking and cheering, some waving bottles from which they drank as they went along. Within twenty minutes, apart from the empty bottles lying about not a sign remained that a meeting had been held there.

At the Maypole Inn, a small thatched roof building, set back from the junction of the roads that gave the hamlet its name, the man who had spoken last was in quiet conversation with the landlord. Amongst those who raised their voices against the iniquity of the conditions that surrounded them, the feelings of the landlord of the inn towards the coal and land owning gentry was well known. Anyone who spoke up against them was assured of a welcome and it was rumoured that meetings of an organisation much more dangerous than the Cattle took place under the roof of his hostelry. The inn was well frequented by the local farm workers and miners standing as it did at the road junction, but for all that it was hardly more than a beerhouse. The mail coach stopped there but only to give the horses a breather and the coachman a chance to sample the beer before they set off once more. Evenings such as this when large numbers of militants held their meetings on the waun were a welcome bonus and with industrial strife rampant in the valley, such evenings were becoming frequent. As the men who had spoken at the meeting drifted in, they approached the landlord and muttered in his ear. They then disappeared into the room outside which, stood a burly man who checked for the landlord's nod before allowing anyone past him. At last the little room held about a dozen men who sat around the rough table. The landlord himself served them and when each had a pot of ale on the table before him, the landlord, at a sign from the big man who had called the meeting, closed the door. The man removed his large hat and rising from his place addresses them.

'Is there anyone here who don't know who I be?' he asked. Nobody denied knowledge of his identity.

'Now you be all sworn members of our union and you know the punishment for breaking our oath. I called you here to talk about a strike at the mines and how best to persuade mister high and mighty Moggridge that he had better listen to our claim for a better rate for hewing coal. Another thing. There be a Company Shop at the Rock run by a man called Rees. He calls himself Doctor Thomas Rees now, but he used to be a miner, same as us, 'til he got religion. Then his friends, the coal owners set him up with this shop. Now he be grinding the faces of his old friends in the Rock Colliery. His shop have been smashed once but he don't seem to have learned his lesson. Maybe it's about time he was paid a second visit.'

There were shouts of agreement from the gathering and they settled down to devise the methods of bringing their plan into operation. There were those amongst them who were not content just to stop the collieries from working and frightening the workers. Some wanted more drastic punishment inflicted. One even went so far as to demand that if a miner blacklegged, then he should be shot. This would serve as a warning to all that the Cattle would not be deterred in their fight for justice for the working man. This was turned down by a majority of the meeting, the leader pointing out that although he agreed that no punishment was too bad for a blackleg, to shoot him would only result in the Magistrates on the Bench asking for troops to be sent down from London to keep order. This would hamper the movement. It was agreed after a stormy meeting that a strike should take place in three weeks time throughout the Blackwood and Argoed collieries and demands made on the employers for an increase in wages, and the abolition of the Truck Shops. Any miner who continued to work would be 'Scotched'. He would be warned and if he carried on then a 'herd' would pay his home a visit and burn everything. If he was there, then he would be beaten.

'Maybe get his leg broken accidental like. It be hard cutting coal with a broken leg' said one laughing.

They left the inn after agreeing to meet the next weekend. They would each call a meeting of their 'herds' and tell them what was planned. The leader impressed on them how necessary it was for this to be kept secret.

'We don't want to give Moggridge and his pals the chance to shut the collieries aforehand. We'll do that for them and hit 'em where it hurts. In their pockets. As for Parson Rees and his Shop, we'll see how much he likes having the taste of the hellfire in his shop that he's always promising his chapel goers.'

When Robert paid his usual weekly visit to the manse the following Sunday evening, the minister said he had good news for him.

'Robert. Mr. Moggridge has told me that due to something unexpected happening, he wants the new assistant steward to start training immediately. I've already told him that I feel I have the man to fill the position. I've told him all about you and he's agreed to see you after the service next Sunday. If he's satisfied with you, he'll want you to start straightaway. He hinted that this new business might mean you will be in charge a lot sooner provided you show you can manage the job.'

Robert could hardly suppress his excitement. He thanked the minister who suggested they cancel the lesson for that evening as he didn't expect Robert would be able to keep his mind on it. Reminding the young man how important it was to appear before his benefactor as clean and tidy as possible, he advised him to have a good wash all over in hot water before coming to chapel, then bade him goodnight.

At about the same time that the minister was giving Robert his instructions and advice, two miles along the road at the Maypole Inn, the leader of the gang of men who had sworn to wreak vengeance on the local colliery owner and greedy proprietor of the Company Shop at the Rock, was busy explaining to those assembled around the table, when and how their plans would be carried out.

CHAPTER 11

When Robert, attired in his cleanest clothes, face scrubbed, inwardly apprehensive, in company with the minister, presented himself at the door of the mansion, and was admitted to the house by the maid, he gazed awestruck at the interior. Never had he seen such a place. The hallway in which they stood was as large as the interior of the cottage he and his family lived in. A stairway nearly as wide as the drive along which he had just walked, led upward and they followed the maid up it. At the top, a passage ran the length of the house and from this, rooms led off right and left. It was to one of these the maid took them, and, after tapping at the door, opened it and announced their arrival. Following the minister inside, Robert found himself treading on a thick carpet which covered the whole floor. In a dream he heard the minister thank the man who sat at the desk, for being kind enough to see them. He looked at the man he had known only by hearsay, never having seen him. The minister had told him that he should remain silent until spoken to and when his prospective employer addressed him, he was to call him 'sir'. He stood there while Mr. Moggridge and the minister spoke of various matters. Amongst these was the minister's worries about the state of repair of the chapel. It was in urgent need of a great deal of repair work having stood in the churchyard since 1694. There were he said, some who thought it might be necessary to rebuild it. They discussed other matters relating to the area then at last the minister placed his hand on his shoulder and said,

'This is the young man I spoke of Mr. Moggridge. Robert Morgan.'

Mr. Moggridge looked at the boy before him. He was clean and if what the minister had told him of the lad's work and home, that was something to his credit.

'The minister tells me you can read and write, and do arithmetic young man?' Without waiting for a reply he went on, 'I shall want more than that. You speak English well I understand. The minister says you come from a Christian family and you are polite and honest, sober and hardworking. You look strong' Robert stood there silent. 'Very well. You can start on Monday. Seven o'clock sharp. Is there anything you want to ask me?'

'No sir, thank you sir, except about my family. Can they move into the cottage straight away?'

'You'd better speak to Jeremiah the steward about that. Well if there's nothing else minister, I bid you good morning.'

Thanking him once again, the minister took Robert's arm and they left the study. Robert was silent, his mind alreday taken up with the fact that he had got the job. He would not need to clamber half asleep out of bed in the morning. No more hammering away at the coal face standing in the dripping water. He would be able to breathe the sweet fresh air all day long. He must hurry home and let Mam know that he had finished working in the NantGwrhay. The minister, conscious that his young companion wanted only to dash home to break the news, wasted no more time.

'Off you go Robert. Go and break the good news to your mother.'

Robert thanked him and hurried away. Tomorrow morning he would be starting a whole new life but there were things to do first.

A few minutes before seven o'clock next morning, Robert knocked at the kitchen door of the mansion. A voice called out from the interior and a maid appeared at the door.

'Please. I'm Robert Morgan. I'm starting work here this morning with Mr. Jeremiah.'

'Well you better come in then hadn't you?'

She turned and he followed her into the flagstoned kitchen. A warm smell of cooking enveloped him, reminding him that he had breakfasted an hour ago on a piece of bread and a lump of cheese. Seated at the large table, already some way into his breakfast, sat the steward.

'You be young Robert Morgan then? The master told me you'd be starting work today. Goin' to learn my job are you? Well young man, I hope you got a good 'ead on you. He don't miss much but he be a good employer, if you do your work proper. I hope you're not one of them loud mouthed sort what he's got working at the mine. Forever shouting about their rights. Mr. Moggridge is gentry and we work for him. We should be thankful and know our places. This be a good chance for you Robert Morgan. Work hard, mind your manners and keep your mouth shut, and maybe, and I say maybe, in a year or so, you could be sitting here, steward of Woodfield Park.'

'Yes Mr. Jeremiah.'

The steward finished wiping up the remains of the egg on his plate and pushing the piece of bread into his mouth, stood up.

'Now. Let's be moving. Monday's a busy day. We'll walk around the park first and see if there be any damage done by those drunken hooligans what spend their money in the Angel on Saturday nights. They do break down the fence so the cows and sheep do get out. Come on young Robert, let's see what they've been up to.'

Robert thoroughly enjoyed his first morning's work. Walking in the fresh morning air, he was surprised at the sights and sounds that he encountered. How different from the darkness, the wet and the stench that he had worked in for the last six or seven years. He was further surprised by the steward's breadth of knowledge of the wild things about them. He pointed out the signs of small animals, birds' nests, and even fox tracks in the dewy grass.

'Probably out looking for his breakfast early. Maybe he was after one of the chickens at the house.'

As they moved around the hedges, he pointed out where he considered it would be necessary to effect repairs. When they came to the stream that flowed through the park he stood on the bridge that spanned it. Overhead, branches of the huge trees arched and met.

'Take note of this young Robert. The master have put a bridge here. 'Tis made of iron. This bridge'll last for over a hundred years and never need no repairs.'

From where they stood, they could see the lodge at the end of the drive. The steward spoke,

'Master said you'd want to know when you could move in to the lodge. Well it's empty. Widow Davies have gone to live with her daughter so if your Mam wants to, she can move in tomorrow.' He laughed. 'If I know women, she'll want to clean it right through first though. No matter how clean it be, they've got to do it all over again. You'll be glad to move I'll be bound. I've seen some of the stinking hovels people live in in Blackwood. I'm right glad I work here and got a decent place up on the Graig there. The master have helped quite a few with his scheme but there's a lot of shifty no-goods around who'd rather spend their earnings on drink than buy some land and build themselves a decent place.'

'Yes my Mam will think she's in Heaven' said the young lad. 'She do work hard but it don't matter how much she do, with eight of us to look after and living in one room, it's too much for her. Eirwen my sister do help but...' His voice trailed off. 'Aye lad I know. Well things'll maybe be better once you're settled in. Come on, there's more to look at afore we have a bite to eat.'

They spent the rest of the morning continuing to search for any damage, and it was with a very healthy appetite that Robert sat beneath a large oak tree and ate the bread and cheese that his mother had wrapped for him. As befitted his position, Mr. Jeremiah had vanished once more into the kitchen to sit again at the large table and partake of whatever the cook had conjured up.

In the days that followed, Robert learned many things, not the least of which was a respect for the extent of the steward's knowledge. It was when they sat beneath the trees discussing what they had seen that the idea first came to Robert. Mr. Jeremiah seemed able to recall details that had passed from Robert's mind, so the young boy suggested that when they had their break, rather than Mr. Jeremiah rack his memory trying to recall the numerous items that needed attention, if he agreed, Robert would accompany him back to the kitchen at midday and in the evening and write down all the things that needed seeing to. In this way they would be able to keep a record to present to their employer as evidence of the good work they were doing. The steward was delighted because he said to the boy with a twinkle in his eye, 'I be getting older and sometimes it be a bit of a strain.' Henceforth, each lunchtime and evening, Robert sat at the table inscribing in a large ledger everything that the steward and he considered needed attention.

Within days of Robert starting work, the lodge had been scrubbed throughout as Jeremiah had predicted and Mrs. Morgan and the children piled their belongings on a cart and with glad hearts left the hovel in Blackwood and moved into their new home.

In the months that followed, Robert became more and more a help to the steward and the old man began to rely on the youngster to a greater degree. Soon he was sending him out to do the daily inspections while he dealt with matters needing his attention elsewhere. The Morgan family flourished in their new home and Mrs. Morgan with the help of the older children soon had the cottage clean and tidy. Eirwen's neat appearance came to the notice of Mr. Jeremiah and she was asked to help in the kitchen of the big house when they were entertaining. Dafydd had taken on the role of gatekeeper and when guests arrived, he would open the big gates for the carriages. He had a natural aptitude for gardening and soon the garden of the cottage was under cultivation. He then took it upon himself to trim the bushes and shrubs that surrounded the entrance to the drive. Soon he made himself responsible for seeing that not a blade of grass should show itself above the surface of the drive. All of this was noted by Mr. Jeremiah and duly passed on to his employer.

While Robert and Dafydd had been putting into effect their plans for the improvements they saw as necessary, those who had attended the secret meeting of the 'herds' at the Maypole, had been equally active. As agreed, a strike was called at two of the collieries in Blackwood. When the miners who wished to work put in an appearance they were confronted by a gang of men at the entrance. They had been warned that if they attempted to gain entrance they would be beaten and their homes wrecked. One man had dared to try to get to work and the Scotch Cattle had decreed that he was to be punished. A crowd of men carrying pick handles and other weapons had descended on his cottage and had dragged him out into the street. There they had beaten him unmercifully before turning their attention to his home. Despite the pleas of his wife they had thrown the few pieces of furniture out into the road, torn down the curtains and with the bedclothes had made a heap in the road. There they had set fire to it. With his wife screaming in terror they had warned him and all the onlookers, that the next man who broke the rules laid down by the Cattle would suffer a much worse fate, namely death. This had been only the first of several incidents which evidenced the fury of the miners. Another gang had broken into the offices and buildings on the pithead of a colliery outside Blackwood and smashed furniture and machinery, destroying books and records. A watchman who had attempted to stop them was beaten. The decision taken at the meeting at the Maypole to attack the Truck Shop at the Rock had also been carried out, but not without a set-back to the plans of the Cattle. Whether the shop owner had been warned or perhaps by ill luck on the part of the herd that attacked it, two of them had been recognised. One was called John James but locally he was known as Shoni Coal Tar. He and his fellow conspirator named William Jenkins were apprehended and taken for trial by the authorities. So incensed were the magistrates by the attacks on the properties of their fellow landowners, that the two were condemned to death. Whether the higher authority feared that carrying out this sentence would only serve to further enrage the Cattle and the rest if the workers, or perhaps because more Christian feelings prevailed, the sentences were commuted to transportation for life.

Mr. Moggridge as a magistrate was well aware of the growing unrest and had warned his manager to take precautions should there be any attempt to cause damage or harm to his mine or workers. There had been no demands made by his workers up until then but following the trouble at Blackwood, a large number waited at the head of the shaft after they came up and demanded to speak to Mr. Paget. Their spokesman told the manager that in accordance with a general agreement throughout the valley, they wanted an increase or would have to call a strike. Although mindful of the trouble that had taken place at the other collieries, Mr. Moggridge refused their request and work in the mine came to a stop. The strike lasted for two weeks during which time there were tales going about of the vengeance being wreaked upon those named as blacklegs who attempted to work at any of the mines where a strike had been called.

Robert did not have a lot of contact with his employer and it came as a shock when he did see him at close quarters, to note how careworn and ill he looked. It was now common knowledge in the kitchen that their employer was feeling the strain of the continual unrest that prevailed among the working classes, and the methods which they were employing to bring home to the mine owners the fact that they considered the latter to be to blame for many of the ills that befell the workers and their families. The whole valley was now involved in strike action and crowds roamed the area seeking trouble. There was talk that the magistrates had appealed to the authorities for troops to be brought in to help maintain public order. The trouble came even nearer home one night. One of a gang of mischiefmakers had been apprehended by the watchmen employed by Mr. Moggridge to safeguard his mine and he was being held at the pithead office until he could be brought before the Bench. A crowd of a hundred or more stormed the office and rescued the man. As Mr. Moggridge and his family were sitting at dinner that same evening, he became aware of a noise approaching down the back drive. Aware of the trouble besetting the valley, he had given orders that at dusk all outside doors were to be locked and bolted in order to protect his home and family. As the dog barked an alarm, stones could be heard smashing against the outside of the house. Windows were broken and from the darkness, threats of violence were hurled against the mineowner and his family. The demonstration continued for the best part of an hour before the crowd withdrew. Like his employer, Robert and his family had heard the noise and had locked themselves in their cottage.

Next morning when he went to the house to meet the steward, he saw the evidence of the crowd's fury. Shrubs and small trees had been torn from the ground and lay about. Slates fronting the house had been smashed by the impact of stones and some windows held broken panes of glass. When he went inside, he was told that Mr. Jeremiah was closeted with the master and he was to wait. After about ten minutes, the steward appeared and together they went out to see what the total damage amounted to. Apart from the immediate surroundings of the house, the crowd had done very little except at the entrance to the drive where they had torn the gate from its hinges and it lay on the grass verge. They re-erected it and continued their walk. When they returned at lunch time to the kitchen, the steward went upstairs to report to their employer. A maid appeared and told Robert he was to go to the master's study. She led him upstairs and after knocking at the door, left him. Answering the call to enter he went in and found his employer seated at his desk and the steward standing before him.

'Ah! Come in Morgan.'

Robert who had not seen his employer for some time, was shocked to see how he seemed to have aged. There were lines in his face that he felt sure had not been there when he had last spoken to him.

'Morgan. Mr. Jeremiah has been giving me his report on the damage caused by those hooligans last night. He has also given me a report on your capabilities. Unfortunately he has also advised me that he would like to retire from his position as soon as possible. I have agreed to this and so from next Monday I intend that you should take over Mr. Jeremiah's duties. So far you have only dealt with the work outside. Your duties from next week will include helping me with the books. With the extra work that I am faced with due to the troubles we are having, it is essential that I have someone capable of dealing with the simple bookkeeping. From what the minister told me and a study of your maintenance ledger it seems you are the answer to my problem. Your wages will be increased by a further ten pounds a year, and if I am satisfied with your work then I think I can promise another increase to start the new year.'

Robert was only too happy to agree to the new arrangement and it was with a light heart that he went home to the lodge that night.

The industrial strife went on for a few weeks but there were no more attacks on the big house. At last the mine owners offered the strikers an increase of a shilling a week for men working at the coal face and smaller rises for others. Although there were grumbles the offer was accepted and the mines re-opened.

In his capacity as steward, Robert was now brought much more into the confidence of his employer regarding the working of the estate. One morning toward the middle of summer, he was summoned to the study where he was informed that a special visitor was expected within the week. Sir Henry Siston would be coming to stay for at least a month. He would be accompanied by his daughter and his agent, a Mr. Morgan. Mr. Moggridge wanted his visitors to enjoy themselves and required his steward to ensure that there would be plenty of game, fowl and red meat for the table. There would be several occasions when as many as twenty or so guests would dine. He was to speak to the cook and arrange to supply whatever she required. Promising that his orders would be carried out, Robert left to discuss the details with the cook. He was confident that he would be able to supply whatever she required as rabbits abounded in the fields and woods nearby, chickens and geese cackled and crowed in their pens near the kitchen door and he would arrange with one of the nearby farmers to slaughter a bullock. The vegetable gardens were crammed with an abundance of greenstuff and potatoes and other roots. It would be the first time since he had started work there that he would have the chance to show the master how well he could carry out his duties. A chance to show the visiting gentry also.

In the time before the arrival of the visitors he spent every moment checking that the hedges and fences were in good repair, that Dafydd was continuing his good work on the drives and that the cook had received all she needed in order to cater for the appetites of all who sat at the master's table.

Daniel Morgan, Sir Henry's agent, was the first to arrive. He had travelled from Newport on horseback and he climbed stiffly down from his saddle when he arrived at the main gate. His arrival had been noted by Dafydd who had been detailed by his older brother to ensure that every rider or carriage was to be greeted at the lodge. While the agent stretched his legs, Dafydd opened the large gates while one of his younger brothers held the horse's reins. Morgan was impressed with the difference that had taken place since his last visit. The cottage was now surrounded by a well attended flower and vegetable garden and the two boys who had greeted him were clean and tidy. He remounted his steed and tossing a penny to the older boy, rode toward the house. He brought the news that Sir Henry and his daughter Lady Gwendoline would arrive tomorrow. They had travelled from London and both were in need of rest before continuing their journey up the valley. They would leave Newport about eleven o'clock and expected to arrive in the late afternoon.

With the news that their important guests were definitely arriving the following day, the housekeeper and maids dashed about adding the final touches to all the preparations they had made since the visit had been first announced.

When Sir Henry had returned to London after his inspection of the London Fuel Company's land, he arrived only twelve hours before his wife went into labour. When she had retired to her bedroom, Sir Henry, having previous knowledge of such events, had retired to his study with the papers that awaited his attention, and a bottle of port. The birth of children was woman's business and he was prepared to allow his wife and the woman who had been present at the births of their other children, to get on with it. Some six hours later after a lot of scurrying back and forth by maids, and some unseemly cries that emanated from the bedroom, he was brought the news that he was the father of another daughter. Both mother and child were well and he could see them.

Susannah lay in the huge four poster bed, pale and exhausted. It had not been an easy birth. Sir Henry kissed his wife and inspected the red faced screaming bundle held by the woman who had assisted at the birth. He excused himself by saying that he was sure his wife needed to rest and went back downstairs in company with the doctor. In the privacy of the study Sir Henry poured them both a glass of port. The doctor raised his glass and said,

'Congratulations Sir Henry. You have a lovely daughter. Let's see. That's five children?'

Sir Henry nodded. The doctor took a drink then spoke again, 'If I may offer a professional judgement Sir Henry. Lady Siston has just had a most difficult time. It was not an easy birth and I feel that it would be most unwise for her to have any more children.'

'But she's only a young woman Smithers.'

'True Sir Henry, but I feel I should warn you that should Lady Siston become pregnant again, she could not only end up losing the child, but might end up as an invalid.'

Sir Henry was badly shaken by this news and after thanking the doctor for advising him, bade him goodbye, then sat down to consider what he had been told. The possibility of Susannah becoming a sickly invalid was not one he relished. He had never considered her to be his social equal but over the years she had given him the support a man in his position needed. Not only had she given him three male heirs, but had proved an estimable hostess when the occasion demanded it. She never bothered him with household details and never taxed him about his comings and goings. She may have suspected that periodically he sought satisfaction elsewhere, but had never faced him with her suspicions. He would just have to restrain himself when the need arose and consider it a small price to pay. There were after all plenty more fish in the sea, and many of them quite willing to accept the bait of an illicit affair. Having, as he saw it, satisfactorily resolved the dilemma in which the doctor's news had placed him, he filled his glass and settled down to study the papers before him.

At a meeting with his fellow directors the following day, he reported his findings and outlined what he considered to be their best course of action. As a result of this, when he declared that he intended returning to Wales and spending at least a month there putting their plans into action, there was no opposition. He was after all the biggest stock holder and if he wanted to absent himself from the delights of the capital to visit such a Godforsaken area, that, thought several of his business friends, was his business.

When he broke the news to his wife, her main reaction was to point out to him that plans had been made to take a break away from London after the birth of their latest child. For herself she stated, she did not mind too much as she still felt rather weak, but the children had been so looking forward to it. Also there was the question of Gwendoline. She was growing up rapidly, and on the few occasions when it had been possible for her mother to accompany her in the carriage, it had become increasingly obvious that young men were attracted to her, and more to the point, their daughter was displaying increasing attention to them. With Sir Henry in Wales and her mother confined to the house, it was a situation that needed considering. The child could not be kept indoors all the time. Henry and Jeremy were at school and Simon was much too young to be away from his mother. Could not Sir Henry take her with him to visit this place? If, as he had told her, the Moggridge household was so well appointed, then would it not be possible for her to stay there? Being in the heart of the country too, there would not be much to tempt a young and impressionable girl? He could excuse his wife's absence on the grounds that she was still recovering from the birth of their second daughter. Gwendoline, bored with the restricted life her mother was subjecting her to, during the absence of her father, added her pleas to be taken away. Sir Henry, anxious to return to Wales to ensure that an early start was made on the new plans for NantGwrhay Colliery, and to take up the option of buying coal cheap and selling it dearly, finally gave in to his wife's and daughter's pleas, and despatched a letter outlining the changed circumstances, and further stated that he and Lady Gwendoline proposed travelling to Wales during the first week of September. He trusted that it would be in order for his agent Daniel Morgan to accompany him on this visit as there would be much to see to.

Whilst Sir Henry had been facing up to his wife and daughter in their combined pleas, Mr. Moggridge sat studying a report that had been delivered to him from Mr. Paget, manager of NantGwrhay Colliery. What he read there was causing him some concern. Added to the problems that had arisen during the recent troubles in the valley, the contents of the letter served to help him make up his mind to discuss certain matters with Sir Henry Siston. Coal production, despite the most strenuous efforts of management, had fallen. This was due in part to the geological features of the new face, and the increase in flooding, both of which were making it almost impossible to maintain the expected production. The men working on the face, were complaining continually of the danger due to the influx of water which now stood at an average depth of two inches throughout the face and was causing the writer great concern. He wrote to express his fears that unless some form of pumping was introduced, the main roadways upon which the colliery depended for input and output, would become impassable.

The installation of pumping gear would entail the expenditure of quite a large sum and added to the falling output, could only have an adverse effect on profit figures. Mr. Moggridge shook his head. Such news and its consequences, arriving as it had so soon after the disastrous stoppage due to the strike, finally convinced him that it was time he quit the coal mining industry and found some other niche in life. At 57 perhaps it was time to retire. First though, he must try and persuade Sir Henry, that despite the problems, NantGwrhay Colliery could be a solid and profitable investment. Relieved that he had reached a decision he carefully placed the letter in one of the drawers before going down to greet the first of his guests. Tomorrow he would send his steward with a letter to Paget authorising him to purchase the pumping equipment. Whether Sir Henry Siston fell in with his plan or not, the fate of NantGwrhay Colliery could not be left to chance. If an agreement could be struck, then some at least of the new equipment would be included in the price to be paid.

Summoned to his master's study next morning, Robert received his instructions and was on his way before eight o'clock. Unlike his predecessor he made the journey to the colliery on foot. However he did not take much longer. Knowing the shortcuts he arrived at the familiar pithead within the hour and went straight to the manager's office where he handed over the letter. Telling him to wait, the manager sat at his desk and read the missive.

'Well that's good news' he said as he put it on the desk. He looked up at the young man standing before him,

'You're young Morgan who came to tell me about the flooding in the new face aren't you?'

Robert admitted his identity.

'You're Mr. Moggridge's steward now then? Well done lad, bettering yourself like that. Though I wish I had a few more like you down below. There's a lot of trouble down there now. A lot of roof falls and there's a lot of water coming in. Maybe the new equipment will keep it down. Let's hope so or we'll have a real problem. All right lad you needn't hang about. Thank you.'

Robert bade him good morning and left the office. The surface of the colliery which once had been as familiar to him as his own home, had now taken on a completely different aspect. Everywhere he looked was covered with coal dust. Puddles of dirty water lay around. Discarded and broken machinery, tubs awaiting repair, the debris of industry, all coated with the same cloak of industrial grime. He could see the women who worked at the windlass, struggling to turn the long handle that wound the iron chain that brought up the bucket from below. In their rags of clothing, sweating from their exertions, filthy from contact with the coal they tipped out, with greasy unkempt hair hanging down, they bore little or no resemblance to the women and girls he now came into contact with daily. At the point where the coal was tipped from the tubs on to a system of steel mesh of varying width one below the other, other filthy creatures picked out the stones and other rubble that had been shovelled in with the coal below ground. They were if anything even dirtier and unkempt than their sisters at the shaft head.

Working in the open except for a rough shelter over their heads, they were at the mercy of the weather. Come rain or sun, snow or hail, it was their task to stand there sifting through the coal that had been tipped onto the sieves, in an effort to ensure that only coal passed into the empty trams waiting to be filled before starting their journey down the tramway. In summer, they choked on the dust. In winter they froze in the winter winds and rain. But it was a job that spelled survival. The few shillings they were paid each week, enabled them to eat, though some there were, who chose to spend a portion of it, in an effort to drown their misery, in ale and gin, or puffed tobacco in a clay pipe, held between decayed and blackened teeth.

Standing there in the sunshine, dressed in clothes that stamped him as one apart from those who toiled within his sight, he knew that never again would he become a part of the scene he surveyed, except as an onlooker. Silently he thanked the minister who had given him the chance to escape. With a last look around, he set off on the return journey to the mansion.

CHAPTER 12

The atmosphere both below and upstairs in the Moggridge household, was one of excitement and great anticipation. To the family, the arrival of such distinguished personages as Sir Henry Siston and his daughter coming to stay as house guests for a month, had caused some upheaval. To Mr. Moggridge, the visit was considerably more than a visit from a business acquaintance. The visit of a titled nobleman who had large business interests, could mean the opening of a door into a comfortable retirement. To his wife, the visit meant something entirely different. As a helpmeet to a husband she adored, the need to make absolutely certain that everything was well, that the guests enjoyed themselves, that the planned social evenings, brought enjoyment to the guests and credit to her husband, were paramount. She was aware that all was not well at the colliery, and her husband had given her a hint that he hoped that the visit might well be the answer to his problems. The one problem that had caused her most concern was Lady Gwendoline Siston. It was a problem she spent two days trying to solve before a possible solution came to her. Since no mention had been of any maid travelling with them, she assumed she would be expected to provide someone to attend to the many needs that young ladies of her station would impose. She would undoubtedly want to see as much of the surrounding country as possible. Her father would probably be too busy to accompany her every time she wanted to go out, so she would need a chaperone to travel with her whenever she went out in the carriage. It was essential that the running of the house should continue in its well ordered way. She could not afford to deplete the staff who were busily engaged in cleaning and polishing. A trained lady's maid was out of the question. They were a rarity in households in this area. Even she had to make do with the ministrations of Ceinwen, whom she had trained herself. What was the name of that young girl who came in to help occasionally? Eirwen, that was it, the steward's sister. She might do. She was clean and tidy and if she had a talent for learning as quickly as her brother, then all might yet be well. Robert was instructed to see that his sister reported to the housekeeper and when they appeared at the house Eirwen was taken to the drawing room where Mrs. Moggridge sat engaged in embroidering a piece of material. She curtsied as they entered and stood silent, awaiting she knew not what. Whenever she had assisted in the kitchen or as a cleaning maid, she dealt only with the housekeeper. To be brought before the mistress of the household could only mean something important.

'Eirwen. Mrs. Watkins has told me that when you have been brought in to help, you have always given satisfaction, and for that reason I am prepared to offer you a temporary position of extreme importance. As you probably know, we are expecting important visitors next week and Sir Henry's daughter, Lady Gwendoline is accompanying her father. I find I have need of a maid to help Lady Gwendoline. I am aware that you have never done anything like this before but at this short notice I have no alternative. I want you to take on the position while our guests remain here. Ceinwen my maid will instruct you in your duties and help whenever possible. You will be issued with a suitable uniform. Do you think you can manage?'

Eirwen, who had been expecting possibly a reprimand for some fault in her work, was astounded. A lady's maid! The sort of position that a young girl dreamed of. To help a real lady dress. To look after her fine clothes! She almost gulped as she answered.

'Oh yes Ma'am. I would do my best, Ma'am.'

Mrs. Moggridge was still doubtful.

'How old are you child?'

'Nearly thirteen Ma'am.'

'Can you press clothes properly without burning or scorching them? Sew buttons on?'

'Yes Ma'am. My mother have showed me how.'

Mrs. Moggridge made up her mind.

'Very well. Mrs. Watkins, send Ceinwen to me. We'll just have to try and teach her as much as possible. We have a week to turn this child into some sort of lady's maid. Goodness knows how.'

Mrs. Watkins bobbed a curtsey and left the room.

A minute or so later there was a tap at the door and a young freshfaced woman entered.

'Ceinwen. This is Eirwen, Robert the steward's sister. I want you to take her away and teach her how to be a lady's maid.' The young woman looked at her mistress in disbelief.

'I beg your pardon Ma'am?'

'Look Ceinwen. When you came to me you knew nothing about being a maid. Now at least you know the right dress to put out for the occasion. You know Sir Henry and his daughter are coming next week. I need a maid for Lady Gwendoline. You'll have to teach her as much as possible before then and keep an eye on her. Now take her away and do your best. Let me know how she gets on.'

The days that followed were a nightmare to the young girl. From morning till night, Ceinwen seemed forever to be scolding her, calling her a stupid girl who didn't deserve to be given the chance to become a maid to a lady of quality. When the child collapsed into her bed at night she cried herself to sleep but as the week progressed, she found that little by little things were becoming easier to remember. Although thanks to Ceinwen standing over her and making her nervous, and causing her to burn herself once or twice when handling the big iron with it's live coals, she was able to press the mistress's under garments with their lace frills sufficiently well for the maid to pass them without comment.

On the Sunday morning. Ceinwen took the frightened Eirwen to her mistress's bedroom. Sat in bed propped up with pillows, a lace cap on her head, Mrs. Moggridge was sipping tea, a tray across her knees.

For the occasion, Ceinwen had clad Eirwen in items taken from the other staff's indoor clothing. Her hair was hidden beneath a maid's white hat that was held on by a black ribbon, the ends of which hung down her back. A black bombazine dress that reached to the floor, begged from Mrs. Watkins, and an equally long white apron the property of one of the maids, completed the uniform. There had been some difficulty when it came to shoes. Normally, Eirwen went about barefoot except on Sunday when attending chapel. To have to wear them continuously had been a misery but now they peeped out from under the hem of the dress.

The mistress studied the new addition to the household. The dress was too big and hung over the apron top in a sausage like roll. It would have to be taken in. Somehow too, the cap needed extra fastening to stop it sliding down over the child's face. She pointed out these needs to Ceinwen then said,

'Do you think she'll be able to manage?'

'She's worked hard Ma'am and picked up quite a lot. She's good with an iron I must say.'

'Well child, we'll just have to hope that Lady Gwendoline isn't too demanding. Run along then and see if someone can do something about that dress.'

Outside the door, Ceinwen took Eirwen by the shoulder, 'Now do what I told you girl and don't let me down.'

As if to make up for the threat in her voice, she smiled.

'Be off with you and ask Mrs. Watkins if she can do something about the dress. I'll get some ribbon to pull the cap tighter. Come back after and you can help me sort out the mistress's dresses.'

The young girl ran off to find the housekeeper. She could hardly contain herself. Tomorrow she would be a lady's maid. Not only that, she would be a maid to a titled lady. Who knows where it would all end?

To ensure that the household would have sufficient warning of the arrival of their distinguished guests and so be on hand to greet them, Robert had arranged with his brother that he, Dafydd, should open the main gate. Iorweth, younger by two years, would be stationed on the bridge that Mr. Moggridge had caused to be built across the stream in the middle of the park. Immediately he saw Dafydd make preparation to open the gate, Iorweth would wave a white rag. This could be seen from the house, and since all the staff would already be dressed in their best uniforms, and waiting for the signal, all they would need do, would be to troop outside, and await the arrival of Sir Henry and Lady Gwendoline. As befitted a servant of his standing, Robert would accompany his master and stand behind him. There being no

98

butler, it would fall upon him to see that the staff were lined up, and ready to curtsey when the guests passed them. He would also be responsible for seeing that their luggage was taken to their rooms. He had no doubt that there would be several trunks to be carried up the stairs. Titled guests did not travel lightly when staying for a month. Dafydd and Iorweth would have to follow the carriage to the house, and help their eldest brother.

Robert had never seen any lady of quality and his imagination worked overtime. He had seen the quality of Sir Henry's clothes and knew that, whether his daughter be as ugly as could be, or as pretty as a picture, her clothes would be of the finest cut and material. Poor Eirwen! She would need all her wits about her. For himself, he was satisfied that he had done everything possible to ensure that whatever happened, the master's table would be short of nothing. The larder and kitchen were full of differing meats, while the gardener was ready to pull from the ground, whatever the cook desired. There was no more to be done, but to await the arrival of Sir Henry and Lady Gwendoline Siston.

CHAPTER 13

The great day arrived and from early morning everyone seemed to be dashing about, engaged on last minute tasks. Robert had reported to Mr. Moggridge on his plan to warn the household of their guests' arrival and had made a circuit of the parkland immediately adjacent to the house but could find no problem that could not wait until the next day. At lunchtime, sat in the kitchen, he listened to the chatter of the cook and maids as they speculated on the looks and clothes of Lady Gwendoline. He had to admit to himself that he too was not unaware of a curiosity as to what the young lady looked like. After lunch, the female staff retired to their quarters at the rear of the house, re-appearing some time later attired in their cleanest and tidiest uniforms. Robert explained to them what was to happen. When the signal was given, they would line up outside the main entrance and as the guests passed into the house, they were to curtsey. They were not to chatter. Eirwen would wait in Lady Gwendoline's room until her new mistress arrived, then help her refresh herself and unpack for her.

The afternoon passed slowly, until at four o'clock, Robert anxiously watching for the signal, was galvanised into action as he saw the white rag, tied to a stick, being vigourously waved to and fro. Well before the carriage had traversed the bridge, Robert had marshalled the staff outside the main door, and rushing back indoors, had advised his master of the imminent arrival of their guests. The arrangements for the greeting of the guests and the disposal of their luggage all went quietly and efficiently with one exception, unnoticed by anyone except Robert and Lady Gwendoline Siston. As the carriage drew up before the door. Robert stepped forward to open the door. As he grasped the handle he found himself looking into the face of an angel. In a daze he unlocked the door and stepped back, unable to tear his gaze from her face. Her features framed in a bonnet of some velvet material, dissolved into a smile as she became aware of the impact she had made upon him. With a smile of welcome, Mr. Moggridge stepped forward and extended his arm to help the vision alight. As she placed a dainty foot upon the step Robert regained sufficient of his senses to bow, thereby hiding his face from her gaze. Well aware of the impact she had made upon the young man, Lady Gwendoline set foot on the ground and bestowed a radiant smile upon Mr. Moggridge.

'Welcome to Woodfield Lady Gwendoline.'

Her father alighted and extended his hand to his host.

'Gad sir, I must say I'm glad to be standing on my two feet. The springs on this carriage are in urgent need of replacement.' He nodded to his agent, 'Morgan.'

'Good afternoon Sir Henry.'

Mr. Moggridge laughed and shook Sir Henry's hand.

'Come along Sir Henry. Perhaps we can find something to ease the pain.'

He led them past the line of servants who in accordance with instructions, all bobbed a curtsey. In the hall, Mrs. Moggridge waited to greet the guests. Mr. Moggridge introduced Lady Gwendoline to his wife. Sir Henry smiling, bowed low over her hand and said how happy he was to renew her acquaintance.

'I am sure you would both like to refresh yourselves after such a long journey Sir Henry. My housekeeper will show you to your rooms and perhaps you would care to join us for tea afterwards in the drawing room?'

'Delighted my dear Mrs. Moggridge.'

Preceded by Mrs. Watkins they went upstairs where Sir Henry was glad to find a decanter of port awaiting him on the bedside table. There was a tap on the door and in answer to his invitation to enter, Morgan appeared.

'I trust you had a pleasant journey Sir Henry?'

'Damned dry one. Pour me a glass of port Morgan.'

His agent did so then said,

'If you'll excuse me Sir Henry. I'll go and see that your trunks are brought up immediately, and if you wish sir, I'll lay out your clothes.'

'Good idea Morgan.'

Sir Henry sat down and sipped his port. Whatever the shortcomings of Moggridge, he kept a damned fine cellar.

Meanwhile, Lady Gwendoline in her room found herself

confronted by a blushing young girl who curtsied and announced that she was Eirwen and was to be my lady's maid, and would my lady like her to unpack?

From the superiority of her position and sixteen years, Gwendoline considered the child standing before her. At home she sometimes was allowed to share the ministrations of her mother's maid. Sir Henry did not yet consider his daughter old enough to warrant the full and exclusive use of a servant and to find one awaiting her command was both unexpected and pleasant.

'Very well Eirwen. I shall have to get out of this dress. The dust on the road was beyond belief. Put out my grey silk one. My hair will have to be redressed but I suppose it's hopeless to expect you to know how to do that.'

'Begging your pardon my lady. Mrs. Moggridge said I was to call Ceinwen her maid if you wanted your hair seen to.'

'Oh very well. See to the unpacking then girl. I suppose my hair can wait until bedtime.'

Once they had been unloaded from the coach the trunks were carried upstairs on the shoulders of Robert, Dafydd and Iorweth, and duly placed in the two bedrooms where Morgan and Eirwen began their tasks of unpacking and stowing away the seemingly endless piles of clothes brought by Sir Henry and his daughter.

Next morning the household awoke to a day of brilliant sunshine. Leaving her bed and crossing to the window, Gwendoline gazed at the scene set out before her. There had been little chance to view their surroundings as they passed through the park leading to the house, and she was amazed at their extent and nature. Near to the house shrubs bearing blossoms of all colours grew in profusion. Trees, the like of which she had never seen before towered above the house. A swathe of green grassland sloped away to the south allowing a panoramic view of the valley, with its river silver in the sunlight, winding away into the distance. Nearer, she could see the drive along which they had come, bounded on either side by tall oaks, elms and sycamores. She turned and crossed once more to the bed, just as a tap at the door announced the arrival of breakfast, carried by her new maid.

'Good morning my lady. I've brought your breakfast' she said unnecessarily.

Gwendoline jumped into bed once more, allowing Eirwen to place the heavily laden tray upon her lap.

'It's a lovely morning my lady. Mistress asked if you would like to take a drive in the carriage after breakfast?'

Gwendoline thought this was an excellent idea and instructed Eirwen to set out an outfit suitable for such an excursion, while she partook of a most satisfactory breakfast.

Downstairs Mr. Moggridge having finished his meal, strolled out in the sunshine. He had much to think about, as he intended to put his suggestion to Sir Henry this very day. If as he hoped, they could come to an agreement which would allow him to retire, the sight of this lovely spot was one thing that he would miss above all else. When years before, he had stated that he intended leaving Gloucester to settle in South Wales, his friends had been aghast. To leave such a place to go and live in an area known to be the centre of coal mining, with its dirt and dust! He must be mad they had said. Little had they known. This spot in the Sirhowy valley was a haven of beauty and solitude and he would miss it sorely. Nevertheless, he must try to persuade his guest that what he proposed would be of equal benefit to both of them.

Sir Henry, breakfasted, bathed and clad in what he had been assured by his tailor was the latest in country wear, descended the stairs and he too moved out into the sunshine.

'Good morning Sir Henry. I trust you slept well?'

'Excellently thank you John. I may call you John?

'I should be honoured Sir Henry. Had you any plans for today? I thought perhaps you might appreciate resting for a day or so before you start putting your plans into action.'

'Capital idea.'

'We could take one of the carriages and go for a drive. There's something I'd like to talk over with you. My wife tells me that Lady Gwendoline is taking advantage of this glorious weather to take a drive and see something of the countryside. I have instructed my steward to drive her and her maid will accompany her.'

'Excellent. I must confess I do not feel like clambering around that blasted mine this morning.'

'Right then Sir Henry. I'll arrange for the carriage in about an hour?'

Robert was both delighted and dismayed when, on reporting to his master's study, he was told that he was to drive the carriage for Lady Gwendoline. Delighted to have the chance to be in close proximity to such a vision of loveliness. Dismayed that for most of the time he would have to sit with his back to her and gaze at the horse's hindquarters. He had been able to think of little else since her arrival the previous afternoon. That he had nearly made a fool of himself he was well aware, and he wondered if she had noticed the effect she had had on him? It was unlikely he knew. Ladies of nobility hardly noticed the servants who waited upon them. To her, he had probably just been a figure who had come forward to open the door, and as was to be expected in someone she probably regarded as a country bumpkin, her presence and appearance had caused him to gape like some village idiot. Unwittingly he was doing himself an injustice. True, Lady Gwendoline did not often notice the people who ministered to her needs, but quite apart from deriving a female satisfaction in causing such an effect upon an impressionable young male, she had noticed him. Briefly at first because Mr. Moggridge had spoken to her, but a more searching look, disguised as an interest in her surroundings, had revealed the young man to be quite goodlooking. Of course he was only a servant but it might be fun to bait him a little. It would help to pass the time.

When she descended from her room accompanied by the little maid, an open carriage was drawn up awaiting her. The young man stood with the door open waiting to assist her to climb in. He greeted her civilly and held out an arm for her to rest her weight upon as she mounted the step. Once seated the young maid tucked a rug around her knees and began to climb up on the seat alongside the young man. Gwendoline spoke sharply to her,

'Eirwen. You will sit inside.'

Her face aflame, the young girl clambered down and seated herself opposite her mistress. Ashamed that she had undoubtedly shown her lack of experience as a lady's maid, the young girl sat silent, her head bowed. Robert clicked his tongue and the carriage moved forward.

Gwendoline was not a heartless girl and the discomfiture of her young maid made her regret her tone. She leaned forward and spoke quietly to the child,

'Eirwen. I am aware that you have very little experience as a maid but it is important that you learn how to do things properly. I might want you to do something for me and it would be inconvenient for me to have to stop the carriage while you climb down from the driver's seat. Your duty is to attend me, not gossip with the coachman.'

The child raised her head. Her eyes were bright with unshed tears. She sniffed and wiped her eyes with the corner of her apron which she still wore beneath the cloak borrowed from Ceinwen,

'Beggin' your pardon my lady, but I always ride with Robert when he drives anywhere.'

'I'm sorry child but I'm afraid that won't do. I'm sure that the coachman wouldn't want to be distracted by your chatter while he has passengers in the carriage.'

'Oh he doesn't mind my lady, my brother's used to me chattering away. I don't suppose he's listening half the time.'

'Did you say your brother?'

'Why yes my lady. Rob's Mr. Moggridge's steward but the master needed the coachman to drive the other carriage. He's taking Sir Henry and the master out this morning, so Rob's driving us my lady.'

She stopped breathless.

Gwendoline spoke, 'I see.' With a glint of amusement in her eye, she moved sideways on the seat and patting it, indicated that she wanted the maid to sit next to her. When they were settled once more, Gwendoline said,

'Now Eirwen. I want you to tell me all about your family. How many brothers and sisters you have? What your father does? Everything.'

This kindly enquiry encouraged the young girl to recount all the details of their family life as far back as she could remember. While the horse ambled along, Robert sitting almost motionless on the seat, straining his ears, could hear his sister disclosing details of his family's life before and after they had moved from the hovel in Blackwood to the lodge. Now and again he caught the delicious sound of Lady Gwendoline's gurgling laughter as some particularly funny episode was disclosed by his young sister. He squirmed silently as she chattered on, aware that much of what she disclosed might be related in some London drawing room by Lady Gwendoline, evoking laughter from her noble friends as she recounted the details of her holiday in the country. There was little he could do as he sat there his face and ears burning, while his sister innocently revealed details he would rather had been left undisclosed.

Gwendoline was enjoying herself immensely, laughing at some of the things Eirwen had told her. She was also kind-hearted enough to be almost to tears as the child spoke of the death of her twin baby brothers, and the appalling accident in the mine which had left the family fatherless. She looked with more than passing interest at Robert's back as Eirwen told how her brother had taken on the mantle of breadwinner at twelve years of age. She had never had any close contact with the lives of ordinary people and she wondered how her eldest brother would have coped had he been faced with the task of replacing their father at that age. Some of the things that this little girl spoke of as everyday occurrences, the lack of food, the filth, the disease and brutality of life, caused her some distress. Eirwen however, with the innocence of the young, seemed to consider that their family at least, were very fortunate, thanks to her brother Robert.

They had been quietly travelling along the route which her father had taken, on his visit to his newly acquired property, and when Robert pulled on the reins and the horse stopped, she saw they were outside a thatched cottage at the crest of a hill. Robert jumped down from his seat and tied the reins to the branch of a tree. Taking off his hat, he approached the side nearest to Gwendoline and explained that the horse needed to rest for a while. While they waited he enquired if her ladyship would like something to drink? A cordial perhaps or a drink of ice cold water? If not these, maybe a glass of buttermilk?

Taken aback by the choice offered she looked at the cottage. 'Surely Morgan, the tenant of the cottage is not able to supply all of these?'

His eyes twinkled. 'No my lady. Perhaps the water or the buttermilk. The cordial I packed in the box behind the seat before we left.'

Biting her lip in vexation at the way she had allowed herself to assume he would not have planned to carry refreshment on such a warm day, and slightly put out by the twinkle in his eye, she said,

'In that case I'll have a glass of cordial.'

He served them both from a bottle wrapped in a wet cloth, in glasses which normally graced the sideboard of the dining room, and then retired to a spot from which he could look down on the valley spread out below. The only blot on the landscape was the colliery's shaft head which was just visible, almost hidden by the oak trees that swept down to the river's edge in the foot of the valley. Why did people have to desecrate the land?

The cordial drunk and the horse rested, he climbed on to the seat once more and continued on the road which ultimately would lead to the little hamlet of Manmoel, hidden in a fold of the hills. His immediate object however was to drive as far as the stretch of water some two miles along the road. It was a wild spot but had a particular kind of beauty, lying as it did on the summit of the hill. Not much moved there. Some sheep roamed aimlessly about, cropping at the grass growing from the springy turf. Heather intermingled with whin bushes spread all around. Curlews uttered their plaintive cries, and occasionally, a skylark would spiral upward into the sunlit sky singing its song.

He loved the solitude and silence of this lovely spot, and had decided that for her first glimpse of the beauty of the country, he would bring her there. Somehow he felt she would like the feeling of freedom that the boundless acres of moorland must induce in one normally surrounded by streets of houses, however palatial.

He was not disappointed in her reaction to the scene,

when after a gentle climb, they reached the top of the bank surrounding the stretch of water.

He sat silent on the seat not moving, gazing out at the landscape. Behind him he heard her say,

'Oh it's beautiful! What is it called Morgan?'

'Pen-y-fan my lady. It's a reservoir to feed the canal which lies in the next valley.'

'Thank you for bringing me up here. It really is lovely.'

They stayed a while, then he suggested it was time they started on the return journey in order to be back in time for lunch. Very little conversation took place between Lady Gwendoline and her maid. Gwendoline had much to think about. Eirwen's disclosures of the struggle of her family and her brother's part in it, together with his obvious love of the beautiful country he lived in, had caused her to alter her first impression of the young man whose body swayed on the driver's seat. Her small companion had nodded off to sleep, but instead of issuing a reprimand, her mistress gently tucked the rug more closely about her.

While his daughter listened to the words of her new maid, Sir Henry listened to the words of his new friend and business associate John Moggridge. They had taken their seats in another of Moggridge's open carriages, and he had instructed his coachman to drive them to the Penllwyn. This was the site of an old monastery and at one time, the home of a branch of the Morgan family. He was not particularly interested where they went, but he needed time to expound his plans to his guest. He felt too that if he showed Sir Henry that even the powerful Morgans had been enthralled enough with the beauty of the area, to make their home there, it might help convince him that living in Monmouthshire would be no hardship.

As they rode quietly along Mr. Moggridge pointed out various points of interest, then approached the real object of their drive. Feeling that he should be direct in his dealings with Sir Henry, he came straight to the point.

'Sir Henry. I told you yesterday that there was something I wanted to talk over with you. I'll not waste any of your time beating about the bush. I want to retire. All my life I've been involved in business and politics. I must admit that I've enjoyed it most of the time, but I'm come to feel this last year or so that I'd like to get out. I'm fiftyseven and my family's grown up. Mrs. Moggridge has been nagging me to retire and enjoy what time we have left. I'll not lie to you Sir Henry. Since the strike last year and the continued unrest, not to mention those terrorists who call themselves the Scotch Cattle, I've given more and more thought to the idea. If I could find a buyer for NantGwrhay Colliery and Woodfield, I would retire. Would you be interested?'

Sir Henry said nothing for a while, his mind already busy with the implications of what had just been said.

'John. I thank you for both your offer and your honesty. What you suggest is too big for us to settle sitting in this carriage. I'm tempted I admit but there are some things that we need to talk about. We're both business men and what you have said about the unrest must have an effect on the price I might offer. If I bought NantGwrhay Colliery it would save me sinking a shaft into my new mine, and I could work both areas from one shaft. But if I'm going to suffer the attentions of those blackguards, then the advantage is outweighed by the disadvantage. We will need to discuss your offer at some length John. Let us leave it for now and enjoy the drive. You've given me a lot to think about and I suggest we talk about it this evening.'

'Very well Sir Henry. After dinner in my study. I'll try to influence your decision with a bottle of my best port.'

They both laughed, Mr. Moggridge content that as yet his offer had not been dismissed out of hand, and his companion equally pleased that something he had already thought about, had been offered to him as a buyer, instead of him having to approach Mr. Moggridge to sell the properties, thus giving him the advantage of naming the price he was willing to pay. A price that at first would be well below the true value, but one that he could increase and still get an excellent bargain. Friendship must not be allowed to interfere with business. Well not too much.

Robert did not have to act as driver of Lady Gwendoline's carriage again that week or the next. Now that the subject of selling his property to Sir Henry had been broached, the need for the regular coachman to take his master and guest for rides had disappeared, so that when Gwendoline had expressed the wish to be driven anywhere it was Jenkins who sat holding the reins. There had been increasing speculation at the servants' meal table as Mr. Moggridge and Sir Henry talked about business in the valley. They had agreed, that subject to the clearing up of a few details, the sale of the colliery and the house would proceed. A price had been agreed that had satisfied both, and Sir Henry would become the head of the company owning the colliery, on the first of January 1829. A separate deal had been struck regarding the sale of Woodfield. This would become Sir Henry's personal property on a date agreeable to both of them. Mr. Moggridge had offered to vacate the premises on the same date as that agreed for the sale of the colliery but Sir Henry had dismissed the idea. His friend was to take his time as Sir Henry had no plans to move his family into the house. He would obviously have to use it while he oversaw the working of the colliery, but he would be travelling back and forth to London for consultations with his fellow directors. He suggested that if his gracious host and hostess agreed, he would have the use of a few rooms in order to have a base from which to operate. As the transfer of ownership need not now take place in the middle of winter, this suggestion was agreed to with grateful thanks. This would enable Mr. Moggridge to enter into negotiations to purchase a property in Swansea, that being the place which he had decided should be his home.

Although the discussions between Mr. Moggridge and his guest had been confidential it was inevitable that with their continuing discussions at the table, word of their dealings filtered down to the servants' quarters, albeit not always completely accurate. It soon became evident however there was to be a change of ownership when Robert's employer officially broke the news to him. He had been summoned to his master's study and Mr. Moggridge had advised him of the sale of the colliery to Sir Henry, and that the new owner would be a frequent visitor to Woodfield. Accommodation must be kept ready for him at all times. It was then he disclosed the fact that he and Mrs. Moggridge would be leaving Woodfield to retire to Swansea. There had been no mention of this at the meal table and Robert was shocked. Mr. Moggridge then told him that Sir Henry was to be the new owner of Woodfield and had stated categorically that there would be no staffing changes. He hoped that Robert would give the new owner the same service he had rendered to the Moggridge family and that all the staff would remain loyal. There would be no change in the running of the estate or the house, at least until April or May of the new year. He was to say nothing to the rest of the staff as yet. Mr. Moggridge would tell them all in good time.

CHAPTER 14

Much had changed since the days when John Moggridge had built his mansion in Woodfield. Blackwood had expanded from a few cottages to a town, the largest between Newport and Tredegar. Coal and iron were pouring down the valley via the tramroad and there was much talk of what had been called a locomotive, steam driven, to take the place of the horses which daily laboured to drag the long convoys of tubs. Already Mr. Moggridge had heard that Samuel Homfray of the Tredegar Ironworks was discussing the possibility of such a method of transport being used to take his products down the valley. However, intrigued as he was by this prospect, he had now taken the first step toward divorcing himself from the march of progress and was immersed in the search for a suitable residence in the Swansea area.

Sir Henry was busy with his new acquisition and spent almost every day at the colliery or dealing with paperwork. Daniel Morgan, although a guest, was still Sir Henry's agent, a fact that his employer did not allow him to forget. Every day he either accompanied him on his journey to the colliery, or spent hours in his room dealing with matters requiring his attention as agent. In this he was glad that he had the benefit of his host's experience of local conditions, and a great respect arose in both men for each other. Mr. Moggridge was surprised at the extent of Morgan's knowledge of business practices and the agent recognised his host as a man of great integrity and not a little compassion.

Gwendoline spent most of her days riding, both in the carriage, and in the saddle of one of her host's horses. This latter only came about after some wheedling of her father. Since it was essential she have an escort in case of accidents, Robert was pressed into service. He was not a skilled horseman and usually trailed along behind her. She, clad in a becoming riding habit which she had included with her normal day to day wear, rode well and took mischevious delight in riding ahead until she was out of sight, causing him not only considerable discomfort as he urged his mount to go faster, but worry in case he might find her lying injured. There was not much other entertainment and when her plan to go riding with Robert in attendance was thwarted due to the need for him to go to Gelligroes on his employer's business, she was annoyed. Although she had been at Woodfield for nearly a month, she had not yet been into the nearby town. Her father and Mr. Moggridge had warned her that it was no place for a young well brought up lady to frequent. It was full of the worst sort of person. Dirty, and dangerous with the continual traffic on the tramline which ran through its centre. Being a young and headstrong young lady, these admonishments only served to make her more determined to investigate, and when the coachman asked her which road he was to take, she told him to head in the direction of Pontllanfraith. This village, a mile or so down the valley stood at the junction of roads leading south to Newport and east to Pontypool and the English border. There was a quite large hostelry in this village, which like its much smaller counterpart, the Maypole at Croespenmaen, was well known as the haunt of the new breed of political troublemakers known as the Chartists. This fact however did not interest her whatsoever. She was aware that the village was en route to Blackwood and this was her intended destination. Settling back on the cushions of her seat, with Eirwen facing her, she pretended a more than passing interest in the scenery, as if her sole object was to appreciate the beauty that lay on either side.

Robert had been despatched by Mr. Moggridge on his errand well before Gwendoline's carriage had left the house, so was unaware of the direction she had taken. He had decided that on his return journey, he would make a detour from his normal return route and instead, travel the road into Blackwood, and then take the path leading down to the river and thence home. As he walked along the roadway running alongside the tramway, he reflected on the changes he had seen take place in the last year or so. He had not had much cause to go into the town as most of his time was spent in and around the estate. His memory of the stench and filth of the place had also been a deterrent, so it was almost as a visitor that he looked about him as he drew nearer. A new tollgate had been erected across the road and line to extract tolls from anyone wishing to use it. He was surprised to see that a carriage stood nearby, its shape and livery marking it as belonging to his master. It was a fifty yards or so distant but he could see that there were two passengers and there appeared to be some angry words being spoken. He began to hurry but before he had drawn much nearer, he saw the driver flick his whip and the horse started forward, heading toward the town. There was no doubt who the occupants were, his sister and Lady Gwendoline, but he was too far away to attract their attention and the carriage drew steadily away as the horse trotted on.

The altercation that Robert had seen take place, had arisen because Gwendoline had overridden the coachman's objections to driving two unaccompanied young ladies into the town. When they had reached the tollgate, he had stopped the carriage and asked if her ladyship would agree to him turning about. She was probably unaware that there was no way to return to Woodfield other than by retracing their present path. He explained that it was impossible to get the carriage across the valley, there being no proper track and the hill from the river being so steep that it could only be climbed on foot.

This revelation only served to annoy Gwendoline more. To be thwarted when almost in sight of the town was the last straw! She would go on no matter what the fool of a coachman said. Wasn't she Lady Gwendoline Siston a guest of his master? When she told him to drive on, he begged her to reconsider. The town was no fit place for unescorted young ladies to frequent. There were all sorts of ruffians roaming about and he felt sure his master would not approve.

'Your name is Jenkins I believe my man?'

'Yes my lady.'

'Very well Jenkins. Listen carefully to what I am saying. I want you to drive me into the town. That is an order. Do I make myself clear?'

Poor Jenkins was in a dilemma. Failure to carry out her ladyship's wishes probably meant that when she reported him to Mr. Moggridge, he would be sacked. If he did as she ordered and they were involved in any trouble he would get the blame and probably be sacked anyway. There was no-thing else for it, he would have to take them into Blackwood. Privately his thoughts ran that it was a pity somebody hadn't taken a stick to the young lady when she was younger and taught her to treat servants properly. He shook the reins and the carriage moved forward.

They had not gone for more than a quarter of a mile when the horse's ears pricked up. He could hear something that the humans had not yet made out. A rumble, continuous, punctuated by bangs and rattling heralded the approach of a journey of tubs, making its way along the track through the town. He snorted and threw up his head causing Jenkins to pull on the reins. Something was startling the horse but Jen-kins could not make out what. He calmed the horse and start-ed forward once more. They were within a hundred yards or so of the beginning of the main buildings, when the tubs came hurtling from amongst them, the attendant hauliers hanging on for dear life. The horse now thoroughly fright-ened, reared up in the shafts. Jenkins, taken completely un-awares, tumbled from his seat to end up sprawling in the mud, the reins flying from his hands. With a whinny of terror the horse wheeled about and with the reins dangling, tore back along the route they had just covered, pursued by the rattling tubs.

Screaming with terror, the two girls clung to each other as they were thrown about by the bouncing of the carriage in the rutted track. Jenkins had staggered to his feet and raced after them. There was little hope that he could catch them and as he ran he prayed that the carriage would not overturn.

As the horse galloped on, the carriage bounced and swayed from side to side, throwing the occupants back and forth from one side to the other. Thankfully the cushions of the seats saved them from any severe injury but had the doors fallen open, they would undoubtedly have been hurled to the ground and probably killed. Robert had con-tinued hurrying after them and had gained a few yards when his horror stricken eyes beheld what had happened. As the horse and carriage flew toward him, he knew that he would have just one chance to stop it. If he failed, then both he and

115

the girls might easily be killed. He had spotted the trailing reins and knew that his one chance of success lay in grasping them as the carriage passed. Whatever happened he had to hang on and hope that his weight on the end of the reins would drag the horse's head down, and eventually bring it to a halt. He waited, and prepared to fling himself forward. If he misjudged it, he knew he could easily impale himself on the end of the shaft. At best he would be hurled to one side with several broken ribs. At worst, the metalwork on it might end his life in the next few seconds, or he could end up under the horse's flying hooves. To make the horse swerve away from him, giving him a better chance to grasp the reins, he waved his hat above his head. The horse wavered slightly but thundered on. As it drew level with him he hurled himself downward, his fingers scrabbling for the leather reins. the hooves striking sparks from the stony track, seemed almost to be scraping his head as he hit the ground. With a jolt that nearly pulled his arm from its socket, he knew that somehow he had got his arm through the looped reins. Desperately he reached up and took a hold with his other hand. He was being thumped up and down on the stones, mud spattered him and the clash of steelshod hooves near his face warned him that any moment, he might receive a kick that would render him unconscious. Shutting his eyes, he hung on, grimly determined that nothing short of being knocked senseless was going to make him release his grip. For what seemed an age, he was dragged helplessly along, his coat torn, his trousers ripped from knee to ankle. Blood from cuts caused by the flying stones ran down his face and he felt that his arms and shoulders had been stretched as if on the rack. At last, when he felt he could not hold on much longer, there was a slackening of speed as the weight of his body began to pull the horse's head downward and around. Unable to see where it was going, the animal slowly came to a halt and stood trembling, its flanks heaving.

Robert lay where he was, barely conscious, his arms twisted in the reins, looking more dead than alive.

Gwendoline had been torn from Eirwen's arms and thrown from the seat. She lay on the floor of the carriage, her clothes in disarray and her bonnet, squashed by her weight, beneath her back, held on only by the ribbon now around her throat. Eirwen, her face buried in the cushions, was lying on the seat immediately behind the driver's, still holding tightly to the framework that supported that seat.

Jenkins came puffing to the spot, gasping for breath. He did not recognise the body lying close to the horse's hooves, but could see that whoever it was, had suffered badly as a result of his bravery. Pausing only to ensure that neither of the young ladies was hurt, he bent down to untangle the reins to release the young man. It was then, beneath the mud and blood covering his face, that he recognised Robert's features. As gently as he could, he unwound the leather from his arms and pulled him clear of the horse's feet. Taking the reins, he pulled them up and over the horse's head and tied them to the seat support, out of harm's way. The train of tubs meanwhile had come to a halt some distance away. The hauliers, recognising the fact that the noise of the journey had frightened the animal into bolting, had thrust their pieces of timber beneath the wheels and brought the tubs to a halt. Several of these had jumped off the rails and the men were busy lifting them back on and replacing the load of iron which lay scattered about. One of them had run forward and while Jenkins was busy securing the horse, had opened the carriage door. On seeing the two girls inside, he had climbed in and made to lift Lady Gwendoline to her feet. Opening her eyes and seeing a filthy creature bending over her, apparently intent on robbing her or even worse, she screamed and hit out at the poor man. Eirwen had cautiously raised her face from the cushions and seeing her mistress defending herself against the ruffian, beat at his head and neck with her fists.

Attacked from the back and front, he left Gwendoline lying where she was and retreated to safety. With the help of her maid, Gwendoline struggled to rise to her feet from between the seats. She was wedged in tightly, the hoops of her dress making it almost impossible for her to rise. At last, redfaced, her hair falling over her face, and extremely angry, she managed to stand. She ached in several spots where she had bumped against the coachwork, and as the realisation came to her that what had happened had been the direct result of her waywardness, she became even more infuriated. To be seen in such a state of disarray not only by that fool of a coachman, but that other filthy ruffian who stood bent over the figure on the ground! Between them they seemed to be trying to raise up the prostrate man whoever he was.

'Jenkins. Come here and help us.'

'One moment my lady. It's Mister Robert my lady. He's hurt bad.'

Despite her concern for herself and her appearance, she felt a great shock as Jenkins revealed the identity of the injured man.

'Robert. How..?'

'It was him what stopped the horse my lady. 'S wonder he didn't get himself killed. He's unconscious. I reckon as how he's been kicked or hit his head on the track. If it hadn't been for the reins wrapped around his arms, he'd 'ave gone under the horse's hooves or the wheels. I reckon he saved your lives my lady.'

When Eirwen heard Jenkins reveal the identity of the blood spattered figure she screamed and made to descend from the coach.

'Rob' she cried.

Gwendoline stretched out an arm and restrained her,

'Stay here Eirwen, there's nothing you can do, leave it to Jenkins.'

Raising her voice she called to the coachman once more,

'Jenkins. Bring him over here and put him on the seat of the carriage.'

Between them, the two men carried Robert to the carriage and laid him along the seat. He was still unconscious. It was Gwendoline who took charge of the situation.

'Jenkins find some water.'

The coachman looked about him. Where did she think he was going to find water? It was the haulier who solved his problem.

'We've got water on the tubs ma'am.'

He added as if an explanation was necessary.

'It's for the horses what pull 'em back up. I'll fetch some.'

He dashed off and soon returned with a leather bucket from which the water slopped as he ran. Gwendoline searched in her reticule for something with which to bathe Robert's face. The tiny piece of cambric that served as her handkerchief was quite useless. Jenkins pulled from his coat pocket a large piece of red and blue material and held it out to her. Taking it she dipped it in the water and gently began wiping away the blood and mud. There was a nasty cut across his eyebrow and his chin was badly grazed. Apart from these two cuts, his only other injury appeared to be a large bruise beneath his right eye. A moan escaped his lips and his eyelids quivered as he began to regain his senses. As he opened his eyes and saw Gwendoline's face peering anxiously at him he tried to smile. The graze on his chin caused him to grimace and he raised his hand to his chin.

'Oh Rob you're alive. I thought you were dead!'

In her relief at her brother's return to consciousness, Eirwen threw her arms around his neck, causing him to groan.

'Oh I'm sorry Rob.'

He struggled to rise and Jenkins helped him to sit up against the cushions. Slowly he turned his head to look about him. His head felt as if it had been kicked and without looking, he knew that his legs would be minus a large portion of skin. Jenkins took the handkerchief from Gwendoline and dipping it in the water wiped Robert's hands. The water stung them and showed them to be lacerated, with blood still seeping from the cuts. Feeling his shoulders he was aware that his coat had been rent in several places and looking down he could see his knees showing through his trousers. Gwendoline had been watching him closely and when he made to rise she spoke,

'Stay where you are Robert. Eirwen, cover Robert with the rug and sit by his side. Jenkins. We'll have to get Mr. Morgan back to Woodfield as soon as possible.'

'I'm all right your ladyship. My head's aching a bit but I've had worse than this underground.'

'Sit where you are and be quiet! Come along Jenkins, climb up on your seat and take us back,' she hesitated then uttered her apology, 'and Jenkins I'm sorry. All this is my fault. I shall explain everything to Mr. Moggridge.'

What she had just said, had taken a great effort on her part and revealed to the other three that beneath the wilful, spirited and apparently spoiled young girl, there was also someone prepared to acknowledge her faults when the need arose.

With his sister alongside him and the object of his devotion opposite, both looking concerned about his wellbeing, Robert lay back, content to rest his aching head and dream of being nursed by the vision who had bathed his brow.

Jenkins had kept the horse to a steady trot and within the half hour the carriage pulled up at the main gate. Dafydd, attentive as ever to the coming and going of anyone to or from the house, opened the gates and they passed through, leaving a very puzzled boy wondering what his elder brother was doing sitting alongside his sister, while her ladyship on the other seat looked so worried.

Despite his protestations that he felt quite well except for a headache, the combined orders and pleas of Gwendoline, Mrs. Watkins and the rest of the female staff, finally convinced him that he needed to rest in bed. Once beneath the coverlet, his mother having been summoned by the housekeeper, came to his room and cleaned his injuries, then left him to the ministrations of a houseful of servants all willing to dance attendance upon him.

Gwendoline, in company with Eirwen, had gone straight to her room without waiting to explain what had taken place. Jenkins could do that. She had another task facing her. If her father was in his room she would face him immediately and tell him that thanks to her, Mr. Moggridge's steward had nearly been killed. She allowed Eirwen to help her change her clothes, now soiled and badly crumpled. Her bonnet was a ruin and of no further use to her. Her hands, which normally did nothing harder than play the piano badly or convey food to her mouth, were stained with blood from Robert's cut forehead. She washed and after dressing and letting Eirwen brush her hair, made her way to her father's room. She entered to find him sitting at a desk reading some papers. He looked up as she entered,

'Hullo poppet. Have you had a ....Are you all right child?'

'Papa..' her determination dissolved into tears.

He rose and took her in his arms.

'What's wrong Gwen?'

She sobbed for a while then sniffling into her handkerchief, dried her eyes.

'Papa. Robert was nearly killed this morning and it was all my fault.'

'I'm sure...'

She broke in,

'It was papa. I made Jenkins drive the carriage to Blackwood. He didn't want to but I made him. The horse was frightened by some tubs on the tramway and bolted with my maid and I. Jenkins fell off and if it hadn't been for Robert throwing himself in front of the carriage and holding on to the reins and being dragged along we might have been killed. Robert stopped them but he was all cut and covered in blood and...' she broke down again.

He held her while she sobbed once more.

'My poor lamb.'

'I'm not your poor lamb papa. I'm a nasty ungracious girl and I shan't be able to face Robert or Jenkins ever again.'

Semi hysterical young women were something beyond Sir Henry's knowledge and he had no way of knowing how to deal with his daughter, while she was in this state. He wished his wife was about, she would know how to deal with this. He placed her on the chaise longue where she sat quietly weeping into his handkerchief. There was a tap on the door and it opened to reveal the face of his hostess.

'Sir Henry. Is something wrong? Lady Gwendoline's maid told me there'd been an accident and her mistress was upset. Is there anything I can do?'

Sir Henry was greatly relieved to have someone as mature as Mrs. Moggridge to help him deal with the situation and when she indicated to him to leave her alone with his daughter, he was glad to accede to her wishes.

Mrs. Moggridge sat next to the sobbing Gwendoline and folded her into her arms.

121

'There there child.'

She held her until the sobs turned into an occasional hiccough, then releasing her stood up.

'Come along my dear. Let's go to your room and talk about it.'

Gwendoline allowed herself to be conducted to her bedroom then when Eirwen had loosened her clothing, lay down on the bed. Mrs. Moggridge dismissed Eirwen and after pouring a little eau-de-cologne on a hand towel, put it on the girl's forehead, then sat holding the girl's hand.

'Do you want to tell me what happened. Eirwen said there'd been an accident?'

Slowly at first, then more quickly, she recounted the incident, not forgetting to include the fact that it was her order to Jenkins which had brought about the terrifying ride behind a bolting horse.

Mrs. Moggridge did not interrupt. Allowing Gwendoline to recount what had taken place, was she knew, as good a way as possible of helping the young girl get over the shock which she had undoubtedly suffered. Poor Robert too. She must go along and see him. But first this child needed to rest, to sleep if possible. When Gwendoline had finished speaking, her hostess said nothing except to suggest that perhaps she slip under the coverlet and try to take a short nap. She would feel better after, and if she didn't feel like getting up to lunch, she would arrange for a tray to be brought up.

Feeling completely drained, Gwendoline was only too glad to allow the older woman to cover her while she lay with eyes shut, her face pale against the pillow. Her grip on her hostess's hand relaxed and after a few minutes she had drifted into sleep. Mrs. Moggridge quietly left the room and made her way along to the servants' quarters. In company with Mrs. Watkins she went to Robert's room and after being invited to enter, both women sat and listened to his account of what had taken place. When he had finished, his mistress assured him that there was no need for him to worry about carrying out his duties for the next day or so. He was to stay in bed. Her next visit was to speak to Jenkins and having heard what he had to say, she felt she had an accurate picture of the events. All accounts tallied, although Jenkins had made no mention of Lady Gwendoline overriding his orders. She felt sorry for the child and a certain admiration. It had taken a great deal of character to admit her fault. Many in her position would have allowed the blame to rest on the shoulders of the servant. She would tell Sir Henry that nobody was really to blame, whatever his daughter had told him. She had been distraught and hardly aware of what she was saying. It had been an unfortunate accident which thankfully had not been as serious as it might have, thanks to the brave action of Robert. She would make a point of stressing Robert's bravery. It might stand him in good stead in the future. Robert thankfully, had suffered no more than cuts and bruises. Lady Gwendoline had, she hoped, learned a lesson. Sir Henry had not been too disturbed and John her husband would get a watered down version of the whole affair. He had enough worries without the possibility of bad feeling springing up between him and Sir Henry. Like most wives, Mrs. Moggridge knew how to manipulate events that effected the men in their lives.

CHAPTER 15

Summer was drawing to a close and with it Gwendoline's holiday. It had been a month of glorious weather and up until the unfortunate occurence resulting in Robert's injuries, she had spent practically every day out of doors. Whereas Eirwen was quite happy to revel in the sunshine with no hat to shade her from the sunshine, her mistress as befitted a young lady of nobility, had taken great care to ensure that outdoors, her head was covered either with a bonnet or a large widebrimmed hat. It would be most calamitous should her skin take on the nutbrown colouring of the majority of the women she was surrounded by in this backwater. To be seen in fashionable society other than with a milk white skin was something everyone in her circle avoided. Despite this need to shade her face from the sun's rays, she had somehow managed to attain a most delicate tan and a shading of freckles across the bridge of her nose. That it enhanced her looks was evident to Robert. He had been completely enthralled by her beauty ever since the day he had first espied her in the carriage. To him, she was the most beautiful thing he had ever seen, and nature had added the final touches. To her, when first she saw them in her mirror, they were hideous. Somehow she had to get rid of them before she returned once more to the company of her friends in London. In an effort to achieve this, she spent a few days indoors, hoping that with no further exposure to the sun's harmful rays, both the tan and her freckles would fade. To help the process, she applied various potions and liquids to the offending area until she was satisfied that the affliction had left her. Taking care to ensure that her hat, a large straw creation with long ribbons embellishing it, and with a brim that allowed no beam of sunlight to fall upon her face, was securely held by the scarf tied beneath her chin, she ventured out once more.

Robert, now once again carrying out his duties had missed her. Although still limping and wearing a bruise of various colours on his cheekbone, he had insisted after two days in bed that he was perfectly capable of returning to his work. When Mr. Moggridge enquired if he felt capable of driving the carriage in place of Jenkins, suffering from some sort of stomach complaint, he was quite happy to confirm his readiness. He was even more pleased when he discovered he was to drive Sir Henry on a visit to the colliery, and that the Lady Gwendoline was to accompany her father. Sir Henry having business there which he wished to complete before returning to London, had thought that since his daughter must have seen all the surrounding country, it might be of some interest to her to visit the place that had brought him here in the first instance. The novelty of seeing a coalmine actually working, might help to restore her to her usual cheerful frame of mind. For some reason she had stayed in her room these last few days, and had snapped at him when he had enquired if there was something wrong? Thank goodness she seemed to have recovered her spirits and she had seemed quite pleased when he suggested this trip to the colliery. He was glad young Morgan was driving them. That had been a damned brave thing he did and the fellow seemed quite bright. Perhaps if things worked out the way he planned, he might be able to use the young man's talents. John had told him that his steward had worked underground hewing coal before becoming his steward. In the meantime, the fellow could explain to Gwendoline what was going on at the colliery, while he discussed things with Paget the manager.

When they arrived at the colliery, the manager was waiting for them. After telling Gwendoline he would be busy for about a half hour, Sir Henry had told Robert to explain to his daughter exactly what was happening and to show her as much as possible. He had then disappeared into the office with the manager.

From a point where they could look down at the pithead, he pointed out the various features. The shaft, the windlass, the area where the coal was inspected and the rocks and stones taken out. He explained how the tubs came in empty and were routed around the pithead back to loading points. He pointed to the little cabins from which could be heard the clanging of hammer upon metal and the glint of fire as the blacksmiths worked at repairing wheels and shackles and all other things necessary. This was a new world to her and she followed his words with interest. Then he pointed to the windlass and they watched as the huge iron backet, full to the brim with coal was finally brought to the top of the shaft. Figures clustered around it and tipped it into a tub, then pushed the tub along the rails to where it was tipped on to the screening grid to be sorted. It was not possible to discern the figures with any clarity due to the coaldust that hung in the air around the shaft and so Gwendoline's mistake was quite natural.

'I suppose the men winding up the bucket must be very strong?'

'Those are women my lady, and the ones pushing the tubs. All the jobs that don't need skill are done by women and girls. They are employed underground as well to haul the tubs from the coalface to the bottom of the shaft.'

'But that is terrible! Surely such work should be done by men, or at least by boys. Women can't be strong enough to do that sort of work day in and day out?'

'It would cost too much to employ men to do the sort of jobs that the women and girls do, my lady. There are boys employed as well underground, and they also do jobs like opening the ventilation doors to let the tubs through. I used to do that when I started work. I was nine years old then. After a year or so I began working with my father. He was a hewer and I used to help him.'

She was silent for quite some time. She knew that she lived in a different world from those she watched, but she could not visualise a situation where a woman or girl need work as they did. Of course there was poverty in London. Hadn't she seen it when they had driven out? There always would be those who were not as well off as their neighbours. That was the natural way of things wasn't it? And yet. She turned away from the scene which now disturbed her, not knowing quite why. Anyway it was not really her business. Robert pointed out one or two more aspects of the working world of a colliery, but somehow the sun had gone from the morning.

'I wonder how long father is going to be?'

she asked, more of herself than her companion. Her one wish now was to leave this place. She shivered as if a cold wind had sprung up.

'Come along Robert. We'll wait for Sir Henry in the carriage.' They made their way back over the dusty ground. The hem of her dress picking up reminders of the scenes she had witnessed.

In the privacy of the manager's office, Sir Henry was engrossed in a study of the figures presented to him by Paget. If things continued like this, he and his fellow directors were sitting on a goldmine. He smiled at the thought. That's what coal was, a new type of gold! He became aware that Paget was pointing out the figures for the output from the new face that had been opened about a year previously. As far as he could make out from the manager's enthusiastic report, the place had threatened to be a disaster what with water pouring in, but thanks to Mr. Moggridge having installed the new pump, the men were now able to concentrate on cutting coal from a seam that was about five foot high and seemed as if it would last forever. Sir Henry questioned his manager about the water. Was this from the stream that formed the boundary between NantGwrhay and the other property he had purchased?

'Yes Sir Henry'

'Couldn't it be dammed, or diverted? It'll always be a danger won't it?'

'More of a nuisance Sir Henry now that we have the pump.' This appeared to satisfy his employer and he went on to talk of other things. At last satisfied that he now had the figures his partners would be delighted with, he ended the discussion and walked out into the sunshine accompanied by Paget. As they walked along, Sir Henry asked if Paget had any information regarding the other collieries in the vicinity? Paget declared that as far as he knew, they were at least breaking even; but not being in possession of the reserves that NantGwrhay had, he doubted that their owners were getting such a good return for their outlay.

'Paget. Make a few enquiries would you? Don't arouse any suspicion if it can be avoided, but try and find out if a reasonable offer would be accepted?'

'Am I to take it Sir Henry that you might be interested particularly in those collieries immediately adjacent to NantGwrhay?'

'Yes, but don't appear too eager. I don't want the price going up if they suspect my interest.'

'I'll be discreet sir never fear.'

'Good man. Now I shall be returning to London in a day or so and I'll be away for about three weeks. If there is any problem contact Daniel Morgan my agent. I hope you'll have some good news for me when I get back.'

They shook hands and Sir Henry walked on to the carriage leaving Paget with a few things to think about.

'Well my dear, did Robert explain everything to you?'

'Yes papa.'

'Good. Right then Morgan, let's be off and see what our hostess has provided for lunch.'

Robert clicked his tongue and the horse moved forward. Gwendoline cast a glance over her shoulder at the scene they had just left, then tried to take an interest in the scenery. But her mind kept returning to the sight of those filthy creatures wrestling with that huge bucket; those creatures who, if bathed and dressed could well have looked like her!

Sir Henry, busy with his own thoughts and plans did not take much notice of his daughter's silence, and was startled when she spoke.

'Papa. Why do they have women to push those tubs about and pull that big bucket up the shaft? Wouldn't a horse be stronger?'

'Bless my soul child. Whatever put that into your head?'

'I was watching them and I thought they were men. Then Robert told me they were women and girls. Isn't it a very hard job for them to do. A horse could do it much easier couldn't it?'

'Probably my dear, but I can get twenty women to work for what it would cost me to buy and feed a horse. And don't forget if the horse falls sick, what then? Most of them are quite happy and if I bought a horse, I'd have to sack them, then they'd have no money to buy food with and who knows how many would starve to death? Don't worry your pretty little head about such things my dear. Leave such things to the menfolk.'

Satisfied he had explained the intricacy of the employment system, he relapsed once more into deep thought about the forthcoming meeting in London. His daughter thought about what her father had said. It was true that women were cheaper than horses, and they would starve if people like her father didn't employ them. Oh dear it was all so confusing. Perhaps papa was right. It was best to leave business to men. They understood such things. In a couple of days they would be returning to London and there would be so many other things to do and think about. She had enjoyed her holiday in the country. It had been very interesting and the countryside was beautiful. She would have quite a lot to tell her coterie of friends. How they would laugh at some of the things she had to tell them. And if papa agreed she would be taking her own personal maid back with her. She would have to speak to Mrs. Moggridge about that. She could speak to Eirwen's mother and see if she would let her daughter go to London to be a lady's maid. She would speak to papa after lunch. He was more likely to agree after he'd eaten. Smiling to herself, she settled back on the cushions. It was a lovely day once more.

Things had worked out exactly as Gwendoline had hoped. She had long been able to wheedle things out of her father and she was quite right in her assumption that he would be more amenable after he had eaten and partaken of his host's port. She approached him as soon as he had settled down in his room. Subject to Eirwen's mother agreeing to her daughter leaving home, he had not the slightest objection to his daughter acquiring a maid. Gwendoline was soon to figure very prominently in his plans and giving her a maid would be a small price to pay.

She gave him a kiss on the cheek and dashed off to ask Mrs. Moggridge if she would approach Eirwen's mother and ask for her consent. She had become quite fond of the child in the month they had spent as maid and mistress.

Sir Henry and Gwendoline left Woodfield on the first part of their long and tiring journey to London. Jenkins drove them to Newport where they were to stay the night. Tomorrow they would catch the mail coach to London and hopefully they would be back in London within two days. Their departure had been marked by tears from their hostess and to a lesser extent by Mrs. Morgan. Since their talk after the accident in which Robert had been injured, Mrs. Moggridge had grown to like Gwendoline, appreciating that under the imperious facade, there was a caring girl. As for Eirwen's mother's feelings, the fact that her daughter might not return to see her for several years was a sad fact, but to know that she was now employed as her ladyship's personal maid and would not become a workworn drudge living in some loathsome hovel was enough recompense.

When Robert kissed his sister goodbye, he begged her to write sometimes and let him know how she was.

'I will, I promise and I'll make sure to let you know how her ladyship is' laughed his sister mischievously.

CHAPTER 16

Sir Henry did not come back to Woodfield for nearly six weeks. Immediately he returned he was closeted with Mr. Moggridge in a meeting that lasted a considerable time. He asked his host if he would consider acting as representative until such time as the plan he had under consideration could be implemented. When Mr. Moggridge suggested that Daniel Morgan be considered for the position, Sir Henry had turned down the suggestion. Sir Henry wanted someone who was on the spot and as Morgan was his agent for the whole of the west, it meant he could not give the position his complete attention. Sir Henry advised Mr. Moggridge of his intention to try to purchase two more collieries. If he was successful, he would need someone who could give the matter his full attention. Eventually, Mr. Moggridge agreed provided that, as soon as he had been able to find new accommodation in Swansea, Sir Henry would release him on receiving a month's notice. Pressed as he was for time, Sir Henry agreed to this and left for London a few day's later, to initiate his plan.

Things had returned to normal after Sir Henry left and within a few weeks the memory of Gwendoline's visit was a faint one except in one person's memory. No matter how hard he worked or how busy he was, never a day passed that Robert did not recall the face of the girl he knew he had given his heart to. The fact that she had hardly noticed him, and at all times had treated him purely as a servant, made no difference. He knew that from the first moment he had set eyes on her, there would be no-one else. How, if ever, he could declare his love to her, he did not know, but somehow, sometime it would happen.

When Mr. Moggridge received the news of her impending marriage, and broke the news, Robert was shaken to the core of his being. If he had known the full extent of the story behind that bald announcement, he would probably have given up his post. By the time he became aware of the circumstances, time had dulled his feelings somewhat and other things had taken place that made it impossible for him to leave.

It was in the May of 1829 that the first event happened that was to ensure that Robert remained at Woodfield. His mother, worn down by years of childbearing, overwork and semi starvation, finally succumbed to the pain within her. Robert had been to the colliery with a message for Paget the manager. On his return Dafydd was waiting for him.

'Rob. Can you come home straight away? Mam is bad. She fell down in the garden and couldn't get up. We managed to get her into the house and Eleri is staying with her. Mrs. Moggridge sent Jenkins for the doctor.'

Hurrying home they found the doctor in the small room that served as the family's living room.

'How is my mother doctor' Robert asked.

'I'm afraid I have bad news for you Mr. Morgan. Your mother has been ill for years, and I'm afraid there's very little I can do for her. It's only a question of time. I've given her some laudanum to kill the pain and I've left some with your sister. Any time the pain gets too much you can give her a spoonful. I'm sorry. I'll call in again tomorrow.'

Robert went to the door with him. Once outside, the doctor spoke again.

'I didn't want to say too much in front of the children Mr. Morgan, but I don't think your mother will last through tomorrow. I think you should be prepared. I'm sorry.'

He raised his hat and climbed into the carriage.

The doctor's prediction came true. Mrs. Morgan finally gave up the fight against the pain that night. Robert had sent his sister to her bed and was sitting by his mother's bedside holding her hand when she whispered to him,

'Robert bach. I'm sorry you've been dragged away from your work but I'm glad you're here now.'

'Hush mam. It's all right. Mr. Moggridge told me to stay with you. Try and get some rest now and we'll talk in the morning. Is the pain bad? I'll get you something for it.'

'No bach. I want to talk to you. I haven't got much time. You've been a good son and I want you to be happy. I've seen the look in your eyes when you've been with the young lady from London. Forget her bach, there's no hope for you there, only a broken heart. You'll probably never see her again so find someone else and try and forget her.'

'It's all right mam, you don't have to worry. Mr. Moggridge had a letter from Sir Henry. Lady Gwendoline is getting married soon.'

'I'm glad son. I know it hurts but it's for the best you'll see. The likes of her isn't for you.'

She lay back on the pillow, holding his hand. They were both silent and when he looked she had gone to sleep. Her grip on his hand relaxed and he gently released it and went into the other room. Eleri had left some bread and cheese on the table and he ate this while his mind was busy with what the doctor had said. If, as he feared his mother died, he would have to make plans. It was while he was trying to foresee what he could do that he heard his mother call out. He rushed into the bedroom. His mother was sitting up in the bed her hand held out.

'All right mam I'm here.'

'Oh Evan hold my hand it's so dark.'

Realising that his mother thought she was talking to her late husband, he put his arm around her and took her hand in his. This was how Eleri found them when she came in a few hours later. Robert asleep, their mother also asleep, but she wouldn't awake.

They buried Myfanwy Morgan alongside her husband and twin babies. Mr. and Mrs. Moggridge stood next to Robert and his brothers and sister while the coffin was lowered into the hole. The children sobbing bitterly were clustered around their big brother, who stood with tears running down his face. He was truly the head of the household now.

There had been tears in the home of Sir Henry Siston too, principally from his wife. Lady Siston, well aware of the position of the wife in the home, was not surprised when her husband told her that he thought it time that Gwendoline was wedded. She was now nearly seventeen, only slightly younger than her mother had been when Sir Henry had asked for her hand, and already several young men had begun taking more than a passing interest in her. Her mother had hoped that she might have been able to enjoy at least another year of freedom. Freedom to go to balls and parties, to dress up and go riding in the parks. Too well she knew that, in the normal course of events, her daughter would spend the best part of the next ten years producing children. There would be little chance of the sort of freedom she had envisaged for her daughter. She sighed and agreed with Sir Henry. Whatever she may have thought, he would have his way, that was the way of the world. Accordingly, in the accepted manner, Gwendoline was launched on to the marriage market. There was just one exception to the usual planned assault on the eligible bachelors. Her father wasn't looking for a marriage that would endow him with a rich son-in-law who could and would ensure that his bride was maintained in the style to which she was accustomed. Rather, he wanted one who would feel indebted to him and prepared to carry out his wishes, for a consideration. He didn't require the successful suitor to do much, just to act on his behalf but to leave any important decisions to Paget the manager.

When Gwendoline's mother announced that after the Christmas festivities, her father and mother intended opening the house for parties, dances, and other gatherings, she was overjoyed. She had been afraid that her father, now that he had property in Wales might want to move the whole family there, and she would be cut off from all her interests and friends. She was not so naive as to think that the forthcoming functions were for purely enjoyable reasons. All her friends who had married, had been launched thus. It was undoubtedly her parents' way of informing London society, that Sir Henry Siston's daughter was now of marriageable age and any eligible suitor would be welcome to try to ensnare the lovely Gwendoline into marriage, or at least, into a firm understanding. There were quite a number of memorable festive occasions over the Christmas and many a young man, sons of Sir Henry's business friends, came, saw Gwendoline, and were conquered. Thus when the first dinner and dancing invitations were delivered, many of those who had met her then, and now knew from their parents that the host's daughter was available to be courted, turned up.

The months that followed, were a period of sheer enjoyment to Gwendoline. Never had she had so much attention.

Her mother had taken her to the most fashionable couturiers in Bond Street where she had been allowed to choose ball-gowns, dresses for almost every sort of occasion and hats of all shapes and designs. They had spent hours, day after day, discussing material, designs, and colours, returning home with the carriage loaded with boxes containing the products of needlewomen who spent nights stitching on sequins and other decorations.

The events too were almost too much for a young girl to cope with. Never a dance went by when she was not whirling about the floor, her dance card full of the names of the very best bred young and not so young, bachelors of London's society. Each night she would fall asleep, her mind awhirl with the names of those who had begged her favours. How handsome this one was. What a dashing figure another was in his uniform. That there would be a price to pay she had no doubt, but for now let her enjoy herself. Each week brought invitations to go here or there, to meet and dance with gallant young men, or visits to the theatre.

Sir Henry paid two visits to Wales after Christmas and when he returned in the early spring he called another meeting of the London Fuel Company. At this he announced that he hoped to negotiate the purchase of two more mines. This purchase would make them the largest coal owners in the valley, and they would be producing more coal than any other. This was excellent news for his fellow directors, but one, more cautious than the rest, raised the question of who would oversee the day to day working of this combine? Sir Henry who had known that this was bound to arise at some point, then made known that he had a plan to install someone in overall charge. Someone who while being responsible for keeping coal pouring from the shafts, would be amenable to any suggestions to improve output that might come from London; no matter how unpopular the methods required might be. He would say no more but promised that the position would be filled in the very near future.

During the months since Christmas, he had made numerous enquiries amongst his friends and business acquaintances regarding the financial standing of all the families of the young men who seemed attracted by his daughter, and whom Gwendoline seemed pleased to have attend. Several he noticed had been regular guests and of these, two seemed to fill the requirements he desired. Both were in their early twenties and impecunious. True both received small incomes from their titled fathers, but having been born second sons, neither had much hope of ever succeeding to the titles. One, young Jocelyn Tremoir, was not only poor, he was reputed to have card debts. He seemed to spend much of his time at clubs where gambling was the principal occupation of the members and his clothing while being of excellent quality was not quite the best. Tailors who had not been paid were loth to put their best products on the backs of young bucks who could not be relied upon to foot their bills. The other, Marcus Appleby son of the Earl of Mountchester, was in much the same position and while having no debts of honour, was said to be fond of the brandy bottle. Sir Henry did not hold this against him, provided it didn't interfere with his plans, should he be the one chosen.

Gwendoline's birthday was to be in the month of May, and to celebrate the occasion, her father planned that a most sumptuous ball should be held, with a guest list numbering some two hundred. Amongst these would be the two he had chosen as the contenders for his daughter's hand. He felt that young Appleby might be the better choice for what he had in mind. It wouldn't do to find that his son-in-law was gambling with the profits from the collieries. If Appleby did over indulge in brandy he would not be allowed to endanger the source of the Siston family wealth, Paget and the other managers would see to that. He determined to try to influence his daughter in her choice of suitor. It might be difficult. She was a spirited young thing and might dig her heels in, but if he could persuade Susannah to favour Appleby, surely Gwendoline would listen to her mother? To this end, he brought the subject up when they had retired for the night, pointing out that he had noticed that their daughter seemed attracted to several of the young men he had seen about the place. Susannah played right into his hands when she said that Gwendoline had expressed a preference for only one or two.

Professing complete ignorance he pressed her to disclose who these were.

'After all, if either of these is going to be my son-in-law, I need to know something about them.'

'I think young Tremoir is her favourite. Of course he's got no money and I hear that he has some debts, but what young man hasn't these days?'

'Gambling debts you mean? I suppose he's hoping that Gwendoline's dowry will clear his debts for him. Who's the other?'

'Marcus Appleby. His father's the Earl of Mountchester. He's not so dashing as Tremoir, but if it was me, he'd be my choice. Still young girls don't look any further than the end of their nose. I expect when the time comes she'll make up her own mind.'

'Well I think you should drop a hint to her that you don't think her father would be too pleased if she married someone who might end up gambling away everything. I've no intention of keeping him in gambling money.'

Satisfied that he had sown the seed, he was wise enough to let it germinate in its own good time and adjusting his night-cap, he settled down to sleep.

When preparations were nearly completed for the big birthday ball, Sir Henry once more raised the question with his wife. He was extremely pleased with himself when she told him that Gwendoline had confided to her, that she hoped Marcus Appleby was on the guest list. Her mother had inquired whether she had any particular reason for hoping he would attend? Blushing, Gwendoline had confessed that she thought the young man in question was on the point of declaring his devotion and speaking to Sir Henry. She stressed that on no account was Sir Henry to admit that should this happen, he had had any prior knowledge of the state of affairs. He was only too happy to agree and retired to his study, content that things seemed to be working out as he wished.

When, on the night of the ball, the young man had asked if he might speak to him in private, Sir Henry had acted the gracious host, appearing anxious only to help his young guest in some matter unspecified. When Marcus had declared his love for Gwendoline and wished to ask for her hand in marriage, he had expressed his astonishment that his little daughter was ready for such a step. Marcus assured him that he was sure Gwendoline felt the same way he did, and that if Sir Henry would agree to him paying court to her, he would strive with might and main to prove his devotion. Faced with such an earnest declaration, Sir Henry rang for Jevons to tell Lady Gwendoline that her father wished to speak to her at once. She must have been in the immediate vicinity, as she entered within a very short time.

'Gwendoline. This young man has asked me for permission to pay court to you and to grant him your hand in marriage. He also tells me that he is sure you reciprocate his feelings. Is this true?

'Oh yes papa. I love Marcus with all my heart.'

'Well! I must say I had no idea you harboured such feelings for any young man. Why you're not much more than a child.'

'Oh papa, you never notice anything. Today is my seventeenth birthday. You and mama were married when she was hardly older than I am now.'

'True, true. Well if you're sure. Does your mother know how you feel about this young man?'

Blushing, she confessed that when she had seen Marcus accompany him to his study, she had gone to her mother and told her that her beloved was at that moment speaking to Sir Henry.

'What did she say?'

'That I was too young, but, if we were in love she hoped we would be very happy.'

Aware that by now, her husband must have given or withheld his consent, Lady Siston entered the study opening the door just in time to hear her husband declare,

'Hm. Very well. It all seems to have been settled without my knowledge but I shan't deny two people their happiness. I shall want to speak to you again young man, but I think that the best thing I can do is to announce your betrothal tonight.'

He kissed his daughter fondly and shook the young man's hand, then followed by the happy couple, arms entwined,

Sir Henry and Lady Siston left the study to announce to their guests that it gave them both great pleasure to announce the betrothal of their daughter Lady Gwendoline to the Honourable Marcus Appleby second son of the Earl of Mountchester.

The success of the first part of his plans, gave him hope that the next step would be equally successful, and that after the marriage had taken place, it would not be too long delayed.

CHAPTER 17

With the death of his mother and the absence in London of
Eirwen, Robert was placed in a difficult position. Eleri was
still too young to take on the responsibilty of being housekeeper and a mother to her two young brothers, the younger
hardly more than a toddler. Dafydd was doing almost a full
time job working in the garden surrounding the lodge, and
acting as gateman at the main gate. On occasion he accompanied his older brother on his daily rounds about the estate,
and with the increase in the bookwork which Robert was obliged to undertake, he had once or twice even taken upon his
young shoulders, the burden of performing Robert's outdoor
duties. One such occasion had been the two days when Robert nursing his injuries had lain in bed. Mr. Moggridge had
suggested to Robert that, if as he suspected Sir Henry en-
larged his holdings, he might well engage Robert to act full
time as his bookkeeper. This would be an excellent opportunity for Dafydd to step in and take over the steward's duties.
While this appealed to Robert at the time the subject was
broached, the death of his mother had made it almost impossible. Dafydd would be required to be away from the cottage
most of the day, and the three children the oldest barely six
years of age, could hardly be left to fend for themselves. Robert could see no way out of the difficulty and each time Sir
Henry paid a visit to Woodfield, he was worried that what
Mr. Moggridge suspected might come true. If this happened
then there was only one solution. Somehow he would have
to employ a housekeeper to look after the family. Any gain
that Dafydd's increased wages might bring to the household
would be almost wiped out in paying the new housekeeper.

It was about the middle of 1829 that Mr. Moggridge received the news of Gwendoline's betrothal. When he announced the news to the household, Robert felt as if he had
been stabbed in the heart. He was aware that his employer
was still speaking, but all he could hear were the words in his
head.

'Gwendoline is getting married. My love is marrying someone else.'

He felt sick to his stomach and had no idea how he performed his duties that morning. He was glad when he was required to go to the colliery with a message for Mr. Paget and could get away from the chattering of the maids who were all agog with the news.

For some days he was like a man in a dream, and it was only when he remembered his mother's dying words that he was able to come to terms with the situation.

In September, Mr. Moggridge's long search for a new home bore fruit. His agent in Swansea wrote to advise him, that a house having all the qualities he desired, would come on the market later that month. He strongly advised Mr. Moggridge to pay a visit to Swansea to inspect the property, and if it suited, he would, he thought, be able to transact the purchase so that Mr. Moggridge could become the new owner before the close of the year. Mr. and Mrs. Moggridge took his advice and leaving Mrs. Watkins and Robert in charge of the household, took the coach to Swansea. They returned a week later and immediately on his return, Mr. Moggridge put quill to paper and wrote to Sir Henry to tell him that in accordance with their agreement, he wished to give notice that he intended taking up residence in his new home in late October.

When Sir Henry received the news, he immediately began to put the second step in his plan into operation. It had been intended that Gwendoline's marriage should take place in the spring or summer of the next year. This long engagement had suited Sir Henry as he was very busy. His journeys to and from Wales had meant that his other business enterprises had taken second place. Now that Moggridge would no longer be available to take care of any problems that might arise, he would have to find some way not only to have someone to take care of the mining interests, but also the house at Woodfield. It would not do to have the place empty. He was well aware that the staff would continue to clean and heat the place, if only for their own comfort, but there was the question of the bookwork, and the need for someone with authority to carry out his wishes. His first thought was that his agent would be able to carry out these duties, then remembering that Morgan had of necessity to travel in order to deal with other businesses Sir Henry was interested in, it seemed that he had no alternative other than to travel once more to Woodfield and ask Moggridge's advice as to how he could arrange matters until the new manager could be installed. Having decided he wasted no time and arrived at Woodfield one wet cold afternoon. Mrs. Moggridge had already started to pack up some of the household furniture that could be done without. Sir Henry's quarters however were as he had left them. A cheery fire burned in the grate and he was happy to note that on the sideboard, stood a tray holding a bottle of port, awaiting his attention. At dinner that night he and Mr. Moggridge discussed the problem. When he asked how long he thought it would be before the new manager could be in place, Sir Henry said he hoped that it might be possible to persuade him to take up his duties by February at the latest. It was then that Mr. Moggridge suggested that Sir Henry install Robert for the intervening period.

When asked if he thought the young man was capable of controlling the affairs of the new combine of collieries he planned, in addition to running the Woodfield estate, Mr. Moggridge had no hesitation in supporting his protégé. He was after all a man who had worked in the colliery so was well aware of the conditions that appertained. He had undertaken the role of steward after only a year's apprenticeship and had then added the duties of bookkeeper to his position. Sir Henry could not deny that both roles had been carried out in an exemplary manner. His temporary appointment would obviate the arising of the problems which the installation of a new and untried manager would bring about. He was local, so had the advantage not only of being able to speak to the workmen in their own tongue but also having worked underground could appreciate the problems that the managers of each of the collieries faced.

Sir Henry was impressed with his friend's support of the young man and next morning sent for Robert. He questioned him thoroughly and was surprised at the grasp Robert had of the financial affairs of the colliery. As this was Sir Henry's biggest worry in choosing someone to fill the post, to have a bookkeeper already conversant with such matters was the deciding factor. Robert would take over the duties of overall financial controller answerable to Sir Henry only. He would take up his new duties in addition to his present bookkeeping role at the beginning of November. He would understand of course that this was a purely temporary measure. He would however be recompensed well and no doubt the incoming manager would depend a great deal on his judgement. He hoped that Robert would continue to serve the new manager when he arrived. The offer of such a prestigious post solved not only Sir Henry's problem; Robert accepted the offer with alacrity as he could see the solution to his domestic problems too. Admittedly it was only for a few months, but perhaps it would pave the way for a long term of employment under the new manager as his financial assistant. He thanked Sir Henry and promised that for the time the estate was in his care, Sir Henry need have no worry about its wellbeing. Sir Henry backed up his promise to give him the authority to carry out his duties, by writing a letter addressed 'To all it may concern' wherein he stated that Robert Morgan was to be recognised as his direct subordinate, and all matters affecting the financial status of the estate and colliery would henceforth be under the control of said Robert Morgan.

Now that Sir Henry had made provision for the management of the estate, Mr. Moggridge was able to concentrate on arranging for the packing up of his old home in preparation for its removal to Swansea. There was a tremendous amount of furniture accumulated since he had caused his magnificent home to be built in this quiet Welsh valley. His wife, casting an expert eye over her beloved furniture, had already decided that their new home would not be able to accommodate it all, so some of it would have to be disposed of. When her husband approached Sir Henry regarding this, that gentleman expressed a preference for retaining the furnishings of the rooms he already occupied. As none of this had any great sentimental value, a bargain was struck for its sale. Other furniture would also be left behind, either because of its bulk or lack of space at the Swansea house. Sir Henry could do with this what he chose. Mr. Moggridge, having influenced Sir Henry in his choice of Robert as the new overall manager, made Robert a gift of his magnificent desk. Now that he was a man of position, if only for a short period, he hoped that Robert would accept the gift and would use it to carry out his duties. Having become a permanent member of the household, Robert had his own bedroom and dressing room attached. The furnishings of these rooms too were gifted to him. He was overwhelmed by the kindness of his late employer and his wife and when he thanked them the lump in his throat made speaking difficult.

Then came the day of departure for Sir Henry. He was returning to London for Christmas and to finalise his plans. Time was now of the essence but he felt confident that by the end of February he would have succeeded in marrying his daughter to Marcus Appleby, and persuading his new son-in-law that, life in Wales with his new wife, a magnificent mansion to live in, and a well paid job requiring little or no experience was a something greatly to be desired.

A week or so later, Mr. and Mrs. Moggridge said farewell to their staff and their home at Woodfield. For days, there had been much coming and going of large carts drawn by huge horses, bearing away the contents of the house. Finally came the day when the goodbyes had to be made. There were tears from all the female staff who had served the family almost from the day John Moggridge had settled there. Robert and his late employer spent a short while saying a private farewell. Mr. Moggridge placed a hand on Robert's shoulder then grasping the young man's other hand, shook it vigourously.

'We have not known each other for too long a time but you have served me well Robert. I wish you and your family well in the future.'

Looking out of the window, he continued,

'This house and estate will be in your care now. Love it as I do and look after it, so that in future years, whoever comes to live here, will say 'this was a house and home built with love'.'

The young man nodded and swallowed hard. They went

down the staircase and out to the carriage. Mrs. Moggridge sat awaiting her husband, a wisp of cambric dabbing at her eyes. All around, the maids, the cook and the housekeeper, stood with tear stained cheeks. As the carriage moved away, they waved and called out farewells, as if to a member of the family who was going away, and who they knew they would probably never see again. Nobody moved until the carriage had disappeared down the long drive and passed out of sight as it crossed the bridge. At the main gate, Dafydd and his brothers and sister stood in a forlorn group. When the carriage stopped, Eleri went forward with a huge bunch of flowers she had picked from the cottage garden. These she handed to Mrs. Moggridge, and with a final wave from the late mistress of Woodfield, now weeping unashamedly, the carriage pulled away.

With their absence in London and Swansea respectively, the new and former owners of Woodfield, both missed what was probably the most momentous occasion in the history of the valley. Something that was to have repercussions, not only in Wales, but ultimately worldwide. A week or so before Christmas, the directors of the Tredegar Iron Company at the head of the valley, decided that they would attend the Cattle Show to be held at Newport. They would travel the distance of twentyfour miles in a carriage drawn by the first ever steam locomotive engine to run on the tramroad which passed through Blackwood. Rumours of this had been circulating for some time, and on the day in question, crowds had collected to witness this stupendous event. Robert had taken Dafydd with him to see the progress of this new mode of transport down the valley. There was considerable delay before before the rumble and shrieking whistle of the new engine, announced its imminent arrival. Belching smoke and with clouds of steam pouring from it, the huge locomotive, said to weigh about 8 tons, and pulling behind it carriages carrying Mr. Homfray and his friends, rounded the bend and hove into sight of the waiting crowd. To a crescendo of cheers and the whinnying of startled horses rearing in their shafts, the party went gallantly on their way.

All along the way, their progress was interrupted by the

engine wheels leaving the rails. This caused delays of some hours until they eventually arrived at Tredegar Park. Here the final catastrophe caused the weary passengers to dismount and continue on foot. The funnel of the engine was carried away by a branch of a tree overhanging the track. Despite these misfortunes, discerning men realised that they had just witnessed a tremendous step forward in transport methods.

CHAPTER 18

Custom demanded that it was not permissable for a young and delicately nurtured girl to be alone with a young man even if they were engaged. Consequently, at all times, or so it seemed to the impatient young swain, his beloved was accompanied by some female or other, all determined that the most he might obtain from his betrothed would be a chaste kiss on the cheek or a discreet pressure from her hand. To one, whose very fibre tingled with desire to take this ravishingly beautiful young girl into his arms and imprint a passionate kiss upon her ruby lips, such restrictions were intolerable. No definite date had been fixed for the wedding, although it was thought it would take place in the Spring, so, when Marcus was summoned to Sir Henry's study, and his future father-in-law enquired of him his views on a wedding in February or at the latest, early March, he was more than enthusiastic in his agreement that such an arrangement met with his whole hearted approval. Seeing that the young man was completely besotted with Gwendoline, and would probably agree with any suggestion that would place her in his tender embraces sooner rather than later, Sir Henry broke the news to him that if this could be arranged, then the young couple could expect the following wedding gifts from him. First, Gwendoline's dowry would be the sum of ten thousand pounds. This would not include the value of the gifts of jewellery Lady Siston would wish to lavish on her daughter. He felt sure that Marcus would wish his bride to live in comfort and elegance equal to that she presently enjoyed? Marcus nodded. To enable this to be achieved, he was prepared to offer him employment, light in nature and not needing any great call upon his time. For performing this task, there would be a further five thousand pounds annually.

To ensure that the happy couple would have no need to seek for somewhere to live, he decided to make a gift to Gwendoline as an addition to her dowry and to place it at their disposal, and ready for immediate occupancy, a mansion set in lovely countryside. There was of course the problem, that both the work and residence were in Wales. Seeing the young man's expression change at the news, Sir Henry hurried on. He stressed that there was no great difficulty in travelling to and from there, as witness his own regular journeys. Gwendoline had stayed there and he was sure would vouch for the beauty and comfort of the mansion which would be their home. Added to this was the attraction of a home in the country. That would ensure that the newly weds would have a continuing honeymoon. Of course there was the question of furnishing. Part of the house was already furnished but he was sure that the bride would want to furnish it in her own style. They need not worry about this. They could do this before moving in and the bill should be sent to him. All Sir Henry asked in return was that the wedding should not be delayed any longer than could be helped. Marcus, who had been slightly worried about his ability to maintain a home and life style that his beloved would find suitable, was greatly relieved by the terms offered by Sir Henry. Marcus was patently aware that he was being bribed to use his influence to persuade Gwendoline to forego the girlish pleasures of planning a massive and expensive wedding. His soon to be father-in-law was obviously in a difficulty of some sort and needed his help. Well for what he was being offered he was quite prepared to do his utmost to ensure that Gwendoline became his wife as quickly as possible.

It was his wife and daughter who presented Sir Henry with the arguments he found impossible to overcome. When he asked his womenfolk if they would consider bringing the marriage forward to February or early March, they laughed at him in disbelief. That he should consider such a thing! Didn't he realise what was involved? The choosing of material for a bridal gown, bridesmaids' dresses and pageboy clothes, the bride's trousseau. All of this would then have to be made and fitted. The catering for the reception, the invitations, the honeymoon. Bring it forward? It might have to be delayed. Apparently, the dazed Sir Henry was given to understand, these were only the essentials. There were unnumbered other details and if he thought all this could be accomplished in time for a wedding in March, little did he know. Besides all this, there were the Christmas festivities to be dealt with be-

forehand! Sir Henry retired defeated but at the first opportunity brought up his reserves in the shape of Marcus. Aware
that failure to persuade his beloved to walk down the aisle as
soon as possible could cost them dear, he used all his wiles to
persuade his darling that, while he realised the importance to
a bride of joining her chosen suitor bedecked in beauty and
that the occasion was one which reflected the love she had
for him, all he wanted was to make her his wife. A wife he
could carry off on a honeymoon, where there would be no
chaperone forever coming between him and his heart's desire. It must have had the effect of weakening her resolve, for
she promised that she would speak to mama and see if it
would be possible to grant him his heart's desire before her
next birthday, though she doubted it would be possible. He
then argued that this was another six months distant and he
doubted he could hold out that long. To see her everyday, to
be near her and not to be able to claim her for his own, was
more than a man could be expected to bear. She was heartless to inflict this penalty upon him. Please! She must see that
his love was consuming him. To wait another six months
would bring him to his bed with love fever. Already his
dreams were racked with the fear that he would lose her.
Could she not be an angel and join their loves and lives in
matrimony in February? Even so he had little idea how he
was going to exist until then, but he would endure somehow.

All this fevered pleading took place in a summerhouse in
the gardens of her home. Although it was November it was a
day brilliant with sunshine. The youngest boy's governess
who was acting as chaperone was enjoying a walk nearby
and Marcus had taken the opportunity to plead his case on
bended knee. Gwendoline was taken aback by the fervour of
Marcus's pleas and by the time he had finished, her heart
was pounding in her breast.

'Oh my darling. I had no idea you were so consumed with
love for me. I have been selfish denying you the joy that our
marriage will bring. My heart tells me to say yes to your
pleas. I would flee with you but my head tells me that we
cannot deny our parents the joy of witnessing the joining together of two hearts so in love. My sweet love. You have

touched me deeply. I will speak to mama. There must be some way we can bring our heart's desire closer.'

Whatever she said to Lady Siston, finally overcame that lady's objections, to the extent that it was agreed it would be possible for the young couple to wed in March. However since the honeymoon would be spent in Italy, there was no possibility of them occupying Woodfield before May. With that Sir Henry had to be content.

But for the loss of his mother, and the knowledge that Gwendoline was lost to him forever, the Christmas of 1829 was the happiest Robert could remember. Being nominally in charge of Woodfield, his was the responsibility for ensuring that his younger brothers and sister and the staff at the big house, enjoyed the festivities. The rooms still in use, mainly in the servants' quarters, were garlanded with greenery and he paid a visit to Blackwood to see what presents he could buy for the youngest of his family. He returned with a wooden doll for Eleri and a wooden spinning top for her younger brother. The smallest, was still too young to appreciate Christmas but with dribbling mouth accepted the gift of a sugar confection and proceeded to suck it with relish. Thanks to his promotion, Sir Henry had agreed to Dafydd taking over the duties of steward outside and this had enabled him to employ a rosy cheeked twelve year old, a niece of Mrs. Watkins, as 'foster mother' to the remainder of the family. On the evening of Christmas Day, scrubbed and clad in their best clothes, the Morgan children sat down in the kitchen of the big house with the staff. As befitted his position, Robert sat at the head of the table, and carved the huge goose that graced it. How things had changed he thought. Would that it had been possible for his father and mother to have lived to be part of this occasion. In London at the home of Sir Henry and Lady Siston, similar festivities were taking place. Their home too was garlanded but their goose was only one of several sorts of meat that lay waiting the assault of the appetites of the three young male Sistons. Marcus had been invited to share their Christmas Dinner with them and sat next to his adored. Sir Henry after one attempt at carving, handed over the duties to Jevons who proceeded to dismantle the bird with expertise. At both establishments there was much merriment and a happy time was had by all.

The weather turned much colder and two days after Christmas, the sky took on a leaden hue. The wind, blowing from the north had a biting quality to it and all who ventured out, took care to wrap themselves in as many layers of warm clothing as they could, Dafydd making his first inspection of the grounds immediately surrounding the house, returned at midday to write his report in the book which his brother had started, and which now was an integral part of the routine.

Entering the kitchen with its huge coal fire roaring and casting a warm glow, he remarked that the wind had dropped and if his guess was right, there would be a downfall of snow before morning. How true his prediction turned out. When the first maid stumbled down the stairs to light the fire, huge flakes were falling, silently carpetting the ground and the branches of the trees. There was no break in the steady and remorseless descent of the large white feathery flakes. At lunch time, after working steadily through the morning, Robert stood at the window looking out at the scene, almost fairylike in its beauty. His mind however was not so much on the beauty of the picture before him. Rather he pictured the scene which his experience told him would be enacted at the pithead. While he and his family were warm and well fed, those with whom he had shared his early years, would be working in freezing conditions, fingers and feet numb with the cold, the cold silent snow seeking to penetrate every and any opening in the rags they called clothes. He could almost feel the burn of the cold metal of the huge iron bucket as they struggled to tip its load into a tub. For those working on the screens trying desperately to order their fingers to pick up pieces of stone and other rubbish from the coal that passed in a never ending stream before their eyes, he knew he could do nothing to alleviate their distress, but having suffered with them in their efforts to earn enough to keep body and soul together, he could well imagine how they would view the snowfall.

Now that he was nominally in charge Robert was privy to practically all the details that effected the colliery. Sir Henry he knew, was hoping that before the new manager took over, NantGwrhay would be only one of the three collieries he hoped to have operating. When he was finally able to venture out on horseback and make his way through snow covered fields across country to the colliery and entered Paget's office, he found the manager sitting at the desk with his back to a roaring fire. Paget greeted him and asked if he wished to partake of a drop of brandy to keep out the cold.

Robert who liked a mug of ale but had never developed a taste for the spirit, declined. He took a chair and sat with his hands outstretched to the fire, then directed a question to the manager as to whether the snow had effected the output in any significant manner? Had many of the workers failed to get to work?

Paget replied that as they had not worked on Christmas Day, there had been a small downward trend but his under-managers had assured him that only the odd one or two had failed to appear after the holiday despite the bitter weather.

Robert's next question came as a surprise to Paget. He had thought that only he was aware of Sir Henry's plan regarding the purchase of other collieries. Seeing his expression, Robert hastened to assure him that he was well aware of their employer's plan and he only enquired because if Paget had any information, then he Robert, could include it in his next report to Sir Henry. He did not anticipate a visit from him at least until the wedding was over, but he did not think Sir Henry would be very pleased if he was in possession of vital information and did not forward it as quickly as possible, particularly if the lack of said information cost him the chance to take control of the other collieries. Paget smiled. This lad young as he was, was nobody's fool. He could imagine the repercussions if as young Morgan said, Sir Henry lost money due to an underling's failure to keep him au fait with events. 'Well as you know, Sir Henry wanted me to sound out the owners of the two mines he's got his eye on. I don't think I've aroused any suspicion in their minds that there's a predator on the prowl. From what I could gather, the Waterloo is losing money. They've had quite a bit of flooding and unlike us, haven't the money to spend on pumping equipment. The

Cwmddu is just about breaking even, but I've an idea that the owner would sell out if he got a decent offer. He's been in this business a long time and since there's been so much unrest with the bloody Cattle, I got the impression he wouldn't take a lot of persuading. I think it might be to Sir Henry's advantage to pay another visit to Wales and have meetings with both gentlemen.'

They spent another half hour talking about the problems facing Paget in his quest to maintain output, then Robert left. Mindful of his thoughts on the morning of the snowstorm, he stopped to watch the poor wretches labouring at the pithead. It was a scene of misery as the poorly clad and in some cases barefooted women and girls, strove to move the tubs through the filthy mixture of coal and slushy snow that lay six or seven inches deep. Even as he watched, a tub propelled by two ragged figures, suddenly jumped off the rail and caused one to fall flat on her face in the sodden mess. From where he sat on his horse, he could hear the cackling laughter that greeted the poor creature's misfortune. Her fellow pusher made no effort to help her climb to her feet but stood laughing as the unfortunate faller, her sodden rags clinging to her body made an effort to wipe the filth from her eyes and face but succeeded only in making her dirty features even dirtier. Not knowing quite how he felt at the scene he had just witnessed, amusement at the sight the women had presented or pity for them that they had to work in such conditions, Robert swung his horse's head around and rode off.

He duly included the report of Paget's investigations in his letter to Sir Henry and his belief that it might be advantageous if a visit could be made without too much delay.

A month later he received a letter from London. Due to events outside his control, Sir Henry found it impossible to come before March at the earliest. However he had had a meeting with his fellow directors and they had agreed that if it were possible to purchase both collieries for a sum not exceeding forty thousand pounds, then they would authorise Robert Morgan to act on their behalf to complete the purchase. He should be guided by Mr. Paget in his estimation of the value of the mines but on no account was he to exceed this figure. Both collieries had to be purchased since one would not help the board's plans. They expected to hear within the next month that he had succeeded in finalizing the purchase. Robert made haste to go and see the colliery manager within days of receiving the letter. This was the greatest test of his financial capability yet. Success might mean a future full of promise. Failure could mean that in Sir Henry's eyes he had failed in a crucial moment and he would spend the rest of his days nothing more than a simple bookkeeper.

He and Paget discussed the situation from all angles. Should they make a straightforward approach to the respective owners for their asking prices or play one off against the other? A pretence that they were only interested in one of the two mines might result in a lower bid being accepted. Since both mines were in the vicinity, Paget had a reasonable good idea how and where the seams of coal ran. He knew that the new face which had played such a big part in Robert's life crossed the boundary into the Waterloo. There would be a great advantage in being able to continue mining this rich seam. The Cwmddu had as its boundary, the same stream that bordered the NantGwrhay and the mine that Sir Henry had purchased but never worked. Access to this meant that the stream could be rerouted to enable workers in the Nant-Gwrhay to penetrate and work the coal in Cwmddu.

It was decided that they should make separate but simultaneous approaches to the owners. This would obviate the chances of the owners acting together to force up the price. Paget wrote a lengthy report outlining all he knew about Cwmddu which he presented to Robert for him to commit to memory. Two days later, after arranging meetings at the pithead offices of both mines, they set off on their joint endeavour.

Robert was nervous. Never had he been involved in anything like this. He had agreed with Paget that should either owner ask for more than half the total they had at their disposal, each would express complete disinterest. They would then meet and compare results. If the total came to less than forty thousand, each would return to the vendor and try to force down the price. If the vendor was firm in his refusal to sell at a lower price, they would accept the price quoted and issue a letter of intent to buy. The owner of Cwmddu was a Mr. Leyland. In company with his manager a Mr. Preece, they met Robert in an office that was almost a replica of that occupied by Paget. Robert who did not wish to become too involved in the technical data associated with mining, preferring to depend on Paget's estimations, refused the offer of a drink and instead plunged straight into the purpose of his visit. He was there to enquire if Mr. Leyland was prepared to sell him the Cwmddu Colliery and if so, what price was he asking? Completely unprepared for such a direct approach, Leyland stared at the young man, nay a lad, before him.

'By George sir, you do not waste time I must say. I will be equally frank with you Mr. Morgan. I've heard about you. You worked for John Moggridge when he owned NantGwrhay and from what I hear you did a damned fine job. Now I gather you've become estate manager for some London gentleman who bought Woodfield from Moggridge. Has he put you up to this?'

'Yes Mr. Leyland. I'm acting on his behalf. I have his full authority to purchase at a price. I too have heard a few things about you sir.'

He smiled as he uttered the words as if to take away any offence that they might incur.

'Mr. Leyland. I am no mining engineer. I'm a bookkeeper. I understand figures but I've received an excellent briefing regarding not only your colliery's capabilities but also that, having spent many years in this business, you like my late employer Mr. Moggridge, are more than a little weary of it and the way things are going. I refer of course to the unrest generally and that engendered by the Cattle in particular. I am given to believe that, offered a fair price, you would be prepared to sell me the mine. If I am wrong sir, in my supposition, I apologise unreservedly and will not waste any more of your time.'

Robert's direct approach was quite outside anything Mr. Leyland had ever encountered. Normally, buyers and sellers manoeuvred, trying by any means to outwit their opponent. This lad, no he was too old in the head to be called a lad, was either too young or too naive or he meant every word he had said. He studied the young man. Robert gazed back. Leyland finally made up his mind.

'Mr. Morgan. It is true that I am more than a little dismayed by the turn of events since the big strike in 1822. The workers are becoming more and more militant and it is becoming increasingly difficult to find men who will work for a wage that will allow me a reasonable profit. Now those scoundrels who go around in disguise and threaten and beat anyone brave enough to work for such a wage, are making it almost impossible for me to show any sort of profit. Damme sir, I admit I am tempted to accept your offer to buy me out and get out of this business. What would you say to paying me twenty five thousand guineas?'

'Mr. Leyland. I told you I understand figures. Your output for the last three months has been falling. You have problems with the stream breaking into your best seam. On your own admission you are barely able to make any sort of profit, so it is likely you cannot afford to purchase the pumping equipment necessary. If the unrest continues, and the water problem continues, you might not make anything except losses. My answer to your question sir, is that I have nothing to say. If that is your final price sir I fear I must bid you good day and apologise for wasting your time.'

He rose from his chair and after shaking hands with both made to leave the office.

His air of finality convinced Mr. Leyland that his best prospect would be to negotiate a price that reflected the true value.

'Hold hard Mr. Morgan! Will you make me an offer?'

'Fifteen thousand.'

'Pshaw Mr. Morgan. You jest.'

'I never jest about money sir.'

'Twenty thousand?'

'Now you jest sir.'

'Very well sir. Let us stop this bargaining. I cannot accept....'

He hesitated as if making up his mind,

'less than Nineteen.'

'Sixteen.'

Leyland shook his head.

'Mr. Morgan I started this colliery twenty years ago. I cannot accept such a paltry sum.'

'In that case Mr. Leyland there is no more to be said. Good day once more sir.'

Once more he made for the door. This time there was no attempt to dissuade him and he closed the door behind him.

Mounting his horse he rode off without a backward glance to his meeting with Paget. They had arranged to confer at Paget's office. Whoever got back there first would await the other and when Robert entered the office, he found Paget sitting before the fire studying some papers. He turned as Robert closed the door. That he was anxious to know the outcome of Robert's meeting was obvious by his question.

'Quickly Mr. Morgan. How did it go?'

'Nineteen thousand.'

'Hm. I was asked twenty three. That makes forty two. Looks like we must go back and try again. Do you think Leyland will come down any more?'

'I have the feeling that Mr. Leyland will settle for eighteen, possibly seventeen if I press him. I beat him down from twenty five by bidding him good day and making for the door. We bargained for a while but when I wouldn't offer him any more than sixteen he dug his heels in and it was then I walked out. How did your meeting progress?'

'Price at Waterloo wanted twenty three at first. Like you I pretended I wasn't interested at that figure. I told him that to my certain knowledge the place wasn't worth more than twenty. I didn't pursue the matter too much but I think he could see that I wouldn't entertain his asking price. I've known Price a long time and he's been in business as long as me. I offered twenty one, he said twenty two and that was his final offer. I said I needed to think it over and would go back to him. We mustn't let Price and Leyland know that they've both had bids. Do you think Leyland will agree to seventeen? From what I know of Price, I don't think I can shift him, so my friend I'm afraid that somehow you must convince Leyland that seventeen is your best offer. I'm afraid that only gives you a margin of one thousand, otherwise Sir

157

Henry must look elsewhere.'

To ensure that should their offers be accepted there would be no possibility of the sales falling through, Paget sat down and wrote out two letters of intent to buy, each with a copy, leaving blank the names of the collieries and the purchase prices. Armed with these they set off once more to try to convince the two mine owners that they were receiving a fair price for their properties. When Robert returned to Cwmddu, Mr. Leyland was still closseted with his manager. He greeted Robert with the remark that no doubt his young friend had considered the matter and had come to offer him the nineteen thousand asked?

Having had to return, Robert was conscious that Leyland was now of the opinion that he was in the stronger position. He decided that his first task was to disabuse the gentleman of this thought.

'I have given the matter some thought sir. I felt it would be only courteous of me to allow you a little extra time to think over the matter. I think you will agree that we are both anxious that this matter should be resolved as quickly as possible with fairness to both? With this in mind I have returned to make you my final offer Mr. Leyland. If you refuse this, I promise you that I shall trouble you no more. Seventeen thousand guineas sir.'

A smile lit up Leyland's face.

'You drive a hard bargain Mr. Morgan. Very well. Seventeen thousand guineas.'

It was Robert's turn to smile.

'To show you I am not a hard man Mr. Leyland. Mr Preece if he so desires is to remain as manager.'

Leyland laughed outright.

'Gad sir it's a pleasure to do business with you.'

There were handshakes all round and after asking for a quill, Robert took from his pocket, the letter of intent and its copy. Watched by Leyland and his manager, he filled in the details of the purchase price and colliery name, then appended his signature. He passed the other copy to Leyland for his signature as vendor. Placing it in his pocket he rose from the desk. His feeling was one of great relief. If Leyland had refused to accept less than nineteen thousand guineas he had no idea what he would have done. Now that the sale had been confirmed by both parties, a more relaxed atmosphere prevailed in the little office and he allowed himself to be persuaded to accept a small glass of brandy to seal the bargain as Leyland put it. The fiery liquid burnt his throat as he swallowed it. He would much have preferred to have been offered a mug of ale, cold though the weather was. Wanting only now to return to NantGwrhay Colliery to confirm that Paget had completed his task, he begged to be excused and after once more shaking hands, made his way outside to his horse.

Paget kept him waiting some time before returning brandishing the letter of intent regarding Waterloo, his face creased by a beaming smile. They clapped each other on the back at the success of their scheme and when Paget offered him another brandy in celebration, Robert felt he could not refuse. He left the colliery office and when the cold air filled his nostrils, he was aware for the first time of the effect the drinks had had on him. He felt light headed and his cheeks felt a glow that belied the cold. Very deliberately he climbed into the saddle and set off for Woodfield, the precious papers tucked into the saddlebag.

He was ravenously hungry when he arrived there and striding into the kitchen enquired when he might expect to be served his lunch. The warmth of the kitchen and the effect of the spirits he had consumed had brought a flush to his face and neck. His eyes sparkled and when the cook offered to bridge the gap until lunchtime with a pasty, he accepted gratefully and sat at the long scrubbed table, happily munching his way through it. The amused look that the cook gave him as she surveyed the young manager of the estate, happily munching away like a common labourer, escaped him. He was too intent on assuaging his appetite and thinking over the events of the morning and the success of the mission. His first task after lunch would be to write a letter, express, to Sir Henry, advising him of the facts. Who knows what would be the result of their efforts?

Despite his good intentions, when the maid went to his

room at midday to enquire what he wished for lunch, she discovered him, head down on the papers, gently snoring. She retreated quietly and reported to the cook that Mister Robert was asleep. The cook smiled but said nothing. Knowing how good his appetite was normally, she took the precaution of laying aside, a large platter of meat and vegetables, for when he awoke.

CHAPTER 19

Letters passed back and forth between Sir Henry and Robert during the next months, the one issuing instructions, the other reporting. One unexpected visitor during that time was Daniel Morgan, the agent. He spent a week at Woodfield, and in company with Robert and Paget, inspected the new acquisitions. Robert had no doubt that, Sir Henry had instigated this inspection. Apart from a letter conveying his thanks to Robert and Paget no more had been said. Presumably the collieries were to carry on as before. No doubt, Sir Henry had plans for them, but until such time as he could personally put them into action, he had no intention of allowing his minions to know what they were. Perhaps the visit of his agent had as its purpose, the observance by another pair of eyes, of the possibilities of the two collieries and how they would fit into his plans.

The snow gradually melted and as the weeks passed slowly by, the date of Gwendoline's marriage crept ever nearer. For mother and daughter, it was a time fraught with anxiety. Disappointment, alternating with female joy at discovering something ideal for their purpose. Gwendoline now began to find that as she contemplated the consummation of their love, she began having doubts as to the wisdom of the planned marriage. Was she doing the right thing? Was she really in love with Marcus or blinded by the prospect of being a beautiful bride pledged to a handsome man? When she expressed these feelings to her mother, she was assured that every bride to be went through these pre-nuptial feelings of doubt and inadequacy. Everything would turn out all right and she would find that once she was indeed wed, she would wonder why she had ever felt that she could possibly be making a mistake.

She did have a shock when Marcus revealed that their first home together would be Woodfield and that he would be in charge overall of the three collieries that her father had now purchased. She had given little or no thought to how Marcus would maintain a home. That his father was an earl and made him an allowance was in the usual manner of things.

That her father had no intention of making her an allowance other then her dowry was not what she had expected. On reflection she had the sense to accept that her father had also to consider the future of his other children. Marcus would receive a generous emolument. They would have a beautiful home and it would be furnished at no expense to themselves. Being in Wales was a drawback but having lived there albeit for a short while, it had advantages. There would not be too many distractions while they settled in and Marcus had taken over his new position, they could then explore the possibilities of entertaining. Children would of course appear in due course, but perhaps they would have a little time to themselves. They both loved riding and she knew from her own experience that there was plenty of open country that she and her husband could spend hours riding over. Altogether things might have been worse.

At the end of March, on a day when Spring lived up to its promise Gwendoline and Marcus became man and wife. She was a radiant bride and had never felt so happy. The reception was a magnificent affair and the guests were the cream of London's society. The happy couple left by coach en route to Dover where they would board a packet for Calais, on their way to Italy from whence they would return in a month's time.

Once his daughter had left on her honeymoon, Sir Henry decided that he could now turn his attention to matters of business and wrote to Robert that he would arrive there in the second week of April. He instructed Robert to convene a meeting at Woodfield of all the managers of the collieries under his control. The meeting would be held two days after his arrival and he would disclose his plans for the future of the combine at that meeting.

Whatever fears any of the managers may have had about the tenure of their positions, were put at rest at the meeting. Sir Henry assured them he had no intention of upsetting existing arrangements. They would of necessity have to work in much closer harmony with their fellow managers, to ensure the smooth transition. To enable the new overall manager to co-ordinate plans, he was appointing his estate manager, Robert Morgan, to act as assistant to him. They all knew Mr. Morgan and he felt sure that they would all assist him in his work. Any problems should in the first place be brought to Mr. Morgan's attention. The new manager, who would take up his duties some time in May, was to be his son-in-law, the Honourable Marcus Appleby. He and his wife, who was no stranger to Woodfield, would take up residence in this lovely old house immediately they returned from their honeymoon. He hoped that his plans for the combined collieries would prove successful and that all would work to ensure that success. Sir Henry had not said so directly, but Robert and the managers were under no illusion that it was Robert who was to be the active overall manager. The Honourable Marcus Appleby, might take the credit but it would be they who would suffer the kicks should things go wrong.

Gwendoline had taken her father at his word and interspersed with buying her trousseau, she had taken the opportunity to buy furniture and materials for her new home. There would be little time to do any of this ònce the honeymoon was over. Papa would want Marcus to take up his duties as quickly as possible. Goodness knows whether Monmouth or Cardiff could produce goods of the quality she demanded. It was as well to be sure and buy it before the wedding. It could be sent on and the servants could unpack it and place it prior to their arrival. No doubt she would have to re-arrange it, but that was half the fun. Sir Henry bore with him when he arrived, a letter from his daughter advising Mrs. Watkins of the imminent arrival of crates and cases containing the nucleus of the new home. As they arrived, they were unpacked and under the housekeeper's eye, the servants carried the contents to their appointed places and set them down.

There was great excitement when a letter arrived to announce that the newly weds would be arriving before the end of May. Sir Henry's hopes for a smooth takeover of the mines and installation of a new manager, had been dashed. However he consoled himself that Morgan and Paget seemed to have kept control of things. It was this that had prompted him to appoint Robert as assistant to his son-in-law. He had no illusions about Marcus's ability to control the working of three mines. Morgan would effectively be in control and if Marcus felt he could over-ride him, then he would feel the weight of Sir Henry Siston's position as chairman of the board of the London Fuel Company. Personally he doubted such a situation would arise. If he had judged his new manager correctly, he was more likely to leave the day to day working to his assistant and spend the time with his new wife and seeking such entertainment as was to be found or made.

During the period that Robert found himself in control pending the arrival of Marcus, he spent more and more time visiting the collieries, and making contact with the other colliery owners in the district. It was after visiting a small colliery at Plas Newydd on the outskirts of Blackwood, that he found himself listening to a man whom he knew only by reputation. He had called into a hostelry named the Coach and Horses to slake his thirst. Standing with a mug of ale he could not help but overhear the words that were spoken by a well dressed man who was obviously a gentleman of some quality. What he had to say kept Robert there much longer than he had intended and made him ponder on its significance. Aware at last that he must go, he enquired of the landlord of the identity of the speaker.

'That be Mr. John Frost of Newport. Him and his friend Mr. Vincent will be speaking at a meeting to be held at Pontllanfraith.'

He left the beerhouse and rode slowly back to Woodfield, thinking about what he had heard. Having been a miner he had always been conscious of a feeling of compassion for their lot. In his present position he was in duty bound to put the interests of his employer first, but despite this he could not help consider the unfairness of a system that gave so much to one class of people, while the other, who produced the wealth that ended up in the pockets of the rich, worked and suffered in degrading and brutal conditions. It had always been thus and he could only thank God that he had been enabled to rise above the misery and poverty that had been his family's lot for so long.

He had heard of John Frost. Of his reputation as a Radical, and of his outspoken condemnation of the conditions under which the working classes laboured and lived. He was also particularly vituperative about the system of Truck Shops which had been operating for some years. One such was now situated in the little village of the Gwrhay that was adjacent to the Waterloo Colliery, and he had been made aware of the iniquitous practices that the owner carried out in the name of business. There had been much political talk about the abuses these shops inflicted on their customers, and it was a long felt hope that soon the government would listen to its conscience and pass an Act that would make these places illegal and cause them to be shut down. It was not only the workers who suffered from the greed of the owners. Local traders too complained that, thanks to the system which enslaved the workers by forcing them to deal only at the Truck Shop, trade suffered and they were hard put to make a living.

These shops were only a part of the system which John Frost railed against and there was much talk of a working men's Charter, which would give them not only decent wages and conditions, but a vote in the running of the country. Naturally most of the owners that Robert found himself mixing with in the course of his work, supported the present system and at meetings he had attended where perhaps four or five were gathered, he had heard talk of asking the magistrates to make application for the troops to be sent into the valley if or when the next trouble erupted. The miscreants who roved about creating unrest under the mantle of the Scotch Cattle, were once more active and demands were again being made for an increase in wages, and the abolition of the Truck Shops. There had been a period of reasonable peace but if the meeting he had just attended was any indication of the owners' worries, then he felt that before the year was out, the coalfield would once more be plunged into unrest and strikes, with the attendant misery for the workers and their families.

On his arrival at Woodfield he tried to dismiss the gloomy thoughts that had filled his head on the journey home, and settled down to prepare a statement to give to his new master, who should be arriving within a day or so. Once more too, he would set eyes on the lovely Lady Gwendoline, now the wife of his new master.

CHAPTER 20

The return of Gwendoline to Woodfield was a time of great happiness to all, not least herself. She had enjoyed her stay there that summer as a guest. Now she was returning to the lovely mansion as its mistress. Awaiting her would be the prospect of turning it into a home for herself and Marcus. They would both have so much to do. She with her plans for the furnishing of the house, and Marcus with the task of getting to grips with the need to convince papa that, his faith in Marcus's ability was justified. Robert Morgan would she felt sure, help her beloved husband in every way. Eirwen had turned out to be a jewel of a maid, and many of her friends had been envious of her. Papa thought highly of the young man so both she and papa had been lucky to have had the benefit of possessing two such good servants from the same family.

Marcus despite his noble upbringing, was impressed with his new home. Gwendoline had tried to describe it to him but it exceeded his hopes. The manager Morgan, seemed a sensible chap and he had no doubt that they would be able to work out a routine whereby he would have ample time, not only to continue the honeymoon, but to take to the saddle and explore the countryside. There had been no mention of any hunting taking place in this vicinity. This was something he could try to establish. Once Gwendoline was settled into being mistress of the house, and had finished with all this fiddlefaddle about furnishings and draperies, they could both enjoy themselves. Of course there was always the chance she'd get herself in the family way, in which case he would need some sort of hobby or other. She could hardly go bumping about the country on a horse with the heir to the family bouncing about in front of her. Anyway time enough to worry about those things. First he must sit down with Morgan and see if he could make head or tail of what Sir Henry had in mind.

As he had foreseen, a routine was soon established whereby Robert assumed overall control, but the reports that were expressed to London every two weeks, were signed by Marcus. This routine enabled the two lovebirds to spend most of the day in each other's company. For the first six weeks or so Marcus was only too happy to dance attendance on his new wife. She in turn, was pleased to have him at her beck and call even if his opinion on the siting of the furniture was non commital. His lack of interest in the colour schemes he explained away by saying that she could hardly expect him to be enthusiastic about a piece of curtaining material when he was trying to puzzle out what the manager of Cwmddu wanted him to do about the water that was flooding the place. He solved the problem by placing it on Robert's shoulders and instructing the stablegroom to saddle up a horse for him, which he then mounted and rode off in the direction of Croespenmaen.

In early July, there came the news of the death of the King and the need to hold a general election. 'Sailor' William as he was known in the broadsheets was placed on the throne as William IV. In France too they changed their King but there it was by a popular uprising against the ruling Bourbons. In the election meetings that took place, Robert was once again reminded of the words of John Frost. Radical agitators demanded parliamentary reforms. It seemed all parties agreed that reforms were necessary. The only problem being that each party had a different idea as to what reform meant. All the hubbub about the election however was of no great significance to those at Woodfield. Marcus and Gwendoline were each too busy, either with her plans for the house or his plans to interest sufficient of the few gentry thereabouts, to mount a horse and chase a fox across country.

When Sir Henry had acquired Woodfield, he had managed to persuade John Moggridge to include in the purchase price, the contents of the cellar. Marcus had assumed that his father-in-law had either forgotten this or had intended that the cellar should form part of the gift to his daughter. Whatever the reason, Marcus was happy to discover the hundreds of bottles that lay covered in cobwebs in their racks, all neatly labelled. When he tired of acting as a sounding board for his wife's choice of colour or material to suit an occasion, he would pick himself a bottle and placing it in his saddle bag, mount his horse and ride off to some quiet spot where he would sit and drink while thinking about his future. What had seemed a bargain when Sir Henry had proposed it, now seemed more of a millstone. He was not used to the endless quiet, the lack of drinking companions, visits to the club where a man could gamble an afternoon away. He had great difficulty in even pretending that he was in any way enthusiastic about the progress of the integration of the three collieries into one large combine. What did he know about such things? Let young Morgan get on with it.

As the months rolled by, Marcus began to drink even more and could be relied upon to be well in his cups before lunch. When Gwendoline remonstrated with him, he excused his behaviour by claiming that there was so little for him to do that he took a drink just to relieve the hours of boredom. There were quarrels which ran over into sullen silences at the meal table. One such altercation took place within hearing of Eirwen who was in her mistress's dressing room arranging her wardrobe. She listened as both Gwendoline and Marcus accused each other of having fallen out of love, of not caring and finally each had said the other had never loved truly. She accused him of marrying her for her dowry and the easy living the marriage would provide. Not to be outdone, he in turn charged her with marrying him only for his name. She had never really loved him, but had been in love with the thought of a large fashionable society wedding. He had been the hapless victim, not she. What had started as a married couple's first serious quarrel, was to be only the first of many in the ensuing months.

Both their accusations had been much too near the truth for either of them and Gwendoline had burst into a rush of tears and hurled herself on to the bed, there to lie sobbing. Marcus aghast at what he had said, but relieved to have made known what he felt was the truth, rushed from the room and within minutes was galloping down the drive.

When he had cooled down somewhat, Marcus reined in his horse. He had galloped madly away from the house, with little or no idea where he was going, trusting to his mount to keep them both from harm. Looking about him, he had only the vaguest idea where he was. Before him rose the mountain, topped by the parish church; to his left the ground descended in a steep incline into the next valley. As he was still on a well trodden track, he decided the best thing he could do would be to continue along the same track until he came to some sort of habitation. Allowing the horse to pick its own speed, they meandered along for some twenty minutes, then as they rounded a bend, to his great delight, ahead he saw a low thatched building. It was not very prepossessing but it did mean he would be able to obtain some information as to his whereabouts. His delight became even more pronounced, when as he rounded the corner of the building, he spotted the sign that swung in the gentle breeze. It was a badly drawn picture of a black and white bird. Whatever the artist may have thought his picture was meant to convey, mattered not. Underneath the picture the words Magpie Inn announced to the world that it was a hostelry, and that meant one thing to Marcus. He could get a drink, several drinks.

The door to the place was shut when he swung down from the saddle. Leaving the horse to fend for itself, he moved to the door and hammered on its surface.

At last he could hear the scuffle of feet approaching, then a voice called out,

'We be shut.'

'Open up landlord. I need information and a drink.'

There was the sound of bolts being drawn, and with a creaking the door opened enough for Marcus to make out the features of the speaker. He was short and dark with lank greasy hair hanging down.

'Give me a brandy man, quickly.'

The landlord took a bottle from the shelf and wiping a glass on his soiled apron poured out a glassful of the spirit.

Marcus seized the glass and quickly swallowed a large portion.

'Where is this place landlord?'

''Tis the Magpie Inn sir.'

'I know that man. I saw your sign. Where is it?'

'We'm between Pontllanfraith and Abercarn.'

'How do I get to Woodfield from here?'

'There be only one way sir. You need to go back along the track 'til you come to the crossroads at the foot of the hill. Turn right there and follow the track. It will take you past the main gate sir.'

Marcus swallowed the remainder of his brandy and told the man to fill it up again. He sat himself at one of the rough tables and when the landlord placed the glass upon it, he immediately took it up again and once more swallowed at least half of the fiery spirit. He began to consider his position. Today's disagreement was the first time they had really quarrelled. Many times in the last few months, he had been hard put to it to restrain himself.

Gwendoline's continual preoccupation with the house. The hours spent daily choosing this, then that, then the other. Why couldn't she make up her mind? Or better still let the housekeeper do it. That's what she was paid for. They had been married for several months now and she was still altering the colour scheme or changing the chairs around. When they went to bed and he wanted to make love, she complained she was too tired. Dammit. A man was entitled to a wife who had some thought for a man's needs. He finished his drink and called for a refill, tossing back another large portion of it while he pondered on his misfortunes. When he called for his fourth glass, the landlord could only give him a small amount.

'I be sorry sir but there bain't no more. The bottle be empty.'

Muttering to himself, Marcus swallowed what had been poured. Fumbling in his pocket he extracted a gold sovereign and tossed it on the table, then staggered to the door. Outside, his horse stood cropping at the grass, the reins hanging down. After two attempts to mount, he called the man and while he held the horse's head, he somehow clambered into the saddle. Swinging the horse's head around, and placing the reins in Marcus's hands, the man smacked the horse's rump and it jogged off back down the track. Presumably his mount had travelled the track so often that it automatically took the correct one at the crossroads, because he had no recollection of how he arrived at the main gate. A small boy opened the gate for him and he rode on into the park. Arriving at the house, the horse stopped outside the main door. Marcus sat in the saddle, befuddled and not sure whether he could dismount without falling off. Someone must have observed his progress up the drive, because he was saved from having to make a decision by the appearance of Robert.

'Morgan. Help me down from this blasted animal.'

One glance at him was enough to tell Robert that his master was more than half drunk and incapable of dismounting on his own. Steadying the horse, he helped Marcus to reach the ground. Tying the reins to a nearby branch he slipped his arm around Marcus's waist and supporting him, entered the house. Luckily no servant appeared to embarrass their employer, and together they made their way up the stairs. At the head of the stairs, Gwendoline stood, her hand to her mouth as she surveyed her husband. Without a word she signalled Robert to bring Marcus to the master bedroom. There helped by Gwendoline, he placed Marcus on the bed and took off his boots, while Gwendoline undid the cravat from around his throat. By this time, Marcus had fallen into a drunken sleep and began to snore. Discreetly Robert left the room, leaving Gwendoline to minister to her husband.

In the weeks that followed, Robert was called upon more and more often to assist his master after one of his drinking sorties. Eventually things became so bad that Gwendoline abandoned all pretence that she and her husband were living a normal life, and had Mrs. Watkins prepare another room where Marcus could sleep off his drunken bouts. These became more frequent until hardly a week went by when his horse did not appear with its master slumped in the saddle, his eyes closed and his clothes smelling of spilled drink. It hurt Robert to see the young girl, who had arrived only months before as a young and radiant bride, rapidly becoming a deeply worried woman, her brow lined and with dark shadows beneath her eyes. He could say nothing, though his greatest wish was to take her in his arms and comfort her. Marcus had now given up any attempt to carry out his duties, spending almost every day out riding, returning always, if not drunk, certainly not completely sober. Thanks to the co-operation of the three managers, Robert was able to render the reports advising Sir Henry that his collieries were doing well. The state of his daughter's marriage, was something that Sir Henry must find out from other sources.

That this state of affairs could not last was becoming increasingly obvious. The staff were all aware that to all intents and purposes, the young couple who had arrived straight from their honeymoon to take over their beloved Woodfield, were not living as man and wife. Eirwen reported to Robert that hardly a week went by when Gwendoline and Marcus did not spit hurtful words at each other, not even bothering to lower their voices when they became aware of her presence.

Gwendoline, despite her misery, had not written to her parents, believing that whatever took place between herself and Marcus, as a wife she must endeavour to support her husband and obey him as promised. She was finding it hard to carry out the vows she had taken at her wedding, and was very often relieved to go to her lonely bed, secure in the knowledge that Marcus was lying in the next room, too drunk to be capable of demanding anything of her. Her marriage she acknowledged to herself, was in ruins. Only if Marcus was to give up his addiction to the bottle, was there any hope that they could ever return to the happiness they had shared when they had come here to set up their new home.

Apart from letters, Gwendoline had no contact with her parents. A letter from her mother had enquired when she might expect them in order to spend Christmas. She had excused their failure to join in the festivities in London on the grounds that, as this would be their first Christmas as man and wife, she and Marcus wanted to spend it in their new home. There had been no more visits from Sir Henry, so her secret remained hidden. Whether her mother suspected something was wrong was becoming apparent, as almost every letter contained the question as to when they might expect the news that she was with child? She could only postpone the inevitable by assuring her mother that she too was anxious to bear Marcus's child, but as yet fate had decreed otherwise. Her mother was not to worry, she was in perfect health. She suggested it may be that as Marcus was so busy with the integration of the collieries into the combine, perhaps they needed a holiday which they hoped they might be able to take in the late summer.

The solution to her problem when it came was a tragic one. Marcus's drinking continued unabated and Robert had taken it upon himself to ensure that no matter what time his master came home, he would be there to see that he was safe and sound. Like many a drunkard, Marcus although always returning home befuddled, seemed to bear a charmed life. Although there were numerous occasions when from the state of his clothes, it was clear he had taken a tumble, he had never suffered any serious injury.

On the last occasion he had left home, he had not returned at eleven o'clock. Robert had gone to Gwendoline and told her that he intended going to look for him. He knew that Marcus had taken to frequenting the Greyhound and this would be his first call. Mounting his horse he rode slowly down the drive holding aloft the lantern he had taken the precaution of lighting. He had travelled perhaps half the distance to his objective when his mount snorted loudly and reared back in fright. The light from the lantern cast a golden gleam around him but he could see nothing. Grasping his crop he dismounted looking carefully about him. Perhaps his horse had become aware of a possible ambush by some of the blackguards who hung about the district? As he made to step forward, there was a crashing from the undergrowth. Peering into the darkness he was able to make out the outline of a horse held by the branches in which its reins were entangled.

Deciding it could wait, he walked forward, fearful of what he was about to find. Crumpled in a heap, with arms outstretched, his head at an angle, lay Marcus. Bending over him, Robert made to turn his head then realised that it would serve no purpose. Marcus's neck was broken. Robert knelt to press his ear to Marcus's chest but could hear no heart beat. There was not the slightest doubt. His employer was dead! There was the strong smell of brandy on his cravat. Evidently he had spilled some. There were no marks of any violence on the body except for a bloody mark on side of his head where he had struck it against the stony ground and some scratches on the other side of his face. His purse still containing several coins was in his pocket. Alongside the track, Marcus's hat lay in the grass. Robert looked up. Above his head the branches hung low and could have been responsible for what looked like an accident. He tried to picture the scene. Marcus, probably half drunk, had ridden into the branch which had swept his hat from his head and him from the sadddle. As he fell his head had struck the stones and his neck had been broken. There was nothing that could be done for the young man. Robert stood up from his grisly task and set about the task of conveying his young master home. It took him a while to free Marcus's horse from the undergrowth that held it, then he struggled to lift the inert body from the ground and across the saddle. He gathered up the hat and with a last look around, mounted his own horse and holding the reins of Marcus's horse he set off to deliver the dead body of her husband to Gwendoline.

CHAPTER 21

The death of Marcus was a blow that caused Gwendoline to decline into a state of deep melancholia which caused her doctor a great worry. When Robert had ridden up the drive leading Marcus's horse with her husband's dead body across the saddle, she had rushed to the door anxious to know if Robert had managed to track him down. On seeing the tragic little procession that had now stopped at the main door, she had shrieked in anguish at the sight, and collapsed in a dead faint at the horses' feet. Mrs. Watkins and one of the maids had gathered up her inert body and half carrying, half dragging her up the stairs, had conveyed her to her room where Eirwen awaited her mistress's return, unaware of what had taken place. There they had laid her on the bed and while Eirwen undid her clothes, the housekeeper had endeavored to revive her. Meanwhile Robert helped by the coachman, had taken Marcus's body and between them carried him to the room he had now taken to using whenever he went carousing. Although it was now past midnight, Robert instructed the coachman to take the carriage and fetch the doctor. There was nothing could be done for poor Marcus but his mistress could well be in need of medical attention. Already Robert's mind was trying to deal with the problems that would arise from this tragic accident. Sir Henry and Lady Siston must be advised immediately and it was imperative that he know the doctor's recommendation as far as Lady Gwendoline was concerned. Marcus's family would surely want their son's body to be interred in the family vault not in some little Welsh chapel burial ground. Lady Gwendoline could not stay here unattended. Her mother would almost certainly want to take her back to London until time had healed her mental wounds. What of the future? Would Sir Henry want him to carry on until he sent someone else to take over Marcus's position? Was this to be the last he ever saw of his beloved Gwendoline? As a widow would she perhaps retire into seclusion? When he thought of her he could hardly believe it right that such a young beautiful girl should spend the rest of her days wearing the weeds of widowhood, hiding her dazzling looks behind a black veil. All these thoughts were driven from his head when, as he returned downstairs to await the doctor, the silence was rent by an agonizing cry emanating from the bedroom where she lay. Eirwen came scurrying down the stairs.

'Oh Rob. It's awful. My poor lady. She be breaking her heart up there. Mrs. Watkins be with her but it be a doctor she do need. Somebody to give her something.'

'I've sent for Doctor Evans. Go back up and see if you can help Mrs. Watkins. Tell her the doctor will be here soon.'

It was nearly an hour before the sound of carriage wheels announced the return of the coachman and his passenger. Robert met them at the door, explained what had happened and his mistress's reaction. The doctor nodded and went up the stairs and entered the bedroom.

It was some little time before he re-appeared followed by the housekeeper. At the door of the room he spoke to her, 'Mrs. Watkins. Your mistress must not be left unattended. She'll be quiet for some time as I've given her a dose of laudanum but when she awakes, I would rather she were not alone. She has had a most tremendous shock. Please see that someone is always in attendance. I'll call again tomorrow. I'd better speak to Mr. Morgan now.'

Robert waiting at the foot of the stairs hurried upward when he saw the doctor emerge from the bedroom. He was just in time to hear the housekeeper's words.

'Rest assured doctor, the mistress's maid will stay with her for as long as she's needed.'

'How is my mistress doctor?'

'Is there somewhere we can talk Mr. Morgan?'

Robert took the doctor along the corridor and entered one of the rooms.

'Mr. Morgan. Your mistress has suffered a terrible shock and although I said nothing to Mrs. Watkins, I fear that without careful nursing there could be dire consequences. I will call every day to keep an eye on her, but someone should be with her at all times.'

'My sister Eirwen is her personal maid, doctor, and I know she will not leave her mistress unattended at any time. Depend on that.'

'Good. Now I assume you will send for the young lady's parents. At a time like this a young girl needs her mother. Someone to comfort her and help her during the next few weeks.'

'I shall be despatching an express letter to Sir Henry and Lady Siston this very night. What about my master's body doctor?'

'I'll see it now Mr. Morgan, though from what you've told me, I gather there's nothing I can do except certify the cause of death.'

After the doctor had examined Marcus, he left after promising to advise the undertaker that his services would be needed. He left strict orders that should he be needed he was to be called immediately.

In the week that followed, before the arrival of Gwendoline's parents, Robert hardly slept. He had spent the remainder of the night of the tragedy, writing a letter to Sir Henry advising him of the steps he had taken and of the doctor's fears. He stressed the doctor's wish that Lady Siston come as soon as was possible. He wrote another letter to Marcus's father the Earl, and asked that they advise him of their wishes regarding the burial. He further advised them that rooms would be kept available for any member of the family who might wish to come, either to accompany the body back home or to arrange for the interment locally. There were letters to write to the managers wherein he stated that pending instructions from Sir Henry, he would take charge of all the day to day running of the combine. He had paid a visit to the Greyhound Inn to enquire of the landlord there, if he could remember seeing Marcus there on the night of his death? The landlord had stated that, yes, the young gentleman had been there as he did most nights. No. As far as he knew he was not too much in his cups because he managed to mount his horse without help when he left. What time had he left? Couldn't be sure. Around ten or maybe a bit later. They'd been busy. He could ask the ostler. P'raps he'd remember? Robert decided there was not much point in pursuing the matter any further. Marcus had obviously been befuddled but it seemed as if it had beeen a genuine accident.

Most of all though, he spent his waking hours thinking and worrying about Gwendoline. The doctor made good his promise and daily arrived in his carriage and reported his findings. The initial shock seemed to have passed off, but he was worried as no matter what tempting dishes the cook prepared, she would eat little or nothing and from Eirwen's reports, seemed to spend all time just sitting in a chair gazing blankly out of the window. When Robert asked him whether he should make any approaches to her in the hope that he might interest her in the affairs of the estate, the doctor advised against it.

'I should leave such matters if I were you. I do not think it would serve any good purpose just now. Perhaps when her parents arrive we might see a change. I most earnestly hope so.'

The arrival of Sir Henry and Lady Susannah although an occasion for tears and worried words, relieved Robert. He felt so helpless. Loving her as he did, he could not and dare not, allow his feelings to appear as anything other than those of a devoted servant, but not to be able to take her in his arms and comfort her was almost more than he could bear.

Lady Susannah had rushed upstairs immediately upon their arrival, leaving her husband to discuss the situation with Robert. They repaired to the study and there Robert recounted the entire story. When he had finished, Sir Henry had questioned him.

'Have there been other occasions when Marcus has been drunk?'

Robert hesitated, unsure how much he should reveal of the events that had taken place in the last few months.

'Come on man speak up. I know Marcus liked his brandy. Tell me. Has he been drunk before?'

Robert then revealed what he knew about Marcus's drinking habits and confessed that he suspected that the marriage had suffered because of them.

'Hm. I suppose all the reports he sent me were your work?'

'Yes sir.'

'All right Morgan. I'll want to speak to you again. I'd better go and see what I can do.'

When he entered the bedroom he found his wife sitting in a chair, Gwendoline on her lap, her mother's arms about her. His wife looked at him over her daughter's bent head and reading the message in her face, he retreated. He could do no good there. Better he return to the study and see Morgan again. Must say the young fellow had done all that was possible. What a damn fool young Appleby had been! A beautiful young bride, a sinecure of a job, five thousand a year and a mansion in the country. What more could he want? Poor little Gwen! A widow already. What now? What a bloody mess to be sure!

Thus ran Sir Henry's thoughts as he made his way along the corridor. He re-entered the study and made his way to the cabinet from which he extracted a bottle of port. Filling a glass he sat behind the desk and allowed his thoughts to roam. Once all this business with the funeral was finished with, he'd have to do some sorting out in his affairs. Young Gwen would have to come back home. She'd need her mother for a few months. S'pose there's no chance she's in the family way? She'd have told her mother in a letter if she had been, perhaps it's as well. Bad enough as it is. She might remarry. Young Morgan seems to be living up to Moggridge's estimation. The mines are doing well and he seems to have got a grasp of the business. If what he says is true, and from those reports I'd say they were his work, then maybe it would be as well to let him carry on. Don't suppose Marcus was much help. Sounds as if he was drunk most of the time. I suppose the Board will want to put somebody else in his place, just to give a touch of respectability. Wouldn't do to have anybody without a title heading the combine. I can just see old Sheringham's face if I suggest leaving Morgan in charge. He'd explode!

'By Gad sir, we can't have a common miner running the place!'

Bloody old fool. The door opened and Robert came in.

'I'm sorry Sir Henry I didn't know you were in here.'

'Don't go Morgan. There's one or two more things I'd like to ask you.'

Robert took a chair and sat waiting. Sir Henry seemed to be

choosing his words.

'Morgan. With this tragic accident, you realise that the Board may want to appoint another overall manager? That may take quite a while. What with the funeral and Lady Gwendoline having to return to London, things are going to have to be left in your hands for some time. Would you be prepared to carry on until the new manager is appointed?'

Robert had no hesitation.

'Certainly Sir Henry.'

'Good man. Now. Have you heard from the Earl of Mountchester?'

'Yes sir. Viscount Thexton should arrive within a day or so. The family would like Lady Gwendoline to agree to the burial taking place at Minton Castle. Naturally I've not spoken to my lady about this sir. I was waiting for your arrival. Perhaps you and his lordship could discuss it'

'Very well. This is a sorry business Morgan.'

'Yes sir. The staff have asked me to extend their deepest sympathy both to Lady Gwendoline and to you and Lady Siston.'

'Thank you Morgan. I don't think there's anything else just now.'

'Very good sir.'

He withdrew. He had many things to do.

With the arrival of Viscount Thexton it was possible for arrangements to go forward. He and Sir Henry were closeted for some time and when they finally emerged, Sir Henry made his way to Gwendoline's bedroom. Since her mother had arrived and taken charge, Gwendoline had become a calm but silent figure. The doctor had declared that there was no more he could do except to recommend to Lady Siston that she take her daughter back to London with her, in the hope that distancing her from the scene of the tragedy might have a beneficial effect. Lady Siston and Gwendoline were in the bedroom when Sir Henry knocked and entered. Apart from the time when he had found her on her mother's lap, he had not seen his daughter. He was shocked by her appearance. The dazzling laughing girl of whom he was secretly proud, had given way to a white faced waif like creature. Dark smudges lay beneath her eyes. Her cheekbones seemed to be nearly penetrating the skin, so thin was her face. When her father entered she looked at him, her face betraying no interest, then her glance returned to the window. Lady Siston sitting opposite her daughter, a piece of embroidery held in her lap, raised her eyebrows in mute query.

'Susannah. There is something I must ask Gwendoline.'

He turned to his daughter,

'Gwendoline, Viscount Thexton, Marcus's brother is here. The Earl has sent him. The family have asked that Marcus be buried in the family vault at Minton Castle. If you agree, Thexton will accompany the coffin. If you would rather we take Marcus back to London, I will explain to him.'

Gwendoline was silent for a long time. Her father wondered if what he had said had penetrated the veil of silence which seemed to envelope her.

'Gwendoline...'

'It's all right papa. I heard. Tell Viscount Thexton that I agree to his family's request. Marcus was never happy here and London was just a place to be. Let him go back home.'

Sir Henry moved forward and took his daughter in his arms,

'My poor little Gwennie.'

He kissed her hair then turned and left the room.

Robert would always remember the scene when Viscount Thexton took away the body of his brother. All the family and servants were gathered outside to say their farewells when the coffin bearing a sheaf of roses, was placed in the hearse. The undertaker, garbed in black, his tall shiny black tophat giving him extra height, directed his four minions as they placed the coffin and secured it. Four jet black horses, beplumed with black ostrich feathers, pawed the ground, the driver atop his seat doing his best to restrain them on this solemn occasion. Viscount Thexton, dressed in sombre garb, took off his hat, and bending over Gwendoline's hand, bade her goodbye,

'Farewell dear sister-in-law. Would that this was a happier occasion. Perhaps when you feel stronger, you will do us the honour to visit Minton Castle. My mother would wish to speak to you I'm sure.'

'Goodbye Jonathon.'

He mounted to the carriage and with a crack of the coach-man's whip the little procession drew away. Gwendoline had stood there stony faced and dry eyed. Her mother had sobbed into her handkerchief and Sir Henry had surrepti-tiously wiped a tear from his eye. The servants, white aprons held to their faces, sniffed as they used the garments to wipe away their tears. When the vehicles and their sad burden had vanished over the bridge, all moved back into the house. As if the departure of her dead husband had been the trigger that released her from some sort of mental bondage, Gwen-doline had run upstairs and they heard her calling for Eirwen before she had closed the bedroom door. Sir Henry and his wife made their way to the sitting room, there to sit and quietly discuss plans for their daughter's future welfare. Whatever these plans had been, they were destined never to be put into operation.

She did not emerge again that day, but Eirwen did and made her way to the kitchen. There the cook prepared a tray which Eirwen carried back upstairs. When she next came down it was to report to Gwendoline's parents that their daughter was asleep. This time it was a healthy sleep not brought about by the administration of the doctor's drug. Twenty four hours after she had closed her bedroom door, Gwendoline emerged. This was a different Gwendoline. Still dressed in black but there was about her a different air. She no longer crept silently along, but with a new dignity she moved to the drawing room where her parents sat. Sir Henry leapt to his feet as she entered.

'Gwendoline....'

'It's all right papa. Sit down please, there is much I want to talk about. Let me say what I have to say please.'

She took a seat and holding her handkerchief in both hands in her lap as if taking strength from it, began to speak,

'Papa, mama. I want you to listen to what I have to say. It may shock you. I don't know how much you know about our marriage. We, neither of us were really in love and we both knew it. Once the honeymoon was over we had very little in common except perhaps a love of horses and you can't make a life out of that. Maybe I failed Marcus. I don't know. Perhaps I wasn't ready to be a wife and mother. It was all like a game, setting up our new home. What man wants to talk about curtains and where to put the chairs? He began to drink heavily and I didn't help him. I was too busy playing building our new home. By the time I began to realise what was happening it was too late. You knew that we had separate bedrooms?'

Sir Henry nodded. his wife continued studying her daughter saying nothing.

'I shall never forget Marcus. He was a good man and perhaps if I had been the right woman to be his wife he might have been a happy man. It's too late now.'

Sir Henry nodded. His wife continued studying her daughter saying nothing.

'I don't want to come back to London with you. If you insist I will come but only until I feel strong enough to do what I want to. I am well aware how concerned Doctor Evans was but I assure you that sad as I am, you need have no fears that I might do something silly or become demented. You may think I am hard with Marcus not yet buried, but I would much rather spend my days here than be the widow Appleby in London. I am not yet twenty and I am not ready to spend the rest of my days being an object of pity. If I come back with you, it will only be for a while. I must and will come back to Woodfield. It is my home.'

She finished speaking. There was silence while her parents thought about what she had said. Lady Siston looked at the girl before her. A few days ago she had nursed her in her arms as she had when she was small and had fallen and hurt herself. Now that child had become a dignified and very forthright young woman. The spirit, which she had always feared would cause her daughter problems, had not been quenched by the tragic events that had taken place. There were however certain conventions that had to be considered. Her husband had a position that must not be besmirched. Should Gwendoline insist on remaining at Woodfield, certain of their circle would, she knew, take the greatest delight in conjuring up all sorts of rumours calculated to delight the gossipmongers. She must return to London, if only for a short while. Also, she must visit Minton Castle. What havoc could be wrought if it ever got about that the young bride of Marcus Appleby, married only just a year, had not even paid a visit of condolence to her late husband's family?'

'Gwendoline. I have listened to what you have said. I respect your feelings but there are other matters that have to be considered.'

She then outlined the effect her daughter's seemingly eccentric behaviour would have on her father's and family's reputation.

'It is too soon to be making plans. Wait awhile. Come back and rest. There is the question too of you paying a visit to Minton Castle. You are their son's widow. The least you can do is to visit them. They have lost a son they loved.'

'Mama is right Gwendoline. Society demands a certain code of conduct. Come back just for a while. Get your strength back, then perhaps in a month or so we can talk about it again.'

'Papa. Promise me that when I decide I want to come back, you'll not try to stop me.'

'Very well my dear, I promise.'

'In that case I will return to London with you.'

Gwendoline rose from her chair and pulled the bell cord to summon the maid. When she arrived Gwendoline said,

'Dilys. Please serve tea and ask cook if she has any of those little round flat cakes?'

'Bakestones? Beg pard'n, my lady. Welsh cakes?'

'Yes please.'

When Dilys entered the kitchen and gave her mistress's message to the cook, there was a lightening of the gloom that had hung over it for the past week.

One week later Gwendoline accompanied her parents back to London.

CHAPTER 22

Gwendoline's first and last Christmas at Woodfield as Marcus's wife had been a subdued one. True there had been decorations and carol singing by the staff, but with only the two of them, and with their marital problems still unresolved, it had not been the sort of Christmas that Gwendoline had enjoyed as a member of a large family. When they had sat down in the evening to share the Christmas dinner, she had eaten very little and Marcus too had paid more attention to the bottle of claret than to the offering on his plate. At a little after eight o'clock they had retired to sit in front of a large fire in the sitting room, the bottle now nearly empty, at his elbow. As she sat opposite her husband watching him become more and more drunk, she wondered what she could do to save their marriage, which was like a ship foundering because the crew had no idea what to do to save it? What if she made a determined effort to ensure that Marcus got her pregnant? Perhaps the prospect of a child of his own might just be the spur needed to lift him from his depressed state and encourage him to make a fresh start? They had enjoyed a normal married life for the first few months and she had been quite prepared to find that at any time she might find herself in the family way. Whatever the reason, nothing had happened and perhaps he had become discouraged. She knew that she had several times claimed she was too tired to satisfy his need. That had been true, but as a dutiful wife should she not have succumbed to his demands? Now that the house was furnished as she wanted it and running smoothly, perhaps this was the time to encourage her husband to share her bed more often? They had had their differences but all married couples did, according to mama, and once a child came along they tended to settle down.

Convinced that this could well be the answer to their problems, she rose at ten o'clock and announced her intention of going to bed.

'Will you be up shortly dearest?'

Marcus looked up at his wife standing before him. This was a direct invitation to sleep in the marital bed. There had been damn few of them in the last few weeks. Maybe he was wronging her? He had been hitting the bottle lately. All that worry about the blasted colliery and Gwen forever going on about curtains and drapes. Enough to make any man have a few more drinks than usual. Why not get to bed and celebrate Christmas by accepting the offer she seemed to be making? She'd been quite a delight on their honeymoon.

'I'll be up in a few minutes dear. Just finish this drop.'

He waved the bottle.

'Don't you think you've had enough my dear?'

'Gwen. I'm not drunk. Far from it. You go on. I shan't be long.'

Deciding that silence might be the best tactic, she left the room and went upstairs. She had told Eirwen that once dinner was over, she could have the rest of the evening off to spend with her family. Eirwen had laid out her night attire and she quickly undressed and put on the white satin nightdress. It was one she had taken as part of her trousseau to Italy and she felt her cheeks flush as she remembered how Marcus had gazed at her when she had first worn it.

She brushed her hair and after dabbing a spot of perfume behind her ears climbed into the big fourposter bed to await him. She became aware that her heart was pounding and she felt nervous and slightly breathless. The way she had on their first night spent as man and wife. It was some ten minutes or more before the doorknob rattled as he turned it and entered the room. She shot a quick glance at him in the light of the flickering candle. He looked no different from the way he had downstairs. She watched him as he moved about the room shedding his clothes then put on the nightshirt she had put on the bed for him. She leaned over and blew out the candle that stood on the table by the bedside. In the flickering light from the remaining candle on his side, she watched him pull back the bedclothes then clamber into the bed. She lay quietly awaiting his first caress, the caress that could be the key that unlocked the door that seemed to be keeping them apart. Marcus immediately belied his assertion that he was not drunk, by collapsing on to the pillow and emitting a loud snore. This was Gwendoline's first and only deliberate attempt to seduce her husband into attempting fatherhood. From that night onward she always felt a sense of shame about what she had tried to do albeit for the best of reasons. On later occasions when Marcus did try to make love to her she entered into the proceedings with no very great enthusiasm. Perhaps sensing her feelings he soon became disillusioned and took further comfort in drinking to an even greater degree. Thus they grew further and further apart, two very unhappy people.

When she returned to London she often looked back on those events leading up to the debacle that finally put the seal of failure on her marriage. This only made her more and more depressed, and the determined young woman who had confronted her parents with the history of her marriage, vanished, to be replaced once more by the silent withdrawn girl who had caused the doctor so much apprehension. Accompanied by her mother, she had paid the visit to Minton Castle to pay her respects to Marcus's parents and to lay a wreath at the entrance to the family tomb, wherein her late husband now lay. It had not been a very successful visit. She had only met Marcus's family on the day prior to their marriage. Her feelings of guilt that it had been her behaviour that had brought about the tragic death of their son, had not made a sorrowful visit any easier, and it was with relief on both sides that she returned to London. Her mother had been prepared to allow her daughter a period of mourning, then had intended trying to rouse her from her depression. Custom would not allow Gwendoline to re-enter society other than as the young widow of the Hon. Marcus Appleby, but her mother felt that perhaps after a suitable period she might once more take part in suitable outings. Gwendoline's determination not to stay in London for too long had been forgotten under the weight of her depression and her parents did not remind her. It was about three months after her arrival that her mother suggested she accompany her mother and father to the theatre. She had agreed but not enthusiastically. At the theatre she had spoken to one or two friends who had offered their sympathy. Others had nodded to her then retired behind their fans, no doubt to relate to their companions their versions of the events they thought had led up to the tragedy and her first public appearance as a widow.

When they returned home at the end of a rather strained evening, she confronted her parents.

'Papa, Mama. I am sorry if I spoiled your evening but you might as well know. I have no intention of remaining in London to be treated as an object of pity. I intend returning to Woodfield as soon as possible. If papa does not intend travelling to Woodfield very soon, then I do. If necessary, I will travel alone. Since it is only a month or so to Christmas I am content to remain here, but as soon as the festivities are over, I shall want to leave.'

Her parents were taken aback by this volteface. Her mother though was slightly relieved that her daughter was once more showing unmistakeable signs that she had put the recent past behind her and seemed intent on facing up to life once more.

Poor Sir Henry who had all his life declared that he would never understand women, was even more taken aback when Gwendoline bearded him in his study one morning.

'Papa. I am sorry if I have given you cause for alarm with my behaviour but I have done a lot of thinking this last month or so. I cannot and will not remain in London so I must go home. However, I shall be going home to an empty house. No matter that Marcus and I did not make a success of our short married life, at least we shared Woodfield and I am going to miss him. I shall need to do something to help me pass the time. I know that Marcus was only nominally in charge of the collieries and that your steward Robert Morgan is the real overall manager so...'

She paused, took a deep breath then,

'would you consider letting me take over Marcus's duties?'

As Sir Henry opened his mouth she stopped him.

'Let me finish what I was going to say. I know all the objections. The Board will never allow it. What would my friends think? It's no work for a woman.'

He subsided in his chair.

She ticked off on her fingers her answers to the objections.

'One. The Board will do whatever you tell them to. You own

most of the stock.'

He smiled.

'Two. I'm not interested in what my friends think, and any-way I shall be in Wales. They'll soon forget all about me.'

'Three. Whether it's a woman's work or not remains to be seen. No woman has ever tried it, and if Robert Morgan is there to keep his eye on me, then I can't see that having Marcus or me as the boss is going to make the slightest bit of difference. And the two very most important points. Woodfield is my home. You gave it to me and if you want to install some stranger as manager, he'll not live there. I won't sell it, and I don't think he'll be happy having the chairman's daughter living so near. He'll think I'm peering over his shoulder. Last but certainly not least, the very best reason of all for letting me take on the task. I'm your daughter.'

Sir Henry said nothing for a while then,

'My little Gwennie. Do you realise what you're asking? What do you know about mining and keeping accounts?'

'Papa. Who's responsible for the running of the mines?'

'Paget and the other two managers of course.'

'Who takes the decisions if you're not there?'

'Robert Morgan.'

'So it doesn't really matter who other people think the overall manager is, does it? You only created the job in order to bribe Marcus didn't you?'

'Well...'

'That's all right papa I forgive you. Now listen to what I'm going to say. You were paying Marcus five thousand pounds a year. I'll do the job for half that, and remember papa, I want to do it, Marcus didn't. I promise you, that if you let me become the overall manager, I'll not interfere with the ways things are run until you are satisfied I'm competent. If you aren't happy with my progress after six months then I'll withdraw and become the Widow Appleby from the big house in the park. What do you say? Please papa!'

He laughed.

'You truly are my daughter you scheming little minx. Six months you said? When do you want to start?'

She threw herself into his arms laughing in delight.

In the third week of January 1832 Gwendoline in company with her father, returned to Woodfield as mistress once more and, after Sir Henry and Robert had talked in the privacy of the study, she became the prospective overall manager of the colliery combine under the tutelage of her steward. Her father, despite yielding to his daughter's wishes, was still enough of a business man to ensure that she understood, that, until the six months probationary period was finished, Robert Morgan, was the true manager and had the last word where matters of the collieries was concerned.

CHAPTER 23

Robert's reaction to Sir Henry's decision to make Gwendoline the overall manager in succession to Marcus, was one of delight tempered with some trepidation. The prospect of being in even closer contact with the woman to whom he had long since lost his heart, was one he looked forward to. No longer would the barrier of Marcus be between them. True he was only a servant and the situation would probably have to continue in that vein, but he could dream, that with their close proximity day after day, maybe in time a friendship would develop that might become on her part, a love to equal that which he had for her. The trepidation he felt, was based on what little knowledge of her he had been able to accumulate, during the year or so that she had been mistress of Woodfield. He was only too well aware of the turbulent spirit that sometimes possessed her. He was glad that Sir Henry had seen fit to make it abundantly clear, that in any matter of policy disagreement, his was to be the deciding voice.

So when Gwendoline sent for him, and informed him that she wanted to begin learning all he could teach her about keeping the accounts, he took his courage in both hands and asked that he be allowed to speak as the financial controller of the combine rather than as her devoted servant? If they were to be able to work together as pupil and teacher then he must be allowed the authority to correct her.

'If my lady feels that I take too much upon myself then I must respectfully beg to be allowed to resign my position.'

Gwendoline, well aware that the loss of Robert Morgan as the controller of the combine's finances, would be a bigger blow to her father than her failure to succeed in her mission, had no choice but to agree to Robert's request. This she did with good grace and it was on these terms that they settled down to become a very successful team.

Gwendoline had had the normal young lady's schooling. Not too much time had been spent by her governess in the teaching of arithmetic. True she could write a good hand, and was well versed in the reading of the works of such writers as Shelley, Byron, Keats and Coleridge. She spoke some

French with an execrable accent, and had been schooled in how to conduct herself in public. These accomplishments however did not help her, when it became necessary to add up a long list of figures, or to convert so many tons of coal at so much per ton into figures that satisfied Robert. Painstakingly he took her through the mysteries of the multiplication tables, making her repeat them until she felt she would scream. He introduced her to sums that grew increasingly more difficult as she mastered the examples he set before her. As a break from the often tedious lessons he considered necessary to give her a grounding in mathematics, he drew on his own experience of underground working to illustrate how, what she was engaged in doing, identified with the actual work of the collieries. When she saw that output of a certain mine had decreased according to the figures supplied by the manager, she was better able to appreciate and understand why, when she read the report that explained that due to flooding or roof falls, small explosions and other difficulties, it had been impossible to maintain the projected figures. He in turn pointed out that this understanding would also allow her to keep a check on the truth of the reports. She was a willing pupil and occasionally surprised Robert by making an observation on something that had escaped him. Because of her upbringing, there were certain aspects of the working life of those who toiled in the mines that would forever be a closed book to her. When Robert tried to explain the necessity to keep costs to a minimum, she remembered the example her father had quoted why it was more advantageous to employ twenty women than one horse to pull the tubs. Why though, she queried, was it not possible to build a shelter that had walls to protect those who searched the coal for stones and other rubbish? Surely in the winter they must be numb with cold from the biting winds? Wouldn't this slight and relatively cheap improvement mean they would work more efficiently and do a better job if they were warm? Robert was impressed with her idea and made a note to take it up with Paget.

As the months went by they settled into an easier familiarity. Sitting side by side, while he explained some particular piece of involved bookkeeping, he never varied his mode of address. He always addressed her as 'my lady', whereas she had now taken to calling him Robert. He was always aware of their relative positions, and of how easily the present arrangement might be destroyed by some simple incident that would escalate into something much bigger. She might take offence at some remark and very soon their pupil teacher relationship might become mistress servant. It was a never ending mental battle to remember, that despite anything Sir Henry had said about who had the last word, in the event of his having to chose between them, there would be no choice. Balanced against this was the sheer delight of being near her, to sit alongside her and feel the warmth of her. To have the scent of her in his nostrils, and always to nurture the hope that one day she would be his. No longer 'my lady' but his 'darling Gwendoline.'

Spring came and went. Still the lessons went on. By her twentieth birthday, Robert acknowledged to himself, that there was very little else he could teach her apart from the reality of working underground.

The combine had continued to prosper, and content to leave well alone, Sir Henry had not visited Woodfield since bringing Gwendoline home. A letter however arrived, to say that he would be coming to make a tour of inspection sometime in June. Gwendoline had no doubt that he would take this opportunity to assess her capabilities. The six months probation was finished and she knew that her dream of becoming the local head of the combine would depend on Robert. She had given her word to her father that should he feel she was not up to doing the job, then she would withdraw. She was not foolish enough to imagine that his decision would be based on what he saw. He would want Robert's opinion and as yet he had not expressed one.

From the time the letter arrived, until the day of her father's arrival, she could hardly conceal her nervousness. She told Robert that she would have to take a break from their daily lessons, in order that she prepare for the visit of her father. No doubt, he would also wish to be undisturbed while he prepared a report for Sir Henry. As she uttered these last words, she gave him a long glance, but he maintained a bland countenance and thanked my lady for her consideration.

Sir Henry arrived and he and Gwendoline spent the evening talking. He brought her up to date on the news of the family and the events that were taking place in London. What had once been the main topics of conversation at one time, now seemed just so many trivialities. The goings on of her onetime circle of friends kindled little or no interest in her, and she was much much more intent on trying to wheedle from her father some idea of his plans. When was he going to give his decision about her becoming the official manager?

'You must wait and see my poppet' was her father's rejoinder.

Sir Henry had no intention of being rushed into a decision that would have far reaching consequences whatever the result. To allow a young woman to become involved in business was almost unheard of. He had had a devil's own fight to get the Board to agree to the idea of a probationary period, let alone an official appointment. As his daughter had pointed out, the Board did what he told them because he was the biggest stock holder, but despite this, one or two had expressed profound disagreement with the whole idea. But for the fact that Morgan would be there to keep an eye on things, he might have to take drastic steps to see that Gwen had the chance to prove her worth. Even so, if Morgan expressed the slightest doubt about her capabilities, then daughter or not, he would have to look elsewhere for a manager. He spent the next day journeying on horseback with Robert to the NantGwrhay Colliery where he held a meeting of the three managers. He talked long and plainly, leaving them in no doubt of his plans.

'From the figures so far given, I can see that the collieries are making a profit. I do feel however, that with your co-operation those profits can be increased. Of course, such increases would naturally benefit you too. You will see from Morgan's report that we would like output increased by ten per cent. If this can be accomplished, I as chairman see no reason why you should not expect an increase in your salaries of at least two and half. Of course there will be difficulties. The workers will say they can't work any harder. Well they always say that, but I leave it to you to convince those under you, that failure to produce more coal will probably result in job losses. Amongst both workers and others. It is of the utmost importance that output be increased. There are big things happening in the coal industry and to keep up with events, more money must be spent. This can only come from bigger profits. I am known as a hard man, but I think you will agree, a fair one. I realise that mining is a filthy, dangerous job. If all else fails and as a very last resort, then perhaps the Board will consider offering an increase to the hewers, of say, two pence per week; provided the target is reached. This is generous we think. Mark you gentlemen, the Board will need to be convinced that such an increase is absolutely necessary and it will not be granted lightly. Its implementation will be closely scrutinised. Do I make myself clear?'

He looked around the circle of faces.

Each nodded. He had made his wishes eminently clear.

Robert had wondered when Sir Henry would approach him and seek his opinion of Gwendoline's capabilities. He had expected that this would be one of his employer's first questions. It therefore came as a surprise when, as they jogged along on the return journey, Sir Henry suddenly said, 'Morgan. You heard what I said to the managers. Do you think the Board's plans are feasible? Can we produce another ten per cent?'

'Not without some re-organisation sir, and the introduction of some new methods.'

'Just what sort of reorganisation and methods?'

'Well sir....'

He got no further before Sir Henry interrupted him.

'One moment Morgan. Before you say any more, what is your honest opinion of my daughter's plan to become the controlling manager? Don't be afraid to say what you think. Could she do it?'

'Sir Henry. When my lady came to me and said she wanted to learn everything I could teach her about the financial accounts system of the combine, I admit I was dubious. From what she told me, it was obvious that she had no knowledge of bookkeeping and very little mathematical knowledge. She said she was prepared to accept me in the role of teacher and would grant me the authority of that role. She then told me that you had agreed to a period of six months probation and that, at the end of that time she would abide by your decision, as to whether she was competent enough to take on the position held by her late husband. I agreed to her request, and for the past six months we have worked together. I have formed an opinion, and knowing that at some time you would require me to voice it, I have taken the liberty of putting it on paper. I would ask you sir, not to read it until after you have formed your own views. Doing it this way, I think that whatever your decision is, I shall not be open to an accusation of having influenced you.'

'Damme Morgan! You should have been a diplomat! Very well. Let me have your report and I'll give my daughter her answer after dinner tonight. I know she's on tenterhooks to know what I intend doing, and if I keep her waiting any longer, she'll have an attack of the vapours. Now back to what we were discussing before.'

'Could we delay discussion until after you have informed my lady of your decision sir? You will understand why when I disclose some of the ideas that have been put forward.'

'Oh very well Morgan, though I must say I am curious as to your reasons.'

Robert was relieved that his employer had chosen to be patient. He had not relished having to disclose his views on Gwendoline's suitability for the vacant position until Sir Henry had made known his. If they agreed, all well and good. If they differed in their opinions, then Sir Henry could in all honesty tell Gwendoline that his decision was based on his opinion and his alone.

Arriving back at Woodfield, Sir Henry retired immediately to his own quarters, there to refresh himself. Having partaken of two large ports, he rang for a servant and bade her find Lady Gwendoline and ask her to wait upon him immediately.

Gwendoline arrived within minutes, her nervous mien evident.

'Ah Gwen my dear, come in. You look nervous child. Well I'm not going to keep you waiting much longer. I've had a talk with Morgan and I've had a good look at the books and one or two other things. I promised Morgan that I would tell you my decison after dinner this evening. Before I do so, I want you to know that, I have yet to read Morgan's report on your work, so what I think has not been influenced by him in any way. Now leave me child while I read what he has to say.'

Pouring himself another glassfull from the decanter, he settled down to read what Robert had spent more than two hours writing. When Gwendoline and her father sat at opposite ends of the table that evening there was a marked contrast in their demeanour. Sir Henry, fortified by a nap after eating an excellent lunch, was in a mood to talk about his plans. While he talked on, Gwendoline too nervous of the outcome of her father's ponderings about her future, could hardly restrain herself. As each course was presented, Sir Henry set to with a will while she picked at her food, taking quick nervous sips at the glass of wine at her elbow. By the time the servants had cleared away and Sir Henry, replete, had pushed back his chair, Gwendoline could hold back no longer.

'Papa. For heaven's sake! Please tell me what you've decided.'

Filling his glass her father looked at her.

'My dear Gwendoline. In the world of business one must learn to keep calm under all conditions. Nervousness will be seen as a sign of weakness, so I would advise you to learn control if you wish to succeed in your chosen profession.'

The significance of his words eluded her for a moment then she burst out,

'Does that mean I am to be the new manager?'

'Yes my dear.'

She rose from her seat and rushed the length of the table to throw her arms around him.

'Oh papa. Thank you. Thank you very much.'

'Mind the port child, you'll have it all over the table.'

She kissed him on the cheek then seated herself on one of the vacant chairs.

'When can I start?'

'I see no reason why you shouldn't take over from Morgan as soon as possible. From what he says in his report, you have been an excellent pupil and he feels that you are perfectly capable of carrying out the duties. I will advise Paget and the others of your new appointment. One thing my dear. Morgan is a very valuable servant of the company and I hope you will continue to rely on him to help you, particularly when dealing with those three gentlemen. They will think you have been appointed purely and simply to ensure control remains in the family, and being a woman I have no doubt they will try to bamboozle you on certain things. Let Morgan be your guide. The young man is nobody's fool. Also, certain members of the Board disagree with my decision to give you the chance and they will undoubtedly be keeping an eye on your performance; particularly in view of the recent output. I hope that I shall have no cause to regret my decision. There! I've said my piece as chairman of the Board. As your father Gwen, you have my support and love and I'm proud of you.'

This was the first time that she had ever heard her father speak in such a way and it was with tears in her eyes she gave him a hug.

'Thank you papa. I'll not let you down. Now if you'll excuse me, I'd better go and find Robert and let him know that the new manager has been appointed.'

If Sir Henry had noticed that she referred to his financial controller by his first name, he gave no indication, but moved from the table and made his way to the sitting room, taking a glass and the decanter with him. There he settled down in an easy chair. It had been a busy day and tomorrow he had no doubt the new manager would want to discuss the re-organisation and new working methods that Morgan had mentioned. Noticing his glass empty, he filled it and looking out of the window at the evening sky, he fell to wondering how his friend John Moggridge was enjoying his retirement.

CHAPTER 24

It had been an eventful four months for Gwendoline. Remembering the warning words of her father, she had been careful in her dealings with the colliery managers and had followed his advice. Whenever she had felt that she did not have the experience to deal with a particular situation, she had called upon Robert for advice. He had given this unstintingly and she was grateful. Having been in control of the combine for so long, it would have been only human for him to have placed all sorts of obstacles in her path, when she had asked for his help in securing her present post. She had thanked him for having given her father a report that she knew, whatever her father said to the contrary, must have had an influence on his decision to give her the job she now held. Once the three managers had come to realise, that while the new manger was a young woman, she was as capable of interpreting a page of figures as any man, they began treating her with respect. Sometimes too, she revealed by her questions, that she might be giving them the benefit of the doubt this time, but next time their reasons had better be a little more convincing. What disconcerted them even more, was the impression they got, that all the while they spoke to her, an invisible Robert Morgan was looking at them over her shoulder.

The first and only time there was a confrontation between them, was when she called them to a meeting at Paget's office to lay before them, the plans she and Robert had formulated to increase output. The managers' efforts had resulted in a small increase in the amount of coal that left the pithead, but nowhere near the desired figure. Gwendoline had not interfered in any way while she felt her way cautiously along. She had studied the reports Robert made out and discussed them with him before adding her signature at the bottom.

After two months she felt the time had come to initiate some new methods, and it was to acquaint the managers with these that she called the meeting.

Gwendoline and Robert had been driven over by Jenkins to the colliery in an open carriage. It was a beautiful summer's morning, one more suitable for a picnic than a meeting that threatened to be anything but friendly. The little office was crowded as the five of them sat around Paget's desk. Once they had settled in their chairs, Gwendoline invited them to smoke if they wished. She took off her large shady hat and with Robert sitting at her elbow she opened the meeting.

'Gentlemen, I have called this meeting because, in accordance with the wishes of the Board, it is my duty as controller of the colliery combine to see that between now and the end of the financial year, output will have been increased by ten per cent. I intend that the Board's wishes, no Board's orders would be better I think, shall bear fruit. Do not think for one moment gentlemen, that because I am a woman, I do not have the authority or will to ensure my orders are carried out. I am aware that Sir Henry has given you an ultimatum; even going so far as to promise that the Board might consider giving the workers a rise of twopence per week as a last spur, to see the target figure is reached. Your reward of a two and a half per cent increase in your salaries depends on you attaining the required figures. I want you to have that increase gentlemen, but while I have a certain sympathy with the miner, working in what is a dangerous and dirty job, I do not propose giving them twopence per week.'

There was a stirring around the table. She lifted her hand.

'What is the biggest obstacle to our obtaining an increase of ten per cent in output gentlemen?'

She listened as each manager listed the various causes he believed were responsible for the difficulties facing them. When they finished she said,

'I sympathise with you gentlemen. Some of these are beyond immediate solution, but I am surprised that nobody has mentioned that every day, many hours are wasted while bringing the coal to the surface. Correct me if I am wrong, but is it not a fact that there are always several tubs waiting to be unloaded into the bucket, because we are now sending all coal through NantGwrhay? Doesn't this mean that, the women employed to bring these tubs to the shaft are standing around waiting their turn, thus wasting valuable time? I understand this situation arises owing to the length of time taken to wind the bucket up the shaft, unload it and return it to the bottom of the shaft. A shortage of tubs at the shaft head adds to the problem, because it takes so long for the women to push them to the screening area for unloading and return. To give the three hundred hewers we employ twopence each week would cost us one hundred and thirty pounds per year and we shall still have the problem unless we solve it somehow. I intend doing just that and saving some money. We will install two buckets which will be raised by using a horse. The number of windlass woman used at present will be reduced and used only to empty the buckets into the tubs. For the time being those not wanted can be used to push the tubs to and from the screening area. I estimate that once these plans are working, we shall be bringing up coal much more quickly. I also want some sort of shelter built over and around the screening area. I am going to hand over the meeting to Mr. Morgan now. He has drawings to show you which will explain what I require. I want work on these new plans to start immediately. Good morning gentlemen. Robert. If you will see me to my carriage please?'

She rose, put on her hat and swept out of the office with Robert in her wake. Once outside she said,

'I'll take the carriage and send Jenkins back. I have work to do at home.'

The meeting was effective in two ways. First and foremost, it instilled in the managers, a respect for the authority of the new overall manager, and when the winter winds howled down the valley bringing rain and snow, those unfortunate enough to spend their days picking stones from the coal, blessed the name of the new manager. Due to the necessity to widen the shaft and carry out some alterations to the headgear, it was nearly Christmas before the plans were fully implemented. By then, time had ceased to be their biggest enemy. It had been replaced by one whose impact was immediate and deadly.

Cholera! The very mention of the dreadful disease was enough to strike terror in the hearts of all who heard its name. Until 1817 it had been unknown outside of Asia, then it had started spreading steadily westward. In 1830 Russia had felt its deadly grip. Moscow and St. Petersburg had suffered terribly, their populations cut down like corn before the scythe. As was the custom with all these plaguelike epidemics, it was the poor part of the population that suffered the greatest impact. Their living conditions, filthy and unsanitary, were breeding grounds for the disease. Its westward march had been remorseless and in 1831 it had reached the shores of Britain where it soon gained a foothold. The death toll soon left the survivors with the feeling that once again they had been visited by the Black Death which had rampaged through the country in the Middle Ages. Four months after Gwendoline took her place as overall manager of the colliery combine it struck the valley communities of South Wales. The epidemic was to last until the following March. It was the industrial villages and towns that suffered the most. With their crowded streets of filthy houses, with cesspits seeping into the streams and wells that supplied their drinking water, the populations were decimated. Reports filtered through to Woodfield of conditions in Tredegar, only about six or seven miles distant, where it was said conditions were so bad that people were fleeing into the comparative safety of the countryside to try to escape. Blackwood had its quota of victims and before the disease had passed on to seek further victims, the churchyard at the nearby chapel in Penmaen held several new graves.

The speed with which the disease struck, brought a special kind of terror to all who were involved. Within hours sometimes, a seemingly healthy person would collapse and exhibit the symptoms that betokened a desperate fight for life was imminent. For those who nursed them, the picture the disease presented was one that shocked. It seemed that nothing could stop the unceasing vomiting and endless diarrhoea that caused the victim to visibly shrink, as the constant loss of fluid dehydrated them. Weight loss and muscle cramps together with the cold clammy feel of their skins, and a tongue that became dry and leathery, between lips that turned blue, added to the onlooker's horror. Since the cause of disease was unknown, there was little that could be done for the unfortunate victims, and people tended to shun each other in the hope that somehow they would escape the clutches of this deadly killer. Pity then the poor family, one of whose members fell victim to this killer. Many, in an effort to help the sufferer, only hastened their deaths by giving them water to drink that was already contaminated. Left alone to try to nurse an unfortunate sufferer, they could only wait and hope that somehow, they themselves would escape the disease.

Woodfield, being isolated, escaped the ravages of this dreadful disease. Unknown to them, their very isolation was probably their salvation. Unlike those living across the valley in crowded and filthy conditions, drinking contaminated water, easy targets for infection, the water supply was pure and safe. Drawn from an underground stream that passed beneath the house, a well had been dug through forty or more feet of earth and rock to gain access to it. Clear sparkling water was available in unlimited quantities simply by lowering a bucket.

Despite the epidemic, work went on. Daily, those who could, stumbled in the darkness of the winter mornings to the pithead, to climb into the bucket that took them into the bowels of the earth. Now though, as they descended, an empty bucket ascended to be filled by more workmen. When all had been transported below, coal would begin to be hauled up the shaft at twice the volume of previously, and much more quickly. Thanks to the idea to install two buckets passing each other in the shaft, and the use of a horse to pull one up, while the empty one descended, Gwendoline and Robert's plan to increase output was a great success. A horse had been purchased from a nearby farmer, at a price that allowed Gwendoline to buy another to share the work. She had been a little nervous that she might have been too enthusiastic, so she was very happy to note that within three months, output had exceeded the target of ten per cent. When Robert presented her with his report for the Board, and pointed this out to her, she thanked him for his efforts in making it possible. When he left it with her for her signature, she wrote a letter to her father pointing out that since the target had been achieved and the colliery managers were to receive an increase in their salaries, as overall manager, she felt most strongly that as financial controller and part author of the plans, Robert Morgan should be equally rewarded. With the coming of Spring, the number of cholera cases lessened, and as the months passed it gradually died away, to become just a memory of the nightmare it had been. There would be other times when it would once again claim victims, but for now, the ragged, underfed, and ill-housed unfortunates who were its most likely victims, enjoyed the warm days of summer, and carried on their struggle to keep body and soul alive.

CHAPTER 25

During the time that Gwendoline was imposing her authority upon the combine and achieving success with her new methods, there had been very little activity on the part of the Scotch Cattle, at least in the Blackwood area. That they were busy in other places was evidenced by the reports of burnings and beatings taking place, that appeared in the columns of the 'Cambrian' and 'Monmouthshire Merlin', two local newspapers. These two journals occasionally appeared in Woodfield and Robert would read them avidly. Parliament had been active in its effort to reform the working conditions of the young. He noted that there had been a law passed to limit the length of the working day to twelve hours, for those between the ages of twelve and eighteen working in the textile factories; and those between nine and thirteen were not to work more than nine hours. A great boon too was the ban on anyone under nine from working in these factories. Meal breaks had to be given, and schooling provided for those in the nine to thirteen age group. Times were changing, but how slowly. Perhaps the continual efforts of men like John Frost to obtain a workers' charter would someday bear fruit.

Other changes too were taking place. Gwendoline who had first appeared at Woodfield in the very latest creations in dresses and hats, had now taken to wearing clothes of a dark hue. Whether she did this as a concession to her marital state, or thought it the appropriate dress for a woman engaged in business, Robert did not know. All he did know was, that to see his beloved thus, was both unbecoming and unnatural. To disguise such young beauty was to him, a sin. She was born for light and colour. How he longed once more to see her dressed as she had been when first he had laid eyes on her. Poor Eirwen too was depressed. No longer did she have the pleasure of bringing out dress after dress for her lovely young mistress to choose from. Each day Gwendoline would don something black or dark grey, unrelieved by any jewellery other than an occasional string of black jet beads. She had taken also, to having Eirwen brush back her hair and pin it in an unfashionable bun on the nape of her neck. How he longed to pull those pins from her locks and allow them to cascade down to her shoulders. She no longer seemed to laugh much, and had taken on an air of seriousness that lay strange on such a young face. No longer did she seem to care, that in the stables her favourite horse grew fat for lack of exercise. Whenever she did go out, it was in a closed carriage.

All these things worried Robert but there was little he could do about it and he was forced to stand by and watch, as daily his mistress began to become a stern business woman, totally unlike the gay and beautiful girl who had stolen his heart.

When Sir Henry paid a visit he too noticed the change in her and taxed her with working too hard. She should take a holiday. Why not return with him to London and see the sights and renew acquaintance with some of her friends?

'There is much to do father and I cannot spare the time nowadays to gallivant about. My friends are probably all married and busy with babies and husbands. What could we find to talk about? I know nothing about children and I am sure that if I tried to describe what I do all day, they would think I was a mad woman. No. I shall remain here, there is much I want to do.'

Colliery owners normally did not live anywhere near their collieries, choosing to leave the running of the mines in the hands of their managers or agents. That Gwendoline as representative of the London Fuel Company inhabited a house within walking distance of the mines under her control was not only unusual, it meant that the managers were under her watchful eye. It was fortunate that the company paid their workers in coin and not tokens. None of those employed in the combine were at the mercy of the owners of the Truck Shops that operated in the district. Maybe because of this, the combine had not suffered as badly as some, at the hands of the Scotch Cattle. Robert had explained to her the infamous ways in which these establishments exploited their workers. The agents, managers and contractors, working for the absentee owners, took full advantage of their positions, and at times had driven the workers to take the law into their own hands in sheer desperation.

In two of the collieries at the Gwrhay, the managers had instituted a system of paying their workers that was a source of despair. This was known as the long pay system. The managers settled with their workers not on a weekly basis, but at lengthy intervals of four to six or seven weeks. Payment was made on a Friday with tickets on which were written the advances made, together with the charges for rent, coal, soap, equipment, the surgeon and sick fund. Once the deductions had been made from their wages, contractors were bound by law to pay them with gold or £5 notes. To obtain the necessary change, payment was often made in the public house, which very often was owned by the manager or contractor. When men asked for advances against their wages, these advances were not in the form of cash. Instead they received notes which could only be exchanged for goods at the Truck Shop, often owned or backed by the manager or colliery owner. Prices were often higher than in ordinary shops but having only the tokens, families had no choice but to shop there. Sometimes too, they paid out the wages in the Shop and then and there families were expected to change their money immediately for goods, which were not always what they wanted. The quality was often very poor and the measures debateable.

It was practices like this that had probably been one of the reasons for the birth of the Scotch Cattle, and were a continuing source of aggravation to the workers. There was a Truck Shop in the little village of the Gwrhay, and it was inevitable that some day trouble would come because of the desperation felt by those having to deal with the Shop. Trouble in the form of strikes and riots that this sort of establishment were responsible for. That day came in 1834 and culminated not only in damage to property but also in the deaths of two people.

For some weeks there had been a gradual increase in tension and there had been several instances of strikes being called at various collieries in the area. Feelings were running high, and when Gwendoline in line with other colliery owners had refused an increase in wages, strikes were called in every mine throughout the valley. Nearly all the miners stayed away from work, but one or two attempted to defy the Scotch Cattle who were behind the strike.

They took the opportunity to settle accounts not only with the blackleg miners but also the notorious Truck Shop in the Gwrhay. Paget had sent a letter to Gwendoline warning her that he and the other managers expected trouble. When she asked Robert why the miners at the collieries under her control should want to strike, he tried his best to explain their viewpoint. He was in an unenviable position. As one who had worked below ground, he had known what it was like to spend twelve hours a day, wet and dirty, hammering at coal and rock. Fearful always, that the creaking of the wooden posts and the unexplained groaning of the roof above them, meant that at any moment they would be buried beneath hundreds of tons of earth and rock. To have bosses of the calibre of Dai Williams placed in positions of authority over them. Men appointed very often, purely because they were bullies and prepared to carry out any order handed down from above. How did one explain such things to a lovely lady whose life had been lived in luxury, waited upon, her almost every wish granted by rich parents? These men worked for her papa, she argued. He had invested a great deal of money in the forming of the combine and surely he was entitled to make a profit? He could offer no argument against this, except to say that the miners claimed, that they only wanted what they considered a fair wage for the dangerous job they did. Enough money to ensure that their families ate properly and an end to the Truck Shop system. She countered this by asking him what would happen if the Board authorised an increase? Wouldn't the other owners have to do the same? And wouldn't this mean that some of them would have to close down because they could not afford it? Then there would be more miners out of work wouldn't there? More families would suffer. Why couldn't they just carry on working and be thankful they had a job?

Seeking to distract her from arguments that had raged ever since one man had employed another, he asked what she thought they should do to protect the mines? Should Paget be told to employ some men to stand guard? This was normal practice but there had been no trouble for several years and they had long ago dispensed with those they had used then.

Gwendoline however had taken the bit between her teeth and ordered Robert to tell Jenkins to have the coach brought around straight after lunch. They would go to the colliery and see Paget and find out what he intended doing. He must have some plan surely?

Robert then suggested that they postpone their journey until the following morning, but she was adamant.

It was past three o'clock when they arrived at Paget's office and already the light was beginning to fade. This was what Robert had feared. The return journey would have to be made in the dark and with the situation as it was, there was always the possiblity they would run into malcontents look- ing to stir up trouble.

Almost as soon as she entered the office and seated herself at the manager's desk, Gwendoline demanded to know what steps Paget had taken for the protection of the collieries? Had he taken on any men to act as guards? If not, she suggested he should do so immediately, preferably some dogs too. What about the office records? There had been some damage done in the office before hadn't there? It might be better if the books were taken in her coach back to Woodfield. They'd be safe there and since there was no work being done while the strike was on, there was no object in leaving them for some rascal to set fire to them.

'I want this colliery guarded well Paget. See to it'

Paget looking ruffled explained what he had in mind. Yes he had employed twenty men. They would be armed with clubs and he had ordered them to use them on anyone they thought was looking to cause damage. He would get a couple of mastiffs too. The men would be split up into groups. Some would patrol the colliery while some would be kept in re- serve to go wherever there was any sign of trouble. Without a fence around the pithead there was no way they could stop miscreants getting in, but by patrolling they would stand a good chance of catching them. Anyone they caught would be beaten then handed over to the authorities for trial. He had no doubt that the local Bench would make sure they didn't cause any more trouble for a long time.

Gwendoline seemed satisfied with this and after instructing Robert and Paget to collect the books and place them in the coach she bade Paget 'good day'.

It was while they were loading the record books that the sound of shouting reached them. It seemed to be coming from the centre of the little village and was increasing in volume.

Robert hurried to the little mound in the vicinity of the shaft head and was able to see what was causing the commotion. Already it was evident that this was more than just a drunken fight. In the gloom he could make out numerous figures milling about. They were shouting and waving their arms. Many had sticks which they were waving above their heads. The focus of their attention seemed to be the building that stood at the end of the row of hovels, which comprised that part of the area known as the Waterloo. He turned his head as he heard footsteps and was surprised to see Gwendoline being assisted over the rough ground by the manager.

'What's happening Robert. What's all that shouting?'

'It looks like some sort of riot my lady. I can't quite make out what's happening, but there seems to be at least a hundred of them down there and they look as if they are attacking some building. Paget! That building on the end of the row nearest the Waterloo. Isn't that the Shop?'

'Yes'.

'Robert! Help me up I want to see what's going on.'

'My lady. I don't think...'

'Robert! I want to see what's happening.'

'Very well my lady.'

He took her arm and encumbered as she was by the long cloak and dress she wore, Gwendoline had difficulty in getting a foothold on the slippery slope on the summit of which Robert stood.

'Paget. Give me a push.'

'My lady!'

'Paget. Push!'

'Yes my lady.'

Paget gingerly placed a hand on either side of Gwendoline's waist and with Robert pulling, and Paget exerting a very light pressure, she struggled to the top.

'Robert! There's a fire down there!'

Robert had been too busy assisting her to notice that flames had sprung up near the building, but now he could see that the crowd appeared to be hurling things on to a large bonfire. Figures could be seen running back and forth between the shop and the fire and every time some object went into the flames, a cheer broke out. Even as they watched, someone, probably the owner, was trying to prevent two men from going into the shop. They engaged in a struggle with him and the next thing the watchers saw, was his figure being hurled into the crowd. It was impossible to see what befell him as many of the crowd linked arms and were dancing about the fire, as if happy to see the contents of the shop go up in flames. It was impossible for the three to distinguish any of the crowd, but it seemed evident that what they were watching was an attack, probably by the Scotch Cattle, on one of the objects of their hate. Whether the attack on the owner of the shop had injured him it was not possible to tell, but if he had been manhandled by the crowd then it was certain he would be badly mauled.

At last the crowd began to disperse, streaming off down the tramroad toward Rhiw Syr Dafydd, laughing and cheering at their success. They had probably come from Blackwood or some other place further down the valley. If they had been members of the Cattle, this would be in accordance with their ways of doing things. Nobody local would be involved, so it would be impossible for the authorities to put anyone from roundabout on trial for what had happened.

They watched for a little longer, then Robert suggested it was time they left. By now it was dark so Robert offered his arm to Gwendoline and she placed her hand lightly upon it. They had some difficulty in walking back to the coach as much of the ground was strewn with discarded bits and pieces of wood and metal. Several times but for Robert's assistance, Gwendoline would have stumbled as she tried to keep the hem of her dress out of the black mud that lay underfoot.

Jenkins had taken the precaution of lighting the lamps on each side of the coach. Although only candlelit, their gleam was enough to guide them back and it was with relief that Robert handed his mistress into the coach. Perhaps because she was so busily engaged in keeping her balance in the darkness, Gwendoline had said nothing about the scene they had just witnessed. However when Paget had closed the coach door, and they had started the climb up out of the valley, she spoke.

'Robert. Who were those people?'

'Probably some of the Cattle and some others from Blackwood and further down the valley. From what I could see they seem to have brought the stuff out of the shop and burnt it. Probably wanted to destroy the records and teach the owner a lesson.'

'Do they do this sort of thing very often?'

'Well this is the second or third time they've done it in this area. The shop at the Rock has been attacked twice. There is a great deal of hatred against these shops my lady, and it is hoped that Parliament will make them illegal.'

'What about the owner. Would they have ill treated him?'

'Possibly but unlikely my lady. Mostly they just try to damage the shop so badly that it has to close. It's the blackleg workers that they beat.'

'Well I hope we have no more trouble at NantGwrhay. Paget seems to have done all he can about protecting the place. Do you think we might suffer an attack?'

'It's hard to say my lady. From what Paget has told me, most of our workers seem satisfied with their wages but there's always some who will try to create trouble. We can only wait and see.'

The rest of the journey was passed in silence as each sat thinking about what they had seen, and the possibility that the Cattle might once again decide, that it was now time to teach the new owners of NantGwrhay a lesson.

The next attack however took place not against the property of the coal owners, but against a miner and his family, and this time with tragic results.

Robert only became aware of the trouble that had taken

place in Blackwood from talk in the kitchen. One of the servants was relating what she had been told when he entered. He overheard the words, 'and they do reckon it was that Morgan what shot her.'

He interrupted the girl,

'What's that all about Megan? Somebody shot his wife?'

'No mister Robert. It be them Cattle. There's talk as how some poor woman 'ave been shot and she's dead. Seems 'er man was blacklegging and the Cattle came and burnt everything and somebody shot 'er and now she be dead. They got somebody and he be in prison.'

The story appeared some time later in the news journal and Robert, anxious to find out the truth of the matter, read it with great interest. If the industrial unrest was becoming so bad that some of the workers were resorting to the use of firearms, then it was quite likely that the colliery owners would soon ask the authorities to send troops into the area to maintain peace. What had happened had taken place only a week or so after the affair at Waterloo, and it seemed that the Scotch Cattle were making a direct attack on the Blackwood area. The two were very likely linked.

The news report stated that,

'On Tuesday the 28th October, the Scotch Cattle attacked the house of a certain Thomas Thomas living in Blackwood. He was a miner employed at one of the local mines, and despite the strike in force had been brave enough or foolish enough to attempt to go to work. He had been warned to stay away from the mine but had persisted in his efforts and what had taken place was the consequence of his actions. A crowd brandishing sticks and other weapons, had gathered outside his house, shouting for him to come out. It was intended obviously to beat him but he did not appear. The miscreants had then battered their way into the house and began throwing out the furniture, curtains and clothes. These they had piled in the street and set on fire. During the attack the man's wife, Joan Thomas, hiding inside had received a gunshot wound above the arm, from a weapon discharged by someone in the crowd. Some onlookers claimed that Thomas had been hiding inside too, but had been so frightened by the mob, that he had stayed hidden until the following morning, before leaving the house to find a surgeon to attend to his wife. In spite of the efforts of the doctor, the wound had turned septic, and Joan Thomas died on the Monday following the fracas. The authorities were pursuing the matter with great diligence.'

There was no mention of anyone having been taken into custody for the shooting as stated by Megan, so presumably the authorities were still looking for the man responsible. In another part of the paper, a small section of the print was taken up by a report that a Shop situated near the Waterloo Colliery at a village called Gwrhay, had also been attacked by a mob thought to be the notorious Scotch Cattle. The contents of the shop had been destroyed by fire. These included candles, paper, tea, grocery and clothing. There was an element of good fortune however, both for the shop owner Mr. Jones, and the ruffians themselves. Mr. Jones was able to rescue the shop ledgers from the fire before they were damaged, and it was later discovered that the mob had overlooked a barrel which unknown to them contained gunpowder. It was stated by a reliable person, that, had the barrel been consigned to the flames along with the other articles, the resulting explosion would not only have destroyed the shop but killed them all. The report went on to say that it was high time the authorities took active measures to ensure that property was protected. No more attacks on property or persons took place and after a period of some weeks the strikers returned to work.

Sir Henry had been kept up to date with reports not only of the increased output figures, but also of the unrest that was causing so much trouble in the valley. Gwendoline had reported fully on the precautions that had been taken to ensure that the mine should not be damaged in any way, and also she gave her father a first hand account of how she had witnessed the looting of the Shop at the Waterloo and the burning of its contents. Perhaps it was her report of this affair that decided her father that he should pay a personal visit to see for himself the position. He arrived one dark winter afternoon bringing with him news for both Gwendoline and Robert.

Lady Siston had been disturbed when her husband had returned after his visit and reported how Gwendoline seemed to have changed. She had expressed her disappointment in a letter to her daughter that Gwendoline had refused to take a holiday away from the problems of the colliery combine, and had taken this latest visit as a chance to write once more urging her first born to please come and spend Christmas with them. She was sure that 'that estimable young man Morgan is quite capable of looking after affairs for a short time', and not having seen Gwendoline for some years she felt it was time that they be together as a family once more. The tone of the letter caused Gwendoline some unease and she questioned her father closely about the state of her mother's health. Was mama all right? Sir Henry was forced to admit that since the birth of Gwendoline's baby sister, her mother had not enjoyed the best of health. He then told her of the doctor's warning about the danger to her mother of having another child. Since the wedding, her mother seemed to have lost the energy and vitality she had enjoyed. Gwendoline could see that her father was more than a little troubled by the state of his wife's health and because of this, she promised that she would return to London with him. They would need to speak to Robert and make the necessary arrangements. She had no worries about leaving the running of the mines in Robert's hands, although for some months they had divided the work. She had determined that all administrative decisions were to be hers and Robert concentrated purely on the financial affairs of the combine. Although they consulted each other frequently and worked closely together, the division of labour had given them both more time and freedom to study the affairs of the combine and make their decisions.

She rang and told the maid to ask Robert to come to her study. Robert entered a few minutes later and after greeting Sir Henry he listened while Gwendoline told him that she intended taking a short holiday. They discussed the various points that she felt might need watching then Sir Henry took a letter from his pocket.

'I'm afraid I have some bad news for you Morgan. I received this letter a few days before I left and since I had decided to come to Wales I thought it better I should break the news to you myself. It is from Mrs. Moggridge. She has written to tell me of the death of Mr. Moggridge.'

There was an involuntary gasp from Gwendoline.

'Oh no.'

Sir Henry went on,

'I did not know John Moggridge for very long but I was proud to have his friendship. He was a man of great integrity and someone who cared for his fellow men. I have written to Mrs. Moggridge expressing my deepest sympathy. In her letter she says that her husband often spoke of their time at Woodfield as being some of the happiest days they ever had. She asked that I pass on a message to you Morgan.'

He opened the letter and after searching for a while found what he was looking for,

'Ah here it is. She says, John has told me of the talk he had with Robert before we left, and of his request that Robert take great care of Woodfield. I know how much Woodfield meant to John, and I would ask that when you see Robert again, you tell him that I too ask that he continue to care for it. John built Woodfield as our home and both he and I loved it. I hope that while he lives there Robert will be as happy as we were.'

Robert said nothing for a while then taking a handkerchief from his pocket wiped away the tear that was coursing down his cheek.

'Thank you Sir Henry. If my lady will excuse me.'

He rose from his seat and quickly left the room.

'That young man was very fond of John I think'

said Henry, then added as an afterthought,

'and John of he.'

Sir Henry only stayed a few days and having succeeded in persuading his daughter to go back with him, was anxious to be on his way. Gwendoline had told Robert that she would return as soon as Christmas was over. This time she did not take Eirwen back with her, a decision that did not displease the young maid. She was not so much at the beck and call of her mistress as had once been the case, and it was common knowledge amongst the servants that she was being courted on her time off, by the son of a farmer from nearby Cyncoed. She was now in her seventeenth year and the young man was anxious to marry her. Eirwen too had felt for some months that a lot of the fun and joy had gone from her work. With her mistress so busy with the running of the collieries, and forever wearing clothes that Eirwen privately thought would be better suited to someone as old as Mrs. Watkins the housekeeper, there was very little for her to do. Since there was no likelihood of my lady returning to London to live, she felt she would rather be the wife of a young strong farmer, than end up as maid to a dried up old widow who was wasting her life away, while a young man, her brother, was so desperately in love with her.

Robert, completely unaware of his sister's feelings, was taken completely by surprise when, during the time Gwendoline was away, Eirwen told him she wanted to leave my lady's service and get married. He had had no idea of her feelings, being so completely absorbed in his work, but had the sense to see that it would serve no purpose to try to persuade her to remain. Evidently her mind was made up, so, after extracting a promise that she would stay until the Spring, he promised to speak to Gwendoline. One thing he had not bargained for was the remark she made to him as she left the room,

'Why not make it a double wedding Rob? Me and William and you and my lady?'

Before he could reprimand her or call her back to explain herself, she had closed the door behind her and all he heard was the sound of her laughter. He smiled. Was it so obvious?

Gwendoline returned in mid January, looking less serious. Her visit had done her good and relieved the anxiety she had felt about her mother. Once back however, she plunged once more into her work. When Robert approached her regarding Eirwen, she asked him to leave the matter in her hands. She wanted to speak to her maid in the privacy of her room.

There had been no more outbreaks of violence in the valley since the shooting affair in October, and unfortunate as it seemed to him, the Truck Shop had re-opened at the Waterloo. Robert had taken to purchasing a copy of the newspaper in order to try to keep in touch with what was happening in the world outside Woodfield, and was surprised when the more serious of the two instances reported previously in the news journals, surfaced again in the Spring of 1835. Megan's remarks, although premature proved to be correct. The authorities had captured somebody and put him on trial for the crime. He was shocked when he read the account of the execution carried out. The details were particularly gory and he there and then determined that he would destroy the paper rather than let it fall into the hands of his mistress. According to the report, a man named Edward Morgan had been arrested for the crime of shooting and causing the death of Joan Thomas. Throughout his trial, Morgan had maintained his innocence. Nevertheless he was found guilty. The jury however recommended mercy on the grounds that they did not believe that the prisoner had fired the shot. Despite this, on Monday April 6th, 1835, Morgan was hanged at Monmouth jail.

From the report on the trial, Robert gained the impression that the reporter was of the opinion that, having waited so long to bring a member of the Scotch Cattle to trial, the authorities were in no mood to listen to any pleas for leniency. The hanging was seen as sweet revenge.

The arrest and hanging of one of their members had the opposite effect on the Cattle to that which the authorities expected. Far from being cowed, there were more instances of beatings and burnings and some said that this came about because the wrong man had been hanged. There did not seem to be much doubt that Morgan had been engaged in the activities of the Cattle, but rumours were going about that far from being the culprit, Morgan had been the victim of a miscarriage of justice. It seemed from the reports floating about that he had been in the crowd attacking the house. He had been captured sometime after, but the real murderer had escaped to America, from where he had written a confession but it was too late to save Morgan who had already paid the penalty.

It seemed the authorities were determined that they would

not tolerate any sort of working men's unions to be formed. In the March of the previous year, Robert had read an article about the arrest of some farm labourers from a village called Tolpuddle in Dorset who had tried to form a union. The sentence of seven years' transportation imposed had caused an intense outcry throughout the country and they became known as the Tolpuddle Martyrs. No matter what the governing body tried to do to suppress the workers they seemed to fail. In the beginning of August Parliament had proudly announced that slavery was abolished throughout the Empire. In the middle of the same month, they had passed the Poor Law Amendment Act. The harshness of this new piece of legislation was enough to give rise to the cry that while slavery was being abolished in the Empire it was being installed in Britain. Copies of the papers bearing all these items were now coming regularly into Robert's hands and were causing him some misgivings. His working class upbringing, had instilled in him a sympathy with the workers who were striving for the right to decent wages and a vote in the way the country was being run. Every Sunday his chapel minister warned his congregation against joining in the activities of these troublemakers. The Union clubs to which many of the workers belonged, had been formed as an aid to resist reductions in wages. All members had to take an oath when joining, and these oaths were considered blasphemous by the nonconformist chapels. The fact that most of these clubs held their meetings in public houses was a further cause for their disapproval. Being a deeply sincere believer in the teachings of his minister, Robert was pulled one way then the other as he read and heard arguments first for one side then the other.

Trouble much nearer home drove from his head all thoughts of the rights and wrongs of the struggle taking place, when an urgent message was recieved from Paget. There had been an explosion in the NantGwrhay. Much of the roof in the new face had come crashing down and several workmen were missing!

Having been involved in the opening up of the new coal face, Robert asked permission of Gwendoline to be allowed to go to the mine, and see for himself what the damage was and whether he could help in any way? When she had agreed to his request, he had donned his oldest clothes and mounting a horse had made haste to get to the scene of the disaster as quickly as possible.

CHAPTER 26

The scene at the pit head was one of chaos and shock. Everywhere, workers were milling about. When the explosion had taken place its effects had been felt right through the colliery. The noise of the explosion had carried along the tunnels and the resulting blast, smoke and dust had frightened miners, women and door boys into abandoning their places and retreating to the bottom of the shaft. There they had clamoured to be raised to the surface before the whole mine exploded, but once in the fresh air, they had not known what to do and were waiting for someone in authority to give them instructions. When Robert arrived, Paget had already descended the shaft together with some volunteers. He had left a message that as soon as Mr. Morgan arrived he was to be told where the manager had gone and ask him to follow. Stopping only to confirm that the explosion had taken place in the new face, he climbed into the bucket and signalled for it to be lowered. At the bottom of the shaft, the winder was talking to another man left there by Paget to bring him into the face. The winder had given him two candles, one lighted, the other obviously a spare. Holding the lighted one above his head, Robert and his companion made their way into the tunnel. Despite not having been down the mine for several years, Robert felt he would have been able to find his way, but he was glad of his guide when they came to a junction that he did not remember. His guide however did not hesistate, but plunged straight into the smokey darkness and they had only stumbled on for a few more minutes, when he became aware that there was a lightening of blackness surrounding them. A few more yards and they came to a small group.

'That you Mr. Morgan?'

It was Paget's voice. He was in the front of the group and seemed to be inspecting a barrier which blocked the tunnel.

'Yes. What's the problem?' asked Robert.

'This.'

He indicated the mass of rock and coal that confronted them. 'The roof has come down and blocked off the face. Everybody working in there is trapped.'

'What happened?'

'Firedamp.'

He had no need to say more. Everybody who had worked below knew the danger they faced, should the flame of their candle come in contact with the deadly gas that existed in the tunnels they bored in their search for coal.

'Who's in there?'

'Dai Williams the faceboss and about fifteen others. There's no other way into it. We had to make a new tunnel. The original, the one you helped dig was so blocked with traffic after we joined up with Cwmddu, that we had to drive this one to take some of the load. Thank God we did. The main one's blocked as well, but that only happened after we arrived. With the water that's been coming into the face, it's possible it's already flooded. There's only one way we can get 'em out. We'll have to dig our way through.'

'I'll go back to the pit head and get volunteer teams to help with the digging. If each team works full out for about an hour, we might be able to save them. What about all this?' Robert indicated the barrier facing them.

'Since the main tunnel is blocked already, we'll put it in there. We'll have to reroute the traffic once this problem is cleared up.'

Robert left them and even before he had turned into the main tunnel, he could hear them working on the task which faced them. Despite the fright they had suffered, once Robert had called for volunteers and explained what they intended doing to release the trapped men, the biggest task was to sort them into teams, so eager were they to help their less fortunate comrades, now trapped and possibly dying behind the wall of rock.

Once the teams had once more descended the shaft and had stationed themselves in the tunnel, there to wait their turns to advance on the barrier and try to break through as quickly as possible, there was not much that Robert could do. Paget had left the work to the experienced facebosses with their teams and returned to his office. Robert joined him there and together they studied the maps of the underground workings. Paget was worried that the buildup of water in the blocked main tunnel, might be such that it would penetrate or even wash away the blockage and flood along to the foot of the shaft. If that happened, the colliery was doomed, and possibly those men waiting to try to save their comrades, might themselves be drowned in the deluge.

Robert felt that he should return to Woodfield and advise Gwendoline of the position. Paget agreed to this and promised that should there be any change in the situation, he would send someone with a message. He did not expect the diggers to break through for some hours and intended trying to nap in his office as he fully expected to be there all night. Anxious now that Gwendoline should know the whole story, and Paget's worry about the possibility of the colliery being totally flooded, he urged his mount homeward, unconscious that he himself looked like a vagabond riding to escape the clutches of the law. His face and hands were black and his trouser bottoms soaked. After some furious riding, he turned in at the entrance to the back drive and galloped along it to the house. He threw himself off his horse and hurried indoors where he confronted Dilys the maid who was crossing the hall on her way to the kitchen.

'Mercy me Mister Robert! Where have you been?'

'Where's your mistress Dilys?'

'In the morning room. I've just.....'

Whatever it was she was about to tell him, he didn't stop to find out but shot along the corridor to the door, and after a perfunctory rap on it, entered without waiting.

Inside, Gwendoline seated at the table turned to see who had come in.

'Good Heavens. Is that you Robert? You're filthy!'

'I'm sorry my lady but I felt you should know what's happened.'

'Of course. Come along, you obviously can't stand there dripping water all over the place. Come to the study.'

She led him out of the room. As they climbed the stairs she called out to those in the kitchen to fill a bath for Mister Robert. Inside the study, she sat at her desk and while he recounted what had taken place, and what arrangements had been made to try to rescue the trapped men, she made notes.

The whole affair would need to be contained in the report to London and she wanted to get it down while it was still fresh in Robert's mind. Finished at last, he asked to be excused to take his bath and put on some clean clothes.

'What if Paget sends to say things are not going well?'

'Then I must go back and try to help.'

Despite his foreboding that at any moment during the long night, he would be summoned by someone hammering on the door to tell him there was bad news, he was persuaded to to go and lie on his bed. If he was needed, better he be rested. It was just after six o'clock next morning when he awakened by Mrs. Watkins shaking his shoulder.

Sleepily he peered at her,

'There's a man from the colliery here. He's got a message for you.'

'Where is he?'

'I've put him in the kitchen. The girls are getting him something to eat. His name's Evans. Poor devil looks tired out.'

He got up from his bed. Somebody must have seen he was fast asleep and covered him with a blanket. Pulling on his boots he hurried downstairs.

The man was sitting at the big scrubbed table, wolfing down a big bowl of soup and some bread.

'Did Mr. Paget give you a message for me Evans?'

'Yes Mister Morgan. He said I was to tell you that the fall is bigger than they thought. Seems like there wasn't enough roof supports and the lot's come down. Manager said I was to ask you to come straight away.'

While they had been talking the cook placed another bowl of soup and some bread on the table.

'Here Mister Robert. Get this down you. You can't go out with nothing in your stomach.'

Robert recognised the sense of what she said and settled himself opposite the workman, who was now spooning his second bowlful into his mouth. As they ate, Robert asked him if he'd been one of the teams. The man answered that he had been with the manager when Robert had been brought to the face and had spent two spells of digging at the barrier. Mr. Paget had sent half of them home at midnight but told them to return at six o'clock, then the other could go and get some rest and food. Due to the narrow tunnels, only about a half of them could work at one time so he had decided on this action to make sure he had rested men working all the time.

'Right Evans. Come with me.'

He led the way out into the cool morning air. Jenkins who had been warned by the housekeeper was already sitting on the seat of the closed carriage.

'Evans. You sit up there with Jenkins.'

As the man climbed up Robert spoke to Mrs. Watkins,

'Tell my lady what's happened. I'll be back as soon as possible but it may not be for some hours. If I'm not back by lunchtime, could you send Dafydd to the colliery with some food for Mr. Paget and myself?'

'Cook's already packed something. She gave it Jenkins, but I'll make sure there's some more if you're not back. You be careful now Mister Robert.'

He climbed into the coach and they trotted off.

Paget was sitting in his office when he got there. His face was drawn with fatigue and he looked as if he hadn't closed his eyes all night.

'The cook sent you some breakfast' he said as he placed a napkin wrapped package and two bottles on the table.

Paget unwrapped the bundle and exposed a cooked chicken and some bread, which to Robert's nostrils smelled as if it had just come from the big oven that flanked the big fireplace in the kitchen. To one who was a firm believer in a good breakfast, the sight of the food before him was enough to tempt him to tear off a plump leg and gnaw at it.

'What's the position now?'

Paget his mouth full pointed to the map he had been studying when Robert had come in.

'We'll go on digging but I've been looking at the map. You remember the water that came in to the face when it was new? Well I think it was a pocket from seepage from the stream. Look. See where it swings around and forms the boundary between NantGwrhay and the place Sir Henry purchased originally? Now look here on this map. See there?'

He put his finger on a spot.

I reckon if we go into the unworked mine, we might be able to get through a lot quicker. I don't know how far in that tunnel goes, but I'm hoping that it's right up to the stream. Perhaps that's why they gave up. They run into the stream and couldn't control the flooding. What do you think?'

'What's the other mine like. Won't it be dangerous?'

'I don't know. But I'm willing to try anything. Those men have been cut off for nearly twenty four hours. Unless they're getting some air in there from the old tunnel, they could be dead by now. If they're still alive then we've got to try everything to get them out.'

He got up. There was more life in his features now that he had eaten and had a plan of action however unlikely of success.

'Let's see if any of the men ever worked in there. They might be able to give us some idea what we're up against.'

There were crowds of men around the pit head, patiently waiting to take their turn to go down and carry on the digging. Paget climbed up on an upturned tub and called for their attention.

'Is there anyone here who worked in that disused mine the other side of the stream?'

There was no answer for a moment then a hand was put up.

'Who's that? Come forward man.'

'It be me, Elias Shepherd, from the West face, Mr. Paget.'

'Good man. Shepherd. Come with me.'

He led Robert and the elderly hewer boss back to the office and when they were gathered about the table, he pointed once more to the map to where he considered the two mines were closest together.

'Shepherd. This is a map of that old mine. How far in did they go?'

'Right up to the stream sir. It were that what made them give oop.'

His accent betrayed that he was one of those who had been an immigrant to the coalfield.

'When did it shut down.'

Elias considered for a while.

'Ten year. Maybe a bit more.'

'Look Shepherd. Do you think we could get through as far as the stream if we went in there?'

'I doan't rightly know. There weren't much water 'cos they knew they were near to it, so they stopped. Mind, the roof'd need a lot of posts.'

His expression altered.

'Ah. You be thinking of getting to new face? You'd be above it Mister Paget. That be a drift mine.'

'Yes and the tunnel goes in on a downward slope. Once I've worked out the angle I'll know how much digging we'll have to do. If we can continue that tunnel we could drive right into the new face.'

'It's worth a try' said Robert not fully convinced 'but a lot will depend on the state of that old mine.'

'Well let's get some men and go and have a look.'

Paget pulled on a dirty old cap that he wore when he went below ground and hurried out.

Elias Shepherd called out some names and several men gathered around him. He spoke to them, and shouldering their picks and shovels, the gang marched off behind him.

Once they reached the abandoned mine, Paget accompanied by Elias and Robert cautiously ventured inside. Each carried a pick, to be used for testing rather than digging. As they moved along in the flickering light of the candles they held, they could make out the state of the roof and walls. Thankfully underfoot was dry, but the further they progressed, the more dilapitated became the state of the mine. Everywhere, posts had broken or splintered and they had to negotiate the small falls of rock that blocked their path. After they had penetrated some distance, Paget looked back at the dim spot of light that marked the entrance. He seemed to be trying to calculate something.

'Come on let's get back to the office. I've got some sums to work out.'

They retraced their steps and when they emerged once more into the daylight he spoke to the men waiting there,

'Make a start clearing the entrance but don't go too far inside the tunnel. It wants timbering. I'll send some men over with some posts and you can start putting them up. Be careful!'

Back at the office, he immediately spread out the map of the old mine which had come into his possession when Sir Henry had purchased the NantGwrhay. With a quill he started jotting down figures on a sheet of paper muttering to himself as he did so. He seemed to have forgotten Robert and Elias. After a while he rubbed his chin as if speculating on the value of his figures and the problem they presented.

'Morgan. If my figures are correct, and I hope to God they are, that tunnel slopes about ten degrees. If it continues at that inclination right to the boundary stream, I reckon the tunnel should end up about thirty five feet above the new face in the NantGwrhay. Give or take a few feet, I think we'll have to break through nearly forty feet to reach those men. I'm banking on the stream having seeped through over the years. It'll be wet but it shouldn't be too hard to remove. If it's rock, remembering what the new face was like before Jonas Pritchard blew it out, then God help those poor devils in there.'

Outside once more he called for volunteers. The work would be dangerous he said, but with any luck they should be able to reach their comrades before the night fell. Teams were quickly assembled and those not required for digging, each carried two posts from the stack of wood and hurried toward the other mine.

Paget returned to the old mine, there to supervise the rescue work. Robert remained in the office just in case there was any word from those working in the NantGwrhay. He looked at the clock in the office. It was already eleven thirty and he realised that he was hungry. The bowl of soup and the chicken leg he had eaten was now just a memory, and he hoped that Mrs. Watkins did not delay too long before sending Dafydd with further refreshment. No matter what happened, he was not going to leave the colliery until, either the trapped men were brought out, or Paget had acknowledged defeat and all hope of a rescue had been abandoned.

At the old mine, Paget, Elias Shepherd and one team went in to see what they were facing. In single file they stumbled along, taking note of the state of the timbering, trying to count how many posts they would need just to make it reasonably safe. When they eventually came face to face with the wall of rock that was the end of the tunnel, Paget's heart sank. If this extended downwards then there was little hope. He took his pick and drove it at the floor of the tunnel. The blade sank into the earth and he levered it to see if there was any resistance. It came out quite easily and he instructed four of them to attack the bottom of the rock wall. He could hardly believe his luck when all four found the rock petered out only inches below the surface. Retreating back some thirty feet, he indicated the spot where he wanted them to start digging. Telling the rest of them to take it in turns to dig, he showed them the angle he wanted to achieve and satisfied that they would do what he wanted he left Elias in charge and made his way back to the entrance. A stack of posts had been started near the entrance and was being added to continually. He looked toward the NantGwrhay and was taken aback to see a procession of women coming towards him. On the shoulders of each team of four they were carrying empty tubs. Of course! He had forgotten that to clear the muck dug out, they would need tubs to clear it from the hole. He had completely forgotten! Each woman was wearing her harness and it was obvious that they intended to be included in the rescue work. This was something they could do better than any man. He gave the signal and the various teams, anxious that their trapped comrades be reached as quickly as possible, moved into the tunnel to begin the rescue taking with them posts from the stack. Soon a stream of material was moving into the tunnel, including the tubs being pulled along by the women. Satisfied that there was no more to be done, he returned to the shaft head, and descended into the NantGwrhay. Making his way along the main tunnel he peered around him in the light of the candle he held. Thankfully, there did not appear to be any change in its condition and he made his way into the tunnel leading to the blocked new face. There too, there appeared little difference from his previous visit. Two men were hacking away at the barrier while others sat around waiting their turn to continue with the attempt to break through. He spoke to the team boss who seemed pessimistic about their chances of getting to the trapped men before it was too late. He told them what was happening in the old mine but urged them to continue their efforts as there was no guarantee that those working there would be any more successful. When Paget re-entered the dimly lit entrance to the old mine he could see all around him evidence of the work that had been carried out while he had been absent. Timbers had been erected to support the roof and extended far into the darkness. Gone were the rocks and piles of debris that had restricted their pathway when first he had ventured inside. He was able to make his way into the tunnel for some considerable distance before his progress was temporarily barred by a gang of men digging at a mound of stone and coal.

The man in charge hastened to assure him that they would soon have it cleared. Apparently, when those ordered to put up new posts had moved in with the timber, there had been a small roof collapse and it was this they were attempting to clear before pressing on. The wisdom of the women who had come prepared to drag away the tubs was plain to see. Already four of them stood waiting while the men shovelled the debris into their tubs. As soon as one was full the women hooked their harness on to the shackle on the tub and throwing themselves forward, made to move back to the entrance dragging their burden behind them. Now however, unlike their efforts when working in the colliery, they were assisted by some of the men, who stationed themselves behind the tub and added their strength to getting the load moving back along the tunnel.

In a very short time, the obstruction had been cleared and Paget was able to proceed. Behind him as he made his way along, he could hear the noise as the teams battled to make the tunnel safe. After a short period when he was completely alone, he came upon some of the gang he had left at the point where he had indicated digging was to commence. The men were sitting with their backs against the side of the tunnel, looking toward the source of the noise that could still be faintly heard coming from the tunnel.

'It's all right. That's the gangs making the tunnel safe. At the rate they're going they should be here in about an hour.

What's happening here. Where's Elias Pritchard?'

'He's down in the hole Mr. Paget.' said one.

Paget made his way forward and found himself on the lip of a hole almost as wide as the tunnel itself. It had been driven in at an angle and he could just see the glow that came from the candles that lit the working area. The area around the entrance had large mounds of soil and rubble banked up against the tunnel walls. The tunnel they were digging out, had become considerably narrower than at its entrance. As they had dug out the soft wet earth, they had been forced to stack it against the sides as there was no means of clearing it away until the tubs arrived with the rescue workers. Realising that this was impeding their progress, Paget told one of the resting men to go back to the following gang and get them to send up some tubs and some timbers. He shouted down to the two men, stripped to the waist, who were hacking away at the face of the earth.

'Elias! Elias Pritchard!'

The man swinging his pick stopped and looked up at him.

'It's Mr. Paget, Elias. What's happening down there?'

Elias dropped his pick and crawled back up the slope. Squatting on his haunches he wiped his forearm across his face.

'We be making a bit of progress Mr. Paget. The ground's a bit soft 'cos of the water like you said. I don't think we can go much further tho' without some props Mr. Paget or we'll 'ave the top come down on us.'

'How far d'you reckon you've dug?'

''Bout eight feet I make it. This muck'll have to be cleared out or there won't be no room.'

'I've sent back for some tubs and props. What about water, is there any coming in?'

'None so far. I don't think we're near enough to the stream yet.'

'I'm going back down the tunnel. If there's anything you want, send one of the men down. The other gangs should be here soon then you can take a breather. I'll hurry them up with those timbers and tubs. Keep your eyes open for any water and let me know if any comes in.'

He left them and stumbled back through the semi darkness. A rumbling stopped him in his tracks, activating fear of a roof fall, then he realised it was the sound of tubs being dragged over the rough floor. In the distance he could see the wavering of lights as the candles flickered in the hands of the gang pulling the tubs. There were at least a dozen men and women pulling three tubs each loaded with the props and in the last tub, a quite large barrel stood upright, water slopping over its rim. He stood to one side as they went past him, silent, intent only on getting to the rescue site as quickly as possible. Once they had passed he hurried back to the entrance. All along the tunnel, new props stood supporting the roof, or awaiting the attention of the gangs who were busy along the tunnel's whole length.

He made his way from the tunnel entrance through the crowd of workers still waiting to take their turns in the tunnel. As he went along there were shouts from men asking how things were progressing? He stopped to tell the assembled crowd that things were moving well. Already Elias Pritchard's gang had penetrated about eight feet. If all went well, he hoped that before the night was out, the trapped men would be safe.

At the office Robert was waiting for his report. Mrs. Watkins had been as good as her word. Dafydd had been driven over by Jenkins and a large basket of food stood on the desk, flanked by several large bottles of beer and one of brandy.

Paget lifted the cloth that covered the basket and looked at its contents,

'By George, Morgan, I must say I'm ready for some of that.' They sat at the desk and attacked the food. Between mouthfuls, Paget brought Robert up to date on the position below ground in both the old mine and NantGwrhay. Both were ravenous and when they sat back replete, only the skeleton of a chicken and half a pie remained as mute evidence of their appetites.

Paget opened a drawer of his desk and pulled out a clay pipe which he proceeded to stuff with some black tobacco. As he applied a light to the mixture and puffed at it, tamping the glowing mixture down with his finger, he settled back in his chair with a contented sigh.

'Morgan. Here I am sitting here with a full stomach, a pipe of baccy and a choice of drinks, but my conscience bothers me. When I went out there and called for volunteers, there wasn't one who hesitated, without thought for food or rest. Can't we find some way to reward them?'

'Your sentiments do you credit Paget, but I don't think any of them will be thinking of a reward for trying to rescue their workmates. It could be their turn one day.'

'I suppose you're right. I'll just have to try and make sure it doesn't happen again.'

'When do you reckon they'll break through to the new face?'

'Well if all goes well sometime around midnight.'

After assuring Paget that he would return about ten o'clock, Robert took his leave and rode back to Woodfield, there to report to Gwendoline what was happening.

Almost as soon as he had arrived, Gwendoline called him to the study where she was busy writing out a report for her father.

'What's happening Robert?'

Robert took a seat and recounted all that Paget had told him. When he said that the manager reckoned that it would be another seven or eight hours before they would be within reach of the trapped men. Gwendoline sighed,

'Those poor men. They probably think they've been given up for dead. Maybe they are all dead by now. Oh Robert it's a terrible price to pay!'

It was the first time Robert had ever heard her express anything that could be construed as sympathy for the lot of those who worked in her father's collieries. Perhaps, now living in the coalfield, and having a share in the running of the collieries had given her a new insight into the hardships suffered by the miners. Straightening her back and taking a deep breath, she asked him several questions to ensure that her report should be factual. Even as she wrote it the thought crossed her mind that, by the time her father read it, the fate of the fifteen or so men trapped below, would already have been settled one way or another.

When she had finished questioning him, he asked that she excuse him as he felt that if he was to be of help later on, he needed to obtain a few hours rest. She nodded her head as if absorbed in what she was writing and he took his leave.

When he had gone from the room, she read what she had written, then as if making up her mind, added a footnote. If he had known what she had written, he would have tried his hardest to have dissuaded her from taking the action she intended.

CHAPTER 27

At eight thirty Robert appeared in the kitchen. The cook had laid out a large supper for him together with another basket of food for him to take to share with the manager. Whilst he ate he instructed one of the maids to go and tell Jenkins to get the closed carriage ready to take him to the colliery at about nine o'clock. Having finished his meal he went into his room to collect his Garrick top coat. When he returned downstairs he was surprised to see Gwendoline in the hall, dressed for the outdoors.

'Are you ready to go Robert?'

'Yes my lady.'

'Good. I have had the basket placed in the carriage so we can leave immediately.'

He stared at her in disbelief.

'My lady. You can't be ....'

'Please Robert. Let's have no argument. I shall accompany you to the colliery. It's about time I put in an appearance and I hope that I shall be there to greet the trapped men. Come along, Jenkins is waiting.'

She climbed into the coach and took her seat. He made one last attempt to dissuade her from going to the colliery.

'My lady. The mine is no place for you to be, particularly at night. We don't know what we might find when they break through to the trapped men. Some or all of them could be dead or terribly injured, not a sight for your eyes. I think I should tell you, that besides the many willing helpers working, there will probably also be quite a few troublemakers, who will try to take advantage of the accident and try to lay the blame on the owner. And to most of them my lady, you are the owner.'

'I thank you for your concern Robert, but as you say, I am the representative of the owners and it behoves me to be there and show concern for those who work for me. Now please tell Jenkins to get started.'

From her tone he could see that any further argument would be of no avail. Poking his head out of the window he shouted to Jenkins to get the coach on its way.

It was well past ten o'clock when they finally reached the colliery and as they dismounted from the coach, a man stepped forward and spoke,

'The manager be gone to the old mine. He do tell me to say that they have nearly reached the men.'

Robert turned to Gwendoline,

'I think you should stay in Paget's office my lady until I find out what's happening.'

'No Robert I want to be there when they bring the men out. Can Jenkins get the coach along to the old mine?'

'I doubt it my lady.'

'Very well in that case we'll walk there.'

'But …'

'Robert I am well aware that you think I should be sheltered from all the unpleasant things that happen. That is most gallant of you, but since Sir Henry had enough confidence in me to appoint me as the overall manager of the collieries, then permit me to exercise that right. I intend going down to the mine and if I fall down and get covered in filth, it will be no more than that unfortunate woman suffered when pushing that tub. Unlike her, I shall be able to bathe and change my clothes. I am not a weak helpless woman, no matter what you may think, so if you will arm yourself with a lantern we will make our way to the mine. My mine.'

Lost for words, Robert went into the office and came out a few minutes later carrying a lantern in which a candle burned brightly. Holding it aloft, he extended his free arm which she grasped firmly, then holding up her skirts with her other hand, they began the walk to the mine.

They had barely gone more than a few steps when she stumbled over something in the dark and clutched at him with both hands. In his haste to save her from falling, he dropped the lantern and his arms went around her, holding her tight against his chest for long seconds. They stood there in the darkness, then, as she moved in his arms, he released her. She adjusted her bonnet then once more took his arm. He relit the candle and silently, slowly and uncertainly they made their way along the track. There was now a constraint between them that neither could define. A line had been crossed. An intimacy, however tenuous, had been reached by the touch of each other's bodies and each was aware of it. Neither spoke except when he warned her to beware of some obstruction. At last, the lights surrounding the mine entrance came into view. As they were congratulating themselves on reaching their destination without further mishap, Robert stepped on a rounded piece of wood that was used for slowing the tubs. He felt his feet go from under him and to his horror, as Gwendoline clung to his arm, his weight pulled her to the ground with him. Luckily his fall was somewhat cushioned by the mud but the breath was driven from his body as the whole weight of Gwendoline's upper body preceded by her elbows, drove into his stomach. Fortunately his head had missed crashing on the iron rail that carried the tubs, but he was quite unable to move, and his mouth opened and shut as he tried to draw breath into his lungs. Gwendoline meanwhile, on her knees, her skirts trailing in the mud and water was trying desperately to push herself off him, but she only succeeded in putting more weight on him. Thrusting her hands into the squelching mess that surrounded them she was at last able to gain some purchase, and lifted herself clear of him. On hands and knees, she could feel the wetness soaking through her garments and struggled to her feet. Robert was still lying where he had fallen, the lantern lying by his side. Her hat had fallen off and her hair was beginning to uncoil from the bun on her neck. She stood there, shocked, the evil smelling water dripping from her clothes, muddied almost from the waist down. Robert, at last having regained his breath, struggled to his feet, his overcoat plastered with mud clinging to him.

'My lady. I beg you to forgive my clumsiness. Are you all right?'

In her embarrassment she snapped at him,

'I am not all right Robert! My clothes are wet and dirty. I have lost my bonnet, my hair is falling down and I have no doubt my face is filthy, and you ask me if I am all right? Oooh!'

The last sound was a most unladylike sound, almost a snort of exasperation at the stupidity of his question.

Once again he relit the lantern and recovered her bonnet

which she jammed on her head stuffing the offending hair inside it.

'Come along, let's get to the light before we have any more accidents.'

This time Robert held the lantern low, determined not to fall over again, and with her hand on his muddied arm, they covered the remaining distance.

There were quite a few men standing about in groups and when they emerged into the lights, Robert took care to stand in front of his mistress in an attempt to hide her dishevelled appearance from their gaze.

'Where's Mr. Paget?'

'He be inside at the face. They be nearly through.'

He turned to her,

'If my lady will wait here I'll go in and find out what's happening.'

'I'm coming with you.'

'But my lady, it could be dangerous in there.'

'No more dangerous than walking with you I'm sure,' she snapped. 'I can't get any wetter or dirtier and I mean to be there when they get those men out. Now lead the way.'

'Very well my lady, but stay close behind me.'

They moved into the tunnel and began making their way through the darkness, lit only by the fitful gleam from Robert's lantern. Thankfully, once they had left the immediate entrance, candles had been lit and left in crevices to throw their pitiful yet welcome light. Determined to stay in close contact, she clung to the hem of his coat and stumbled over the rough ground, straining her eyes to make out her surroundings. Robert stopped and she bumped into him.

'What's the matter?'

'There's something coming.'

She listened but could hear nothing other than the sound of her own breathing, then faintly to her ears there came a rumbling.

'Keep into the side my lady. It's probably a tub.'

They moved until they felt their backs against the side of the tunnel and stood there waiting.

A minute or so later lights flickered ahead of them, then to the sound of shouting, a bent figure appeared out of the darkness, straining against the harness that held her captive to the tub. Behind, two men, arms outstretched, urged her on with shouts and curses. The little procession swept past them, totally unaware of their presence and vanished into the darkness once more. A little further on, they came to a patch of darkness totally unrelieved by any light other than that from their lantern. The darkness outside of the circle of light was a palpable thing. It hung there thick and heavy, like a curtain behind which unnamed horrors silently waited for someone to step out of the light and into their world. She drew closer to Robert, conscious for the first time of the darkness and danger that surrounded them. A creaking caused her to swing her head to try to see where it had come from. Blackness. As if sensing her alarm Robert spoke over his shoulder,

'It's all right my lady. That was only a post creaking.'

'How much further Robert?'

'I don't know my lady but we're bound to see someone soon.'

He had no idea of the distance they had travelled and not wishing to alarm Gwendoline any further had deliberately lied. It could be ages before they reached the place where the digging had been started. They could not travel very quickly for fear of tripping over some of the debris that littered the ground.

Praying that they would soon reach their destination he stopped and listened once more. Was that something? Straining his ears he tried to distinguish between the well remembered groans and creaks that occured every few moments. Surely those were voices?

'Come along my lady, I think we're nearly there. I'm sure I heard voices.'

They stumbled on for what seemed ages before the darkness ahead lessened, then bright light surrounded them as they came to a bend in the tunnel. Spread out before them along the length of the tunnel, was a string of candles burning brightly and shedding their light on a scene that was to remain in Gwendoline's mind for the rest of her life.

All along the tunnel, men and women sat, squatted on their haunches, or leaned on shovels gazing intently forward. Motionless. Their very stillness caused them to look like figures in a painting, caught by the artist as something claimed their total attention. A shout from somewhere ahead released them from their poses and they became a crowd of miners once more. Someone must have spotted the light of the lantern and as Gwendoline and Robert moved into the light, there was a buzz of talk. Robert placed the lantern on the floor and moved forward.

'Where's Mr. Paget?'

'Down the hole with Elias Pritchard. Elias do tell us when he wants to listen 'cos he says we'm nearly through.'

'Is that what you were doing just then?'

'Aye but it were no good.'

'Send someone to get Mr. Paget. Tell him Mr. Morgan wants him. Tell him the owner's here.'

The man looked at Robert then switched his gaze to Gwendoline who stood just outside the edge of the light.

'Go on man. Get Mr. Paget.'

The man hurried off along the tunnel then vanished from view as he entered the newly dug hole which it was hoped would lead to the trapped men. Robert returned to where Gwendoline stood.

'I've sent for Paget. They're not through yet but he'll be able to tell us what's happening. They can't have far to go. That man told me they have to stop working now and again because Elias Pritchard is trying to hear if there's any sounds.'

He turned to look at the spot where the new tunnel began its descent into the floor. He was just in time to see the top half of Paget's body come into view.

'Here's Paget now.'

They waited for the manager to come to where they stood then retreated a little further away from the gaze of all the workers.

'My lady what are you doing down here? Don't you realise how dangerous this old place is? Morgan how could you allow her ladyship to accompany you down here?'

Paget was visibly shaken to see Gwendoline. God! If anything happened to her down here!

'Mr. Paget. If it will allay your fears, Robert tried his best to dissuade me, but this mine is my responsibility and I wanted to see what was being done to rescue those poor men.'

Perhaps having been surrounded for the last twentyfour hours by faces black with dust and dirt of the mine, Paget had not consciously noticed the state of their clothing and their dirt smeared features.

'Have you already had an accident my lady?'

'Of a sort Paget, but don't worry it was above ground and no harm had been suffered except to our dignity. Now. What's the position? Are you near to breaking through yet?'

'I'm hoping that we shall break into the new face within the hour. We have to go carefully in case there's any water in there. We've had water leaking into the face for some months but we were able to deal with it with the pump, but with the face blocked off, it's possible the water may have risen in there, and it could burst back into our escape tunnel if we're not careful.'

'Thank you Paget, I'll not bother you any more. You have much to do and I should only be in your way. Robert will escort me back to the office. I shall remain there and I shall be most grateful if you will send someone to tell me when you have rescued those poor men.'

She took Robert's arm and they began their journey back to the entrance. Paget looked at her retreating back and there was a strange expression on his face. Sympathy from mine owners toward the unfortunate victims of disasters in the collieries they owned, was something he had not come across very often in a life time's employment in the coal industry. Heaving a sigh he turned and hurried back to join Elias Pritchard.

When he crawled the last few yards to join his co-worker he was in time to see Elias tapping gently with his pick at the coal face before him. Hearing Paget behind him, Elias turned his head and made a shushing noise, his features set in an expression of intense concentration. He tapped again and placed his ear close up to the barrier.

'Listen Mr. Paget!'

Paget crouched close to the coal face, his ear almost touching its surface, his mind trying to exclude all noise as he strained to pick up whatever it was that Elias had heard.

Almost indistinguishable from the sound of his heart beat in his ears, there came a definite vibration. Without moving he held up two fingers. Elias grasped their meaning and struck the barrier two sharp raps. An age seemed to pass then there sounded in his ear two distant thuds.

'It's them. They're alive!'

Paget shouted. He sat back on his heels.

'Elias. We can't hurry the next part. If there's any water in there we mustn't let it flood back in here. Go on digging quietly while I get some help, but go easy for God's sake.'

He squirmed his way past Elias and crawled up the tunnel. As he appeared those waiting began shouting to him.

'Somebody's alive in there. They answered our signals. Quick now. I want some volunteers. There's not much room in there and there's a chance that when we break through, if there's any water built up in the new face, the tunnel could be flooded. We want to get them out as quickly as possible and up here.'

There was a general movement forward of all the men and Paget picked two dozen of them. He explained that they were to stand on alternate sides so they would not get in each other's way and could pass the trapped men from hand to hand. Six others were to stand by in case there were any injured amongst the trapped men and to render assistance to carry them out.

With the men he had picked, he re-entered the tunnel spacing them out until he was satisfied, then crawled the remaining few yards to where Elias on his haunches was picking at the coalface.

'We'll have to go a bit harder than this Mr. Paget. It could be yards before we're right through.'

Paget considered. If any water showed then could he gamble on getting through before it became flooded? He would have to take a chance.

'All right 'lias. Go ahead.'

Elias shifted slightly to balance himself then commenced

243

swinging his pick. As the blade sank into the coal, with a twist of his wrists, he levered at it until it broke away. Then he repeated the action, time and time again. Paget picked up the shovel with its shortened handle and dug into the pile, then threw it behind him. Together they worked for about ten minutes, then Elias stopped.

'Water Mr. Paget.'

Trickling down the coalface, glittering in the light of their candles, was a thread of water.

'Keep on Elias.'

Reassured, Elias continued swinging his pick and levering away shards of the shiny black coal. The thread of water remained no more than that. When they tired two more stepped forward and sinking into the traditional miners' crouch, proceeded to hack and shovel as they inched forward into the barrier before them. So it went on for some time until one of the men stopped with his pick embedded in the coalface.

'Mr. Paget!'

Paget crawled forward from where he had been squatting.

'Listen.'

Distinctly they could hear the rhythmic pounding coming from the other side of the barrier.

'Somebody's digging from the other side.'

As if encouraged by the sounds, the man pulled at the handle of his pick and brought down a shower of broken coal. Hardly waiting for it to fall at his feet he swung the pick once more. As it struck into the coal, Paget's fears were realised. A spurt of water came from the hole made by the pick's blade and as he levered it out, first it increased in volume, then slowed to a trickle. While the man dug, Paget watched carefully, dreading the moment when the trickle might turn into a flood and thwart their efforts. It would be tragic if having got so near to rescuing the trapped men, their efforts should be brought to nought. The water had not increased and this gave hope to Paget that perhaps they had only struck into a small pocket of water. Should he take the chance and drive forward, not worrying too much about clearing the tunnel? If and when they broke through, speed would be essential should there have been any buildup of water on the other side. Not to know what the situation was on the other side of perhaps only a few feet of coal was a worrying factor, but his instinct told him to go ahead and smash their way through. Turning, he called at the nearest men.

'Get up here and help. Don't worry about clearing the muck, just break through. It can only be a foot or two. Come on lads!'

The two men lined themselves up alongside their companion and in the narrow confines of the tunnel began swinging and levering, the sheen of sweat on their shoulders and backs gleaming in the candle light. Swing, thud, lever, crack, the rhythm was almost monotonous. Around their feet and legs, the piles of coal grew larger, but still the black gleaming face of coal remained a solid barrier, mocking their puny efforts to break through it.

Has he miscalculated? The thought had hardly had time to formulate in Paget's brain before the man on the right of the trio was struck in the head and chest by a flood of water as a large piece of coal surrendered to the twist of his pick. Water poured in on them making it impossible to stand too close to the face. As it swirled around their legs, Paget stumbled forward to where it poured in. To be defeated now, just when success was in their grasp! Wait, was it slackening? There did seem to be a lessening as it poured from the dimly lit hole which confronted them. A hole! They were through! There was a light in there!

'Quick lads. We're through. Never mind the water. Break it down.'

Like men possessed, the three miners splashed forward through the ankle deep water and attacked the barrier, hacking and smashing at the edge of the hole until it was possible to see into the space where the trapped men awaited them.

'All right lads, we'll soon have you out' shouted Paget into the darkness. 'Is anybody hurt? How many's in there?'

The darkness within was broken by the guttering of a small flame. Somebody had managed to keep a candle end to comfort them as they had waited for their comrades to save them. A weak voice came from the darkness.

'Thanks be to Jesus, we're saved.'

As Paget peered into the space before him, he could just make out the pale outline of a man's face.

'It be me Mr. Paget, Dick Morgan. There be twelve of us alive. Sam Jones got a broke leg and Dai Williams the face-boss is knocked out. He 'it his 'ead on some 'ut when he slipped. Thank God you come Mr. Paget. We been praying ever since we could hear the sound of the digging. Hurry up and get us out Mr. Paget! There's a lot of water in here and it's up to my waist now. Hurry Mr. Paget for God's sake or we could drown!'

As the hole was enlarged, the rate of water coming in increased and Paget wasted no time. He scrambled through on hands and knees and dropped into the other face. The man's fear that the water would result in their drowning seemed unfounded. It came up to his knees but no further. Candles were passed through and quickly they were lit and placed to afford some light in what the trapped men had feared to be their grave. Standing in the water, he helped the first of the tired and weakened men into the tunnel that had been created, and quickly they were passed from hand to hand out into the main tunnel. Sam Jones, although injured was conscious. Dai Williams's gross body was propped up on a large rock against the side, his upper body well out of the water. Together with one of the rescue team who had climbed through, the manager sloshed through the water to where Williams lay. He did not appear to be suffering from any obvious injury, but if, as the first man said, he had slipped and struck his head, that would account for his unconscious state. Together they half dragged, half carried the huge man to the escape hole and struggling, lifted him into the space where willing hands grasped him and dragged him from sight. Having seen to those unable to help themselves, they turned to the remainder who had stood patiently waiting while the injured had been seen to and lifted them into the hole. There, the eager hands that had dragged the injured man through, ignoring his moans of pain at the rough handling, now reached out and grasped the last of them and quickly transferred them hand to hand out to safety. When the twelve had been sent through, Paget looked about him. In the dim light he could make out that the men had been trapped in a space not much more than a dozen feet in each direction. It was a scene of complete devastation. Posts, few in number, stood drunkenly, barely supporting the roof. Paget wondered at this but dismissed it from his mind. He had much more pressing things to do.

Signalling his helper to precede him, he climbed into the escape hole and emerged into the tunnel. Water stood inches deep but had not climbed very far up the incline. Again he thanked his stars that they had only had the overflow from the new face to deal with. If, as he had feared, they had been dealing with water breaking through from the stream now directly above them, there would have been a different tale to tell and women who tonight were relieved wives, would probably have been grieving widows.

When Gwendoline had returned to the office to await the news from the old mine, she sat herself at Paget's desk. For a long while she sat staring sightlessly, her mind far away below the ground with those trapped there. Robert did not interrupt her reverie but stood gazing out of the window at the lights of the colliery also thinking of the trapped men. Her voice brought him back to the present.

'Robert. Has anyone sent for the doctor? There could be injured amongst them. Even if none have suffered hurt, they will need medical attention.'

'I doubt that anyone has thought that far yet my lady. I could send Jenkins with the coach to rouse the doctor and bring him back here.'

'Do that Robert.'

He hurried off to do her bidding. When he returned she was still sitting at the desk but had removed her bonnet and cloak. She was busy pinning her hair into its customary bun on her neck. When she had finished she said,

'Robert. I wish to apologise for the way I spoke to you tonight. It was no fault of yours that we ended up in the mud and I had no right to speak so sharply. Now if you know where Mr. Paget keeps a towel I would very much like to wash my face and hands.'

Robert searched the cupboards of Paget's desk and unearthed a piece of towelling that he had seen Paget use to wipe his hands.

'I'm afraid this is all there is my lady.'

'That will do. Now if you'll leave me I will try and repair the damage caused by our mishap.'

She smiled as she said this and Robert left the office feeling that once again, his mistress had shown him another facet of the character that lay beneath the skin of the hard headed business woman he called 'my lady'.

Walking toward the shafthead he wondered what progress was being made in the desperate gamble Paget had undertaken. He had to stay where he was despite the need he felt to be down there, helping. Paget would be able to do anything that needed doing and had promised to send a message as soon as there was anything to report.

He walked back and forth, trying to visualise the scene. How long he spent hoping so he had no idea, but a shout roused him from his thoughts. Looking toward the old mine there seemed to be an increase in the number of lights and he was sure that the shouts were in fact cheers. He hurried back to the office and pausing only to knock and receive the invitation to enter, he faced a much tidier and fresher looking Gwendoline.

'Something has happened my lady. I'm sure I heard cheering and there seems to be many more lights. With your permission I will go and see what is happening down there.'

'Very good Robert, but hurry back. Make sure you bring back a couple of lanterns. I have no wish to greet my workers looking like a mud spattered scarecrow a second time.'

He hurried away and she waited as patiently as she knew how. That something had happened was obvious. She could hear the cheers that rang out every now and then. Paget had succeeded of this she felt sure. Oh hurry Robert!

At last she heard the sound of hurrying feet and a breathless Robert came running toward her, waving his hat.

'They've got them my lady. Twelve of them. All alive.'

'Oh Robert I'm so pleased. Are any of them injured?'

'Only one my lady. A broken leg. There's another, Dai Williams the face boss. He's unconscious but doesn't seem hurt. One of the men said he fell and hit his head.'

'Did you bring the lanterns Robert?'

'One of the men is bringing four along my lady. I thought we'd better have some spares in case the doctor needs them. I told them to pass a message to Paget that you'd sent for the doctor my lady and that you would go down there as soon as the doctor arrived.'

'I noticed that the basket of food is still in the office Robert. I think it would be a good idea to take it with us to the mine. I expect those poor men are starving and I don't suppose there's a bite to eat there.'

Once again Robert was taken aback at the way this young aristocratic highborn lady cut through to the essentials. Of course they would be hungry, having been without food for nearly thirty six hours or so. Nobody else seemed to have given a thought to the matter, being much too tied up wondering how they were to get them out of the trap.

There was the sound of footsteps and a miner came into sight carrying the lanterns.

'Shall I be lighting them sir?'

'No. Leave them on the desk in the office. Is there any more news?'

'They be all brought out sir 'cept the one with the bad leg and the faceboss. They be bringing them out in tubs. Mr. Paget is still inside with 'Lias Pritchard.'

Just then there was the welcome sound of carriage wheels and they were able to make out the lights of the coach as it drew to a halt some distance away.

Robert made his way to the carriage to greet the doctor then led him back to the office where Gwendoline was waiting. She tendered her apologies for having had to call him out at such an hour but she was sure that when the situation was explained to him, he would understand the need. She then related what had happened and went on to tell him that it would not be necessary for him to enter the old mine. But in view of the exhausted state in which he would probably find the men, she hoped he would agree to go to the mine entrance with her and carry out his examinations there. One of the men had a broken leg and possible other injuries, while another was unconscious, have suffered a blow falling. If he was ready, they could make their way to the scene immediately. All this was uttered in a business like tone that made it plain to the doctor that, no matter what his private feelings may have been at being dragged from his bed in the middle of the night, she wanted him to commence ministering to his unfortunate patients without any further ado. Stopping only to take some food from the basket and placing it with the bottle of brandy on one side, she and Robert gathered up the basket and bottles of ale. After lighting the lanterns, the three of them led by the miner, made their way back to the mine. On arrival, the doctor quickly examined the wet and tired out but uninjured men, and having declared them fit, left them to the care of their comrades while he waited for the arrival of the other two. At this point, Gwendoline instructed Robert to issue the food and drink to the men who sat around still in their wet clothes in a state of shock. When it became evident what was being done for their benefit, a cheer broke out from those gathered around and one of the rescued even went so far as to shout. 'The good Lord bless you Ma'am', before falling upon the lump of cheese and fresh bread that Robert had handed him, like someone in the last stages of starvation. It was a good twenty minutes or more before another cheer announced the arrival of the tubs carrying the injured men. Once willing hands had laid Sam Jones on the ground, the doctor, watched by a crowd who gathered around him holding lanterns and candles, began his examination. Despite the care with which the doctor handled the injured limb, there was no doubt that he was in a great deal of pain and he moaned continually. At last, the doctor taking a large scissors from his bag, sliced through the material of the trouser leg revealing a mass of torn flesh through which the splintered end of a bone protruded. The torn flesh was badly discoloured and the doctor's nose wrinkled as he bent to look at it. It was an injury that already had suffered from being unattended for too long, and, having been immersed in the dirty water in which they had been trapped he had little doubt that the only way to treat the injury was to amputate the leg, and as soon as possible. After questioning the man as to whether he had any other pains, the doctor bound the man's two legs together and tied a rough splint to hold the injured limb steady. Leaving the injured man, the doctor joined Gwendoline and Robert.

'The leg is badly broken and the flesh is beginning to putrefy. It will have to be amputated if he's to have any chance, and the quicker the better.'

'Could you do it doctor?'

'Yes my lady, but we'll have to get him to my surgery as soon as possible.'

'Robert. If we can get him up to the office, he could go in the coach when the doctor leaves. We need a stretcher.'

'I'll get one my lady.'

She turned to the doctor,

'Robert will arrange to carry the man up to the coach doctor while you examine the other one.'

Within a few minutes, the stretcher arrived and slightly more comfortable but still groaning occasionally, Sam Jones had begun his journey, first to the office, then the surgery.

While a team of six men carried their injured comrade away, the doctor was busy examining the unconscious Dai Williams. After five minutes feeling various parts of the inert body seeking injuries, the doctor had transferred his attention to Williams's head. He was seeking a reason for the man's continuing state of unconsciousness, but was having no luck. The only visible mark was a swelling along the jawline. The skin was grazed but there was no sign of any blood. The only explanation the doctor could think of was that when he had fallen, his face had come in contact with one of the wooden posts; it was something falling on his head that had caused him to trip and hit his face? It was of no great consequence unless the skull was fractured, but feeling gently with his fingers, he could detect no sign that indicated this. Heaving a sigh, he climbed to his feet, then spoke to Gwendoline.

'Quite frankly my lady, I don't know what to make of this man's unconscious state. There doesn't appear to be any serious injury. He has a lump on his head which I assume was the cause of his fall, and a graze on his jaw where he must have hit one of the wooden posts as he fell. Apart from that I can find nothing else wrong. I suggest that he too be stretchered to the coach. He can stay at the surgery until he regains consciousness, then I will send him home.'

Now that all the miners had been examined, there was nothing else to keep Gwendoline or Robert at the colliery, but at her suggestion, the doctor with his two patients was given the use of the coach and they settled down to await the return of Jenkins. They were joined by Paget, who had delayed his return in order to make sure that the tunnel was as safe as could be, until such a time as he could institute full repairs. He had already decided that the new short tunnel they had driven to the existing coal face in the NantGwrhay, could prove to be valuable. It would provide another entrance and exit to the face and an alternate roadway in and out until such time as the blocked tunnel in NantGwrhay had been repaired. He was obviously very wet and tired after the part he had played in saving the men and sank on to a chair. Gwendoline placed the food and drink she had saved on the desk and told him to eat it. Any discussion could wait she said until he had eaten. Paget rose to his feet and went outside from where they could hear the sound of water being splashed about. He returned drying his hands and face on a large neckerchief, then sat down and attacked the food. Satisfied at last he asked that he be allowed to smoke and having received Gwendoline's assent, settled back in his chair and having charged and lit his clay pipe, puffed away in contentment. He described what had taken place and how the rescue had seemed threatened when the water had come in. He related how he had found Williams propped up out of harm's way, and the curious fact that there seemed to be only a very few timber posts in the part of the face that had been the scene of the rescue. When Gwendoline suggested that perhaps the explosion had blown away the others, Robert and Paget exchanged glances but said nothing, Both had suspicions but it was not the time to talk about them. At last the sound of the coach's wheels was heard and they took their leave after Gwendoline had extracted a promise from Paget that he would come to Woodfield to dinner one week from today. They had much to talk about and he no doubt would want to have effected the clearance of the blockage at NantGwrhay before turning his mind to social affairs. Though, as she said with a twinkle in her eye, 'she was sure that he would appreciate eating a meal in surroundings a little more congenial than a colliery office.'

When they climbed into the coach, Jenkins told them that Williams had regained consciousness. After helping to carry the injured man into the doctor's surgery, Williams had been sent home. When he had left, the doctor had been busy making preparations to deal with Sam Jones's injury.

CHAPTER 28

There were repercussions to the explosion and the rescue which followed. Sad to say, three days later, when Gwendoline sent Jenkins to enquire of the doctor regarding Sam Jones's injuries, the coachman returned with the news that the unfortunate man had not survived the amputation of his leg. The doctor was of the opinion that the wound had putrefied and poisoned him, and after being transferred to his cottage in Blackwood had died. As far as Williams was concerned, he had professed to feeling no ill effects of the blows he had suffered, although he seemed vague as to how he had received them, and the doctor had sent him home. He had heard nothing since so presumed he was well.

Sam's death caused Gwendoline considerable upset and she sent for Robert. It was her intention, she stated, to visit the dead man's home and console his widow and family. No doubt Robert agreed that in the circumstances, she would be in order to offer the family compensation for the loss of their breadwinner?

Robert, remembering the way his family had been treated after the death of his father in the selfsame colliery, could hardly believe his ears. Then as he thought about the differing circumstances he began to realise what had caused his mistress to consider such an action. She was, in addition to being the overall manager of the colliery combine, a woman, a caring woman. Should he agree that her action was right, there would be strong opposition from the three managers under her as well as from the Board. Once the story had become common knowledge in the district, there would be uproar amongst the other colliery owners. Compensation indeed! They were lucky to have jobs! Other owners would claim she would be setting an example that would have serious repercussions. Every miner who suffered any sort of injury that would keep him home from work for a day or so, would be claiming compensation as a right. Despite her kindness, she must be dissuaded from such a course. It would be seen as a typical example of the sort of thing that happened when a woman became involved in business. So ran Robert's thoughts. How best to answer her question?

'By all means send a letter of condolence my lady. I will deliver it and read it to Sam Jones's family. It is not likely his widow can read. I would advise against publicly giving them any compensation though my lady. It is a most praiseworthy thought but have you considered the consequences of such an act?'

He then went on to recount what he considered would be the reactions, not only of the local owners and managers, as well as the miners themselves, but also of the Board and her father Sir Henry. Would not such an act be seen as a weakness, a womanly weaknesss? No doubt Sam Jones had money due to him for the period he had worked before the explosion. It would be possible for the payment of such money, to be made through the financial controller's office instead of through the usual channels. He himself could deliver it with my lady's letter. If a sum equal to a normal full week's wages were paid, it was unlikely that anyone would ever discover that something more than was due had been paid.

'Thank you Robert. You are a good servant, both to me and to the Board. I see there are things I still have to learn. I agree with what you have said, but as I feel a responsibility, would I be thought odd if I attended the poor man's burial?'

'I am sure the family would appreciate such an act my lady. I will enquire as to when the burial is to take place. I expect it will be tomorrow as these things are not long delayed.'

His subsequent enquiry of the parson confirmed his statement. Sam Jones was to be buried the next day at eleven o'clock and after they had talked it over, Gwendoline decided that they would both attend the burial and she would speak to Mrs. Jones rather than send a letter. Robert would take her the money as an official payment of wages due so that there would be no public awareness of their gesture.

To Robert, the scene at the little churchyard was almost identical to that which had taken place when his father had been laid to rest; but to Gwendoline it was the first time she had ever been present at a burial. When she and Robert descended from the carriage at the little gates of the churchyard, the parson was waiting. Telling Jenkins to return to Woodfield as she intended walking back, they greeted the parson. Apart from a visit to welcome them to Woodfield after the honeymoon, and a further visit to offer his sympathy when Marcus had died, the parson had not had any contact with Gwendoline. In the course of the talks he and Robert had on the occasions when Robert had been able to attend service, he had learned of the decision which had resulted in this young aristocrat becoming the overall controller of the collieries. He had been taken aback as everyone else at such an occurence, but had learned from various sources that she was now much respected as an astute and hardheaded business woman. When Robert had enquired about the burial and his mistress's wish to attend, he had expressed surprise to Robert. It was an uncommon experience for the colliery owner to be present when one of his workmen fell victim to the conditions that existed in the mines that abounded in the district. He now looked at her with renewed interest. When he had first seen her, she had given the impression of a typical young highborn lady who had little interest in anything other than her own enjoyment and comfort. She was indeed still a beautiful woman, if somewhat severe looking, but the loss of her husband in such a short time and the subsequent taking up of the duties she now performed had given her, a dignity and authority that belied her years. He was well aware that she was even now only a very young woman and he wondered if during the years to come she would become embittered as a result of the blow that fate had dealt her, or would fate be kind and let her find happiness once more with some fortunate man?

Gwendoline had been looking at the little chapel with some interest. She knew that it was quite old and when she had first arrived at Woodfield, it had been in a state of some disrepair. Mr. Moggridge had told her that it was being renovated but she had not been particularly interested in the events taking place in those bygone days. Now however it had the appearance of having been extensively repaired and she remarked upon this to the parson.

'Not so much repaired my lady as rebuilt. It was finished in Eighteen Twenty Nine, the year Mr. Moggridge went away.

It had become so dilapidated that it was in danger of falling about our ears. The old building was erected in Sixteen Ninety Four, although there has been a chapel here since Sixteen Forty. In those days, they used to worship in the houses of the church members, because it was forbidden by Parliament, but after Cromwell's time they had their first church here. It was the second Independent church to be built in Monmouthshire.'

He paused, then spoke again.

'I beg your pardon my lady. I tend to run on when I get on the subject of our church.'

'I would appreciate it parson if you would allow me to look at your new church sometime.'

'It would be a pleasure my lady.'

Looking down the hill he spoke again,

'Perhaps you and master Robert would like to wait inside the church my lady? I see the burial party are approaching. I will come and conduct you to the graveside when they arrive.'

Gwendoline turned and before accompanying Robert had just time to see the approaching farm cart bearing the rough wooden coffin. Behind it, bent forward as if the slope of the hill was exhausting them, a small group trudged. As they walked along the flagstoned pathway to the church, she thought of the splendid coffin that had borne Marcus away. Of an elegant wood, with solid brass handles, its corners chamfered, the lid carved with the family crest and his name engraved into the brass plate. Magnificent black horses, beplumed had drawn the hearse. How different to the heavy carthorse that even now was digging its large steel shod feet into the ground, as it leaned into the big collar round its massive neck, and took the strain as it climbed the last hundred yards up the hill. No tophatted coachman this time, just the farmhand, one hand holding the reins, a stubby pipe clenched in his teeth as he urged his horse upward. Entering the cool dim building, they sat in one of the long shining hard wooden seats. Robert in a lowered voice, pointed out the various features of the building then lapsed into silence. They sat there for about ten minutes, not speaking, until the creaking of the door announced the arrival of the parson. He held the door open for them, then led the way down the slope to the foot of the churchyard. There a mound of newly dug earth to one side of a gaping hole, proclaimed the last resting place of Samuel Jones. His family, six in number, together with the same two gravediggers who had prepared Evan Morgan's grave, were gathered about the hole. His widow, surrounded by her five children, wept quietly, her head bowed. The children varying in ages from about six to twelve, overcome by the solemnity of the occasion, stood with heads bowed until they heard the footsteps of the little party approaching. Curiosity overcame them and all heads tilted to one side to inspect the newcomers, then once more they stared at the coffin resting on the wooden planks above the hole.

The parson took his place at one end of the grave with Gwendoline and Robert facing him, the family ranged along one side while the gravediggers, their shovels at their feet, stood one on either side, ready to remove the planks and lower the coffin into its final resting place, by means of the thick ropes already in position.

Glancing around the little group, the parson opened his bible and began to intone the service for the dead. Since it all was in Welsh, Gwendoline had no means of knowing what was being said, although the word which sounded something like 'yissy', seemed familiar and she assumed it was a reference to Jesus. At last, Robert and the family all uttered an Amen and she hastened to follow their example. To the sound of increased sobbing from the widow the coffin was lowered slowly into the grave. When it came to rest each child cast a handful of dirt on to its surface and retreated to stand grouped around their mother. As if unsure what to do next, the little group stood looking into the grave until the parson moved to join them. He spoke quietly to the widow and resting his hand on the smallest child's head, ruffled her hair as she clutched at her mother's skirt and moved to stand tightly pressed against her legs. The gravediggers, as if anxious to break up the silent immobile group, picked up their tools and watched intently by the children, proceed to shovel the damp earth into the hole. At last, as if shooing away a flock of hens, their mother, spreading her arms, moved up the slope, herding them before her. The parson waited until Gwendoline and Robert left the graveside and then followed them. At the top of the churchyard, the family had gathered by the church gate as if loath to leave. Gwendoline, hesitant, moved closer to the group and perhaps sensing this, the parson spoke in Welsh to the widow. She in turn said something to the eldest, a boy, and the children went through the gate out on to the track. Already, the solemnity of the occasion was receding from the minds of the youngest and first one, then another, bent down and picked up stones which they flung at the trees nearby. As the missiles rattled against the branches, two or three large and very black crows, uttered angry sounding caws and took wing. Their mother turned and shouted at them in Welsh then turning back to the parson and Gwendoline, she bobbed a curtsey.

Gwendoline not quite knowing what to do, reached out and took the woman's hand. As if the touch of another woman had unlocked her grief, they came together, and with Gwendoline's arms about her, she cried bitterly, her face pressed against the girl's shoulder. Feeling they were intruding on something they didn't fully understand, both Robert and the parson moved away, their backs to the couple.

After a while, the widow drew back and wiped her eyes, 'I'm sorry my lady. I didn't ought to 'ave done that.'
'Don't worry about it Mrs. Jones.'
The widow obviously wanted to say more, but seemed unable to. Gwendoline took the opportunity to express her sympathy for her and her family, saying how sorry she was that, having being present when Mr. Jones had been rescued from the mine, she had learned of his death.
'My Sam. He told me 'ow you and mister Robert, come to bring food when they brought him out. He didn't blame you nor mister Paget. He said 'tweren't no fault of nobody.' Her voice dropped and she seemed afraid to utter the words, "cept Dai Williams.' She started to weep once more and Gwendoline stood holding her hand.
'What will you do now Mrs. Jones?'
'I doan' kno' my lady. I got a brother got a farm outside Ma-

chynlleth. P'haps we'll go there. Yorrie, thass my oldest boy do work in the Islwyn, but his money do not be a lot. We managed when Sam was in work but....'

Her voice trailed off and she fell silent.

'Have you any money?'

'I 'ad to spend most it for food my lady, and then the coffin maker wanted paying so there's only the rent money left. Yorrie'll be paid in a couple of days so us'll manage somehow 'til then.'

Not knowing what else to say to comfort the woman, Gwendoline turned to Robert. Seeing her discomfort in the unusual role she had cast for herself, Robert stepped forward, slipped a package into the widow's hand, whispered something in Welsh, then spoke,

'I think we should be leaving now my lady.'

'Very well Robert. Good day parson. Goodbye Mrs. Jones, I hope things improve.'

They passed from the churchyard and walked slowly down the hill, passing the children. Having been admonished by their mother, they had stopped throwing stones and instead had taken to playing some sort of game that involved chasing each other. Having caught their prey, the chasers immediately shouted out some words in Welsh which seemed to cause them great merriment as they were all shrieking with laughter. They stopped as Gwendoline and Robert passed and Yorrie as his mother called to him, took off his cap. They had only gone a few yards more, when Gwendoline, who had been fiercely berating herself for not having been able to utter some appropriate words of comfort, stopped.

'Robert. Do you have any money?'

'Some my lady.'

'Give the oldest boy something suitable. A half guinea if you have one. God knows they'll have need of it now.'

'My lady...'

'Robert do as I say please. I feel bad enough as it is not being able to comfort that poor woman. Perhaps it will help ease my conscience to know that I've given them the one thing they need most. Apart from a father and a husband. Hurry now before their mother comes.'

Robert turned back and took some coins from the purse he carried. He spoke to Yorrie and Gwendoline saw him hand over something. The boy looked at what he had been given and said something, then turned toward Gwendoline and in a gesture that was both dignified and almost comical, he bowed before leaving his brothers and sisters and climbing back up the track to where his mother was taking leave of the parson.

Not wanting to become involved in any more emotional scenes, Gwendoline walked quickly down the track followed by a bemused Robert who hurried to catch her and offer his arm over the rough ground. As he carefully guided her over the stony track he looked at her from the corner of his eye. What an amazing creature his lady was. Apparently a hard business woman who could hold her own in the difficult world of mining, yet a shy girl, fearful of being thought too caring. A lady who had taken someone of much lower station in life in her arms and held her, comforting her. A woman who herself had lost a husband, but who, because of her up-bringing had been annoyed with herself for not being able to say the words to convey her feelings of sympathy to someone else who had now suffered the same misfortune. He shook his head. Would he ever understand her?

The walk back had taken toll of Gwendoline and when they at last turned into the back drive, she breathed a sigh of relief. The day was quite warm and she was conscious of a beading of perspiration on her upper lip. Turning her head away from Robert she dabbed gently with her handkerchief. It would not do for a lady to be seen to be feeling the heat. It was all right for a man. One expected them to sweat and no-body said anything. The soles of her shoes had not been much protection against the roughness of the track and well before they had reached the lodge, she was regretting her decision to dismiss the carriage. As they slowly walked along her thoughts roamed idly.

'Thank goodness for the soft grass in the middle of the drive. When I get in I'm going to have a long cold drink and spend an hour or so on the bed with my stays loosened. My God!

What we women go through just to appear fashionable. How I shall miss little Eirwen at a time like this. Little indeed. She'll soon be married and not yet as old as I was when I married. Probably have a houseful of children by the time she's twenty five. Maybe if Marcus and I hadn't both been so selfish I'd be a plump matron with three or four sons and daughters instead of managing papa's mines. What must Robert think of me? He's a man even if he is only one of the servants. He's intelligent and must have some thoughts about women and marriage. Wonder what he'd say if I asked him if he thought it was right for me to be in business instead of being married and having a child every year?'

She glanced at him as he walked by her side. He had taken off his hat and was wiping the inside. Evidently he too was feeling the heat. Suddenly she remembered the night she had stumbled and he had saved her from falling by putting his arm about her. She felt herself flush. 'It was like having an iron band to rely on, but how gentle it had been. How strong he must be. Of course he worked cutting coal and that would have given him his muscular arms.' She flushed again as a mental picture of him stripped to the waist, his body gleaming with sweat as he plied his pick, came into her mind. Years ago if she had thought such thoughts she would have considered them unmaidenly, and she would have willed herself to dismiss them. But having been married and seen Marcus, a woman couldn't be expected to act like a shallow girl, could she? Besides, Robert is only a servant.'

As she had promised herself, Gwendoline retired to the bedroom, and after Dilys had brought her a cold drink and helped loosen the strings of her corset, she lay on the bed. She drifted off to sleep and into a dream where the bizarre events that took place seemed perfectly normal. That she should be walking along the drive, not only barefooted but clad only in skirt and camisole, her feet sore, and her corset cutting into her, seemed a natural thing to do on a warm day. When a man carrying a huge bible had opened it and pointing his finger at her mouthed some gibberish, that too was normal. As she continued along the drive she found herself dancing to a song sung by some children who all bowed to her, then ran away shrieking as the figure of a man naked to the waist, wearing a large hat, suddenly appeared. As he hurried to catch her, no matter how she tried, her legs seemed unable to go any faster as she tried to run from some unknown danger he represented. The strings of her corset became untied and hung down just beyond the reach of her pursuer's reaching hand. Suddenly she was indoors, running from room to room. Each room had a door that she had to shut just as the hand was about to grasp the strings. In and out of innumerable rooms, along passages that seemed endless. All the time, his footsteps grew nearer. A terrified glance over her shoulder showed his body glistening with sweat that ran down his chest and fell to the floor. At last she ran into the kitchen, and out into the courtyard. As she cleared the doorway, she felt the strings wind around her ankles and she tumbled forward. The dark opening of a grave-like hole in the flagstones gaped at her feet, the glitter of water in its depths clearly visible to her eyes, when suddenly an arm encircled her waist pulling her back against the hard muscular body of her captor. As she closed her eyes in despair, the crushing pressure of his lips on hers, brought a sense of delight that shook her very being. She opened her eyes and beheld Dilys's hand gently shaking her shoulder.

"Tis nearly noon, my lady. Are you alright my lady?'

'Thank you Dilys. I was having a dream but I'm fine now.'

She sat up in bed, conscious of the emotion that still gripped her. She felt breathless as if she had truly run for her life. The events were still vivid in her mind and her heart hammered in a way it had not since the first night she and Marcus had .... She smiled a secret smile as she recalled the feel of the arm about her and the bruising, hunger of his lips on her mouth. One thing eluded her. His features had been shaded by that ridiculous hat he wore and no matter how she tried, she could recall no detail of his features.

CHAPTER 29

In the office the next day, Gwendoline enquired if Robert knew the identity of a man called Dai Williams. Apparently this man was responsible in some way for the death of poor Sam Jones. Mrs. Jones had told her that her late husband had laid the blame for his injuries on this man. Who was he? He reminded her of the other man who had been brought out from the mine, unconscious, having suffered a blow on the head.

'But surely, he was injured himself.'

'Yes my lady, but not badly. Somebody said he probably hit his head when he fell. He's the face boss.'

No more was said of the matter, but Robert determined to bring up the subject with Paget. Why should Sam Jones blame Williams when it was the explosion that had caused the cave in?

The problem of the cave in and subsequent rescue was foremost in Paget's mind. The barrier which had blocked off the face from the main tunnel had finally been cleared and soon he hoped it would be possible once more to start cutting coal. The flooding in there had not increased and the pump was quite capable of keeping it down to manageable proportions. The men didn't seem to mind as long as it didn't interfere with the way they cut the coal. He would have to make sure there were plenty of posts to shore up the roof. As this last thought struck him, he stopped as if a bright light had shone into a dark corner of his mind. Of course! The posts. Or rather the scarcity of them in the coalface. That's what he had been struck by during the rescue. There hadn't been enough there! Despite the explosion, there should have been enough of the remains left to show where they had been erected. He had not been able to see more than four or five. Shattered and splintered though they were, they still indicated their position. Whoever was responsible for erecting the posts had not been doing his job. No wonder the roof had collapsed along almost the whole face. It was a wonder it hadn't come down of its own accord. He took from a drawer his report on the explosion and the ensuing investigation he had undertaken. A search revealed the names of the dozen men who they had been able to rescue. He would see them all and question them. Except for poor old Sam Jones, they were all back at work but whether they would want to return to that face when it was reopened was something only time would tell.

Robert sat in the office reading Paget's report on the state of the now cleared face. A lot of work had gone into bringing it back to a safe condition and he anticipated the first tubs of coal to start coming from it in the next day or so. Paget stated however that he was still carrying out investigations into the cause of the cave in. He would make a further report when he had completed them. Robert stared at this last sentence. It reminded him of something but he could not think what it was. Never mind it would come to him. In the meantime he would need to visit the colliery and see for himself how things were. Lady Gwendoline had changed once more from the caring employer who had attended the burial of Sam Jones, to the business woman worried by the fall in output, who wanted to be able to report to the Board that once again, the colliery combine was exceeding its output target. So it came about that two days later, he sat opposite Paget in the colliery office. On the desk before him lay the report Robert had just finished reading.

'You are saying that despite the explosion, the new face would not have collapsed had the right amount of timbering been done?'

'Yes. I'm convinced that if the men had carried out their orders, we would not have had to dig them out. The explosion's blast would have certainly caused some damage, but with the roof being so badly supported, the whole lot was bound to collapse from the shock waves through the workings.'

'You questioned the men and the faceboss Williams?'

'Aye and all the men tell the same story. They put up all the posts that they were allowed to. Each and everyone of them says Williams wouldn't give them time to do the work. He reckoned it was more important to keep the coal coming out and if they didn't like it, they knew what they could do.

Called them a load of old biddys, afraid of a bit of coal hitting them on the head. Also said he didn't intend losing his job because they couldn't keep up. Well, he's going to lose it now. I'm sacking him.'

Robert spoke as if to himself.

'Of course! That's what Sam meant.'

He recounted what Mrs. Jones had said about Sam blaming the faceboss for being responsible for his injuries.

'Sam was right. There's something else I didn't put in the report that helped me make up my mind about getting rid of him. I've suspected for a long time that the man's a natural bully and that some of the men under him were afraid of him. Well someone, was determined that if they were going to die when they were trapped in that hole, he going to make sure Dai Williams was not going to be alive if and when we got to them. Ten men all told me that, when they realised they would have to wait to be rescued, it was decided that they would pool the food they had and ration it out. Sam Jones being injured couldn't do anything so they gave him the job of keeping it and doleing it out. Apparently the pain must have made him lose consciousness at one time, and when he recovered somebody had taken a good half of it. Since it was almost pitch black in there as they had hardly any candles left, anybody could have done it. Anyway whether Sam must have had some suspicions or just hated Williams, he accused him of stealing the food. They made Williams turn out his pockets but found nothing. You can imagine what it must have been like in there. One of them was a thief, so it was decided to split up the remaining food. Sam was in a bad way and kept passing out. They only had one candle and a bit left so they decided to save them. Sitting there in the dark they heard Sam yell out, and they reckon he must have come to and with his mind confused and thinking he heard somebody moving near him, lashed out with the lump of wood he was using to help him move. When they got the candle alight there was Williams lying with his head broken. We shall never know the truth but they all say Williams who was left on his own after he had been accused had no reason to be moving about. Maybe somebody knowing where Williams was sitting took advantage of the dark and hit him. In the confusion he could have pushed Williams towards Sam. Who knows? Maybe Sam hit him with a lucky blow in the dark. Anyway. I'm not having a faceboss working in any colliery I manage who doesn't obey orders, and one who might meet with a fatal accident brought about by his methods.'

'Have you told Williams yet?'

'Yes. I sacked him yesterday. He blustered and said he had only tried to keep up with the demands for higher output. Accused the men of wasting time when they were putting up the roof supports and that they needed driving all the time. I pointed out I couldn't be responsible for the safety of a man who the next time he was carried out in a tub, unconscious, might be suffering from having a broken neck, brought about by getting in the way of a pick handle. When he left he was muttering all sorts of threats but he doesn't frighten me.'

'Good riddance I say. But keep your wits about you if you meet him and any of his cronies.'

'Don't worry, I've dealt with his sort before.'

He opened a drawer in the desk and took out a small pistol. 'I always carry this with me after dark. By the way, I've put Elias in his place. He deserves some reward for the work he did in getting through to those trapped men.'

'Good. I'll take this report back with me and let my lady see it. I won't mention what you told me. Before I leave, my lady asked me to remind you that she is expecting you to dinner tomorrow evening. There will only be the three of us. Seven thirty.'

Whatever had been said between Gwendoline and Eirwen when his sister had expressed a wish to finish as her personal maid, had not been disclosed to Robert. The relationship between mistress and maid however continued as before and it was some months before Eirwen finally began to make preparations to marry her suitor. As head of the family, Robert would be giving her away and one of the bridegroom's brothers was to be the best man. Gwendoline as befitted her position declared she intended to be matron of honour and that the wedding breakfast and celebrations were to be held at

Woodfield Park.

The wedding took place on a beautiful July morning. The house had not echoed with such laughter and gaiety for years. Eirwen's hair, shining and holding several small flowers, framed a face that made Gwendoline remember her own happiness on her wedding day. She uttered a silent prayer that life for the girl, who had come to her as a bewildered little 13 year old maid, would be happy. Her wedding dress was of sprigged muslin and for the ceremony, she wore a large shady hat. Around her neck, she wore one of the two pieces of jewellery she possessed. Gwendoline had given her a chain and locket that Eirwen had seen many times in the jewellery box that usually lay on the dressing table. Robert's gift was a bracelet that he had purchased on a rare visit to Blackwood. Her husband to be, William, was a large fresh faced young man with a mop of flaxen curls that no amount of water could subdue. His eyes, when they alighted on his bride as Robert escorted her down the aisle, showed how much in love he was.

When they returned to Woodfield in the open carriage bedecked with garlands and driven by Jenkins, resplendent in a scarlet coat and cocked hat, he had driven them to the main gate thence through the park. The whole household, together with William's parents, and several equally large brothers and solitary sister, waited to greet them when they alighted. The wedding breakfast had been laid on the lawn. Chairs had been carried from the house and the huge table which normally stood in the kitchen had been placed end to end with the magnificent dining room table. Mrs. Watkins had ransacked her cupboards for linen, and the damask table cloths, decorated with embroidery so painstakingly worked by some unknown needle women, gleamed snowy white in the brilliant sunshine. Seated at the smaller headtable, the bride and groom, supported on either side by Gwendoline, Robert and Dafydd, and William's parents, laughed and blushed as the festivities got under way. Two large barrels of ale stood on trestles and jugs containing the golden liquid were carried to and from the tables to be filled in rapid succession, as the sun beat down on the happy scene. Unused to drinking the rough brew, Gwendoline had arranged for several bottles of claret and other wines from the cellar, to be placed within reach of those sitting alongside the couple. However, after a solitary sip or two, when drinking the various toasts to the bride and groom, William's father, a larger edition of his newly married son, touched his forehead, leaned across the bride and groom and begging her ladyship's pardon, asked if he could be excused from drinking the wine as he was not used to it and feared the effect it might have on him. Hiding a smile, Gwendoline assured him that she understood his dilemma and replied that she drank wine because she feared the effects of ale. Taking her words as a general dispensation, everybody apart from herself and Robert, immediately demanded that they be supplied with tankards of ale. The wealth of food that had awaited the onslaught of young healthy appetites sharpened by hard outdoor labour, diminished rapidly and when it appeared that everyone was satisfied, by common consent, and to the accompaniment of the fiddler specially hired for the occasion, led by Eirwen and William, everybody joined in the dancing. The sun had moved across the sky and it had become considerably warmer. Several of William's brothers had divested themselves of their coats and as the jollity increased, could be seen to be mopping their brows and paying more frequent visits to the barrels to have their tankards replenished. Assuring the happy couple that it was because of the heat, Gwendoline who suspected that if she was absent, the company would enjoy themselves even more, begged to be excused and retreated indoors. She insisted that Robert should not accompany her to the house but remain to enjoy the festivity. Indoors she went to her bedroom and loosening her clothing sat in a woven basket chair near the window. From her vantage point she was able to see the wedding party and could plainly hear the shouts and laughter. How different her wedding had been. Solemn words spoken by the Bishop in the huge church her family attended. Her parents and friends, aligned along one side of the church, with Marcus's family, friends, and retainers, filling the seats opposite. It had been like the coming together of two small armies, each side displaying the loyalty they felt to the family of bride or groom. In the little chapel, there had been none of that. Friends, guests and fellow workers, had all been mixed up higgledy piggledy, there to share in the enjoyment of watching two young people joined together to start out on the long hard road of married life. She remained seated there, musing on what might have been, idly watching the scene below. When the fiddler tired and begged to be allowed to rest awhile, they sat down in groups or couples talking and laughing. Robert had also divested himself of his coat but had retained his colourful waistcoat and cravat. He had danced and laughed with the rest of them, but now sat in serious discussion with William's parents. She wondered what they talked about. The price of cattle at the market? The increasing unrest as the supporters of the Chartist movement waxed louder and louder in their demands? One or two couples lay under the trees in close proximity to each other, in some cases the girl's head rested on her swain's shoulder. Other couples strolled amongst the trees, enjoying the shade cast by the mighty oak and elm trees. Already she surmised, other romances could well be blossoming down there amongst those couples. What of Robert? Was there any one down there who might have caught his eye? She searched amongst the crowd. He had moved away from the table and was walking alone in the direction of the main lodge. She watched as he strode along. How tall he was. Not as tall as William, but his carriage was more graceful. He appeared slim but she knew that despite the hours he spent sitting at his desk, his body was hard and muscular. Had she not felt it when she had tumbled upon him that night on the way to the old mine? Dressed as he was today, at this distance he could well be mistaken for one of the gentry out for a walk in the park. All he needed was a silver topped cane. She became aware of the way her thoughts were leading. Of course there was more to being a gentleman than dress. Courtly manners, the way to address a lady and pay compliments, social chitchat. All these things he lacked. Except manners. Those he had. Never had he been anything but a gentleman. Never had he crossed the line that separated them in any way. As for being amusing and paying her compliments, his life, from what Eirwen had inadvertently disclosed during the early days, had hardly been the sort that encouraged him to talk amusingly. As for paying her compliments, that could never be. He was a servant. Of course there was no denying that on that day so many years ago when she had first come to Woodfield on holiday, he had paid her the greatest compliment he could. She had never forgotten the look in his eyes as he had looked at her for the first time. It had amused her then and the prospect of having a lovesick servant at her beck and call had promised all sorts of fun. How she had planned to torment him and then tell all her friends about the way she had led the clodhopper a merry dance. Come to think of it, she hadn't. Oh she'd teased him a little, true, but wasn't it a woman's privilege to be able to make a man, any man, respond to the little wiles a woman practised?

Well he was no clodhopper now and she wondered whether he still retained that same devotion, or had he his eye on someone unknown to her?

While Gwendoline sat in her room musing, Robert walked alone along the drive thinking about his future. He was nearly twenty eight. Seeing his sister marrying William today, had brought home to him how life was passing him by. Oh he had a good job, a comfortable living, and her ladyship was a kind and thoughtful employer. That was the trouble. She was his employer. How true his mother's words had been when she had warned him to look elsewhere for his heart's desire. There never had nor never would be any chance that one day, Gwendoline would be his. He could still recall the feeling he had had when he had seen her for the first time. The way she had looked as she had stepped down from the carriage to greet Mr. Moggridge. Never had he seen a more beautiful picture. He had just been a servant to her then, someone to run and fetch, to obey her whims. He was just a servant now. His position had not changed, despite his responsibilities. Lying on his bed sometimes, unable to sleep, he indulged in fantasies. A favourite one was when he saved her from some danger that her stubborn nature had got her into. How he had berated her for risking her life that was so precious to him. She in turn would stamp her dainty foot and demand to know by what right, he a mere servant, dare talk to her in that tone. He would respond by taking her in his arms, slipping the big shady hat she wore from her head, and loosening her glorious hair from the knot she wore. As it cascaded over her shoulders, he would declare that servant or not, he was a man, who because he was in love with her had a right not to allow her to risk danger. She would gaze at him in wonder, her flashing eyes would soften, then his lips would meet her's in a kiss that both knew heralded the start of a life together.

Absorbed in reliving this fantasy, he had been unaware that he had left the wedding celebrations so far behind. He must return at once. Although his official duties were now over, he felt a responsibility to see that nothing untoward happened. They were all his friends, but with the amount of ale that had been drunk and the natural high spirits of the young, goodness knows what might come to pass if some sort of restraint was not placed upon the proceedings. His beloved would not be well pleased, should any damage befall any of the items that had been brought out from the house. At the thought of one of William's large brothers indulging in some horseplay and falling on to one of the fragile chairs, he turned about and hurried back.

CHAPTER 30

After the wedding of Eirwen and William, life at Woodfield settled down once more. Only one thing had caused Robert mild concern, but he had put it from his mind. William, had been drinking in one of the local taverns and had been told that Dai Williams who frequented that same place, had been heard uttering threats against both Paget and Robert, blaming them for his dismissal. Eirwen knowing of the hate that still festered between Williams and her brother, had warned Robert at the first opportunity. Robert had chosen to ignore the warning, putting it down to Williams's bluster. Things were going well at the colliery and the Board in London had had no reason to regret allowing Sir Henry to override their objections to his making a young inexperienced widow, the controller of a large combine. Output had once again soared after the repairs had been effected in the new face, and Paget in his inspections of the workings was satisfied that the prospect of another such collapse, was remote. He was however a man who was only too well aware of the danger of having naked lights in mines. Years ago, in 1815, Davy had invented a safety lamp, which it was said not only gave much better light to work in, but also blotted out the chance of explosion by the igniting of any fire-damp present in the workings. Despite the obvious advantages of the Davy lamp, mine owners were loth to spend money on equipment that showed no profit. Miners had worked with candles for years and were quite happy with them they said. Paget brought up the subject at various times in his talks with Sir Henry and later with Gwendoline, but had had no success in persuading them to purchase them. The main argument against them was their cost. Not only were they made of expensive metal, but had a wick that would need renewing or trimming all the time. There was the question of keeping the lamps fuelled, more expense. The Board could not afford to employ somebody to look after the lamps to keep them in working order, and the miners would certainly not agree to pay a charge for the use of these new wonder lamps. After the explosion, Paget thought it might be a good time to raise the question once more. He estimated what it would cost to purchase enough lamps for use in the new face and having also estimated what the explosion and consequent closure of the face had cost in output, placed the figures before Robert when he visited him in his office.

Robert studied the figures and although doubtful that the Board would pay any more attention than they had previously, agreed that it could do no harm to place them before Gwendoline. He tucked them into his coat pocket and bade Paget goodbye. Mounting his horse he left the pithead in the deepening twilight. He had gone about two miles when his horse began limping. Dismounting he peered at the offending foot and discovered that a stone had become lodged in the shoe. He struggled for a while before managing to remove the obstruction, but could see that there was no possiblity of riding the horse any further without some further attention. Holding the reins he began walking the remaining couple of miles to Woodfield. By the time he had reached Croespenmaen, it had become dark. Thankfully, a full moon was rising steadily in the starlight sky as he trudged on, but it was with relief that he spotted the lights of the Maypole Inn. He was aware of its rather unsavoury reputation as a haunt of Chartists, but had always found the landlord, a man named Henry Walters, civil enough on the few occasions he had frequented the place for refreshment. Tying up the horse, he opened the door and entered the gloomy interior. A potman, lighted taper in hand, turned as he heard the latch rise. He was in the act of lighting a collection of oil lamps hanging at various points about the room. He raised a forefinger to his eyebrow.

'Evening sir.'

'Evening. Give me a tankard of your best ale please. My horse has gone lame. Stone bruised its foot and I've had to walk from the Cherry Tree.'

'Where be you bound sir?' the man asked as he drew the liquid from one of the barrels and passed it to Robert.

'Woodfield.'

Robert took a deep draught then placed a coin on the bar. The potman took the coin and rummaging in a tin box gave him his change. Relighting the taper he continued lighting the lamps.

'Not busy this evening?' said Robert.

'Not in here 'sir. Landlord be busy in back room. There be some sort of meeting going on. Thirsty lot I must say, but it be good for trade.'

Robert wondered what sort of meeting would be held in such a place. He had heard various rumours about it but had not paid a lot of attention. There were meetings being held everywhere these days. The Chartists were forever ranting about the rights of the workers. There had been trouble in various parts of the country and even tales of an armed uprising in support of their aims. Well it was nothing to do with him. Thinking of the walk still before him, he lifted up his tankard and quaffed what was left of his drink. As he replaced it on the counter, the door leading to the back room opened and the landlord appeared followed by a file of men. Amongst them, conspicuous by his bulk, was Dai Williams. As Robert turned to let himself out, he heard Williams's voice across the room.

'What's the matter Morgan. Company not good enough for you? Take a good look lads. There be one of them what's stamping on the faces of the poor workers.'

Robert whirled about to face him. He could feel the hate he felt for this lout welling up in him,

'What would you know about work Williams? You haven't done any for years.'

'Listen to the high and mighty Mister Morgan lads. Got hisself a nice soft job squeezing me and my mates in the NantGwrhay. Him and that highborn doxy of his. Reckon he spends a lot of time squeezing her, but in a different way eh boys?'

Robert saw red at the mention of Gwendoline and hurled himself across the room at Williams.

Before he could lay hands on him, the others had grabbed him and held him fast.

Williams pushed his face close to Robert's.

'What say we show this jumped up collier boy how we workers be going to give the likes of him a taste of the way we be treated? Let's show him what we think of workers what turn on their mates.'

The landlord stepped between them and pushed Williams back.

'I don't want any trouble in here Williams. I could lose my license if there's any fighting on these premises.'

Williams looked at him for a moment then turned to the men holding Robert,

'Come on lads. Take him out on the Waun. We won't have nobody poking their noses in out there. There's plenty of light from the moon. The landlord don't seem to like the sight of a bit of blood.'

The men holding Robert's arms hustled him out through the door into the night, the others crowding after them. They were excited by the prospect of seeing a fight. Several of them were old cronies of the huge Williams and had seen him beat quite a few miners into bloody submission, or grasp them in huge muscled arms and crush their ribs until they screamed in agony. These men Morgan and Williams obviously hated each other and there was the prospect of a good mill before Williams beat him unconscious.

The full moon had risen and everywhere was lit by its radiance. The gang of men and their captive, struggling and kicking in desperation, moved away from the inn out on to the springy turf. All around the inn were beds of peat with one dangerous spot some thirty or forty yards distant. There the ground was boggy with some peat dyed water standing in pools, as if waiting for some unfortunate to stumble into their depths and vanish. Skirting the danger, they made their way at least a hundred yards into the darkness until Williams shouted.

'This be far enough. There won't be no nosey parkers coming out here. Right Mister Stuckup Morgan, let's see how you like this.'

As he finished speaking he swung a huge fist at Robert's body. The two men holding him staggered back, but still retained their hold on him. The strength and unexpectedness of the blow had knocked the wind from Robert and for a moment or two he hung in their arms, desperately trying to suck air into his lungs. As he straightened once more, Williams closed in and hammered at his jaw. Robert ducked his head but was not able to evade the blow and he distinctly felt the flesh rip as the man's knuckles tore into his left eyebrow. This second blow was enough to cause him to sag to his knees and his captors, sure that he had submitted, let go of his arms. As he lay on the turf, wiping at the blood streaming down his face, his opponent stepping forward, drew back his foot and drove his steel shod boot into his helpless victim's side. For one awful moment, Robert his head ringing, was sure that his ribs had caved in. The pain was like nothing he had ever felt before. Williams laughing, prepared to kick him again, when one of the men stepped between him and the prostrate figure of Robert, gasping for breath.

'That's enough Williams! We didn't come out here to see you murdering him by kicking him to death. You couldn't wait 'til he was free could you? Now if you're so anxious to beat him, you'll do it fairly. We'll give him five minutes to get his breath back, then if he can stand up and wants to fight, we won't interfere any more. Pick 'im up boys and walk 'im about a bit.'

Two of the men took Robert beneath his arms and lifted him. He hung there, then as they started to move, his legs began stumbling forward. Blood was still running from the cut eyebrow into his left eye and as his head hung forward, dripped on to his coat. His scattered wits began to function once more as he sucked the air into his body. Every time his chest expanded, he felt as if a knife was being driven into his ribs. He knew that if he was to escape from a beating that could leave him a cripple for life, somehow he would have to keep on his feet and out of Williams's reach until the strength came back into his aching body.

"Ow you feelin' mate?'

The question voiced by one of his companions took him by surprise. He had thought all those in the crowd were just toadies of the sacked faceboss, and it came as a surprise that perhaps there were one or two amongst them, that because of their belief in justice for all, were mixed up in what seemed to be a Chartist meeting. He turned his head toward the speaker and mumbled,

'I could do with a drink. I can hardly see out of my left eye.'
One of the men put his hand into his pocket and pulled forth
a bottle.

'Try some o' this.'

He held the bottle to Robert's lips. As the fiery liquid went
down his throat Robert gagged, then started to cough.
Brandy!

The man laughed,

'It's not only the bosses what likes a drop of the real stuff.'
He put the bottle back in his pocket.

'Can't do much about yer eye lad. D'yer think you can stand
up on yer own?'

They released him and he stood there swaying. Gradually
the world stopped spinning and he took a few more deep
breaths.

"ow about it. D'yer want to fight 'im? If he gets his arms
round yer, yer'll be a goner with them ribs o' yourn.'

Robert sucked in his breath and winced as the pain shot
through him,

'I'll fight him.'

'Come on then. If it's gonna be a proper mill with rounds and
rests after knock downs, I'll give yer a knee to sit on.'

They walked slowly back to the circle of men grouped around
Williams. The man who had intervened looked at Robert.

'Alright?'

Robert nodded his head then wished he hadn't.

'Right. We're gonna do this proper. Up to the mark. One that
can't get up to the mark after a knockdown will be counted
out to ten. No biting or gouging. No rests. Fight to a finish.
Get your coats off. Ready at the mark. Go'

As he said the last word, Robert whose coat and waistcoat
lay on the ground at the feet of his recent captor, stepped
back banking on Williams swinging his huge fist in a round-
house blow at his head. Sure enough, his opponent grunting
with the effort, let fly. Finding no resistance, his body followed, presenting Robert with an undefended target stretching from the hip to the top of his head. He swung his left fist
at the man's bull neck feeling the shock run through his arm

as the fist connected just below the jaw. Williams gagged as his breath was cut off, and for a moment stood gasping like a fish out of water. Taking advantage, Robert swung his other fist and had the satisfaction of landing it on Williams's right eye. With a snarl of rage Williams reached out to grasp him but, aware that to be caught would mean the end of him, Robert moved out of reach. Now that he was actually engaged in the fight, he was only vaguely conscious of the ache in his side. If he could keep hitting Williams about the eyes, eventually closing them, then he would have him at his mercy. To do that he would have to stay out of reach of those arms. The ground was springy beneath his feet and being so much lighter, he was able to move quickly around the ring that had been formed. Like a bull being baited by a quick snapping terrier, Williams slowly turned trying to get within reach of his more nimble opponent. Several times when he thought he had Robert in his grasp, he found there was nothing in front of him, then a fist would hammer into his face. Robert was aware that having suffered such vicious punishment before the fight proper, he could not expect to be able to keep on dancing out of reach. He would slow down the longer it went on and Williams would have him. He made no move to take the fight to Williams, preferring to take advantage of the openings that the man's crude roundarm swings and misses afforded him. So far he had escaped heavy punishment. He had had to take some punches but mostly on his arms and he felt he had the measure of his man. Already his accurate and continuous punching had practically closed the right eye and the other man was having to peer in the moonlight to see where his will-o-the-wisp tormentor was. Urged on by his supporters he made another determined effort to get within reach and, as Robert dodged back and forth, one of them stuck out a foot. Too late, Robert felt the obstruction, but could do nothing about it and tumbled backwards to end up lying spreadeagled on the turf. With a turn of speed surprising in so big a man, Williams leapt at him as he struggled to rise. Before he had properly regained his feet, Williams had him in a bear like hug, his face within inches of Robert's. 'Gotcher Morgan. Let's see how you like this.'

He increased the pressure of his arms and it was as if a vice was being slowly tightened around his ribcage. Struggle as he might, he could not break the grip. He could hear the crowd shouting for him to be finished off. His arms luckily had not been imprisoned in Williams's grip and he hammered at the man's head. Williams laughed and buried his head in Robert's chest, squeezing harder. The breath was being driven from his lungs and he knew that in another minute he would be senseless and completely at Williams's mercy. He grabbed a handful of hair and exerting all his remaining strength pulled as hard as he could. Williams's head was gradually lifted from Robert's chest. Squeezing his forearm beneath the man's chin he levered it backwards until they were struggling eyeball to eyeball. Knowing that if he did not do something desperate and unexpected he would soon be a senseless heap, he released the hair and managed to get the palm of his hand under the chin to help increase the pressure upward. The muscles on Williams's neck bulged as he tried to stop the upward movement of his head. The further back his head was forced, the less pressure he was able to exert on Robert's ribs. Knowing that it was now or never. Robert lunged forward with a head butt. It was no time for niceties, and as his forehead smashed into Williams' face, he felt the bone crack in the man's nose, and simultaneously with the scream of pain, there came a gush of blood that soaked his shirtfront. Williams his hands clutching his face staggered back howling at the pain and Robert gratefully tried to suck air into his tortured lungs. His ribs felt as if they had completely caved in and he had difficulty in expanding them. It had been a very close thing as he felt groggy. The impact of his forehead against Williams's frontal bones was making itself felt and his head was beginning to ache. Mercifully, his opponent was in no shape to take advantage, being fully engaged trying to breathe himself. His nose was broken, of that there was no doubt. It lay at an angle with blood running from it. While they both stood there trying to summon up strength to continue, some of the crowd were screaming at Robert to go in and finish it while Williams held his head in agony. Exhaustion or some sense of fairplay held Robert back until Williams, shaking his head to clear it, advanced once more. His face was a ghastly sight, bloodstreaked, his nose a smashed mess, with one eye now firmly shut and the other with a swelling above it. His hatred of Robert drove him forward, and with arms reaching out, his fingers crooked like claws, he moved within reach. This time Robert did not retreat or move out of his way. Instead, as Williams touched him, he took a short step forward and with all the strength he could muster, aimed a blow into the huge belly of the man. His fist smashed into the region just below the breastbone and sank into the flesh to his wrist. For a moment it seemed to have no effect on the advance of the huge bull like figure, then as the breath whistled from his lungs, he seemed to rise on his toes and his arms flopped to his sides. Quickly as he began to sag forward, Robert moved to the man's blind side and as coldly and calculatingly, as if measuring his distance when chopping at a tree, he smashed his fist once more into the bloody mess that had been Williams's nose!

It was doubtful whether the battered bully was capable of feeling any pain from the savage blow to his nose. Already, the nerves that controlled the senses in that area, were sending the maximum amount of information to his brain. What had really turned him from a vigorous mountain of flesh and blood intent on killing the man before him, into a hulk of a man with no wind in his lungs was the first blow delivered. It seemed to rip into him like a sword. There was no pain after it had landed. Just an awful deadness that was pervading his whole upper body. He could not breathe. He had no control over any limb and the bright moonlight had disappeared like a candle snuffed out. To those around, their shouts cut off in mid breath, it was like watching a tree, strong and deep rooted, suddenly tumble to earth. As he had risen to his toes, then started to bend from his middle, the delivery of the second blow, its thud distictly heard in the silence, had dictated the direction in which he would fall. Backwards. Arms outflung, he fell to the turf. No movement. No sign at first that he was even alive. Then from his mouth, wide open, came the first gargles as he tried to replace the breath that had been driven from his body. Several of the onlookers, crowded forward, looking at the hulk that minutes before had seemed indestructible. The man who had appointed himself referee of the contest, stepped forward and shouted,

'Up to your marks.'

Robert hardly aware of what he was doing, stumbled into the middle of the ring, swaying. The referee began his count, standing over Williams, but might well have saved his breath. Williams still lay there, gasping and gurgling, blind in one eye, a beaten man. Robert felt someone trying to push his arms through the armholes of his waistcoat, then his coat. He allowed them to do up the buttons. He felt so weary, and now that the excitement of the action had drained from him, his very bones ached. His hands, blood smeared where he had hit Williams, were a mass of pain. Perhaps he too had broken bones? He felt too tired to care. All he wanted, was rest. Hands pounded his shoulder congratulating him, nearly knocking him to the ground. The man who had given him the brandy once again proffered the bottle. Robert wearily shook his head. His lips were bruised and he could taste blood. The punches that Williams had thrown while he was being held, had left their mark. He shook his head, trying to clear it, and mumbled,

'My horse. Mus' get to Woodfield.'

Flanked by the two men, he walked on legs that threatened to give way, across the moonlit turf to the inn. As they approached, the door opened and a figure, outlined against the lamplight within, stood looking out.

As the trio came within his vision, the landlord stepped forward. His eyes fell on Robert's battered face and unsteady gait,

'Hell's teeth! Williams has gone too far. He's half dead.'

The men laughed, then one said,

'This un's the winner. Williams is back there, flat on his back and out for the count. Never seen nuthin' like it. He shut Williams's eye and butted his nose flat, then just one punch and Williams was finished. Lying there like a stranded whale when we left. Where's the genelman's 'orse?'

Robert had lapsed into an almost semi conscious state as the men, now fully supporting him, led them to where Robert's horse stood tied.

The landlord said,

'It's lame. He told Jabez the potman when he came in. Thass why he stopped here. He had to lead it from the Cherry.'

'Lame or not, it'll have to carry 'im. He won't be walking any further tonight. Best get 'im aboard and let the horse find it's own way home.'

The craven landlord nodded his head,

'Aye. 'Twouldn't do to 'ave anyone connect 'im with this place. We don't want any snoopers about 'ere just now. If he get's 'ome they'll think he's been set on.'

Between them they hoisted him into the saddle and placed his feet in the stirrups. They gathered the reins and as he sat swaying above them, they shook and cajoled him into partial awareness.

"ere lad, take the reins and get off 'ome.'

Hardly knowing what he was doing, Robert obeyed them. As one of them gave the horse a smart rap on the rump causing it to start off, he nearly fell off, but some instinct kept him in his seat. The horse favouring its bruised near front fore, limped off along the moonlit track.

Racked with the pain in his chest and side, his eyebrows bleeding, and his jaw feeling as if it had become unhinged, Robert had only the vaguest idea what was happening to him. Several times he must have lapsed into near unconsciousness, coming to only just in time to stop himself from falling to the ground. The horse, limping even more, the further they went, had only one gait and it was probably this which saved him. When at last they passed down the hill by the chapel, Robert slumped forward, his hands slipping from the reins. As he bent forward he took grasp of the mane and hung on. The Angel beerhouse, in total darkness, appeared and was left behind. Soon he knew, he must fall. If only he could hang on just a while longer...

That was his last coherent thought. Without warning, a sudden blackness, blotting out everything, descended. He was not even aware that he had hit the ground.

CHAPTER 31

Gwendoline reached out and pulled the bellrope. A minute or so later, Dilys appeared in the doorway.

'Dilys. Has Robert come in yet?'

'No my lady. He said he would be back before supper. Cook's put a meal by for him.'

'Very well. When he does come in, tell him I would like to see him right away.'

'Yes my lady.'

She withdrew her head and the door closed. Returning to the papers before her, Gwendoline continued reading. After ten minutes or so she glanced at the ornate clock that adorned the mantelpiece. It said eight fifteen. Robert was late, it was unlike him as he was one of the most punctual people she knew. She wondered whether there had been any trouble at the colliery which had kept him there. No doubt he would appear very shortly.

Immersed in the contents of the report, she raised her head as a sudden hubbub broke out below. As she rose to her feet to pull the bellrope, the door burst open and Dilys's worried face appeared,

'Oh my lady! It's Mister Robert my lady, he's lying out there all covered in blood. He looks to be terrible hurt my lady.'

Gwendoline rushed past the girl and lifting her skirts ran down the stairs. At the main door, were clustered the cook and two of the servants. They were trying to lift the inert form but only succeeding in getting in each other's way.

'Cook, Mary. Put Robert down. One of you. Go and get Jenkins. Quickly now.'

As Mary ran out into the night to fetch the coachman, Gwendoline shouldered aside the others and knelt down by the side of the unconscious Robert. He was breathing but his face was a mask of blood from a terrible cut over the eyebrow. There was blood on his lips and a huge bruise along the line of his jaw. She lifted his head and cradled it in her arms,

'Robert. Robert. Can you hear me?'

There was no response. The sound of hurrying footsteps heralded the return of Mary with Jenkins.

Gwendoline began issuing orders to the servants who stood there uttering small shrieks.

'Dilys. Get Mrs. Watkins, then go with her and prepare Robert's bed. Get hot water and some bandages. Cook. You and Mary take hold of his arms. Jenkins, will you lift Robert while I take his head?'

Between them they lifted him from the ground and staggered up the stairs to his bedroom. Mrs. Watkins had appeared and was busy turning back the bedclothes. Once they had lain him on the bed, she removed his halfboots, noting how caked they were with some dark soil. Dilys appeared bearing a water jug of hot water which Mrs. Watkins indicated she should pour into the flower patterned water basin, standing on the marble topped washstand.

Stripped to the waist, the full extent of his injuries could clearly be seen. They both gasped at the bruising around his ribs. His arms were mottled with small bruises where he had warded off many of Williams's punches. Mrs. Watkins spoke.

'I have a salve in my medicine box that I am sure will ease his bruises. I will go and fetch it if you will watch Robert, my lady.'

Leaving Gwendoline staring down at Robert's bruised and battered body she left the room. As she stood there, Robert uttered a groan and tried to move. Quickly she held his shoulders to the bed leaning across him. He was mumbling something and she lowered her head to his mouth to try and catch what he was saying. Perhaps he might give a clue as to what had taken place. She could make out nothing but the odd word one of which was 'waun'. She had no idea what it meant but put her face nearer to his lips. Again he struggled to raise himself, and his lips touched her face as once more the almost inaudible words came from his bruised mouth. What was it he was saying? She strained to catch the muted sounds then suddenly as if in anger she distinctly heard him say,

'A lady. No doxy of mine.'

Then more muttering that died away. She raised her head and stared at him. His eyelids were moving as if he were struggling to awaken but had not the strength. Had she heard him correctly? It sounded as if he were denying some accusation. As she sat puzzling at the possible meaning of his words, the housekeeper returned holding a glass jar containing some white creamlike substance.

'Sorry my lady, I couldn't lay my hands on it, then I remembered I had loaned it to Jenkins so I had to fetch it. He found Robert's horse my lady. He said it's lame but isn't hurt. If you'll hold Robert I'll rub this on. It smells a bit but I swear by it for strains and suchlike.'

While Gwendoline once more put her arms about Robert, Mrs. Watkins dipped her fingers into the jar and began smearing the strong smelling cream on his bruises. When at last they had covered almost all of his torso, Mrs. Watkins suggested it might be a good thing if Robert was dressed in his nightwear as the ointment she had put on might stain the bedclothes. Not waiting for agreement, the older woman began rummaging in the chest of drawers that held Robert's clothing. She pulled out a nightshirt and while Gwendoline could not restrain the flush that came to her cheeks, between them they stripped off his trousers and long woollen pants, pulled on the nightshirt then pulled the bedclothes up around him.

'He should be all right my lady, but I think I'll sit up with him in that basket chair there. If he's taken bad or wants anything, I'll be able to see to him.'

Aware that in the most delicate way, her housekeeper had dismissed her from the sickroom, Gwendoline went to her room. Mrs. Watkins had brought it to her attention that, widow or not, a young man's bedroom was not the place for a young woman to be. She sat thinking about the words that Robert had mumbled.

'A lady. No doxy of mine.'

She had no knowledge of any young woman that Robert paid court to and knew that the term doxy was one given to those women who were kept as mistresses by philanderers. He was no rake, that she was certain of. It was ridiculous to think of his being accused of being connected in such way with any woman...She stopped as a possible solution struck

286

her like a blow. Oh no! It wasn't possible.

'Why not?' said a voice in her head. 'You live in the same house. You are a widow, therefore free. Young women who spend every day in the company of personable young men, no matter what their stations in life, must expect to have their names linked.'

The more she thought about it the more she became convinced that she had stumbled on the explanation of his injuries. He had not been set upon by footpads. He had been in a fight defending her good name against the foul accusation levelled against her. But who could hate her so much that they would say such a thing? Another thought struck her. If such an accusation was being bandied about then it must be stopped immediately. If it ever reached her father's ears, then that would be the end of her position in control of the combine and her immediate removal to London, there to live as the Widow Appleby. Poor Robert would lose his job, his defence of her good name counting for nothing. To ensure that neither of these things came to pass, there was only one solution. When Robert had recovered, he would have to move out of Woodfield. No doubt he would be able to move into the lodge with his brother though they would be a crowd. Still better than dismissal, and knowing how hard her father could be, he might decide to sell his interests in the mines and force her to sell Woodfield. Robert must leave.

The subject of her thoughts came to his senses to find himself lying between the sheets of his own bed. He lay still for a while trying to piece together the events of the previous night. He could hardly remember what had happened after being assisted to the inn. He had a hazy recollection of riding his horse, but how he had arrived home was a compete mystery. As he tried to turn over, the pain that shot through the area around his ribs made him gasp and he subsided. His face felt sore and as his fingers explored the line of his jaw, he could feel a puffiness and his lips felt twice their size. He clenched and unclenched his hands to relieve the stiffness and when he held them before him, he could see the grazes on the knuckles. Whatever punishment he had handed out to Williams, he had not escaped unscathed himself. He tenta-

287

tively tried a deep breath and was relieved to find out that he could fill his lungs, although he needed to be cautious. His head ached and as he recalled the punch that Williams had hurled at him while he was being held, he knew that he must have a black eye to go with the cut that had dripped blood during the fight.

His inspection was interrupted by the opening of the bedroom door and the entrance of Mrs. Watkins.

'Ah Mister Robert. Awake then? Do you think you could eat some breakfast? I'm afraid you'll have to make do with gruel this morning. Maybe by tomorrow your jaw will have gone down enough to manage some toast. Can you raise yourself up so that I can wash your hands and face?'

'How did I get here?'

'Never mind that now, the mistress will explain. I'll go and get some water and tell cook to prepare some gruel. I'll be back in a minute.'

Robert painfully levered himself up against the pillows and lay back suddenly realising how sore he was. He looked at the nightshirt he was wearing. How had he managed to put that on? The return of the housekeeper carrying a jug of hot water and a towel answered his question. He had been put to bed by her for the second time. He watched her as she filled the basin and placing it on the bedside table, sat on the bed and commenced washing him. As she touched his jaw, he winced.

'Sore?'

'Mm'

She gently patted his face dry then washed his arms and hands.

'Pull your nightshirt up.'

As he hesitated she said,

'Come Mister Robert. I've seen you undressed before. I want to have a look at your ribs.'

He pulled the garment up from beneath the bedclothes and she helped him lift it over his head. As she saw the state of his body she clucked her tongue. The whole of his lower ribs were swollen and the marks surrounding his waist were even redder than she remembered them from the night before.

There was extensive bruising but at least he had been able to raise his arms. She touched his ribs and he retreated from her touch as if burnt.

'That needs a doctor. I'll go and tell the mistress to send Jenkins.'

She helped him put the nightshirt back on and poured water from the basin into the bucket beneath the washstand.

'I'll send Dilys up with your breakfast. Mistress will probably be in to see you when I tell her about your ribs. I could see she was worried last night.'

'She was here last night?'

'Well of course. Who do you think helped me undress you and put the ointment on?'

'Undress me? You mean....'

'Of course. She's a married woman. She's seen a man before.'

Leaving him to digest her words she left the room.

Within minutes Dilys came into the room carrying a tray on which reposed a solitary steaming dish.

'Good morning Mister Robert. Do you want me to spoon this gruel for you?'

Hurriedly he denied needing any help and she placed the tray on his lap. She tucked a napkin into the neck of his shirt then stood back to watch him eat.

When he picked up the spoon, try as he might, he found that he was unable to close his fingers about the handle. Feeling as helpless as a baby he looked at her imploringly. She picked up the spoon and began feeding him.

Dilys removed the napkin and wiped his mouth very carefully then picked up the tray and went out. As he settled back once more, Gwendoline came into the room.

'Good morning Robert. Mrs. Watkins tells me she thinks you need a doctor to look at your injuries so I've sent Jenkins. Do you feel up to talking about what happened?'

'I can't remember everything. How did I get here?'

'Presumably on your horse. Jenkins found it wandering about in the park after you had fallen from it. Mary heard a noise outside and when she went to see what it was, she found you lying in the driveway. Between us we got you up here and attended to you. You were practically unconscious but you kept muttering something. Now perhaps you will tell me what happened to you? You have been in a fight haven't you?'

'Well not the way you mean my lady. It was not a drunken brawl.'

'Robert! Tell me what happened.'

He was silent for a while.

'There was a fight but I had no choice.'

He then recounted the events leading up to his being taken prisoner by the gang in the beerhouse.

'Williams said something and before I could stop myself I went for him. I couldn't help it. I've hated that lout since the day my father was killed and I've always known that one day there would be a reckoning. Before I could get at him, they grabbed me. Williams wanted to beat me up there and then, but the landlord made them take me out on to the Waun. That's the open ground behind the Maypole. It's all peat beds and nobody would be likely to interfere. When we got there, Williams started taunting me and while they were holding me he punched me. It was then he did this to my eyebrow. When I went down, he kicked me. If one of the men hadn't stopped him I think he would have kicked me to death. They gave me time to get my breath back and a drink of brandy then formed a ring. I knew that if I didn't beat him, I'd never get off that Waun alive. Williams blames me for getting him the sack. Paget made it clear in his report that he sacked Williams because he hadn't carried out his orders properly, but seeing me on my own in the Maypole was too good a chance to miss I suppose. Anyway to cut a long story short, I managed to beat Williams, but they had to help me get on my horse and that's about all I remember.'

'You said that it was something that Williams had said that made you lose your temper. What did he say?'

Robert remained silent his head bowed.

'Did he say that I was your fancy woman - your doxy?'

Robert's head lifted and he stared at her as if he couldn't believe what he had heard.

'Don't look suprised Robert. I know what a doxy is. Was it

that that made you try to attack him. You were trying to defend my good name?'

Shame faced Robert replied,

'My lady. I couldn't let a foulmouthed lout insult you without punishing him.'

He paused as if struck by something.

'How did you know what he'd said my lady?'

'You muttered something about 'A lady. No doxy of mine' when you were nearly unconscious. Only I heard it. I thought about it and guessed it was me he was talking about. Thank you Robert for defending my honour. Try and get some rest now. We can talk again when you are feeling better.'

Later, when the doctor arrived Gwendoline allowed Mrs. Watkins to advise him of Robert's injuries and to accompany him to the sickroom. In view of what had happened, and after some deep thought, she determined that she should distance herself as far as possible from the event. If she showed too much concern for him now, goodness knows what construction might be put upon her actions if the story had spread. Robert was a servant, and heads of households, particularly females, did not show too much interest in the well being of good looking young bachelors in their employ, unless there was some bond between them. The doctor's report was encouraging. Robert had suffered severe bruising but luckily the kicking he had received had not broken any ribs. The cut over his eye would heal of its own accord although he would have a scar in his eyebrow. As for the rest of his aches and pains, the doctor was confident that another day or so in bed would see his young body shake them off. As a precaution however, he bound his ribs so tightly that Robert was unable to take any very deep breaths. Until such time as he could hold a spoon, Dilys had been instructed to act in the capacity of his feeder, and the elderly woman took full advantage of this, mothering him like a hen with one chick. Mrs. Watkins insisted that he remain in bed for the recommended two days and allowed him to get up on the third. By this time, Robert was bored to death and when allowed out of bed, insisted on having his clothes and taking a slow walk in the park.

From her room, Gwendoline watched him as he strolled among the trees. She had decided that it would do no good to delay her proposed action, and when he returned to the house Mary was despatched to bring him to her room.

Robert was relieved when Mary told him that he was wanted by the mistress. She had not been to see him since they had spoken in his room. He wondered if somehow he had done something wrong, though he could think of nothing that would deserve a punishment that cut him off from seeing and speaking to her.

He tapped on her door and entered,

'You sent for me my lady?'

'Sit down Robert. We have to talk about what happened the other night. You have explained your reasons for becoming involved in a fight on my behalf. If I understand your reasoning, you believed that this man Williams was insulting my good name by suggesting that we were engaged in some sort of romantic affair. I can understand a man of low intelligence mouthing such lies, if only for the enjoyment of his cronies; but for you to rise to his baiting and by engaging in common fisticuffs, give all those present the opportunity to think that you, and therefore I, had something to hide, showed a complete lack of gentlemanly conduct. A gentleman would have taken his horsewhip to the lout or ignored him completely. You have probably only strengthened their belief that I am your paramour.'

Robert was sitting staring wide eyed, aghast at her words and the cold, steely tone in which they were delivered. Gwendoline's eyes were flashing and as he opened his mouth to speak, she stopped him with an imperious wave of her hand.

'I am not yet finished Robert. You have placed me in a most invidious position. It pains me to have to say this, but I cannot and will not have my name linked with yours other than as employer and servant. Should one whisper of this rumour reach Sir Henry or any member of the Board, my position here would be untenable. You would be dismissed immediately. I would be sorry if you lost your position through what I realise was a mistaken sense of gallantry, but you must realise that we have to take steps to see that this rumour is quashed immediately. To this end I must insist that you move out of this house. For you to remain here any longer will only encourage further gossip. I suggest that you move into the back drive lodge. Mrs. Evans the gatekeeper can look after you. She is elderly but quite capable. You may take your meals in the servants' kitchen. When you are ready to move I will instruct Jenkins to help you with your personal furniture. I hope that this action will undo the harm I feel you have done to my good name.'

Robert's mind was in a turmoil. He could not believe what he had just heard. That his beloved Gwendoline should have taken this view simply did not make sense. Of course he was in love with her, but it was a pure love. He wanted her for his wife. That she should expel him from the house meant that the only time he was going to be with her would be in the office. Why should she have taken this stance? Had the last ten years meant so little to her? True they had only been partners in the business of controlling the finances of her father's mines, but they had shared the problems that had arisen and even the danger, when they had gone into the old mine. Did all that count for nothing? Did she still consider him just another servant? He had never stepped over the line that divided them but she must have sensed that he was devoted to her. It had been obvious to Eirwen. What could he say to the tirade to which he had just been subjected? He was after all just a servant in her eyes, and had been a fool to think that having worked together all this time really counted for anything. If he moved out, the rest of the staff would know that something was amiss. He would have to resign but even as he thought it, he knew that somehow he would have to swallow his pride and accept. He could not afford to lose this position and maybe time would bring a change of heart on her part. Oh my Gwendoline. How could you?

'Very well my lady. I will move out the day after tomorrow. I am sorry that any action of mine has caused you pain. May I take it that I shall have access to the office at all times?'

'Yes Robert. There will be no change in office routine. I am sorry to have to take this attitude but I see no other way to put an end to any gossip.'

He stood up and with a dignity that struck at her said, 'If there is nothing else then, my lady, may I be excused?'

'Yes thank you Robert.'

When he had gone, she sat for a long time staring at the wall. How dignified he had been. Her outburst must have been like a blow in the face. Servant he might be but he had not deserved that. But what else could she have done? She would not have her name the subject of lewd jests in beerhouses. The very idea that she could take a common servant as a lover. How dare they! No, she had done the only thing possible. There would be murmuring amongst the rest of the servants but she would ignore them and they would soon get used to the new arrangement. Satisfied that her actions had been justified, she turned to the paperwork that awaited her.

CHAPTER 32

When Robert declared his intention of moving into the lodge, there was much speculation amongst the rest of the staff as to his reasons. Aware that he would need to give them some explanation, he told them that he had asked the mistress to allow him to do so. He was after all at an age when he should be thinking seriously of settling down and he needed a place of his own. He had been given permission to make alterations to the cottage, and he let them understand that the alterations he intended making were those that any new bride might approve of. After some remarks such as 'Aren't you the sly one?' they seemed satisfied and as Gwendoline had hoped, within a matter of weeks the new arrangements had become routine.

Throughout the whole of 1838, the activities of the Chartists had been a cause for concern to the authorities. A voice was becoming heard, more and more often, a voice that was to bring the valleys of South Wales to the brink of an armed rising. Henry Vincent, had been involved in politics for some years and was a brilliant orator. He had long been a member of the Working Men's Association in London, and came to the area to speak and organise. Such was his success and popularity, that the big industrialists decided that they had no alternative other than to arrange his arrest. The mayor of Newport declared that Chartist meetings were illegal and from evidence he collected by attending meetings at which the young man spoke, was able to charge not only Vincent but several others and they were arrested and placed in Monmouth jail to await trial at the assizes.

A huge petition said to have contained over one million Chartists' signatures, asking for the right to be armed in order to protect themselves against the Industrialists' Association formed by the iron master Crawshay Bailey, had been rejected by Parliament and the magistrates in Monmouth asked for troops to prevent any attempt to release Vincent from jail. The situation was becoming more and more tense and at a rally called at Whitsun in Blackwood it was estimated that there were thirty thousand present. John Frost spoke against Vincent's arrest but nobody suggested that they try to release Vincent.

Now that he no longer lived in the house, Robert was more free to pursue his other interests when he had finished his day's work. He had once heard John Frost speak at the Coach and Horses Inn at Blackwood, and was attracted by the reports he read in the news journals. He soon became familiar with the names of the foremost leaders of the local Chartists and attended a few meetings. He was however careful not to become too involved and at no time did he consider becoming a member. In August the long awaited trial of Vincent took place and when he and his fellow prisoners were found guilty, the Chartists were so angry that they spoke openly of violence. All of this was of great concern to Robert. He was aware that, if and when the armed rising took place, there was every chance that hotheads who attended the meetings being held at Croespenmaen would attempt to wreak vengeance on Gwendoline and himself. He had made a bad enemey of Williams, and the beating he had given the man would only have served to inflame the bully's hatred. If Williams had any influence over his cronies, now that they had witnessed his humiliation, the confusion which would surely exist during the rising would give him the chance to get his own back. And what better way than to attack Woodfield?

Meanwhile, Gwendoline was trying to deal with the problems her action had brought about. No matter that she felt justified in adopting the attitude she had, she felt she had wronged Robert.

She tried to view the situation dispassionately. Robert Morgan was an employee who had been involved in a public brawl. He had reacted to the situation in the only way he knew how.

It was no good saying he should have behaved like a gentleman and have taken his whip to the scoundrel or ignored him. In the first place, Robert was not a gentleman. Well that was not entirely true. He may not have all his social graces, but never had he behaved in any way toward her, other than correctly. He was kind, courteous, well spoken. Of course he had a pronounced Welsh accent, but that was no great drawback. Many of papa's business friends from the north, sometimes spoke in such a way as to make it difficult for her to understand them. Robert had thought he was defending her good name. It was not his fault that his good intentions should have given rise to a situation that may have added credibility to the accusation.

The more she analysed her actions, the more she seemed to be condemning herself. Annoyed, she brought out the final argument. She had reprimanded him and she hoped, made it clear that he was after all only a servant. But somehow even this did not seem right. Her pride would not let her admit that she wished the old easy relationship could be reinstated; consequently some devil within her took delight in making mountains out of molehills. Several times she complained about trivial matters that normally she would have not only overlooked but ignored completely. Robert's demeanour never changed. He accepted the rebukes and apologised. This only made her even more annoyed, both with him and herself.

At last there came the incident that she seized upon to bring this unsatisfactory state of affairs to a conclusion.

Robert had read that a meeting was to be held at the Greyhound at Pontllanfraith, where several of the leaders including John Frost and Zephaniah Williams, were to speak. He had finished for the day and after eating his evening meal with the rest of the staff had made his way to the lodge. It was a lovely evening and feeling restless he decided that he would walk to the inn and listen to some of the speeches. He had told Mrs. Evans that he intended taking a walk and not to wait up for him. She, like the others, believed that somewhere amongst the local girls was one that had taken his fancy, and he was off to pay her court. He had been gone about an hour when there was a knock at the door and when she opened it there stood Jenkins.

'Mistress wants Mister Robert back at the house.'

'He b'aint 'ere. Gorn courting is my guess. Went out about 'alf past seven. Told me not to wait up.'

Jenkins trudged back to the house and reported to Gwendoline.

'Did he say where he was going?'

'Don't think so my lady. Old Mrs. Evans seems to think he's gone acourting, beggin' your pardon my lady.'

Gwendoline frowned, then dismissed the coachman.

As he told the cook while they sat at the kitchen table later, 'Mistress looked proper upset at Mister Robert going out without tellin' nobody where he was going. They don' seem to get on these days.'

When Robert entered the office the next morning, he had no idea of the storm that was about to fall about his head. Mrs. Evans had said nothing about Jenkins's visit so he was totally unaware until enlightened by the cook. He had not returned until well after ten o'clock, having got into conversation at the inn with some miners that he had once worked with, and his elderly landlady as instructed, had long since gone to bed.

Gwendoline had not slept well. For some reason she was unable to fathom, her rest had been disturbed. It had taken her a long time to get to sleep. Thoughts had scurried about in her head like a squirrel dodging from branch to branch, never staying long enough for her to follow it to a conclusion. She had tossed and turned until well after the household staff had finished their duties and retired to bed. Even when she had slept it had not been the deep sleep of a mind at peace.

Having eaten a sparse breakfast, spoken to Mrs. Watkins about the various household affairs that that lady had thought should be brought to her mistress's attention, then dealt with the cook's problems, she entered the office and found Robert immersed in adding up one of the ledgers. She walked to her desk, sat down and ignored his 'Good morning my lady.'

'Robert! I sent for you last evening. You were not at home.'

'No my lady. I went for a walk.'

'Without telling anyone where you were going. I needed to speak to you about Paget's latest report.'

'I'm sorry my lady. I had no idea there was anything in it that was urgent.'

Her tone was chilly,

'I will decide what is and what is not urgent. I spent some time dealing with the problem while you were out walking. I would remind you that I employ you and you are to be ready to answer the demands of the job at any time. Am I to be allowed to know where this important walk took you?'

Although aware that Gwendoline was looking for a confrontation for some obscure reason, he was not going to act like some lap dog.

'I walked to Pontllanfraith my lady. There was a big crowd there listening to some speakers. I met some old friends and we talked and drank some ale. I returned home about ten.'

She knew this would be true, but had gone too far now to retreat. The devil within her took possession of her tongue and she threw caution to the winds.

'Am I to understand that while I was in this office working, you were out drinking and listening to those Chartist blackguards with your so called friends? Friends, who if I read the news correctly, might well murder all of us in our beds? This is too much! I have tried to overlook your previous actions but it seems you are determined to take advantage of your position. Well Mister Morgan, I will stand no more of your insolent behaviour. You no longer work here and I should be obliged if you would leave at once.'

The vehemence with which she spoke did not really surprise him. From the very outset of their conversation, he had been aware that she was building herself up to make some sort of declaration. He was relieved in an odd sort of way that what had been festering between them these past weeks, had finally been brought out into the open. She had allowed her pride to place her in an uncomfortable position and her only recourse was to do what she had just done. Their years of working together were at an end, but what she had said this morning would not make any difference to his feelings towards her. Come what may, he knew that his love for her was as strong as ever. She had enslaved him that first day, and he had over the years, come to know that beneath that proud exterior there existed a woman with all the virtues and frailities of any other. He would wait as he had already waited. Someday she would come to him. Be his.

As she stood before him, quivering with the strength of her emotions, eyes flashing, her last words seemed to linger in the air. He put down the quill pen he held.

'Very well my lady. I admit I am sorry to be leaving after all these years, but if you feel that I am neglecting my duties, then better I go. I will arrange to leave the lodge and will remove my furniture as soon as I can find somewhere. I bid you good day my lady and trust you will continue to prosper.'

The very evenness of his tone and his demeanour served to make her feel both angry and ashamed. She had deliberately engineered the situation and now she felt that it was pure pique that had made her act as she had. What was the matter with her? She could not undo what had been done. Her pride would not let her withdraw one word. It was done. What her father would have to say she hesitated to think. But wasn't she the overall manager here? The dismissal of a servant was an everyday occurence, even a valuable one. Damn you Robert. Why are you so ...noble? Why didn't he argue? He was no coward, that was half the trouble. She could have dealt with him if he had been or had blustered or spoken up, but somehow he seemed to know that it was she that was being punished. She turned her back, dismissing him. She could hear his movements then the door opened and his last words, 'Goodbye my lady.'

As the door closed she let out a long shuddering sigh. She found that during the whole affair she had been standing with her fists tightly clenched. It came to her as an almost random thought, that even when she and Marcus had had blazing rows, they had not effected her like this. What had she done? Her father would think she was demented. To dismiss an employee as valuable as Robert for such a trivial reason, would seem to him to be the height of stupidity. She could hear him now,

'Just where young lady, do you think you are going to find someone with his qualities, to replace him? And for such a small salary? By Gad young Gwen, I would have thought a daughter of mine would have had more sense. So he went out wenching. Oh he wasn't wenching you say, he was talking to some friends. You must have been mad. Well what do you propose to do, having lost half your office staff?'

What was she going to do?

Her first task would be to inform her father and the three mine managers, of the position. From now on, only orders issued by herself were to be carried out. Not that she thought that Robert (why couldn't she think of him as just Morgan?) would interfere in any way with the working of the combine.

She sat down and tried to calm her nerves. Her heart was still pounding in her breast, and rising from her seat she went to look out of the window. The peace of the park spread out before her was in stark contrast to the atmosphere in the room. Her heated words seemed to have taken on a sort of physical presence that created a tension she could feel pressing in upon her. She needed to get out of the house, out into the open air where she could breathe. She hurried from the room and pausing only to put on a cloak and her bonnet, made her way downstairs.

'Dilys! Mary! Where is everybody? Ah there you are Mary. Go and tell Jenkins I want the open carriage immediately.'

She followed the maid outside and stood waiting there until Jenkins brought the carriage to a halt before her.

Without waiting for him to get down and open the door, she climbed in. As he looked at her over his shoulder she said,

'Jenkins. Take me to that big pond. You know the one I mean. You follow the road up to the turn off for the colliery.'

'You mean Penyfan my lady?'

'That's it.'

She settled back against the cushioned seat. Behind her, Mary and the cook stood in the doorway staring after her their faces betraying their thoughts. There was much going on that morning that needed an explanation. First Mister Robert hurrying out and striding off up the drive without so much as a wave. Now the mistress looking decidedly put out, hareing off in the carriage to Penyfan. What on earth does she want up there? There's nothing there but water. The cook turned to Mary,

'Mark my words, there's something very funny going on.'

301

When Jenkins pulled the carriage to a halt on the bank of the pond, Gwendoline said,

'Wait here Jenkins. I'm going for a walk.'

'Be careful my lady. Don't go too near the water. It's very deep.'

Pulling her cloak closer about her she set out. It was her intention to make the complete circle of the pond hoping that the walk and the serenity of the place would restore some sort of peace to her feelings. Apart from a few sheep there did not appear to be another living thing about. The surface of the water rippled as the gentle summer breeze swept across it. The silence was unbroken except for the splash of the water as it lapped against the stones around its edge. As she walked she tried not to think, allowing the silence to soak into her. Beneath her feet the turf was springy, and close to the ground, purple berries peeped from the whin bushes. At the water's edge, pebbles worn flat by the constant movement of the windswept water lay in abundance. She bent down and picked one. She hurled it in a flat trajectory across the surface of the water, counting the splashes as it bounced across the pond. A sixer. She laughed, remembering how she and her brothers used to hurl stones in the very same way. 'Why do we have to grow up' she thought 'it's so much more fun when you are children.'

Sitting on a large stone she looked out across the water. She could see the carriage with Jenkins huddled in his driving cloak and on a sudden impulse, waved to him. After a moment, his hand raised in greeting. She laughed out loud.

'I'll warrant that surprised you Jenkins.'

This was a magic place. Already she felt better. Little wonder Robert loved it.

She had been deeply touched when he had brought her up here that first time she had come to Woodfield. It was as if he was sharing something he valued, knowing that it would mean so much to her. He had been right. It had sprung to her mind as the only place to seek the solace she needed. Now that she had opened her mind to her problems, she let herself think about the way her life had run. All through it, men had pandered to her. Her father had spoiled her. Young men flattered her and had begged for some personal trinket as a memento. When she had danced, her card had always been full, with young gallants pleading for an extra dance. What had they really thought about her marriage? Marcus's liking for drink had not been a closely guarded secret. She had been so innocent in those days. Worrying about the colour or feel of a piece of material had seemed so important. She had learned though. Her first sight of a fellow creature harnessed to a tub of coal had shaken her to her very soul. And yet those same filthy coarse tongued women had been among the first to volunteer to help save their menfolk trapped in that hole. She stirred and rose to her feet. As she walked she recalled incidents that had helped change her from a silly empty headed girl into what she was now. She stopped. What was she now? A Widow. The manager of a mining combine. Wealthy? Certainly. Marcus hadn't had time to drink his way through her dowry. Was she content to go on being the business woman who lived in the big house? Alone now, the thought came unbidden. It was this that stopped her once more. Had she given up thinking of marriage and children? Widows usually retired to become unpaid nannies to relatives' children. That was not for her. She was still young enough to bear children. Was there somewhere a man willing to take her for his wife? To put up with her spirit, her need to be something other than a housewife? Most men just wanted a woman who would keep their homes nice, have the meals ready on time, bear his children and not ask too many questions. But did she want marriage and children. What to do? Give up work, and let papa seek out some middle aged equally lonely person to marry her? Was she lonely? As she stared at the water the answer came to her quite clearly. Oh God! If people only knew how lonely I am! I'd exchange it all for someone to love. Someone to tell me he loves me, and to have his children. Where could such a man be found? Suddenly she knew.

'You fool!' she whispered, 'You blind fool!'

When she returned to the carriage, Jenkins could see the frown had gone from her brow. She looked serene, as if she had overcome whatever it was that had troubled her earlier.

He turned his head in silent query.
'Home please Jenkins.'

CHAPTER 33

Sir Henry stared at the letter he had just read.

'She's mad.'

'Who's mad dear?'

Lady Siston at the other end of the table asked as her husband put the letter down and stared at it as if he didn't believe what he had just read.

'Your daughter Gwendoline. Do you know what she's done? She's sacked Morgan.'

'Morgan? That young man at Woodfield? Why did she do that dear? Has she caught him thieving? You can't trust servants too much. Especially those indoors. I'm sure that Jevons drinks a lot of your brandy.'

'Morgan the financial controller. She's sacked him. God knows why. Seems he wasn't there when she wanted him. Listen to this.' He picked up the letter and began reading, 'Morgan went out without telling anybody where he was going. When I questioned him he said he had gone for a walk, met some old friends and they talked and drank ale. He didn't get back until gone ten o'clock.'

'The girl's gone mad. She can't do all the work on her own, and where she thinks she's going to find anyone who can do the job as well as young Morgan I'm blest if I know. The Board will be up in arms if the financial reports are late. Some of them have never forgiven me for putting her in charge in the first place. Maybe she should come back here. The way things are going down there with those blasted Chartists, I'm not happy her being in that big house all on her own with only old Jenkins now for protection. There's only one thing for it. I'll have to go down to Wales and see if I can persuade her to come back here and see if Morgan will come back. He'll want a rise for sure. I'll be leaving tomorrow morning. Get Jevons to pack my things, he'll know what I want.'

Still muttering to himself he left the table. His presence was required at a meeting that morning. There were certain members of the Board who were all for trying to sell the colliery combine. The tales which appeared in the news journals about the Chartist threats and demands, were making them nervous about having their money tied up in such a vulnerable business. He had had enough trouble keeping them in line when those Scotch Cattle were on the rampage. Perhaps he had better say nothing about the Morgan business just yet. Better leave it until he had seen Gwendoline and found out the truth of the matter. Morgan had always seemed a level headed young man, one who knew on which side his bread was buttered. Had a good head on his shoulders too. Pity about his background. If he'd been something a bit better than a coal hewer, maybe Gwendoline could have been talked into considering him as a husband. Been an improvement on Marcus, despite his noble bloodline. Women! I'll never understand 'em.

His arrival at Woodfield was no great surprise. In fact, after her letter outlining the events, she would have been surprised if her father hadn't come. When he had washed away the dust of his journey, she had tea served in the drawing room looking out on to the parkland. He wasted no time in getting to the point. Almost as soon as Dilys had left the room and Gwendoline had handed him his cup, he plunged straight in.

'Just what is going on here young lady?'

'You read my letter papa. I am in charge here, and Morgan like everyone else is employed to be where I want him, when I want him.'

'But how on earth do you think you are going to manage all the reports and other work on your own?'

'I shall manage somehow. Maybe the parson will know of somebody.'

'I doubt it. Employees like young Morgan don't grow on trees. What on earth made you go as far as to sack him? Couldn't you have given him a good telling off and stopped some of his pay?'

'Papa I told you. I'm in control here and I do it my way.'

'Gwennie, there's something else you are going to have to consider. Both your mother and I are worried about you being in this house on your own. You know what is going to happen around here don't you? If I read the news journals correctly, there's going to be a rising of some sort. You've

306

heard of Vincent the young fellow they've got in Monmouth jail? Well there's reports these Chartists might try and get him out. It's common knowledge that they are forming armed bands and I don't mind telling you, there are plenty of my friends in Parliament who are convinced that before the year's out there'll be an armed rebellion. We don't want you here if that happens. Why don't you come back to London? If it's your pride that's standing in the way, maybe I could persuade Morgan to come back and take charge until things have settled down. By then both of you might have seen the error of your ways.'

'Papa I am not coming back to London. This is my home and I'll not be driven out of it. I shall stay here and you will get your reports as usual.'

Sir Henry could hear from the tone that there was no argument he could bring forward that was going to make her change her mind, so he decided to leave the subject alone, for a while anyway. He stayed at Woodfield for three days, in which time he paid a visit to the colliery with Gwendoline. Paget had been astounded when he received the letter informing him that Robert had been dismissed. Like her father, he wondered where she hoped to find someone to replace him. He made no mention of the matter as he was only too well aware of the way she would react to anyone interfering in what she considered to be her province. He was sorry that Robert had gone. They had become good friends and respected each other's talents. Privately he had thought that perhaps, someday Robert would pluck up the courage and ask her to marry him. They were ideally suited and would make a good match.

The night before he was due to return home, Sir Henry once more brought up the subject of Robert's dismissal. He was sure that he had not heard the whole story. Normally Gwen was a level headed business woman, not given to making stupid decisions. He decided that his best plan would be to ask her right out, if there was anything she had not told him that had caused her to act the way she had.

It was a slip of the tongue that forced her into revealing details of the fight between Robert and Williams. They were discussing ways of cutting down some of the paperwork when she said,

'As you know papa, Morgan and I had our own special duties. He always read Paget's reports then passed them to me for my decision. When I found the report still on his desk, I sent to the lodge for him. He'd gone out.'

'What lodge? Why send to the lodge for him? His room's just along the passage.'

He was sure that if he pressed her hard enough whatever it was she was hiding would come out.

'What was he doing at the lodge?'

She rose from her chair and walked to the window. With her back to him she began speaking,

'Papa. Some months ago after the explosion, Paget sacked a faceboss called Williams, holding him responsible for a lot of the damage that occurred, because of the shortage of posts. Robert and Williams have hated the sight of each other since Robert's father was killed working under Williams. Robert's horse went lame and he stopped at an inn where Williams and his cronies happened to be holding a meeting. Williams made certain accusations calling my good name into doubt and accused Robert and me of being ...lovers. While his cronies held Robert, Williams kicked and punched him until one of them intervened. He gave Robert some brandy to help revive him, and Robert and Williams had a terrible fight. Robert won and was allowed to go, but was in bed three days. When I saw the injuries he suffered on my behalf, I realised that as well as being a devoted servant, he's in love with me.'

There was an exclamation from Sir Henry,

'The devil you say!'

'I realised that if a rumour linking our names was allowed to circulate, I would have to give up my work and Robert would have to be dismissed. I'm afraid I laid all the blame on him, accusing him of strengthening the rumour by engaging in fisticuffs rather than ignoring the lout, and told him that the only way to squash the rumour was for him to move out of Woodfield and live at the lodge. He accepted my view of the matter, raising no objection. I gather he put it about that the move was his idea. He was supposed to be considering marriage to some local girl and the lodge would do admirably for their first home.'

'Bless my soul.'

'What happened next was entirely my fault. Robert carried on as usual but I'm afraid that this only served to annoy me. There was an atmosphere in the office and when he went out that night I saw it as the opportunity to get rid of him. In a fit of pique, I said terrible things, acting like a fishwife. He never said a word, just stood there until I had finished, then apologised, bade me goodbye and walked out.'

Sir Henry rose and approached his daughter, and putting his hands on her shoulders turned her to face him.

'And now you find that you are missing him, and your Siston pride won't let you admit it. Is that it?'

'Oh papa I'm so miserable and lonely.'

Tears shone in her eyes.

'Gwendoline. I've always said that I'd never understand women, but even I can see that you are unhappy. You say Morgan's in love with you. Well in that case you did the right thing by getting rid of him. He's only a common collier boy with a bit of education. You are my eldest child and I'm as proud of you as I am of my sons. You were right, you can't have your name bandied about with Morgan's. He's a good man but he is a servant. Come on now dry your tears, we'll say no more about it.'

'Oh papa you don't understand women do you? Can't you see that I'm trying to tell you that I love him. I only realised it a few days ago. And he is not just an educated collier boy. He's the equal of any noble gentleman I've ever met. I want to marry him and have his children.'

'Gwen! Didn't you hear what I said? It's impossible. You are a Siston.'

'No papa. I'm the Widow Appleby, but he won't want me now I've treated him so badly.'

She started to weep and her father held her as her shoulders shook. Women! Who did understand them? He left the next morning after making another attempt to persuade her to return to London. He had given thought to the possibility of getting Paget to take on the job if she agreed, but she was adamant that nothing would make her leave, so feeling worried but even prouder of his eldest child, he waved goodbye and set off for Newport.

The subject of their conversation had been shaken to the core of his being when Gwendoline had sacked him, but although feeling as if the world had crashed upon his head, he felt he must maintain his dignity. Although he wanted to deny what she said, he bit his tongue and hurried from the house. He needed to think what he was going to do. There was no question but that he must find another job as soon as possible, but what? For years he had worked as a manager, nobody would employ him to hew coal again. What else could he do? His first step must be to find somewhere to live while he searched for work. There was no room at Dafydd's little lodge. That was already bursting at the seams with his own children and his two youngest brothers. He had given Dafydd a small sum of money weekly to help raise them, now that would have to stop. Perhaps Eirwen might be able to help. William's father's farm was a large rambling place, maybe he could find a room there? He had some savings, not much, but enough to keep him for a week or two. Since the fight and the way things had been going at the office, he had given more than a passing thought to throwing it all up and taking a chance in America. He had enough for the boat fare and there were reports of the need for miners in the coalfields of Virginia. It would mean goodbye to all his thoughts of ever making Gwendoline his wife but his mother had warned him that she was not meant for the likes of him.

He was lucky when he called at the farm in the Cyncoed. It was harvest time and another pair of hands were welcome. After speaking to Eirwen's father-in-law, he was told he could sleep in one of the outhouses, eat with the family in the huge farmhouse kitchen and lend a hand in the fields. For the next few weeks he worked from sunup to dusk and fell asleep on his rough bed at night with the scent of the hay in his nostrils.

September had gone and the harvest had been gathered. He had managed to retain most of the money as the farmer had told him that 'he had earned his vittles and the shed be empty anyway', so his plan to take passage had not been abandoned. He spent the first couple of weeks of October helping with repairs to the fences and preparing for the winter, not too far away.

Eirwen was big with her first baby and they would often spend an evening before the big fireplace talking about their hopes. He had told her of the fight and how it had effected his relations with Gwendoline.

Eirwen, content with her marriage and life on the farm, was scathing about her late mistress. One night they were sitting either side of the fire. Eirwen had her feet resting on a stool her belly bulging.

'She be wasting her life working in that office. She must be blind not to know you loves 'er Robert. It were plain for all to see. The servants all knew and I should 'ave told 'er when I left.'

'It just as well you didn't or I should have been looking for a new job a lot earlier. She made it plain that she didn't want her name and mine linked after the fight.'

'You ought to be alooking for some young country girl to wed Rob. It be grand. I knew William was right for me when I first see'd him. Now that our baabie be on the way, us'll be even 'appier.'

She looked at the clock.

'Lor' it be nigh on ten. William'll be in lookin' for his supper. He do like to get over to the Maypole for a drink with 'is brothers now and then. You'll 'ave some bread and cheese with us Rob before you go?'

Robert liked his huge good tempered brother-in-law, and agreed to stop for supper and a chat. Grunting with the effort, Eirwen lifted herself out of the chair and began putting the supper on the table. Robert watched her. She was happy and contented and how different to the girl who had spent her days looking after Gwendoline's clothes and dressing her hair.

'Do you miss the old days Eirwen?'

'I do look back at them sometimes. They was nice in the beginning and Lady Gwendoline was kind. It wasn't very nice after she got wed. All those rows. Both of 'em shouting and spitting at each other like a couple of cats. He was always drunk and she was so tied up with her new house, they didn't 'ave time to love each other. When 'e died and she began to start looking like a dried up crab apple, I knew I'd 'ave to leave, speshly with William keepin' on asking me to get wed. I on'y stayed on the last couple of months 'cos she asked me. She told me that if I would she'd pay for the wedding breakfast. That was a lovely day wasn't it? Aye she were good to me and taught me a lot. Not that I got much chance to show what I learned, not on the farm. It's not an easy life but we be happy. Me and William and the baabie.'

There was the sound of footsteps crossing the yard approaching the house. She laughed,

'Here be the master or so he thinks.'

William entered, bending his head to pass through the doorway. He put his big muscular arms about his wife and kissed her.

'Hullo Rob. You'll stay to supper?'

'I've asked 'im already.'

'Good. I've got something to tell you Rob. A message from a well wisher. He said you'd know who 'e was when I told you he likes a drop of brandy same as the bosses.'

'I know who you mean. What did he say to tell me.'

"e wants you to meet 'im quiet like. Said 'e'd be at the Angel tomorrow about seven. He don't go there very often and 'e'll sit on the wall outside, so's anybody knowing you won't connect you with 'im. 'e said to follow 'im when he finishes 'is drink. 'e says it's real important.'

Having passed on the message William took down two pewter tankards from over the fireplace.

'Fancy a drop of Dad's cider?'

At Rob's nod he filled the two mugs and they all sat around the table talking about life on the farm, until Eirwen yawned capaciously.

'It's bedtime for me. Don't stop talking too long William, nor you Rob. You're worse than women when you got a drink in front of you. G'night.'

She kissed them both then slowly waddled to the other room they used as a bedroom. William's eyes followed her until she passed out of sight.

'Best thing I ever did marrying your sister. Come on drink up. Let's 'ave one more.'

They emptied their tankards and he refilled them; then they settled down once more.

When Robert arrived at the Angel beerhouse the next evening, his mysterious wellwisher was already sitting on the wall outside chatting. Both were careful not to give any indication that they knew each other and Robert went inside. He was greeted by the landlord and having ordered a tankard of ale, stood talking to him for a while. Glancing at the old grandfather clock that stood in the corner he saw it had just gone seven o'clock. From the corner of his eye he saw the man move away from the wall, come just inside the door and put his empty tankard on the nearest table. He called out a 'goodnight' to the landlord as he turned and started to walk up the hill toward the chapel. Robert lingered long enough to finish his drink then remarking that he too had to get back home, he left. Outside, he could see the man about halfway up the hill and he followed slowly. At the churchgate the man turned into the churchyard and disappeared from view. Increasing his pace, Robert passed through the gate and looked about him. There were plenty of places to hide and he stood there waiting for some signal to tell him where his quarry was hidden. A low whistle from the chapel doorway pointed to his hiding place and he hurried along the path.

The figure in the shadows pulled him into the doorway. 'Anybody follow you?'

Robert assured him that nobody had been behind him on the short walk from the beerhouse.

'Can't be too careful, and if they found out I'd told you, I'd be as good as dead! I don't want to hang about 'ere so listen careful. There's trouble being lined up for you and that lady boss. Sometime at the end of the month I don't know 'xactly when, the bands are gonna be on the march. We've mucked about long enough, now the word's gone out that we're armed and ready we're just waiting for Frost to name the day. I was at Waterloo and I've got me musket. I know what to expect and any sojer fires at me is gonna get one back, but I

313

don't hold with what some of 'em are plannin'. There's a couple of 'em that were there that night you had a mill with Williams. Them and a few more 'otheads are going round saying that when we march, we oughter make sure that the 'ouse at Woodfield be set alight. They reckon Widder Appleby is one of them what helps to keep the workers down. There be quite a few what agrees with 'em. We be marching to join the boys under Frost, so we'll be coming down this way and that's when they plan to do it. You'd better get everybody outer there 'cos some of they be real nasty and mean business. Now thass all I know so iss up to you what you do. For Gawd's sake don't let on how you found out. Now I be agoin'. Give me plenty of time to get clear. G'night and remember what I told you.'

He slipped away almost as soon as the last words left his lips. There were questions Robert wanted answered but it was too late. Already he had disappeared into the night leaving him to ponder on what he'd been told.

He did not stir for ten minutes or so, then made his way back to the track and began his walk back to Cyncoed. He had much to think about, not least how to persuade Gwendoline that she must leave Woodfield. There was less than a week to the end of October and if his informant's facts were correct, then it meant that if the rising did come off, it would probably be planned to take place on the Saturday or Sunday. That would be the second or third of November. He must see her tomorrow and convince her that if she valued her life and those of the servants, she must quit the house immediately and return to London. If Woodfield was burned to the ground, so be it.

The week preceding the rising was one of rumour and counter rumour. All up and down the valley, word was that the time had finally come when the yoke of the landed gentry would be lifted from the necks of the workers and they would receive their just reward. All would get the vote and the ballot would be secret. There would be elections at regular intervals and not just those who owned property be allowed to stand for Parliament. The authorities had listened to the rumours and had acted accordingly. There were meetings

314

being held everywhere with talk of open insurrection and after a particularly noisy and riotous assembly at Tredegar was reported, the Mayor of Newport enrolled many constables and posted them in various hotels in the town. Troops were on standby in case they were needed.

All this was yet to come when next morning Robert set out for Woodfield to speak to Gwendoline. He arrived at the main door and hammered on the huge brass knocker that was polished every day until it shone like a beacon. The door opened to reveal Dilys.

'Mister Robert! There's lovely to see you.'

She shouted over her shoulder,

'Cook, Mary, it's Robert.'

There was the rush of footsteps and the faces of her fellow servants appeared over her shoulder, beaming with pleasure at the sight of someone they had grown to look upon as a brother. They ushered him into the kitchen demanding to know where he had been keeping himself.

'Is my lady at home? It is imperative I see her immediately.'

How easily her old title had slipped from his lips, but they seemed to accept it.

'Yes she be in her study doin' those old books she always got her 'ead stuck in. Seems to spend all 'er time there these days.'

This from Dilys.

The cook chimed in,

'Yes. I don't know why I bother cookin' some times. She be always too busy to eat proper. When 'er tray comes back, half 'er meal is still on the plate. She'll be took ill if she don't eat proper.'

'Dilys. Go up and ask your mistress if she will be kind enough to see me. Tell her it is of the utmost importance.'

Dilys left the room and within a very short time she flew down the stairs and into the kitchen.

'Yes Robert she'll see you. She says to go up straight away.'

As he left the kitchen, climbing the main entrance staircase, Dilys was telling the cook,

'You should 'ave seen 'er face when I told 'er he was in the kitchen wantin' to see 'er.'

How many times had he climbed this staircase? Never though had it been on such an important occasion. Tapping at the study door he heard her voice call out for him to enter and he went in.

His first glimpse of her confirmed the cook's fears. She had lost weight and her hair, still tied in an unbecoming bun, had lost it's sheen and looked dull and lifeless. Beneath her eyes, dark shadows showed. He had seen her like this once before, after Marcus's death, and remembered only too well the doctor's fears for her.

'Robert. How are you?'

'My lady. I am sorry to intrude upon you at this early hour but what I have to say, will not wait.'

'Sit down please and tell me what this urgent news is you have.'

'My lady, I've come here to tell you that for your own safety and that of the servants, you must leave Woodfield at once. I've been informed secretly that it is the intention of the Chartist bands to start marching this weekend. I cannot tell you the name of my informant, but I believe him when he says he's put his own life at risk by telling me what is planned. He is no blackguard. Mistaken perhaps in what he sees as his duty, but he says he will not stand by and see innocent people hurt. Because of this he asked me to meet him secretly, and he told me that when the Croespenmaen band march to join with Frost's men, some of those who have been linking your name with those they reckon to be their enemies, intend putting Woodfield to the torch. They will be coming along the track from Croespenmaen and will take the opportunity to set fire to your home in the dark and confusion.'

She stared at him, her eyes wide with the horror her imagination had conjured up.

'But I've done nothing to harm these people.'

'My lady, where many of these people are concerned, if you are not with them, then you are against them. Many of them are just poor ignorant workers who have suffered much at the hands of some unscrupulous bosses. They see this as a chance to right those wrongs and may have been led on by the local leaders. There are men of principle in the Chartist movement, but there are others who are using it to achieve their own ends. I have been told that amongst the band that plan to attack Woodfield, are some who were present that night on the Waun. They are troublemakers and consider that they must punish you because of your connection as my employer.'

'My father warned me there might be trouble before the year was out and wanted me to go back to London until the trouble was over. I told him that Woodfield is my home and I will not be driven from it by anyone. I must give you the same answer Robert. If they attack this house, I shall fight back. Marcus's pistols are still in their case and I know they are still loaded. I know how to use them and I swear that the first ruffian who steps over my doorstep will be shot.'

'My lady, you must not even consider such a thing. These men will be armed, and if I'm any judge, a lot of them will be half drunk. They wouldn't hesitate to shoot you. Who is going to know who was responsible when they find your body?'

'I will not leave here Robert, that's final!'

'I have the merest glimmering of a plan that might work my lady, but it will need some money, and your agreement just in case it doesn't work, that you will do as I ask.'

'Anything you say Robert.'

'If you will excuse me then my lady, I will take my leave.'

While he had been talking, she had been studying him. She had not seen him for some weeks and his work in the open air had given his skin a faint tan. His eyes were bright and clear and his muscular shoulders swelled the cut of his coat. He was speaking to her as if nothing untoward had happened. He gave no indication that he was in any way angry at his wrongful dismissal. All he seemed concerned about was her safety. Oh what a fool she had been! To think that she had considered this man nothing more than a servant. If only she could admit what he really meant to her, but the stupid Siston pride would not allow that. He must make the first move. He must declare his love for her. Tell her what she already knew, that he had been in love with her for all the years they had known each other. Would he ever utter the words she wanted to hear? She had treated him so badly; he had every right to go away and leave her to spend the rest of her life grieving over what might have been.

She realised he had finished speaking and that she had agreed to do whatever he asked. For a brief moment she wondered whether she should ask him what he intended, but he was already on his feet waiting for her to say good-bye,

'When will I hear from you again Robert?'

'I hope to know how much money I shall require by tonight my lady. With your permission I shall return tomorrow and let you know the details of my plan. After that we must hope and pray it works.'

She accompanied him to the main door and watched him stride along the back drive.

When she went back indoors she was smiling, for the first time in weeks.

CHAPTER 34

Robert's plan was a simple one. Knowing that many of the band starting from Croespenmaen, would first sample the brew at the Maypole in order to boost their courage, then quite possibly again at the Ivy Bush, he intended if it were possible, to encourage them to partake of further refreshment when they arrived at the Angel. The only difference being that the drinks they had at the last port of call would be free. Compliments of the landlord as his contribution to the success of the Chartist Rising, which would free the workers and give them what they asked. All he had to do was to get the landlord of the little beerhouse to agree to his scheme. In exchange for an agreed amount, the landlord would allow the marchers to drink as much as they could and should any fighting break out, any damage would also be paid for. Robert knew all too well, that he was in danger of being cheated but to save Woodfield and Gwendoline, no price could be too high. He was in luck when he opened the door of the little building and entered. The landlord who knew him well was alone in the room that served as the public bar.

'Good morning Mister Morgan. A tankard?'

'No thank you, but I would like to have a few words with you.'

'If you will wait while I tap this barrel we can go into the other room. Missus can come out 'ere though it be a bit early for custom yet.'

After placing the spigot on the barrel, he led the way into the living quarters. They sat either side of the kitchen table.

'Well Mister Morgan how can I serve you?'

'How much stock have you got and what value would you put on it?'

'Well I usually have two full barrels ready tapped and a brew ready for barrelling. 'Course at weekends I could get through three barrels.'

'What about rum, brandy?'

'Not much call 'ere for that but I keep a couple of bottles of each in case any gentry want some when a coach stops to water the 'orses.'

'How much would you say three barrels of ale and your rum and brandy would be worth?'
The landlord considered for a while,
'Roughly twenty five guineas.'
'What about the chairs and tables.'
The landlord looked suspiciously at his interrogator.
'What be you planning Mister Morgan? D'you want to buy my place?'
'How much for the furniture' said Robert not answering his question.
'Another fifteen.'
'That's forty guineas for the contents of your drinking room?'
'Aye.'
'Right. Now this is what I want you to do.'

He bent closer across the table and in a low voice outlined his scheme to thwart the marchers. If he succeeded, no-one would get hurt, although there might be a few sore heads next morning.
'And all I 'ave to do is see that they drink as much as they need to stop 'em going any further? 'ere! 'ow do I know they'll come this weekend? I'll need to make sure there's enough ale so I'll have to brew extra. Say another barrel.'
'Alright. Fifty guineas. That's my last offer. Be ready for them though on Friday, Saturday and Sunday. And tell nobody, not even your wife. You just stand outside and get them inside to drink to the success of the march and you'll earn yourself an easy fifty guineas. Now I'll be back this evening with half the money as a token of my good faith. If nothing happens this weekend, it's yours. If the worst happens and they break up your room and drink all your ale, you'll get the balance on Monday. Agreed?'
They shook hands and refusing the offer of a free tankard, Robert took his leave. He would go to Woodfield in the evening and obtain half the money. It was a lot of money but he was sure Gwendoline would consider it a small price to pay to save her home.

He was correct in his assumption. She did not argue but took twenty five golden guineas from her secret drawer in her desk and handed it to him. When he told her what he had arranged, she agreed that in view of the shortage of time it was as good a plan as could be compounded. She did however demur when he asked her to spend the three nights in Jenkins's living quarters above the stables.

'I can't spend three nights cooped up above a stable full of horses.'

'It'll be the safest place my lady. Jenkins can sleep in one of the empty stalls and if they do come there, I think he'll be able to persuade them not to burn it down. Whatever they are I don't think they would harm the animals.'

She finally agreed to his pleas then asked one final question, 'Where are you going to be Robert? You mustn't let them catch you.'

'Don't worry my lady. If all goes well, they'll be too drunk to remember what they are supposed to do. Whatever happens, I'll not be far away, but I have one last request. Let me have Marcus's pistols. Just in case.'

She had to be content with that, and going into the drawing room, took the velvet case containing the silver inlaid pistols from a drawer and handed it to him.

'Be careful Robert. Please.'

'I will my lady. Now I must go. I must speak to Jenkins and the landlord. Don't be afraid my lady, I'm sure everything will work out right.'

He left and paid a call on the coachman who readily agreed to his request to vacate his room and to try to protect the horses.

His next call was to the Angel where he handed over the money.

'Now remember what you have to do. Invite them in for free drinks to help celebrate the downfall of the mine owners.'

'Don't worry Mister Morgan. For fifty guineas I'd invite the Devil in to sup.'

He made one more call and having obtained consent to hide there until the Saturday evening, he set out for the Cyncoed to say goodbye to Eirwen and William. It was possible some people would know he was living at the farm, so he had to leave at once. When he told his sister that he was leaving to go into hiding until the weekend, she asked him where he would go.

'I can't tell you that but don't worry, I shall be quite safe.'
He stayed indoors until darkness fell, then with a large parcel
of food which Eirwen forced on him despite his protests that
his friend would feed him, slipped away from the farm and
met his friend at the appointed place. They went inside and
he was shown where he could eat his meals whilst waiting.
With his top coat and a blanket and pillow thoughtfully
supplied by his friend, he settled down for the night on the
front pew of the chapel! He was forced to spend the whole of
Thursday inside for fear of being seen. He passed his time
reading the large Bible that stood on the lectern. On the Friday when he heard the sound of the key in the lock of the
main door, he scuttled quickly into the little room used as a
store room for brushes, by the ladies who helped clean their
place of worship. The parson's voice called his name and
when he emerged his friend and one time mentor told him he
need have no fear. Only he had the key and if he had to bring
anyone to the chapel he would make sure that Robert was
warned in plenty of time. He had brought some books with
him and when Robert told him how he had spent the day
reading the Bible, he said,
'I can think of no better company for a lonely man.'
He had brought some extra food and bottles of spring water.
'I shall be going out tonight once it's dark parson. If nothing
happens I'll need to come back and spend tomorrow in here.
I'll do the same on Saturday night but I'll not be back. You'll
have a full chapel on Sunday so I've already picked a place to
hide and by Monday morning it should all be over one way
or the other. If the worst happens and the rising is a success
then pray for us parson.'
    When he slipped out into the darkness that night, it was
cold and wet. Huddled in his topcoat, his hat pulled well
down over his eyes, he hurried down the hill and knocked
rapidly on the door of Dafydd's lodge. His brother came to
the door peering into the darkness.
'Dafydd. It's me Rob. I'm not coming in but I shall be hiding
under the park bridge until dawn. I'll be back again on Saturday night once it's dark. I'll be there all day Sunday until late.
If anyone asks you where I might be, tell them that as far as

you know I'm at Eirwen's. If you want me urgently walk to the bridge in the park, stand on it and say what you have to. One more thing. Stay indoors for the next three nights and lock your doors.'

With this last injunction he was gone.

Crouched under the bridge he was glad of his coat and the blanket he had brought with him. All night the rain pattered down and occasionally the wind whistled through the undergrowth. With the first hint of dawn he crept out. He was cold and his limbs were numbed. He hurried through the trees, skirting the house and made his way along the back drive. There were no lights in either place and he was safely back in the chapel before the dawn made it possible to see the gravestones in the churchyard. What he would have done for a drop of rum or brandy. He had no means of making a hot drink and after he had drunk the water and gnawed at the bread and cheese he curled himself up on the pew to try to sleep.

He awakened when the door was opened. The parson stood looking down at him. He shivered as he became aware of the cold atmosphere of the chapel.

'Robert, Robert wake up!'

Peering from beneath the coat and blanket he saw his breath in the cold air. He stretched his legs to try to get some life back in them.

'Robert! Drink this.'

He held out a jug covered with a cloth. As Robert reached up and took it from him, the warmth of its contents gave a welcome touch to his hands. He tilted the jug and felt the soup hot in his mouth, but he persisted and slowly the warmth returned to his body.

'Oh! That was good parson.'

'Robert. If you are going to be out all night tonight, much as I deplore the tendency of some of my flock to take strong drink, I think I must make an exception in your case. If you are not to be found dead from the cold and wet, I suggest you take a flask of brandy with you. Purely for medicinal purposes I hasten to add. It is raining and cold and from the look of it, I think we are in for a wet weekend. If you are exposed to the elements for the next thirty six hours without proper warmth and cover, then I may well be placing you in a grave in the churchyard very shortly. I realise you cannot go to the Angel or any other hostelry to obtain such medicine, so I went to see Mrs. Appleby last evening and told her of my concern. She sent you this.'

He drew a silver flask from his pocket and held it out. Robert took it from him and noticed the coat of arms that was engraved upon it. It was evidently Marcus's. He unscrewed the top and the rich aroma of brandy came to his nostrils.

'I'm sorry Robert, but not in chapel.'

'Sorry parson. I'll keep it and take it when I really feel the need. Purely for medicinal purposes of course.'

The cleric took another package from his capacious pockets. 'I expect you could do with a change of diet. My housekeeper will think I've got an enormous appetite. I took a chance and carved some off the ham and took half a loaf.'

Robert could think of no way to thank this man who had been more than a friend, but held out his hand. Taking it the parson held it then they both squeezed. No words were spoken but a lot had been said.

As before, he slipped from his hiding place as soon as it was dark. He had more need to be careful since it was the beginning of the weekend, and workmen from the mines and farms would be making their way to the inns to drink and talk with their friends. No doubt all would be discussing the events that were crowding one another in this fateful week. He managed to get to his place of concealment and settled down to wait for whatever was to happen. Knowing that he might have to stay there all night and all next day, he ate sparingly and only took a sip of the brandy when he awoke from a doze. Having nothing to drink he cupped his hands and took water from the clear stream that flowed within feet of his hide. The day was as the parson had forecast. Although not particularly cold, the drizzle continued all day. Twice during the day there were footsteps crossing the bridge but they didn't pause and he assumed it was one of Dafydd's brood. As dusk began falling the rain increased.

If it continued like this, the chance of his plan succeeding would increase. There was nothing like rain to undermine anyone's enthusiasm, and he hoped that the chance to get in out of the wet and swallow as much free drink as they could, would seem much more attractive than marching in soaking clothes bound for a possible fight with well armed troops.

At varying times he thought he could hear shouts or cheering coming from the direction of Blackwood, but with the babble of the stream and the hiss of the rain, it was difficult to distinguish quite what the noises were. It was when he looked at his watch just after five he realised he could hear shouting and it was not coming from Blackwood. The night was pitch black and the rain streaming down. He felt that he had nothing to fear if he ventured out of his hiding place and went to see what was happening.

Judging that this was a good time to take some protection against the weather, he pulled the flask from his pocket and took two or three swallows. The fiery liquid burned its way down his throat and spread like a fire lit in his stomach. Pulling his hat well down and turning the collar of his Garrick up around his ears he crept from under the bridge. Everywhere he could hear the hiss of rain but could hardly see his hand before his face. He slipped slowly from the tree to tree until he came to the drive. There was a light in the lodge but he had no fear of anyone being able to see him so as quickly as possible he moved across the drive and into the trees on the other side. The parkland extended well up the track until the fence that enclosed it impeded his progress. On the other side of the track some forty or fifty yards away he could make out the reason for the shouting. Never had he seen anything like it! Crouched down in the long grass he watched the scene before him. About fifty or sixty men were milling about outside the little hostelry. It was utter chaos. Many carried torches which smoked and guttered in the pouring rain. Many were armed with an assortment of weapons ranging from muskets to pitchforks and even scythes. A loud cheer rose from them as the landlord appeared in the doorway. As he struggled to make his way through the press of figures, laughter and more shouting came from inside. He held up his arms and shouted something but it was impossible for

Robert to hear. Whatever he said was good news to the ears of those outside, as they cheered again and surged forward, pushing him back inside. Some minutes later Robert was amazed to see a barrel of ale carried out into the rain and placed on the little wall. Next a collection of tankards was handed out, passing from hand to hand until except for a very few, every man held one and was pressing forward trying to make sure they got it filled before the barrel was emptied.

He pulled his watch from his pocket and tried desperately to see what the time was, but the rain and darkness defeated him. He reckoned it must be about six o'clock, and it looked as if the mêlée before him was unlikely to disperse for some time yet. If only the landlord's supply of ale held out, success was assured. The trouble would come if the supplies ran out and the disappointed marchers, turned nasty. They could then not only smash up the beerhouse, but might well follow those hotheads who wanted to destroy Woodfield. Anxiously he watched the events taking place. Now that everybody seemed to have a drink in their hands, despite the rain still streaming down, there seemed to be a lot of coming and going between those outside and those in the crowded room. The explanation soon became obvious as those inside had only come out in order to empty their bladders against the wall. Those outside were taking the chance to slip in and try to get shelter and be nearer a larger supply of ale. Tired of holding their weapons, they began stacking them against the wall, then the side of the building. Soon the collection of makeshift weapons were lying in piles, and it was doubtful if any man there would have been able to recover his own scythe or hatchet or whatever he had armed himself with, when starting out on the march to Blackwood. As the rain continued, even the torches began failing as they became soaked. A few lanterns still guttered feebly, but apart from the light emanating from the interior there was little or no illumination outside and Robert was tempted to sneak even closer in order to try and find out the mood of the crowd. He resisted the temptation however and soon was rewarded by the sound of singing and clapping. Those inside seemed to have reached the happy stage of drunkenness and it was a welcome sound to his ears. If they kept on like this, in a very short while they would forget their original mission and settle down to have a good time. There was a sudden shout and several of the crowd outside began pushing toward the doorway. The barrel was lifted from the wall and one man lifted it above his head and hurled it out into the darkness. The barrel had been drained and they seemed to be demanding further supplies. Robert prayed that more would be forthcoming and heaved a sigh of relief when another was carried out and placed in position. This time they formed an orderly line and each man in turn held his tankard under the spigot, before moving out of the way. What followed next convinced Robert that his plan had succeeded. Waving their tankards in the air, to the sound of their own voices they linked arms and began dancing around in a circle as if dancing around a maypole. Several fell over and were left lying where they fell. Others came staggering from the beerhouse and soon the outside of the building was once again a mass of shouting, cheering and singing men, most of them so drunk that many began staggering up the hill shouting farewells, as if going home after a drunken night out.

As far as this band was concerned, the rising was over. Robert rose to his feet. He was wet through and stiff but absolutely elated. The plan had worked like a charm. Tomorrow he would pay his second call at the Angel and pay the landlord the balance of the money. First and foremost though, he needed a hot meal and a nip of something to ward off the chill that seemed to have crept right into his bones. Blessing the parson and Gwendoline, he took the flask from his pocket, raised it in a mock salute to the Angel and quickly swallowed the contents. What had been scattered elements of the crowd making their way home, soon became a general exodus and within a quarter of an hour, no member of the Chartist contingent from Croespenmaen remained. The only evidence of their presence was the pile of discarded weapons. Whether they would return to collect them was doubtful. They would not want to draw attention to their participation, in what after all was an armed rebellion against the lawful rulers of the realm. Sure now that there was no danger, he retraced his steps to the drive and walked back up the track to the Angel. The door was open and light streamed out into the darkness. Cautiously he approached the doorway but was not challenged. He could hear no sound, so entered, prepared to turn and run if necessary. The room was unoccupied except for the landlord sat at a table. Hearing Robert's steps he turned.

'Mister Morgan. Welcome to the Angel once again. I'm afraid I can't offer you any ale. Our friends drank the lot. All I was able to save was a bottle of rum. Will you join me in a toast to a very successful night's business.'

At Robert's nod, he poured a generous tot into a glass and handed it to him. Robert looked about him. Surprisingly there was very little damage. A few chairs lay broken and the tables were littered with empty tankards. There were pools of ale lying beneath the barrels. Robert sipped at the rum. It was not a drink he normally took and after having drunk the brandy, he had no wish to end up sleeping the night away beneath some hedge.

'I shall be back tomorrow with the money unless the rising has been successful in other parts. Did you manage to find out where they were marching to?'

'They were to join John Frost's band from Blackwood. They were marching to Newport. There was so much shouting going on I couldn't really hear much. I was too busy serving. When I heard them coming down the hill singing, I went out and stood in the rain shouting out, 'Free ale for all. Free ale.' I had a tankard in each hand. They must have thought I was mad but once they saw I meant it, I was nearly trampled as they rushed inside. My wife and I had lined up our stock of tankards on the table in front of the barrels but we couldn't keep up with 'em, so when those outside started shouting I got another barrel and they carried it outside and put it on the wall and helped themselves. It was a near thing Mister Morgan. I thought we'd run out but I'd taken the precaution of brewing four barrels. I afraid you owe me an extra five guineas.'

Robert was too wet and hungry to argue, despite the fact

there was hardly any damage.

'You shall have your thirty guineas landlord. If I can't come, seek out the mistress of Woodfield. She will pay you. Now I must go. Goodnight landlord.'

'Goodnight Mister Morgan.'

It was his intention to make his way back to the Cyncoed. If anyone had been seeking him there before the march, they would be too busy to think of going back there tonight. What had taken place tonight, had been the failure of just one small band of men. It was possible, nay probable that the thousands who were involved were even now pouring along the valley roads on the way to attack Newport. Tomorrow morning would be soon enough to find out whether he could walk about a free man or whether he must flee, a hunted man. What of Gwendoline? He could not abandon her. He must return at first light and join her. They would have to wait until they had firm news of the outcome of the events taking place. If the danger still persisted then there was only one solution. He would take her to safety in one of the carriages and woe betide anyone who tried to stop him.

The farm was in darkness when he arrived. He beat upon the door until it opened and William's huge figure confronted him. He was clad in a night shirt and holding a lighted candle in his hand, evidence that the knocking had brought him from his bed. Eirwen's voice came from the bedroom, 'Who be it William?'

''Tis Rob. Come in quick.'

He pulled Robert inside and shut the door.

'You be soaked Rob. Best get them clothes off. What's been 'appening?'

While Robert was taking off his clothes, he recounted the events of the evening. William laughed when he described the drunken men dancing in the rain.

'There'll be sore heads this day.'

When Robert asked him if there had been anyone looking for him he said no, but if they did come he and his brothers would give them short shrift.

'I must go to Woodfield early in the morning. There are arrangement to make in case the rebellion is a success. If it is they'll come seeking my lady, and I am going to make sure she's not there to be taken.'

William promised to rouse him at first light, and after eating a bowl of stew from the pot hanging over the dying embers, he lay down in front of the dying fire and within seconds was deep asleep.

It was still dark outside when William woke him. The rain had stopped during the night and there was a dim lightening in the sky to the east. Robert's clothes had been hung to dry but when he pulled them on there was still a dampness about them. William was moving about the room already dressed ready for work. He placed a loaf and some butter on the table and alongside it, a platter holding a large cooked ham. When Robert had finished dressing, Eirwen came out of her bedroom. In her night attire and a boudoir gown that Gwendoline had given her, she looked huge as she waddled to the table.

She filled a mug with milk from a big metal can and began drinking it.

'Come to the table Rob.'

She took a large carving knife and cut off several large pieces of the ham, then hacked off some bread and spread the rich creamy butter on it. A mug of milk was pushed toward him and he settled down to eat while his sister watched him.

William meanwhile had finished his preparations and after kissing Eirwen went out into the darkness.

'What happened last night Rob?'

While he ate, he told her of the events at the Angel and his need now to know what had transpired at Newport. He intended going straight to Woodfield and waiting there for news. If it was bad, he would bundle Gwendoline into one of the carriages and head for safety in the direction of Monmouth where there were troops stationed.

'Will you come back?'

'Only if the news is good. I will be back sometime to say goodbye Eirwen because I'm taking ship to America. I can't stay here any longer and I'll work in the mines until I've saved enough to start my own business.'

She forebore to ask him whether he intended declaring himself to Gwendoline.

When he had eaten his breakfast, it was full light but the lowering sky gave no promise of a fine day. He kissed his sister goodbye and promising that if he couldn't return he would let her know where he was, strode off. There was no-one about and he took the footpath over the Graig and down to the rear of the chapel. He hurried down the hill and turned into the backdrive. When he passed the house he thought he heard noises coming from the direction of the kitchen, but did not stop. Rounding the house he approached the stables. All was quiet and he let himself in. It was warm inside and the smell of the horses and the polished leather harnesses assailed his nostrils. A snore came from one of the empty stalls indicating that Jenkins was not suffering any loss of comfort by giving up his bed. Smiling, Robert tiptoed to the stairs and crept up. At the top facing him was the door to what now served as Gwendoline's bedchamber. He tapped gently but there was no answer. Knocking again, he heard the creak of the bed then the sound of her voice.

'Who's there? I warn you, I have a pistol. Who is it?'

'It's Robert my lady.'

There was the sound of the bolt being drawn and the door opened. Wrapped in a peignoir, her face rosy with sleep, her hair loose and hanging to her shoulders, she faced him, clutching a horse pistol almost too heavy to hold.

He reached out and took it from her. Thankfully he saw that it was not cocked.

'Good morning my lady.'

'Oh Robert, it's so good to see you. What's the news?'

'All well here my lady, but I do not know what has happened down the valley.'

Suddenly she realised that she was standing in her nightwear, talking to a young man, she blushed scarlet and hurriedly retreated into the room and closed the door almost shut. Speaking through the gap she said,

'Robert. Wait for me below. I shall not be long. We can go to the house and you must tell me all.'

True to her word, she joined him in the stables within minutes. Jenkins's snores reverberated in the warm air. Now and

331

again the horses would snort or kick against the partitions, but the coachman slept on. They left the stables and hurried through the cold air to the main door. It opened as they reached it and Dilys worried face greeted them.

'Oh my lady ..Mister Robert!'

At the sight of Robert, whatever had worried her, was forgotten, and she stepped back to allow them to enter.

'Tell the cook we'll have breakfast in a half an hour Dilys. I'm famished.'

She led the way up the stairs to the office that they had once shared. There she left him to complete her toilette. When she returned, her hair was knotted on the neck once more. She walked to her desk and seated herself.

'Now Robert. I want to hear everything.'

He spent the next twenty minutes recounting all his movements and the events of the past three days. When he told her how he had spent the whole of Saturday night and all day Sunday crouched beneath the bridge, she could not stop the expression of sympathy that escaped her. When he then went on to tell her how he crouched in the rain watching the antics of the band of rebellious workers, her expressive eyes showed the depth of her feelings that he should have suffered so much on her behalf. When he had finished she sat silent for some time.

'Oh Robert how you must have suffered from the wet and cold.'

'I must admit that I was very glad to be in possession of the brandy flask my lady. Thank you for entrusting me with it.'

He took the silver flask from his pocket and handed it to her. Now that he had told her of his actions, there only remained the question of why he had been prepared to risk his liberty and this she determined to ask.

'Robert, things have not been easy between us recently, and during the last few days and nights I have wondered why you have been prepared to risk so much. You could not have been blamed if you had chosen to let matters take their course. Was there anything that swayed you to do what you did?'

'Two things my lady. You know my background. I was a coal

hewer who was fortunate enough to acquire some education and a responsible position. However I have never forgotten what my life was before that. For the great majority of those miners and iron workers who marched on Newport last night, I have a great deal of sympathy. They have been cheated and exploited nearly all their working lives and all they are really asking for, is a decent life and to have a say in deciding who shall rule them. Because they believe there is no other way to get them, they are prepared to fight. To save them from getting hurt and to prevent those blackguards from burning Woodfield, I thought the surest way would be to get them all drunk but I had to watch in case things didn't work out.'

'You said there were two reasons. What's the other.'

He stood up and stepped to the desk. She rose from her seat, her heart thumping. Reaching out he took her hands in his, 'You Gwendoline Appleby. For years I have served you, and worked alongside you. I have always called you my lady, when all I have ever wanted was to call you beloved, to tell you I love you and have from the first time I saw you. I wanted you to know before I sail to America where I can be my own master.'

'Oh Rob my darling. How I've longed to hear you say those words. When I sacked you, I went to Penyfan where you took me when I came here first. It was then I realised that I love you. I have been so lonely and miserable since you left. I don't want to be a business woman. Take me with you and I promise I'll always be your lady.'

When Dilys opened the door to tell them breakfast was ready they didn't notice. They were wrapped in each other's arms, lips joined in their first kiss. She went back downstairs and told the cook to keep the breakfast warm. My lady and Robert were too busy.

When at last by reluctant consent they drew apart, she with face rosy with the emotion his kisses had aroused, he breathing deeply, his heart thumping in his chest, they stood searching each other's face as if they were strangers meeting for the first time. Although they had spent years working in close proximity it was if neither had really seen the other before.

Gwendoline reached out and her hand touched the spot on his forehead where a small blue mark declared that at some time he had suffered a blow that had broken the skin and allowed a minute speck of coal dust to lodge there, inflicting on him a brand that would forever mark him as a man familiar with the dangers that awaited those who sought to praise the black diamond like fuel from the earth. Her fingertips gently traced a path about his face, following his eyebrows, the cheekbones, then outlining the lips that a moment ago had ravished her feelings so delightfully, arousing emotions within her that had lain dormant for years. He sought to draw her once more into his embrace, his eyes intense as they gazed deeply into hers. Suddenly she was aware of a frisson of pleasurable fear. Something whispered to her that should she surrender once more to the demands of his lips, she would find herself helpless to control the yearning that rose within her. Oh how she wanted this, but some instinct warned her, it must not be. Even as his arms tightened about her, crushing her against his chest, she moved her hand to cover the lips that threatened to sweep away all her resolution.

'Rob my darling, we must stop. I too want nothing more than to be here being loved by you, but there are many things to do before we can be sure that all danger is passed.'

She placed her hands against his chest and gently pushed him away, desperately trying to ignore the naked hunger that shone in his eyes.

My dearest, don't deny me now. I have waited so long for this moment. Seeing you, being next to you, but never able to reach out and hold you and tell you how much I love you.'

'There will be time my love, later. I too want nothing else, but until we know what has happened down the valley, we cannot count on our safety.'

As the realisation of the precarious position they were atill in, took the place of the passion which had swept him along, he dropped his arms.

'Forgive me my love. I had forgotten the danger that might still exist. Fool that I am. Even now, if they were successful last night, they could be sweeping the countryside looking for anyone they feel opposes their wishes. I must find out what has happened.'

'You mustn't venture out my love. Suppose you meet anyone who recognises you. They will be armed and and in no mood to show any mercy. If anything should happen to you now that we have found our love, I could not bear it.'

'What else can I do? I cannot stay here hiding. If they should come and find me, they might well destroy the whole place and harm you too for hiding me. I must go. Trust me my sweet. I too want only to be allowed to live and love you and I shall take no chances.'

Seeing that he was determined to find out the true state of affairs, she reluctantly agreed but insisted that he stay long enough for them to breakfast together. Unaware that the maid had already been once, Gwendoline tugged the bell rope and was surprised when Dilys appeared with a laden tray almost immediately. When she had gone they sat at the table sharing the meal, frequently pausing to give each other little kisses.

At last Robert wiped his mouth and pushed back his chair. 'I must go my darling. I will make enquiries down the valley. I am not known down there and I'll borrow an old cloak from Jenkins. Nobody will connect me with Woodfield. I will try to get back by evening. Remain indoors my dearest and lock the outer doors.'

He took her in his arms and once more they kissed before he finally tore himself from her arms and without looking back, hurried from the room.

CHAPTER 35

In an effort to occupy her mind with thoughts other than those which had only one concern, she tried to concentrate on the paperwork which had built up. Paget had continued sending reports via Jenkins who had been detailed by his mistress to act as courier between herself and the mine manager. Despite the promise she had made to her father, she had not been able to cope successfully with the reports that, in the days when Robert had shared the task, had been dealt with speedily. As she studied the output figures and tried to work out a comparison with the previous week's figures, her mind kept wandering away from the neatly penned figures and picturing Robert, her Robert now, hiding in bushes as armed men searched, or being held and beaten. At last she gave up any pretence of working and left the study.

Moving from room to room she wandered the house attracting odd glances from the maids who were busy cleaning and dusting. As they bobbed their curtseys she greeted them absent mindedly and passed by without further comment. Robert had obviously instructed someone to lock the outer doors as she found them securely barred when she came upon them. As she appeared in the doorway of the kitchen, the cook and kitchen maid stopped what they were doing and stood awaiting her comments, but other than to look around at the spotless interior with its roaring fire and huge scrubbed table, she only nodded and reclimbed the stairs. The hands of the tall grandfather clock standing on the landing at the head of the stairs pointed to a quarter past twelve and the chime rang out the quarter even as she gained the head of the stairway. It would be hours yet before Rob would return. She tried to imagine where he might now be. He was on foot, fearing that a mounted man would be a target for any Chartists who might be searching the highways. He had been gone about two hours, so proceeding with caution he would not be much further than Gelligroes or perhaps the new village of Ynysddu. When he returned, if he returned, they would either have to flee to a safe haven or with God's grace they could celebrate. She chose not to consider the former

336

possibility. Fate could not now be so unkind as to endanger their new found happiness? She would make preparations to greet her lover. For too long she had been the widow of Woodfield, dull and drab. It was time for her to encourgae the flames of love that had threatened to consume her this morning. She needed, no, wanted, his love. When he returned she would be waiting, a new Gwendoline.

Making her way to her bedroom she sat before the dressing table looking at her reflection in the full length mirror. She touched the various brushes, combs, jars and powder bowls that lay upon the trays, as if trying to place them firmly in her memory, then on impulse raised her arms and undid the bun that hung coiled on her neck. Shaking her head she freed the long tresses until they hung down her back. As if preparing for bed, she undid the fastenings of her dress and standing up, let it slide to the floor. Stepping out of it she tossed it on a chair and as if in a dream took the long curtain of hair and brought it forward over her shoulder. Picking up a silver backed brush, she began slowly brushing the thick mass, her eyes on the mirror before her. What she saw was not a mature woman nearing thirty, but a young fresh faced girl, eyes bright with youth, a new bride. The strokes faltered as her mind raced ahead to what had happened and a low sound, half sob, escaped her; as if the rhythm of the strokes had a hypnotic effect, she saw herself confronting Robert, accusing him of ungentlemanly behaviour and dismissing him. Slowly a tear welled in her eye and began slowly to find its way down her cheek. Her arm stopped and she sat gazing sightlessly, her mind's eye picturing the look on his face as he realised what she was saying, then as he turned and left, a second tear rose and traced a path down the other cheek. She shivered and returned to the present. Like a small child, she rubbed each cheek with her palm, wiping away the tear stains. All that was behind her now. She had made her mistakes and had paid for them. She had been granted a second chance of happiness and Rob had helped her grasp it. They would spend the rest of their days together. She stopped as once more, the terrible thought intruded.

'Please God bring him back safe',

she whispered. Her hair, now gleaming and glistening in the light that entered through the window, lay on her bare shoulder.

Suddenly, she rose and crossing the room, tugged the bell-rope. A few moments later there was a tap at the door and Dilys appeared, curiosity etched on her face.

'Yes m'lady?'

'Dilys. Can you or Mary dress my hair after lunch?'

'I can try m'lady. Eirwen showed me some of the ways she used to dress yours m'lady, but beggin' you pardon m'lady, it's been so long.'

'Never mind that Dilys. Let's see what you can do. Where are all my combs and pins?'

'I think you'll find them in their case in the bottom drawer m'lady.'

Gwendoline reached down and pulled out the lacquered case which held the fastenings which she had once employed to hold her hair in whatever manner fashion had decreed. Her fingers played amongst the fancy combs and jewelled pins then she closed the lid.

'Dilys! I will have my lunch up here. Afterwards I want you to help me with my hair. Tell cook that she is to prepare something extra special for dinner. Something that can be kept warm if necessary. Robert will be my dinner companion tonight but I do not know what time he may return. I shall bathe before we dress my hair and choose a gown. Off you go and tell cook.'

Dilys bobbed and left the room, a smile at the corners of her mouth. Gwendoline smiled, well aware that within the next few minutes, the news would have spread to every servant. 'Robert is dining with my lady this evening. My lady wants a bath and I'm to dress her hair and help her choose a gown.' No doubt there would be secret smiles amongst the staff and guesses hazarded as to whether he would return to his previous position. They would have to wait and see!

Enfolded in the huge warmed towels that Dilys had brought, Gwendoline sank on to the stool before the dressing table. Her face, flushed with the heat of the bath, peeped from amongst the folds as the maid patted her dry. In the fireplace, large red hot coals warmed the room against the dank cold November afternoon. It would soon be dark and already the bare branches of the trees outside showed starkly against the lowering sky. When she slipped the towels off her shoulders and stood up, the maid quickly replaced them with a silky peignoir. Loosening the hair which had been tied up on top of her head in an effort to keep it dry, Gwendoline allowed the garment to slip to her waist, exposing her upper body. Dilys took up the crystal powder bowl and taking from it a soft pad proceeded to dust her back and shoulders with the fine powdered chalk it contained. Gwendoline sat motionless.

'It had been years since she had allowed a maid to minister to her so. There had been no reason to. Tonight though she wanted to roll back the years. When the servants had retired, leaving them alone, and Rob took her in his arms...'

She sighed. Dilys finished powdering and helped her mistress into the voluminous underwear. As she pulled tight the strings that squeezed Gwendoline's waist even smaller and pushed her bosom upward, the clock struck five. All was ready now for the attempt to comb and curl and pin up the shimmering mass of golden hair that hung down over the smooth white skin of her shoulders.

Opening the lacquered case once more, mistress and maid, began the task of dressing my lady's hair.

An hour later they surveyed the result. Eirwen had had a gift for making hair do what she wanted it to. Dilys did not, but despite this, Gwendoline was quite happy with the result. No longer was it dull, strained back, and ending in a most unbecoming bun. Instead, Dilys had somehow managed to lift it and with the aid of the small combs and jewelled pins, keep it raised until her hair resembled a crown around her head. Several times the whole mass had collapsed reducing them both to laughter, but eventually they were satisfied with the result. Taking care to rise slowly from the dressing table. Gwendoline instructed Dilys to open the cupboard that held her dresses. Not for years had she taken anything other than dark dresses from there and as she looked at the row of silk and satin creations that she had once changed into as the mood took her, she wondered which would delight Robert most.

As if preparing for a ball or reception, she bade Dilys pluck first one, then another from within, holding them against her as she considered the effect in the mirror. The pile on the bed grew larger as one after another was discarded. At last a rose pink froth of satin and lace, decorated with tiny pearls, was chosen.

'This one I think Dilys?'

'Oh my lady, it's beautiful!' exclaimed the maid.

Ten minutes later, Gwendoline looked at herself in the long mirror. It had been a long time since she had gone to this much trouble to please anyone she thought, as she looked at the reflected picture. Facing her was a woman. A woman whose eyes searched for flaws as do all women. She was no longer the girl who had so often stood here watching while Eirwen had put the finishing touches. Now, her figure, despite the tightness of her stays, was slightly fuller, but there was more character in her face. Her hair, a shade darker, she thought better suited to the eyes that looked gravely back at her.

'Oh my lady, you look beautiful!'

'Thank you Dilys. Much of the credit is due to your efforts. All we must hope for now is that it has all been worthwhile.'

As she finished speaking, there was a hammering at the main door. Dilys clasped her hands together in a fearful gesture. Gwendoline straightened, took a deep breath and as she walked to the door said,

'That will be Robert. His enemies are not the sort to knock and await admission. Go and tell cook we shall be ready to eat in about half an hour.'

She passed down the stairway and along the passage to the sitting room not waiting to see who would be admitted when Mary finally opened the door. A minute or two would make no difference now. They had waited years.

When Mary opened the door, Robert, looking dishevelled hurried indoors.

'Where is your mistress Mary?'

She pointed along the passage and said,
'The sitting room master Robert.'
He strode quickly to the door and threw it open. Gwendoline was standing before the fire looking toward the door. Not waiting to close it behind him, he crossed the room in a few steps, throwing his hat on to a chair as he swept her up in his arms swinging her around with her feet off the floor.
'My darling. It's all over. We're safe. The rising has failed.'
Allowing her feet to rest on the carpet once more, but still holding her in the circle of his arms, he kissed her lips, then her cheeks and sought to savour the delights of her various features. Eyelids, nose, the column of her neck all received his attention while she wriggled and giggled with delight and confusion. Trying at last to restore some measure of decorum to the situation, she struggled to release herself and finally pushed him away.
'Stop it dearest, please. You must tell me all that has happened before we dine. You must be starving and from the state of your clothes you look as if you have been in hiding in the bushes. We have half an hour. Let us sit down and tell me what has passed since you left me this morning.'
He looked ruefully at his hands, begrimed and stained. Dried leaves clung to his cloak and there were several wet patches on his breeches where he must have knelt on the ground. He took off the cloak and joined her on the cushioned chaise. She took his hands in hers, not caring about the state of them.
'I had only got as far as the Greyhound when I heard the first news. Somebody had brought news that the columns had reached Newport and were making preparations to attack the troops. If that were true then I thought my fears of a successful uprising might be true. However I walked as far as Ynysddu and hung about there. About midday there were quite a lot of men hurrying up the valley. There seemed to be a lot of confusion and none of them seemed anxious to tarry. At last I was forced to stop one man who was on his own and I asked him. Pretending to be a sympathiser I asked for news of the success of our rising. He looked scared to death and after a while admitted that everything had failed. There had been

troops in the Westgate Hotel and they had fired on the marchers. There were many dead and wounded and our leaders had run away. The troops are out hunting for them now.'

'Thank God' said Gwendoline. 'You have not said how you came to be so dirty and wet. Were you in danger from those ruffians?'

'I think not my love. Most of them looked too scared and as far as I could see carried no weapons. I did dirty my hands and face just in case I ran into any of them who were armed. I thought that they would not attack anyone who looked as scruffy as me. I got wet when I hid in the undergrowth while watching the track at Ynysddu.'

He stopped speaking as if something had struck him.

'My own sweet love. I have been selfish. I wanted only to see you so much that I have taken no note of the effect my behaviour has had upon you. I have left you to worry and fret about my safety. When I come back my only thought was to take you in my arms and smother you in kisses. Were I not blinded by my desire to take you and hold you close I would have seen that you had made preparations for my return. My love, forgive me. For so long I grieved that you were hiding your beauty behind a mask of severe dress. Now when you greet me looking as lovely as you did when I saw you first, I am too selfish in my own desires to notice.'

'Hush my love. It is of no consequence. When a woman is in love she wants only to please the eyes of her lover. I would not be a woman were I not thrilled that nothing else mattered except that you take me in your arms when you returned. Kiss me now quickly my dear love. You must wash and brush away the stains before we dine and we have so little time.'

He took her in his arms and their lips met in a long kiss. As the chimes of the clock sounded she struggled free and as he left to clean away the travel stains, she tried to repair the damage his embraces had done to her so carefully contrived toilette.

Despite the actions they had taken, when Dilys and Mary took in the first course of the evening meal, Gwendoline and

Robert sitting alongside each other, and apparently waiting patiently, had not removed all the telltale signs. Dilys, serving her mistress, could not help but notice that several pins in Gwendoline's hair seemed to have become loose, threatening to fall out despite the care she had taken to ensure they were firmly fixed; her face was flushed and she seemed a trifle breathless. Robert's sleeve and lapels both appeared to have come in contact with some sort of white powder. As they left the room both girls heard Gwendoline make some remark in a low voice. They could not hear what it was she said but Robert's reply was easily heard,

'Don't worry cariad, they all know we are in love.'

When servants came to clear away the last of the dishes, Gwendoline said,

'Dilys. Tell cook that was excellent and ask Mrs. Watkins to prepare a room for Robert please. We shan't be needing anyone again this evening.'

They repaired to the sitting room where a large fire burned cheerily and with the thick drapes tightly drawn and the candle flickering, it presented a cosy picture. They had so much to say that it was natural they should seat themselves close together on the chaise once more. As often happens with lovers, much was said the night with lips that spoke not a word.

They breakfasted together next morning and spent the whole morning in the study. There was much to do and speak about. They had no difficulty in agreeing on the most important item, their marriage. That would take place as soon as possible bearing in mind that Robert was still intent on going to America and becoming his own master. However he did agree that Gwendoline could not simply walk away from the control of the mines and they finally compromised by setting a date in the summer. As an betrothed couple, it would not be possible for them to live in the same house, so once again he would take up residence in the lodge and take up his former post. They would marry in the chapel and live in Woodfield until all arrangements had been made to hand over to whoever was to be the new controller. Then they would sail to the New World.

Every day news kept coming to the house of the actions

taken by the authorities in the train of the uprising. The ring-leaders had been captured within days and within a couple of months John Frost, Zephaniah Williams and six others had been tried and sentenced to death for high treason. Perhaps because the Chartist cause had become a national matter, and the government feared even more unrest if the sentence were carried out, these eight men escaped with their lives and instead were ordered to be transported for life and despatched to Australia. In the immediate aftermath of the rising, troops had come to the valleys seeking any who had taken part, but a silence descended and satisfied that there would be no more trouble, the soldiers were withdrawn and an uneasy peace settled once more.

Gwendoline had despatched a letter to her father assuring him that all was well and giving her parents the news of her impending marriage to Robert, and also subject to the Board's approval, his re-appointment as Financial Controller. She made the point that since they intended giving up their appointments anyway to set sail for America sometime after the wedding, she was quite prepared to finish immediately should the Board disagree with her decision to reappoint her future husband! Whatever Sir Henry's feelings regarding the forthcoming marriage of his daughter to someone he considered to be no more than an educated servant, he did not allow them to stand in the way of his wholehearted agreement to Robert taking on the post once more. Whatever he felt, Sir Henry was always a business man.

Paget for his part was delighted and a dinner was held at Woodfield to celebrate the announcement of the return of Robert to the management and their betrothal. On Christmas morning William arrived to tell them that Eirwen had given birth to a boy the previous evening and they intended naming him Robert. Jenkins was summoned to bring around the carriage and within the hour, Gwendoline, Robert and William were gazing fondly at the new baby. At the insistance of his wife, William took Robert to the main room where two large tankards of cider were despatched as the proud father was congratulated. In the bedroom, Gwendoline broke the news of Robert's return to the position he had held, then blushing happily she told Eirwen that in the summer she and Robert were to be married. Eirwen, lying against the pillows held out her arms and the two embraced. When they released each other Eirwen looked at her former mistress, then with a twinkle in her eye said,

'Would my lady like to hold the baby? It'll be good practice.' Gwendoline blushed and moved to the cot where the baby lay. Gently she picked up the little bundle and held it against her.

'Oh Eirwen you are so lucky.'

She sat on the edge of the bed and while their menfolk drank a further congratulatory tankard, they talked about babies.

As the winter months dragged slowly by, snow fell and melted. Storms raged and high winds bent the tops of the trees and tore off loose and broken branches. At the colliery coal continued to pour out, to be loaded into trams and sent down the valley, to be sent to feed the furnaces that demanded more and more. Robert slept at the lodge, returning there late at night having spent the evenings with his betrothed. Gwendoline looking younger as her wedding approached, was busy with Mrs. Watkins making arrangements for the arrival and stay of the whole Siston family. Of necessity she had to be responsible for everything connected with the wedding and each evening she talked to Robert about what was still to do. Spring came and in the park daffodils bloomed, then faded. The chestnut trees grew tall spikey flowers of white and pink and as they too fell, summer was upon them.

On a bright warm morning in July, Sir Henry Siston accompanied his eldest daughter to the chapel at Penmaen to be married to Robert Morgan. The chapel was full with relatives and friends. Gwendoline had insisted that there was to be no question of separately seating the guests according to whether they belonged to the bride or the groom. All were to be seated in the same pews. Robert stood talking to his friend Paget who had gladly agreed to act as his supporter. Only a minute or two late, the carriage containing Gwendoline and Sir Henry drew up at the gate of the churchyard. Eirwen had paid an early visit to Woodfield to dress the hair of her future sister-in-law. Now clad in a long cream coloured gown, her hair brushed and pinned and dressed with a coronet of flowers, father and daughter walked to the church door and were greeted by the minister who then hurried inside to take his place. In a pew right at the front, Lady Siston with her younger daughter, a child who bore a startling resemblance to the bride, was talking to Eirwen who held her son asleep in her arms. Looking only slightly older than the young girl who had come to Woodfield so many years previously, the bride walked down the aisle on the arm of her father. As she passed along, all noticed the smile she wore as she approached the man she was to marry. There was no hesitation in the replies of either bride or groom as they affirmed their intentions to be joined and soon Robert slipped the plain golden ring on to the finger of his bride. As they emerged from the chapel into the sunshine they stopped and to the delight of those gathered there, they kissed.

Once again, the park was the scene of a wedding breakfast but this time a little more decorous. With Sir Henry and Paget available to deal with any problems that might arise, it had been decided that the newlyweds should spend a short honeymoon in Monmouth and shortly after noon, Jenkins resplendent in his coachman's livery brought the carriage to where they waited. To the cheers of the guests they climbed in and with his arm about her, they drove away to begin their new life together.